*Sheikhs and pr...
and to conquer...*

*Soaring tempe...
desire in the desert.*

DESERT
PRINCES

Three complete novels from fabulous
international bestselling authors
Michelle Reid, Alexandra Sellers
and **Lucy Gordon**

DESERT PRINCES

THE ARABIAN LOVE-CHILD

by
Michelle Reid

BELOVED SHEIKH

by
Alexandra Sellers

THE SHEIKH'S REWARD

by
Lucy Gordon

*Published in Great Britain by Harlequin Mills & Boon Limited,
Eton House, 18-24 Paradise Road, Richmond, Surrey TW9 1SR*

DESERT PRINCES © by Harlequin Books S.A. 2007

The Arabian Love-Child, Beloved Sheikh and *The Sheikh's Reward*
were first published in Great Britain in separate, single volumes.

The Arabian Love-Child © Michelle Reid 2002
Beloved Sheikh © Alexandra Sellers 1999
The Sheikh's Reward © Lucy Gordon 2000

The poem "whisper of ambergris" as a re-telling of the Persian
poem by Unsuri was specially written for *Beloved Sheikh* by
Jessica Sellers Stones. Copyright 1999 by Jessica Sellers Stones.
Used by permission.

*ISBN 13: 978 0 263 85553 1
ISBN 10: 0 263 85553 8*

10-0207

*Printed and bound in Spain
by Litografía Rosés S.A., Barcelona*

THE ARABIAN
LOVE-CHILD

by
Michelle Reid

Michelle Reid grew up on the southern edges of Manchester, the youngest in a family of five lively children. But now she lives in the beautiful county of Cheshire with her busy executive husband and two grown-up daughters. She loves reading, the ballet, and playing tennis when she gets the chance. She hates cooking, cleaning, and despises ironing! Sleep she can do without and produces some of her best written work during the early hours of the morning.

CHAPTER ONE

RAFIQ AL-QADIM climbed out of the back of a chauffeur-driven limousine and strode through the plate-glass doors that guarded the International Bank of Rahman. In the clenched fist of one hand he held a rolled-up newspaper, in his eyes glowed a look that foretold of hell to pay for some poor fool. Hurrying behind him, his newly appointed aide, Kadir Al-Kadir, was wearing an expression that suggested he might be that very unfortunate person.

As Rafiq struck a direct line for the row of steel lifts set into a wall of grey marble, people in his path took one look at him and began backing away to give the big man an uninterrupted passage to his target. He didn't notice; he was too consumed by the blinding fury that carried his intimidating six-foot-four-inch frame into the nearest vacant lift. A dark-suited arm shot out; a decidedly murderous finger stabbed at the button for the top floor. The lift doors shut out Kadir Al-Kadir and the sea of stunned faces. No one who'd had any dealings with Rafiq Al-Qadim had ever seen him appear anything but formidably controlled.

But he was not in control. Rafiq had never been so angry. Rage was literally bouncing inside him, fighting to get out and vent itself. The lift took less than fifteen seconds to reach its destination. The doors opened; he strode out. Nadia, his secretary, took one look at his face, paled and shot to her feet.

'Good morning, sir,' she greeted warily. 'There have been several messages for you and your first appointment arrives in—'

'No calls. Nothing.' He cut right across her and kept on walking, each of his powerfully constructed, sleekly toned

5

muscles moving him with stallion-like grace to behind his office door, leaving Nadia staring after him in a state of near shock, for she too had never known Mr Rafiq to be anything but staunchly even-tempered and rigidly polite.

Rafiq's private office was a statement in architectural drama. High ceilings, marble floors, a window that was a wall of glass, in front of which a large slab of grey marble rested on legs of forged steel. As he moved across to it the pale sunlight of a London winter morning shot shards of cold steel through his black hair and added a sharpened cast to his lean dark profile that spoke of his ruthless Arab heritage.

Stepping around the edges of the slab of marble, he slammed the newspaper down on its smooth grey top. It unfurled on impact, showing him the inner-page headline that his aide had helpfully presented to him. It was Kadir's job to scour the world's newspapers, his job to mark those items he believed would be of interest to the acting head of the International Bank of Rahman. But Kadir would not be making the same mistake again very quickly, Rafiq mused as he glared at the reason for all of his anger. He had been duped, he'd been betrayed, he had been taken for a fool by a woman. And there it was, splashed all over the page of a Spanish tabloid: his private life uncovered, picked over and mocked at.

'SHOCK ANNOUNCEMENT,' block capitals proclaimed. 'SERENA CORDERO DROPS BILLIONAIRE SHEIKH TO MARRY HER DANCE PARTNER, CARLOS MONTEZ.'

His skin began prickling against his clothing, sharp white teeth setting behind the grim line of his mouth. Only two months ago she had been clinging to him like a limpet, adoring him, begging him, telling him she could never love anyone else.

The liar, the cheat, the unfaithful little slut. As far back as six months ago his brother Hassan had warned him about Serena and Carlos Montez. Rafiq had dismissed those rumours as mere publicity to add spice to the current world tour the two flamenco dancers were embarked upon. Now he knew the truth and he could taste the bitterness of his own conceit and arrogance at having believed that Serena could not have wanted another man while she could have had him. Only twice before in his life had he ever been betrayed by a woman: once by his mother, and once by the only woman he had ever let himself love. After that last bitter experience he had vowed he would never be betrayed like that again.

Yet here he stood, pulled into the betrayal trap by yet another woman, and he was so angry he could spit nails into the half-page picture of the beautiful Serena, smiling into her new husband's handsome face.

His mobile phone began to ring; dragging it out of his pocket he put it to his ear.

'*Querida*, please don't hang up. I need you to listen to me!'

His face, like his height and the tough, muscled build of his body, made no compromises at the best of times but the low dark sensual tones that hit his ear made his face take on properties as cold as the marble and steel that surrounded him.

'The tour is in trouble. We needed a sensation to put our names on people's lips. I love you, Rafiq. You know I do. But marriage between us was never a possibility. Can you not accept this situation for what it is?'

'You are someone else's wife. Do not call me again,' he incised, and broke the connection before tossing the phone from him as if it was contaminated.

Silence arrived, buzzing in his ears like a thousand wasp wings. In front of him lay the discarded phone and the damning newspaper. Behind him lay the rest of the world who would now be laughing at him. He was an Arab in every way you wished to look at him. Make an Arab look a fool and you win yourself a life-long enemy.

Eyes like black opals turned almost silver at the prospect. Picking up the newspaper, he flung it sideways and watched as it landed in the waste-paper bin. Serena Cordero's name would never reach his eyes again, he vowed as the other telephone sitting on his desk dared to start ringing. Black opals fired as a hand snaked down and long fingers closed round grey plastic as if it was someone's throat. 'I thought I said no calls!' he bit into the mouthpiece.

'By your tone I presume you have seen the news today,' a very dry voice drawled into his ear.

His half-brother, Hassan. He should have expected it. He swung himself down into his black leather desk chair. 'If you have called me to say I told you so, then take my advice and try silence,' Rafiq returned grimly.

'May I commiserate?' Hassan wryly suggested.

'You may mind your own business,' he snapped, then added tautly, 'Does our father know?'

'You think we swap gossip about your love life?'

'I don't have a love life,' Rafiq hit back with bite. This had been part of the problem with Serena. Finding a time when their busy schedules came to together had been almost impossible. If he had seen her twice in the last few months he could well be exaggerating, for while Serena had been travelling the world in one direction with her flamenco dance troupe he had been travelling in the other direction, attending to business duties that usually belonged to Hassan.

'How is Father?' he enquired as one thought led to another.

'He is well,' his brother assured him. 'His blood count is good and his spirit is high. Don't worry about him, Rafiq,' Hassan added gently. 'He means to meet his first grandchild, believe me.'

This time Rafiq's sigh was heavy. The last six months had been a trial for all of them. The old sheikh's illness had been long and miserable, spanning years of waste and pain. But six months ago it had almost taken him from them. With thanks to Allah, he had rallied on hearing the news about his coming grandchild. Now the disease was in remission, but no one could say how long it would remain that way. So it had been decided that from then on one of the two brothers must always be at home with their father. He needed the comfort of their presence. *They* needed to know that one of them would be there if his new-found strength should suddenly fade again. With Hassan's wife Leona in the latter stages of a much prayed for pregnancy, Hassan had elected to stay at home and deal with internal matters of state while Rafiq did all the travelling, taking care of the family's international business interests.

'And Leona?' he enquired next.

'Round,' her husband drawled satirically. But Rafiq could hear the pleasure there, the love and the pride. He wished he knew what those things felt like.

Then, he told himself forcefully, no, he was not going to go down that particularly rocky pathway, and turned the conversation to the less volatile subject of business. But when he rang off he continued to sit there seething and brooding and contrarily wondering why it was that he was so angry.

He had never loved Serena. She had been speaking the truth when she'd said marriage between them had never been a possibility. She was beautiful and hot—the perfect bed partner, in fact—but love had never been the engine that drove them through the passages of pleasure, even if she'd liked to use the word to him. It had been sex, good sex, but just sex for both of them. And sitting here wishing for love like his brother had was a damn fool's game.

But the small lecture brought him to his feet and sent him to stand staring out of the window. He was remembering a time when he had once thought he had found the kind of love Hassan was enjoying—had believed he held it in his hand like a precious diamond only to discover it was merely paste. Since then he had never looked for love;

he had no wish to feel its tortuous grip again, harboured no burning desire to pass on his genetic fingerprint. That delight belonged to Hassan and Leona, both of whom were worthy candidates to make the successful genetic mix. Whereas he…

That muscle within his chest called a heart gave a squeeze and he grimaced at the sensation. Alone. The sensation spoke to him of a bleak dark sense of aloneness that made him envy all of those people he could see moving about in the street below because they probably had good wholesome relationships to go home to at night, while he—

Well, he stood up here in his marble tower, personifying the rich and powerful and enviously privileged, when sometimes, like now, he felt as poor as any beggar you might pick out on any street corner—emotionally anyway.

Serena's fault? No, not Serena but that other woman, the one with hair with the same golden sheen he could see on the woman standing in the street below. Melanie had ruined him. With a calculation that belied her beauty, her shyness and innocence, she had taken a younger Rafiq, full of confidence and optimism, and had turned him into this hardened cynic he was today.

Where was she now? he found himself pondering sombrely. What had the last eight years done for Melanie? Did she ever think of him and what their affair had done to him? Or had she simply moved on, left him so far behind that she would struggle to remember his name if they had the misfortune to come up against each other again? He guessed the latter—he *knew* the latter. Melanie might have possessed the face of an angel but she owned the heart of a harlot. Harlots did not remember names; one merged in with the many.

Behind him his mobile phone burst into life again. It would be that other harlot, Serena, he decided. She was not the kind of woman to give up easily. Did he answer? Did he leave it? Had he dropped down so low in his own estimation that he was actually asking himself those questions? His teeth came together, gleaming white against the satin darkness of his olive-toned skin as he let the phone ring and glared down at the street where the woman with the golden hair was still hovering, as if she was unsure what she was doing or where she was going. He understood the feeling, could even sympathise with it.

In fact, the golden-haired stranger had more chance of getting him to answer her call than Serena did, was his final thought on the subject of female betrayal.

Standing on the pavement outside the imposing marble, glass and forged-steel frontage of the International Bank of Rahman, Melanie tried very hard to convince herself that she was doing the right thing by coming here. The building was big, and it was bold; it spoke of no compromises when she knew she desperately needed many compromises if her plan was to succeed.

Could it succeed? Was she wasting her time by coming here to see a man she knew from experience held no respect for her at all? Remember what he said, remember what he did, a small voice in her head cautioned. Turn around, Melanie, and walk away.

But walking away was the easy option. And easy options had never come to her. It was either do this or go home and tell Robbie nothing, she determined. And if those two options were not the same as being caught between a rock and a hard place, then she didn't know what was.

So, think of Robbie, she told herself firmly, and set her reluctant feet moving towards a giant pair of plate-glass doors reinforced by solid-steel tubing that defended the entrance to one of the most prestigious investment banks in the world. As she approached she glimpsed her own reflection in the polished glass doors and didn't much like what she saw: a too-slender woman with pale hair caught into a neat little topknot and an even paler complexion touched by strain. Her eyes looked too big, her mouth too vulnerable. Overall she looked just too darn fragile to be taking on an arrogant giant like Rafiq Al-Qadim. He'll step on you and not even notice, she warned her reflection. He'll do what he did to you the last time and freeze you out with his black opal stare.

No, he won't because you just won't let him, she told herself forcefully, and kept her feet moving as the pair of doors slid open with a stealthy silence that made her insides curl.

Like its exterior, the International Bank of Rahman's inside was a cavern of more glass, marble and steel. Glass walls for three floors gave her glimpses of open-plan office spaces flickering with busy computer screens and even busier people. Here in the foyer a marble fountain pushed moisture into the air while tall exotic plants tried and failed to soften the cold, cold atmosphere. People wearing statutory grey or black moved about with the confidence of those who knew exactly what they were doing here and where they were going.

It was sharp, it was sophisticated—it was everything she wasn't. A point that would have made her smile at any other time, because she knew who she was and she liked that person. The cut-throat world of high finance held no fascination for her. Never had, never would. But as she stood looking around she was forced to accept the grim truth that, hate all this though she might do, she had still dressed for the occasion in a sharp black suit that blended in perfectly here.

Deliberate? Yes, it had been deliberate. She answered her own question as her high-heeled shoes took her across the busy foyer towards the line of steel-faced lifts. She had dressed to impress, to make him stop and think twice before he tried throwing her out again. Melanie Leggett in jeans had never managed to do that, but Melanie Portreath in a designer suit might.

A stainless-steel plaque set between two of the lifts

listed the names of the departments and the floor on which each was situated. She hovered for a moment or two, unsure as to which department she should be making for, then realised that it could only be on the top floor, because high-powered executives liked to keep their minions firmly beneath them.

As she should know, having been there once upon a long time ago. She'd played the worshipping minion to a superior ego and had learned the hard way what it was like be walked all over. It wasn't the best memory she could have picked to take with her into the lift, Melanie realised as her heart began to pump unevenly. Pressing the top-floor button, she barely felt the lift move it was so efficient, so nerves were putting that sinking feeling in her stomach, she determined. Nerves and just the teeniest hint of excitement about what she was about to do.

Face the truth, an eight-year-old truth, a dark and potentially dangerous truth. The lift doors opened, her knees began to shake as she stepped out into yet another foyer; this one was much smaller and bore the refined trappings of luxury in the soft carpet covering the floor. A steel-framed desk stood in front of a floor-to-ceiling stretch of glass covered by vertical blinds. A dark-haired woman sat working at the desk. She glanced up at Melanie's approach, came to her feet and smiled.

'Mrs Portreath? How nice to meet you.' Her voice, like her smile, was warm and pleasant, the slight accent falling in with her dark and gentle Arabian looks. Coming out from behind her workstation, she presented Melanie with a hand. 'My name is Nadia,' she announced. 'I am Mr Al-Qadim's secretary. I am afraid Mr Al-Qadim is running a little late this morning,' she went on apologetically. 'And the information your lawyer sent ahead of you arrived on my desk only five minutes ago. Please…' she indicated towards several soft-leather chairs '…make yourself comfortable while I check if Mr Al-Qadim is ready for you.'

Not for me, he isn't, Melanie thought as she watched

Nadia walk towards another giant pair of doors, made of solid wood this time. The secretary paused, seeming to need a moment to gather herself before she knocked rather tentatively on the door, opened it, stepped through and closed it behind her.

That small hesitation left Melanie standing there having to deal with the next rush of uncertainty that attacked her resolve. Rafiq was on the other side of that door, and if his secretary had to steel herself to go anywhere near him then what chance did she have of meeting a sane and sensible man?

Arrogance; she was suddenly remembering the hardened arrogance that could add such cold condemnation to his lean face. He was a man who could freeze out the world by just standing in silence, a man who could shatter a person with just two small words: 'Get out.'

Her stomach muscles collapsed on the crippling memory. In the space of six short weeks he had wooed her into loving him. He had asked her to marry him and promised her the earth. He had told her that no one could ever love her as much as he did, then he had taken her to bed and wooed her of her innocence. Then, on the evidence of one cleverly constructed scene, he had simply turned his back on her with those now immortal words, 'Get out,' and had never looked at her again.

Did she really want to subject herself to that kind of humiliation again? she asked herself. Was she crazy to risk exposing Robbie to the same?

The urge to change her mind and just walk away while she still had the chance rose up to grab at her again; panic of the sort she hadn't experienced in a long time actually set her feet swivelling towards escape.

The door behind her opened. 'Mrs Portreath?' his secretary's smooth voice prompted.

Melanie froze—utterly. She couldn't move, not a muscle; she couldn't even bring herself to draw in breath. It was awful. For a horrible moment she wondered if she was going to faint.

'Mrs Portreath…?'

Remember why you are doing this, she tried telling herself. Think of Robbie. He loves you and he's suffering right now, feeling the vulnerability of his own mortality and, more significantly, yours. Rafiq does not know what he turned his back on eight years ago. He deserves this chance to know about Robbie, just as Robbie deserves this chance to know him.

But she was scared of what it was going to mean to all of them. Rafiq was from a different race and culture. He viewed things through different eyes than she did. He might not want to know about Robbie. He might fling this chance right back at her and…

'Mrs Portreath? Mr Al-Qadim will see you now.'

Mr Al-Qadim will see you, she repeated anxiously. Did it matter if he did toss Robbie aside? It would be his loss if he did. Robbie never needed to know about this visit, but if you'd asked him outright, he would say it was worth any risk. So do this one small thing for him and you might start to sleep nights.

Small. She almost laughed, because this was no small thing. It was huge, colossal, as big and unpredictable as the big man himself.

'Get out' her head echoed. What did those two cold words do but expose a man who was unwilling to face up to *his* responsibilities? Let him use them again, she decided as her chin lifted. She could take the rejection for Robbie. She had done it before, after all. Her conscience could be cleared and she could then walk away to get on with the rest of her life, and more importantly Robbie's life, knowing she had at least tried.

'Yes, thank you,' she heard herself murmur, and by the time she turned to face Rafiq's secretary she was back in control again, with her eyes clear and her slender shoulders set into a determined line. One of the doors to the office stood open. Nadia stood to one side of it, waiting for Melanie to step by. With only the smallest increase in her pulse-rate she walked towards that open doorway and through it, with her smile fixed and ready to meet fate full-on.

The room was just another play on steel and marble. It was huge, with high ceilings and wall-to-wall glass that framed a desk built of marble and steel. In front of the desk and standing slightly side-on stood Rafiq Al-Qadim. He was wearing a dark grey suit and was leaning over slightly with one big hand braced on the desk while he read the set of papers in front of him.

Her papers, Melanie recognised. Her requirements. Her nerves began to flutter. Had he seen? Did he know yet? A clammy sweat broke out on her skin as she stood just inside the door and waited for him to lift and turn his dark head so she could make that first stunning impact on eyes that, even after eight long years, still visited her in her dreams.

Rafiq was being deliberately slow in straightening to acknowledge Mrs Portreath. He was wishing he hadn't agreed to this meeting. The woman might have inherited the Portreath fortune, but even her healthy millions were small fry to an investment bank like this. Randal Soames, the executor of the Portreath estate, had talked him into this interview. He was doing it as a favour to Randal because the woman herself was being so stubborn about wanting to use the services of the bank and, more significantly, she had insisted on seeing Rafiq. In his mind, if she'd managed to get the hard-edged Randal Soames to go against his own better judgement it made her one very manipulative woman.

He despised that kind of woman. Was learning to despise the whole female sex with each betrayal they hung upon him. If he had a choice he would have them all locked up in harems to use only when necessary. They called them the weaker sex, the vulnerable sex, when really they were stronger and more dangerous than a whole army of men.

'Mrs Portreath to see you, sir,' Nadia prompted. It was a brave thing to do when his secretary was already aware that his mood was about as volatile as an active volcano.

But it also meant that he had taken too long to lift up his head. So, gritting his teeth together behind the flat-lined set of his lips, he attempted to put some semblance of a smile on them as he straightened up and made himself turn to face the woman he was already predisposed to dislike.

What he found himself looking at shut his heart down. What he saw standing not fifteen feet away made him have to wonder if he was actually losing his mind. He could not believe it. He had conjured her up. Any second now two more women were going to walk through the door and stand right beside her: Serena and his mother. The three witches.

As that dark head lifted Melanie felt her breath begin to feather, felt her pulse begin to accelerate. He hadn't changed, was her first breathtaking observation. He still had the build of a Roman gladiator and a proud cut to his jaw line that warned of no weakness anywhere. His hair was still as black as midnight, his hands as big and strong as she remembered them to be. He could fill a room like this with his size and the sheer electrifying force of his presence.

Yet his height and his size and his deep inner reserve had somehow always made her be very gentle with him. Why was that? Melanie asked herself now as she stood facing her past with the puzzled mind of maturity. It wasn't as if he was a vulnerable giant. If anything, he had been cruel and heartless, utterly ruthless in his method of discarding her.

Her eyes took their time lifting to clash with his eyes. She was expecting to be frozen by cold disdain but what she found herself dealing with shook her to the core. For she was looking at Robbie's eyes, Robbie's beautiful, almost black eyes that were looking back at her with the same sensational long eyelashes that could turn her insides to soft, loving butter. And Robbie's wonderful high slashing cheekbones, Robbie's perfectly, perfectly moulded mouth.

And the beauty, dear God, she'd forgotten the masculine beauty in those lean dark high-born features that could flip her heart over and set her senses singing to the kind of tune she'd experienced with no other man. It hurt, oh, it hurt, because she was standing here staring love in the face again.

How could she not love, when she was seeing the man who had shaped her son's image? she thought despairingly. It was like looking into the future and seeing her beloved Robbie as he would be thirty years on: the height, the riveting dark features destined to breaks hearts just as his father's had done. Did that forecast worry her, or did it touch to life maternal pride, knowing she was in the process of rearing a heartbreaker for a son? She didn't know, couldn't think, didn't even know why she was rambling over such ridiculous things when there were far more important issues to consider.

But her insides were a mass of shakes and tremors, her eyes stinging with the onset of tears. Tears for a lost love, a broken and irreparable love. She didn't want to feel like this; she hurt as badly as if it was only yesterday that he'd thrown her out of his life.

A movement behind her caught her attention. Rafiq's secretary was hovering, probably wondering what was going on. Neither she nor Rafiq had moved or even spoken. Rafiq was frozen, his face held by a shock so profound it was clear that he was in no fit state to say a word.

Which left that mammoth task to her, Melanie realised. She'd planned this moment, spent hours rehearsing it in her head. All she had to do was find the strength and the will to put her plan into action. But it wasn't easy. She had come here believing that Rafiq had killed everything she used to feel for him. Now she knew that wasn't the case, she accepted, as she set her feet moving across a vast space of marble until she came to a stop just an arm's reach away from him.

She looked up—had to—he was six feet four inches, a towering figure in comparison to her five feet eight. It wasn't a bad height for a woman, but compared to Rafiq she felt like a pocket miniature. He had shoulders that were three times the size of her slender ones, hands that could easily span her waist. His torso was lean and cased in hard muscle, and his legs—

No, stop it, she told herself fiercely as things began to stir inside that she just did not want to feel. She lifted her eyes, made contact with the dark, dark disturbing density of his still shocked eyes that seemed to want to pull her like a magnet into taking another step closer.

She resisted the urge, held it back with a fist-grabbing catch of control. Then, with every bit of sophistication she had acquired over the past eight years, she murmured, 'Hello, Rafiq,' and even managed to hold out a surprisingly steady hand. 'It's been a long time, hasn't it?'

CHAPTER TWO

IT CAME as a punch to his stomach. The truth—reality. Melanie was standing here in front of him. No ghost, no spectre dragged up from the depths of his own bitter memory. The same spun-golden hair, darker gold eyes, creamy smooth skin covering perfect features; the same small, soft kiss-needy mouth and that soft-toned sensually pitched voice which brushed across his senses like a long-remembered lover's caress.

Yet in other ways it was not the same Melanie. The clothes didn't match, nor the way she styled her hair. The old Melanie had worn jeans and battered old trainers, not handmade leather shoes with spindles for heels and a slender black suit that shrieked the name of its designer label. Her hair used to stream around her face and shoulders, freely and simply like a child's, though then she had been a twenty-year-old woman.

'What are you doing here?' he rasped out without any attempt to hide his contempt.

'You're surprised.' She offered a wry smile. 'Maybe I should have prewarned you.'

The smile hit his system like burning poison, seared through his bloodstream on a path that had no right to gather in his loins. He shifted, ignored the hand. 'You would not have got beyond the ground-floor foyer,' he responded with a gritty truth that sent her hand sinking to her side.

It also wiped the smile from her face, and with it Rafiq felt the heat in his body begin to dissipate. She shifted uncomfortably—so did someone else. Dragging his eyes across his office, he saw his secretary standing by the door.

20

Fresh anger surged, a burning sense of bloody frustration, because this was the second time today that Nadia had witnessed him behaving like an ill-mannered boor.

'Thank you, Nadia.' He dismissed her with icy precision.

His secretary left in a hurry. Melanie turned to watch her go. Give it an hour and the whole building was going to know that Mr Rafiq was undergoing a drastic change in personality, he was thinking grimly as Melanie turned back to face him.

'She's afraid of you,' she dared to remark.

'The word you mean to use is respect,' he corrected. 'But, in truth, your opinion of my staff does not interest me. I prefer to know how you dare to think you can safely walk in here masquerading as someone you most definitely are not.'

Eyes that reflected the winter pale sunlight streaming in through the window, widened. 'Oh, I'm sorry, Rafiq. I thought you knew who I was. Didn't you receive the papers from my lawyer's office?'

Since those very papers were lying on his desk in front of both of them, it was sarcasm at its infuriating best. But it also made its point. Rafiq's eyes narrowed. 'You mean you actually are the Melanie Portreath who inherited the Portreath fortune?' he demanded in disbelief.

'Don't sound so shocked,' Melanie responded dryly. 'Even poor little country girls can have a lucky change in fortune occasionally.'

'Marry it, you mean.'

The moment he'd said it Rafiq could have bitten his tongue off. It was hard and it was bitter and gave the impression that he might actually still care that she'd been seduced by his wealth.

'If you say so,' she murmured, and turned away to take an interest in her surroundings. As she did so he caught the delicate shape of her profile and felt something painful tug at his chest. Damn it, he thought. Don't do that to me.

'This place is as cold as a mausoleum,' she told him.

She was right, and it was. Leona was always telling him the same thing. His half-brother Hassan's office, which was next door to this one, had received a full makeover by Leona's gifted hand to make it more hospitable. But Rafiq refused to let her anywhere near his office because— because he liked mausoleums, having placed his life in one, he accepted with an inner sigh.

Maybe Melanie knew what he was thinking, because she turned suddenly and their eyes clashed again, golden light touching bleak darkness, and the years were falling away. She had once told him that he was incapable of feeling anything deeply, that his big test in life was to learn to trust his own feelings instead of deferring those judgements to others. 'You'll end up a cold and lonely cynic, Rafiq,' she'd predicted. 'Living on the fringes of real life.'

'What do you want, Melanie?' he demanded grimly.

'To sit down would be nice.'

'You will not be stopping long enough to warrant it.'

'It would be to your loss.'

'The door is over there,' he drawled coldly. 'My secretary will see you out.'

'Oh, don't be so arrogant.' She frowned at him. 'You could at least have the decency to hear what I have to say.'

'You can have nothing to say that I wish to listen to.' With that he turned and walked around his desk.

'Now you sound pompous.'

He swung on her so angrily that she took a shaky step back from the desk in alarm. 'I sound like a *cheated* man!'

The words rang in the space between them. Melanie looked into his face and felt her knees start to fail. Bold slashing features cast in bronze seemed to loom ever closer. Eyes spiked with bitterness threatened to shrivel her where she stood. His mouth was no longer a mouth, but a pair of parted lines between which a set of white teeth glinted with danger. And the cold slab of marble lying between them seemed to be the only thing holding him back from stretching out a large hand and taking hold of her by the scruff of her neck.

She was shocked. Oh, not because of the pulsing threat itself, but because she would never have believed that he could reveal so much of what was raging inside him. The man she'd used to know had been so fiercely controlled that it had taken him weeks to get around to admitting he was attracted to her. He'd used to haunt her family's farm on the pretext that he was considering investing money into it. He'd used to turn up in strange places like the tack room at the stables, or the hay barn, and would stand watching as she heaved bales of hay onto a low-loader ready for transport to the animals scattered about the outlying fields.

'You should not be doing this,' he'd said in husky disapproval.

'Why?' She remembered laughing at him. 'Because I'm a woman?'

'No.' He hadn't smiled back. 'Because you hate it.'

It had been a truth that had confounded her, because she hadn't realised her dislike had showed. She'd been living on the farm since she was ten year's old, had been expected to do her share of the many daily chores. But as for enjoying the life? No. She would have given anything to go back to how things used to be, when she'd lived in London with two loving parents instead of one bad-tempered uncle and his weak stepson.

'You cheated yourself,' she now returned unsteadily. 'And you have no idea how badly you—'

'Quit,' he warned thinly, 'while you still can.'

It was an outright threat. Instinct was telling her to heed it, but anger was already welling up from the dark pit where she'd stored it for the past eight long years.

'As you did when you preferred to believe lies about me, rather than give me a single minute to explain what you saw?' she flashed back at him. 'Is this my cue to come over all tomb-like and walk out of here, Rafiq? Will it make you feel better if I leave you alone with your righteous belief that you were the only one injured eight years ago?'

'Get out,' he incised.

And there they were. Those magic words, delivered with the same black-toned lack of emotion as before, that literally froze her blood. Melanie looked into the cold dark cast of his face and thought, Ten minutes. It had taken just ten short minutes for them to reach the same point where they had finished things eight years ago.

She laughed, though it was a shaky sound, and swung away, aware that she might have mocked herself about those two small words earlier, but they were still having that same crippling effect on her now as they'd had then.

Only there was a difference. The younger Melanie had run; this older version was made of stronger stuff. She swung back, faced him squarely. 'I have something important to tell you first,' she announced.

'I have no wish to hear it.'

'You might regret saying that.'

'Leave, Melanie,' he reiterated.

'Not until you hear me out.'

Where had that damn stubbornness come from? Rafiq glared at her with a mix of frustration and fascination. It had been a hard push to get the old Melanie to argue about anything. Now he could not shut her up!

The telephone on his desk began to ring, and glad of the diversion he picked it up. It was Nadia informing him that his next appointment had just cancelled. 'Thank you,' he murmured, and returned the receiver to its rest, then glanced at Melanie. 'I'm sorry but my next appointment has arrived,' he lied. 'Which means that your time is up.'

Melanie stared at him. He could have done without seeing the hurt glinting in her eyes. 'You never intended to give me a chance, did you?' she gasped.

'Even as Mrs Portreath?' He arched a cold black eyebrow. 'No,' he confessed. 'I have a congenital dislike of machinating women, you see, so using Randal Soames to get you into this room earned you no more extra time than if you had managed to get in here as Melanie Leggett.'

And that, Melanie realised, more or less said it. She had failed in her mission even before she'd arrived here. What a joke, what a sad little joke. For a few moments longer she continued to stand there, looking at this tall dark beautiful man with the romantic face of Arabia and eyes fit to turn a desert to ice, and seeing no sign at all that there was anything worth appealing to beyond those eyes she knew she was going to give up the fight.

'You know what I think, Rafiq?' she said quietly. 'I think you've just lost the only chance you will ever be given to turn yourself into a human being.'

And with that she turned to walk away. From his chance, from Robbie's chance. The threat of tears suddenly overtook her, because she knew deep down inside she was walking away from her own last chance to make this man understand the truth about her.

I was a fool for thinking I could do it, she railed at herself. Rafiq needed a heart before he could care enough to want to listen. Robbie didn't need a man without a heart cluttering up his life. He had already known the best. It would be an insult to William Portreath's memory to now offer her son the worst.

'Wait…'

Her hand had a grip on the door handle. Melanie froze like a statue with her eyes to the door. What next? What now? she wondered tensely. Did she even want to hear it?

Yet she didn't move. Bigger fool that she was, she just stood there and waited, with her teeth clenched tightly and her heart pumping heavily, while behind her there was… nothing. He didn't speak again, nor move, as far as she could tell. And where the silence before had held a smothering sense of failure, this silence screamed with hope. Weak and pathetic, pained and helpless—hope.

She was trembling; Rafiq could see it happening. So

much so that the knot of silk hair was threatening to come loose. Was she close to tears also? He had a suspicion that she was—just as he had a suspicion that he'd just made the biggest mistake of his life by stopping her from leaving here.

But her last remark had got to him; it had touched a raw nerve inside that went back eight years to when he'd regretted not listening to what she'd had to say. The human being part had pricked him, because if anyone knew he was only half-human then it had to be himself. But here stood the woman he blamed for that.

So why *had* he stopped her when she could have been gone by now? Confusion at his own actions set him frowning as he threw himself down into his chair and tried to decide what do next. As he did so his eyes fell on the stack of papers he'd only had time to glance at before Melanie had walked into the room.

'Tell me about William Portreath,' he invited.

Her shoulders sagged a little, her chin dipping towards her chest to expose the long slender length of her nape. A nape he could almost feel against his fingers—fingers that actually stretched out on cold smooth marble in a featherlike caress. He drew them into a fist, sat outwardly relaxed in his chair while inside every muscle he owned had knotted in an effort to cast out what had been daring to take a grip. His gaze dropped to where her hand still grasped the door handle. Like him, she was dubious about continuing this.

The tension rose along with the silence, and his heart began to pump unevenly in his chest. When his mobile phone began to ring he was so glad of the diversion that he answered it without even thinking about it.

It was Serena again. Of course it was Serena. She had just remembered who was financing her tour, and was using her most seductive voice to try and make him see sense.

At last Melanie moved. He didn't. In fact his eyes, ears,

his capacity to breathe had all been lost in a stress-loaded moment as he watched her fingers slacken and finally drop away from the handle altogether. She began to turn. It was slow and uncertain. She began walking back across the room with her eyes carefully lowered so he could not see what was going on behind them.

Serena was turning on the heat now, the fact that he hadn't cut the connection giving her encouragement. She wanted them to carry on as they had been. She wanted him to remember what it had been like for them.

But *he* was remembering what it had been like with Melanie. He watched her come towards him in her smart suit that skimmed her slender body like a smooth outer skin, but he saw tight faded jeans and a simple tee shirt, saw himself peeling both from her wonderful flesh with hands that worshipped what they found. He saw beautifully formed breasts with rose-tinted areolae and perfect nipples that tightened at the slightest caress. His eyelashes grew heavy as his gaze skimmed downwards to recall the flatness of her silk-smooth stomach with its perfect oval for a navel and gently rounded hips that loved to be cradled in his. Shy Melanie, virginal Melanie, with a soft mouth that had trembled because she had wanted him so badly, and eyes glowing like topaz, aroused and ready to offer him her one precious gift. If everything else she had ever offered him had been lies then he knew without question that wanting him so badly she had had to give him her virginity had been Melanie's one truth.

Should that count for something now? he pondered grimly. In his own country it would count for everything. They would have been man and wife on the strength of that one night alone. Indeed, his sense of honour had already made that decision before he had claimed his exquisite prize. It was a prize that still held a power over him as he sat here in the present listening to one woman beg for his passion while the other aroused him without having to try. He recalled a single afternoon spent upon an old-fashioned feather mattress beneath an eiderdown when her arms had clung to him and her body had accepted him with small soft gasps that had rolled his heart around. He had felt the barrier, could still feel it tempting the proud crown of his sex. 'Yes,' she had said in that soft breathy whisper, and it had stirred him beyond anything he could ever remember.

He was in agony, he noted ruefully. But while he sat here struggling with his own discomfort, he also had the satisfaction of seeing Melanie's cheeks grow warm and her eyelashes flicker in a way that placed a wry smile on his lips. She knew what he was thinking and was unable to look at him because she was feeling the effects of those memories just as strongly as he was.

It was sex, nothing more. He could deal with sex—as the beautiful Serena would agree.

If he didn't stop undressing her with his eyes she would change her mind and leave, Melanie decided as she sank down into the chair by the desk. He was daring to sit there looking as laid back as a man could look while listening to a telephone conversation, but his hooded eyes were burning through her clothing. Did he think she was too dense to know what he was doing?

A wry smile twitched his mouth. It was a mouth that should have looked mean and cold, but by some quirk of fate looked anything but. She sighed, dropped her eyes away from him and wished his expression did not re-minded her of sex. One man, one afternoon, only that one experience to call upon—and she was certainly able to call upon it, she noted helplessly. All it had taken was a know-ing glint in those eyes and she could see the man in all his naked glory. The breadth of his wide bronzed shoulders and long muscular torso peppered with soft dark hair and—no, stop right there.

Who was on the other end of the phone that could hold him in silence for so long? she wondered as she shifted restlessly on the chair. She wished he would speak, if only to break this terrible tension that was eddying in the air.

Sexual tension. The man had always had the power to turn her inside out with that heavy-lashed, steady stare. Perhaps he knew it, perhaps the call had finished ages ago but he was stretching out the silence on purpose just to extend the agony. Could he be that calculating?

Yes, she decided, of course he could. He had made it very clear that he didn't want her here, but then for some baffling reason had decided to give her a chance to say what she'd come to say. Perhaps she'd touched a nerve when she'd challenged his status as a human being, and this was his idea of payback. Rafiq had pride enough for ten men. He had an ego as big as…other parts.

Oh, stop it! she railed at herself as a second wave of heat crawled up her cheeks.

Rafiq saw the blush and was reminded of the first time he'd seen her, at a friend's country estate. He had been there as a weekend guest and Melanie had been one of the paid staff. She'd served him throughout dinner, quiet, shy, and wearing a perpetual blush to her cheeks. Every time she'd leant over his shoulder to serve him he'd inhaled the scent of her delicate perfume, had felt the soft brush of her breath and her silk hair brushing his cheek. Electric, clinging… He stopped breathing for a moment in dark recollection. Twice she'd caught his shoulder with a serving dish and had almost died with embarrassment. Twice he'd found himself making a joke about his own size in an attempt to deflect the wrath of his hostess.

'She's new—temporary,' Sally Maitland had explained with the condescending tone of someone who had lived her whole life being served only by the best. 'Leave it, Melanie!' she had snapped in annoyance while Melanie valiantly tried to remove spilled sauce from where it had landed on the tablecloth by Rafiq's plate. Her hand had been trembling, the heat from her cheeks hot enough to heat his own cheek as she leant across him. 'You just can't get the staff these days. Melanie is more used to feeding chickens than people.'

He smiled at the memory, though it was more like a grimace. Melanie had fed him a lot that weekend. She'd fed his mind and his senses by being everywhere he'd happened to be. Her perfume had lingered in his bedroom whenever he'd walked back into it after she'd been there tidying the bed; her shyly lowered eyes had followed him whenever she'd had the misfortune to be serving food. If they'd met on the stairs she'd blush like mad and scurry hastily away from him; if they'd brushed arms or shoulders she'd jump like a startled kitten and refuse, though he'd tried, to utter a single word to him. Nods and shakes had been all he'd got for his trouble.

Nods and shakes that had almost driven him out of his mind.

'Come on, *querida*. Forgive me and let us put this behind us. Carlos is not expecting fidelity from me and I—'

With a flick of the hand he cut the connection. Melanie lifted her face. 'You didn't speak a single word,' she said, almost accusingly.

'No words were required,' he drawled lazily, and smiled the kind of smile that made her feel threatened and edgy and eager to get out of here.

'About William,' she said firmly, 'I think I should start by—'

'Lunch,' he inserted.

'Lunch?' Melanie offered him a perfectly blank stare.

He offered a smile to her. 'I think we will take this conversation away from the business environment and place it in a more…congenial setting.'

'But you have another appointment waiting outside!'

His answer to that was to reach out and pick up the other phone. Several smooth words spoken in Arabic and as far as Melanie was concerned the problem of his next appointment had been consigned to the archives. The phone went back on its rest.

'Problem solved,' he murmured with lying smoothness.

'I really do prefer to deal with this right here.' It was almost a desperate little plea.

'Oh, come.' He stood up. 'Here I am attempting to show you my human side by offering to listen to you, and you throw this gesture back in my face?'

If he thought listening to her talk over lunch was going to be pleasant then he was in for a surprise, Melanie thought ruefully. And why did she feel as if she'd just come face to face with a slippery snake?

She watched him warily as he walked around the marble slab. The dig about his human side hadn't passed her by either, nor the fact that in the space of a one-way conversation with his mobile phone his whole manner towards her had taken a complete reversal. He arrived at the side of her chair. The hairs on the back of her neck began to stand on end. He was waiting for her to give in and stand up, but her eyes were level with a certain part of his anatomy and what she could see happening there sent a wave of shocked heat sweeping down her front.

This had nothing to do with lunch, or talking, or even him showing his human side! It was to do with sex. Let-me-rumble-you-on-the-nearest-bed kind of sex—for old times' sake.

'Stop this, Rafiq,' she uttered tensely.

'Stop what?'

'You *know* what!' Jumping up, she took an anxious step back. The chair was in the way, the marble desk blocking any other form of escape. 'Let me pass,' she insisted.

'Of course.' He took a step sideways.

Flustered beyond daring to think, Melanie went to slither between him and the desk. His hand snaked out, caught her by the waist to bring her to a standstill. It was the first time he'd touched her in eight long years and it turned her senses into live wires that forced her to draw in a sharp breath.

He laughed huskily. 'Sure you want to go?'

She lifted her face to spit out her answer at him. Eyes clashed with eyes, hot and elemental. She parted her lips on a shivering gasp. Rafiq dipped his dark head and covered them. She fell into his kiss like a suicidal lemming.

What shocked Rafiq more was that he did the same thing himself. He had no idea where it all came from. One minute he was toying with her just for the hell of it, the next he was locked into hottest, darkest, most sexually arousing kiss he had ever experienced in his life! He could feel every quivering inch of her as if they were already naked. Her perfume filled his head, and the desperate little groans she was making as she tried to fight what was happening and knew she did not stand a chance vibrated in every one of his nerve cells.

Melanie the harlot, he thought grimly as she arched compulsively then hungrily deepened the kiss. Well…why not? he asked himself as the anger still burning within the desire gave him the excuse to do what he liked. The desk was convenient. All it would take was a lift of his arm and he could be enjoying her on a slab of cold marble. Sex in a mausoleum, he thought grimly, sacrificial and pagan. It suited him very well.

A sound beyond the door infiltrated the madness. With a tug Melanie managed to separate their mouths, then took a jerky step back. Shocked and shaken by the whole experience, she slumped weakly against the edge of the marble and gasped like a sprinter while trying to clear the dizzy fog from her head.

'What made you do that?' she choked out when she could manage to say anything.

He laughed—harshly—as if she'd just told a really bad joke. But the really bad joke was the way he was standing there calmly fastening shirt buttons she must have unfastened! Horrified, she looked down, and saw her jacket was hanging open revealing her skimpy black lace bra. Pure vanity had made her decide to wear nothing else beneath the jacket, so as not to spoil its smooth line. But now she had to deal with the mortifying knowledge that he knew she had come here only half-dressed!

As if she was begging for it. She shuddered. She could almost hear him saying those derisory words out loud. Why not? She had fallen into that kiss like a love-racked teenager.

Her skin was flushed, her nipples hard. 'I don't believe this is happening,' she breathed shakily, while urgently redoing buttons with numb fingers and wishing she couldn't still feel his hands on her body.

'You should not have come here, Melanie,' Rafiq said grimly.

'I didn't come here for this!' she cried.

'Take my advice and get out of here.' Turning, he strode back round the desk. 'And if you have any sense at all you will not attempt to come back.'

Melanie nodded in complete agreement, tried swallowing down the lump in her throat and tried to stand without the aid of the desk. It didn't happen. Her legs refused to support her. It was the final humiliation and she had to put a trembling hand up to cover her burning eyes.

He was a ruthless, heartless, arrogant devil. How could she have let herself forget all of that?

But she hadn't forgotten it. She'd merely shelved it in a box marked, Has had time to change.

'I n-need my papers,' she stammered, and in a last-ditch attempt to leave with some dignity she forced her stupid legs to carry her weight.

He nodded coolly, and began gathering the papers together. Melanie stood at his side and waited in stiff silence for him to hand them over so that she could get out of here and never, ever come back.

'Your uncle is still running the farm?' he asked suddenly.

She frowned at the question, her head still too fluffy to think properly. 'He died five years ago in a farming accident.'

'I'm sorry, I had not heard.'

Melanie shrugged away his commiserations. There had never been any affection between her and her uncle. She was sorry he had died so tragically, but other than that, she still could not bring herself to forgive him for the part he had played in trying to ruin her life.

'And Jamie?'

Ah, he couldn't resist it, could he? A fresh wave of bitterness welled, putting the light of defiance back in her eyes. Her chin went up and she threw that defiance straight at him. 'My papers,' she prompted, holding a hand out.

To Rafiq, this was a challenge and a refusal to make any comment on the person she had betrayed him with. He lowered his gaze to the outstretched hand.

'You've changed,' he remarked. 'Grown more assertive.'

'Life has a habit of changing you.'

'And money.'

'And money.' She nodded in agreement.

'Which you would like me to invest for you?'

'Money is a devil to look after if you're not used to handling it,' she answered.

'Why me?' he asked, suddenly curious when Melanie no longer wanted him to be.

'Because Randal assured me that you were the best.' And that's all you're getting out of me, she added silently.

'Liar,' he drawled. '*You* suggested *me* to Randal.'

Oh, that shook her. She hadn't expected Randal to reveal that juicy bit of information. Still, she rallied. 'Are you trying to tell me that you *aren't* the best?'

His smile this time was disturbing. Disturbing because she'd seen Robbie use the exact same expression, but had never connected it with his father before. She knew that physical things, like the colour of eyes and hair and skin, came as part of the genetic package, but she hadn't realised that smiles did also.

'There you are, then.' She tried a smile. 'I was hoping

your business ethic would put you above bearing grudges. It seems I was wrong. My mistake. I'll find someone else.'

'To...' he glanced at the top piece of paper ''"...invest one half of your inheritance in long-term options while the other half is locked into a trust fund,"' he read out loud.

A frisson of alarm disturbed her breathing. He was beginning to show interest when she no longer wanted him to. 'Randal is setting the trust fund up for me,' she said tensely, her eyes fixed on those long brown fingers set against the white paper that held the details of her entire life.

Her life and Robbie's life.

'For whom?' Rafiq questioned.

'Does it matter?' she countered stiffly.

'If you want me to work with you, it does,' he murmured quietly.

'But I don't any longer.'

He ignored that and went to sit down in his chair—taking her papers with him. 'Sit and explain,' he smoothly invited, then flipped to the next page.

'N-no,' she refused. 'I've changed my mind, Rafiq. I made a mistake to come to y-you. I know that now. You were right. I should leave. I'm s-sorry I intruded.'

Rafiq narrowed his eyes on her taut stature; something inside him went very still. She was afraid, white with it, suddenly no longer defiant but teetering dangerously on the edge of panic.

'For whom?' he repeated very quietly, and watched with deepening interest as her eyes flickered away, nervously scanning anything that did not include him. They settled on the illuminated numbers on the communications console.

'Lunch is out,' she announced jerkily. 'I have to be somewhere else at one.'

Rafiq said nothing. He just continued to sit there watching as her cheeks grew even paler and her tongue made a nervous pass across trembling lips. Lips that still pulsed from his kiss, he noticed. Lips that seemed to have forgotten how to speak. She was tense, she was edgy, she was so nervous he could see the fine tremors attacking her flesh.

A sudden thought made his eyes narrow. She was Melanie Portreath now, not the Melanie Leggett he'd used to know. William Portreath had been in his nineties when he'd died, making his widow very rich. Rafiq knew how these things usually worked: wise men tended to protect their money from the machinations of a trophy wife.

But protect it for whom? 'Answer me, Melanie,' he commanded grimly.

She shimmered a glance at him then dragged it away, swallowed, and murmured huskily, 'M-my son. The trust is to be set up for my son.'

So, the old man had been capable of enjoying the charms of his lovely young bride! Rafiq's skin began to prickle at the very idea of it. She was now so pale her eyes were bruising. Was it shame? Was she beginning to realise that it was not as easy as she had expected to come in here and admit that she had sold herself for a pot of gold to a man old enough to be her grandfather?

Sickness was suddenly clawing at his stomach, disgust climbing up the walls of his chest, as she stood there staring at him through eyes that seemed to beg him for some kind of understanding. But all he saw was her beautiful, smooth naked form lying beneath a withered old man.

Placing the papers on his desk, he stood up and was amazed at the smoothness of the movement, was impressed by the way his legs carried him around the desk. 'Come with me,' he said, and was further impressed by the steadiness of his voice as he gave the instruction.

Melanie was looking slightly bewildered. He had no wish to look into her face any longer so he turned and walked away. As he strode towards the door he could hear her following him. In the outer foyer Nadia was busy at her computer, and Kadir was leaning against her desk while talking on the telephone. He was speaking Arabic, but Rafiq had not a single clue what words were being spoken in his natural tongue.

'Kadir!' With a flick of a hand he brought his aide to attention and kept on walking towards the other side of the room, where the lift stood with its doors conveniently open and waiting for them.

Kadir arrived at Rafiq's side as he was silently indicating to his aide Melanie should precede him. She was frowning as she did so, eyeing Rafiq warily as she passed him by. He ignored her to indicate to Kadir to follow suit. Kadir entered the lift. Rafiq stepped in after them, but only for as long as it took him to hit the ground-floor button. He was taking no chances here.

'Escort Mrs Portreath off the premises,' he instructed Kadir. 'And ensure that she does not gain entrance to this building again.'

With that he walked away, hearing Melanie's shocked gasp as the lift doors put solid steel between them. As he strode past Nadia's workstation he ignored his secretary's stunned expression. With the easy flow of a man completely in control of his own actions, he stepped back into his office and closed the door.

Melanie was staring at the walls of her steel prison. Shock was holding her silent and still. Beside her, the dark-haired young Arab called Kadir was almost as frozen.

She found her voice. 'What happened?' she whispered.

He offered her a very formal bow. 'I'm afraid I do not know.'

Then, before either could say anything else, the doors were opening onto the ground-floor foyer and Kadir was politely carrying out his master's wishes by escorting her all the way to the giant glass doors and even beyond. In a daze of bewilderment Melanie found herself being offered another polite bow before the young man turned and retreated through the doors again, leaving her standing there in a state of utter disabling shock at the slick smooth way

Rafiq had just executed his revenge on her—if revenge was what it had all been about. She didn't know, didn't care. He had thrown her out—publicly. In all her life she'd never felt so humiliated.

Stunned beyond being able to function sensibly, she began moving and almost fell beneath the wheels of a passing car. The car horn sounded; she just stood watching as it brushed by within inches.

Up high, in his marble tower, Rafiq viewed her near-death experience through black eyes and with bone-crackingly clenched teeth. It was only as he stood there fighting a battle between fear for her life and a wish never to lay eyes on her again that he made the connection between Melanie and the golden-haired woman he had watched hovering in the street before.

If he had known then what he knew now she would not have got beyond the building's entrance doors, saving them both a lot of trouble.

The liar, the cheat, the little slut, he seethed in ice-cold silence. And he'd had the pleasure of experiencing two of her kind in a single day! All he needed now was for his mother to rise up from the grave and tell him exactly how much money she had squeezed out of his father before she'd agreed to carry his child full term.

Money. It always came down to money with women, he concluded, as he turned away from the window after watching one of their number safely cross the road. His mobile phone began to ring. Striding over to his desk, he picked it up, opened the back, removed the SIM card, then discarded the lot into the waste-paper bin where today's Spanish newspaper was already showing yesterday's news.

By tomorrow he would have pulled the plug on Serena's finances. And his mother had ceased to be an issue when she'd died on the day of his birth. Which left only Melanie—or Mrs Portreath, he amended bitterly as he picked up the stack of her papers with the intention of consigning those to the waste-paper bin along with everything else.

Only something caught his eye and he hesitated…

CHAPTER THREE

MELANIE had no idea how she managed to get home again. She had only a vague recollection of standing on an Underground train and being strangely comforted because she was just one more blank face amongst many. But now here she stood in her own warm kitchen, surrounded by everything that represented familiarity, comfort and security to her—and she felt like an alien.

An alien being in an alien place, present, yet not a part of. It was an odd sensation, because she recognised everything yet couldn't seem to connect with any of it. The old Aga set into the chimney-breast, for instance, the scrubbed table that took up too much space but was as much a part of the family as Robbie's pictures decorating the cork notice-board on the wall by the door. Assorted mugs hung from old-fashioned cup hooks suspended beneath one of the ancient wall cabinets, and at some point since coming home, she had set the old kettle to heat on the Aga, though she didn't remember doing it. It was puffing out steam in a gentle flow now, telling her the water was hot but not yet boiling. She had lost her shoes somewhere and was standing on cold quarry tiling in silk stockings that had cost her the absolute earth, though it felt as if she was floating above the floor.

Shock. She was suffering from shock. She understood that even if she couldn't seem to do anything about it. Every time she tried to think what had thrust her into this foggy state she experienced that awful sinking sensation of a lift swooping downwards and the claustrophobic sensation of being encased in steel. But what had happened

40

before the lift and what had come after it was refusing to show itself.

She looked at the wall clock, saw it wasn't even one o'clock yet, and realised she'd done well to get back so quickly after...

That lift swooped her downwards again and she fumbled for a kitchen chair then sank onto it, put a cold hand up to cover her mouth and caught a brief flash of Rafiq's stone-like face. She blinked slowly as the part of her brain that stored pictures refused to connect with the part that stored emotion.

He'd thrown her out.

She dropped the hand onto the table, fingertips hovering in the air as if they knew that making contact with anything solid would cause some kind of horrible calamity.

He'd played with her like a cat with a mouse. He'd insulted her, kissed her, had brought her right there to the very edge of panic by suddenly showing an interest in things she'd no longer wanted him to know about. Then, quite calmly and precisely, he had thrown her out.

Her fingers began to curl down towards the table, her stomach muscles coiled into a ball, and at last blood began to pump more oxygen to her brain. Across the kitchen the kettle began to make hissing noises; the clock on the wall chimed the hour. The fingers touched base and she stood up; it was quick and tense and impulsive.

How could she have got it so wrong? How could she have talked herself into believing that he possessed a heart worth pleading with? Where had she ever got the stupid idea that he was a worthy father for her very precious son?

The telephone mounted on the wall behind her began ringing. Forcing herself to go and answer it took most of her self-control.

'I saw you come back,' a female voice said. 'How did it go?'

It was her neighbour, Sophia. 'It didn't go anywhere,' Melanie replied, then burst into tears.

Sophia arrived within minutes, banging on the back door with a demand to be let in after having come through the hole in the hedge that separated their two gardens. She was a tall, dark-haired, sex-seething bombshell with lavender eyes and a lush mouth that could slay the world. But inside the stunning outer casing lurked a legal mind that was a sharp as a razor and as tough as the glass ceiling she was striving to break through.

'Dry those tears,' she instructed the moment Melanie opened the door to her. 'He doesn't deserve them, and you know he doesn't.'

Half an hour later Melanie had poured the whole thing out to her over a cup of tea. By then Sophia's amazing eyes had turned glassy. 'It sounds to me as if you and Robbie have just had a very lucky escape. The man is a first-class bastard. I did tell you, you should have stuck with me, kid,' she added sagely. 'I'm a much better father-figure for any boy child.'

It was such a ludicrous thing to say that Melanie laughed for the first time. But in a lot of ways Sophia was speaking the truth, because her neighbour's curt, no-nonsense approach to life had always appealed to Robbie. When he was in need of something other than his mother's loving softness he would disappear through the hole in the hedge to search out Sophia. So did Melanie, come to that.

'What did your lawyer have to say when you told him?' Sophia asked curiously. 'The same as me—I told you so?'

Randal. Melanie's brain ground to a halt again; she went still, her eyes fixed and blank. Then—

'Oh, dear God,' Melanie breathed, then jumped up and made a dive for the telephone.

'What?' Sophia demanded anxiously. 'What did I say?'

'Oh—hello.' Melanie cut across Sophia with the tense greeting. 'I need to speak to Randal Soames, please. I'm M-Mrs Portreath... W-what do you mean he isn't there? I was supposed to be meeting him there for lunch!'

'Mr Soames was called out on urgent business, Mrs

Portreath,' his secretary told her. 'I was expecting you to arrive at any minute so I could offer you his apologies.'

She didn't *want* an apology. 'I have to speak to Randal!' She was becoming hysterical. 'When will he be back?'

'He didn't say…'

'W-well…' Melanie took in a breath and tried to calm herself '…I need you to get him on his mobile phone and tell him I have s-speak to him urgently.'

'Yes, Mrs Portreath. I will try to contact him for you but I can't promise. He tends to switch off his mobile when he's in a meeting, you see.'

Melanie placed the receiver back on its rest, then sank weakly against the wall and put a hand up to cover her aching eyes.

'What was all that about?' Sophia questioned.

'I left my papers on Rafiq's desk,' she breathed. 'How could I have been so *stupid*!'

The covering hand began to tremble. On a sigh, Sophia came to place an arm across her shoulders. 'Okay, calm down,' she murmured soothingly. 'I think you need to remember that he didn't give you much chance to do otherwise,' she pointed out.

No, he hadn't, Melanie agreed. He'd just got rid of her. He'd heard enough—*had* enough—and had just got up and marched her out! Sophia almost copied him by marching her back to the kitchen table and sitting her down again, only her friend used a guiding arm to do it whereas Rafiq hadn't even spared her a glance, never mind touched her! As if she was unclean. As if he would have contaminated himself if he'd remained in her company too long.

A shudder ripped through her. 'Stop shaking,' Sophia commanded. 'The man isn't worth the grief.'

But Melanie didn't want to stop shaking. She wanted to shiver and shake and remember another time when he'd done almost the same thing. She had followed him back to London, had almost had hysterics in her desire to get inside his embassy and plead with him. What she'd met with when she'd eventually been granted an audience had been Rafiq locked into his Arab persona, about to attend some formal function dressed in a dark red cloak, white tunic and wearing a white *gut rah* on his head. He'd looked taller and leaner, foreign and formidable. His face had taken on a whole new appearance: harder, savage, honed to emulate some cold-eyed, winged predator. 'Get out.' He'd said those two immortal words then turned his back on her to stride away.

'Melanie, if he still despises you as much as you think he does, he will probably consign your papers to the bin without bothering to read them.'

'Yes.' She liked that scenario.

'But would it be a very bad thing if he did read them?' Sophia then dared to suggest. 'At least he would know everything—which is what you wanted, remember? It was why you decided to go to see him in the first place.'

Sophia was holding onto her hands while trying to talk some good sense into the situation. But she hadn't been there this morning; she hadn't seen the size of the mistake Melanie had made. It had been huge; she'd been damned by her own foolish optimism, letting the years soften Rafiq's hard image until she'd actually begun to question whether *she* had been fair to *him*.

William had helped by gently nudging her in this direction. Dear, sweet, gentle William who, like herself, hadn't liked to see bad in anyone. But even William's advice had only been wise with all the facts laid before him. If Rafiq did decide to read those papers they would only tell him half the story. As for the other half—

Well, that half belonged to his eagerness to believe badly of her simply because people had told him to.

But, no. She sighed. There had been so much more to it than words of poison spoken into his ear. He had *seen* her with Jamie. It had all been so desperately damning. And explainable, she reminded herself, if he had only given her the chance to explain. He hadn't and still wouldn't. That hadn't changed. He still looked at her and saw her through the unforgiving eyes of a half-Arab man with his feet firmly entrenched in cultural principles and a deep-rooted belief that all women were natural sinners.

And she no longer wanted a man like that to come anywhere near her son so he could contaminate him with his poisonous view of her.

'Melanie—'

No. She scrunched her hands free, then got to her feet. She didn't want to talk about it any more. For what was the use in talking when it was basically too late? All she could hope for now was that Randal would come through for her and manage to retrieve her stuff before Rafiq decided to feed his hatred by reading things that he really did not want to know.

'What are you doing at home at this time of the day, anyway?' she asked Sophia as an abrupt change of subject. 'I thought you were supposed to be wowing them all in some court or other.'

'The case was adjourned,' Sophia explained. 'And I'm off to wow them in Manchester tomorrow, so I decided to come home to pack a bag and catch a flight up there today. I've got friends there I haven't seen in ages—but I've changed my mind,' she then added swiftly. 'I'm going to stay here with you, just in case—'

'No, you're not.' Mouth set in a stubborn line, Melanie glared at her with a warning look. 'I had a bad experience today but I'm all right,' she insisted, and to prove it she gathered up the tea mugs and took them to the sink. 'Maybe I even needed it to help me move on from the past.'

'You believe you can do that?' Sophia sounded sceptical.

Maybe she was right to. 'I have no choice.' Just as soon as I've got my papers back, she thought with a shiver. 'Because I won't be repeating the same mistake twice.'

It was such a complete, final statement that Sophia

didn't even attempt to say another word. Ten minutes later she'd gone, leaving Melanie with the rest of the afternoon stretching out in front of her like a long dark road filled with nerve-stretching uncertainty—and a heartache she didn't want to feel.

She called Randal's office three times with no satisfaction. Actually picked up the phone to call Rafiq's secretary, only to change her mind when his final words came back to hit her full in the face. She would not even get beyond the main switchboard.

How could a man fester in such hatred that it could make him want to humiliate her like that? Tears threatened again; she swallowed them down and went upstairs to change out of her suit. As she removed the jacket she caught sight of herself in the mirror, saw the black lacy bra and relived the feeling of long brown fingers staking their claim. She shuddered, despising herself for being so easy, finished removing the suit and scrambled into a pair of faded old jeans and a roll-neck top that covered everything. By the time she walked downstairs a few minutes later she was the casual Melanie her son was used to seeing when he arrived home from school. No sign of designer clothes left anywhere for him to pick up on. No hint that she'd been doing anything today that was different from any other day.

Robbie arrived with a shout and a bump of his school bag against the polished hall floor. She turned from chopping vegetables at the sink to watch him come in through the kitchen door. His maroon and gold striped tie had flipped over his shoulder, and beneath his gaping school blazer she could see the white tails of his shirt hanging free from grey school trousers. One grey sock was up, the other was down, and his glossy black hair looked as if it had been in a fight.

Her heart dropped like a stricken bird, because even with his rumpled appearance he was hitting her hard with his father's image.

'Hi,' he said. 'Guess what we did today?'

'What?' she asked.

He frowned. 'Are you catching a cold?'

Melanie shook her head and tried swallowing the tears again. 'Just need to clear my throat.' Which she did. 'So what did you do today?' she prompted.

'We went to the park to collect fallen leaves that looked like skelintons, then took them back to press some into a books and draw round others.'

'Skeletons,' Melanie corrected.

'Skeletons,' he dutifully repeated. 'Do you want to see?'

'Of course I want to see,' she answered. 'But not before I get my hug.'

With a grin that could knock her eyes out he came towards her, a tall boy for his seven years. Melanie squatted down and opened her arms to receive him. As she hugged him close she felt another wave of emotion threaten. She must have sniffed, because Robbie jerked his head back.

Eyes as dark as his father's looked into hers, only they weren't the same, because this pair of eyes were darkened by love and warmth and concern whereas that other pair...

'Are you sure you're not catching a cold?' he demanded.

'Robbie,' she said firmly, 'I am not catching a cold, all right?'

It was a mother's voice, the I-know-everything voice. He continued to study her for a moment, then nodded his head. 'I'll go and get my bag.'

End of small developing crisis, Melanie thought with a sigh. Since William had died Robbie had lived in fear that she was going to follow him. Every sneeze, every twitch, every minor *ouch* could shake him to the core with fear.

They played with the leaves, drew some more, ate supper, watched some television then eventually went upstairs to play games in his bath before curling up on his bed to read stories. By eight o'clock he was fast asleep and Melanie had given up on expecting Randal to call.

For the next hour she tried to keep herself busy doing

the usual mundane chores. They'd used to employ a house-keeper, but she'd decided to retire when William had died and there seemed no point in employing another when there was only two of them to be looked after now. But the house was big—too big for both of them. A large Edwardian terraced home, with five bedrooms and four main reception rooms, it deserved a large noisy family to fill it, not two people who seemed to rattle around in it these days.

Melanie missed William, she missed Lucy the house-keeper, and she missed having only to open a couple of doors to find someone else there when she felt in need of company. As she felt now, she admitted, when she found herself standing in the front living room just staring into space.

Diversions, diversions, she told herself forcefully, and had just decided to go upstairs and indulge in a long hot bath in the hopes that it would ease some of the stress from her aching body when the sound of a car drawing up outside caught her ear. On legs that had suddenly turned very heavy she walked to the window and twitched back the edge of a curtain. As soon as she saw the low black monster crouching by the front gate she knew the long anxious wait was over.

Rafiq climbed out of his car and set the central locking system, then turned to view Melanie's home. It stood in the middle of an Edwardian terrace, brick-faced and solid-looking, with an iron gate leading to a small garden and a narrow porch with a half-stained-glass front door. One big bay window sat on each side of the porch and three flat windows faced the upper floor.

Did one of those windows belong to his son's bedroom?

Even thinking the word son threatened to lock him up inside. He saw a curtain twitch in a downstairs window, felt a cold winter gust of wind wipe what was left of the colour from his face.

An omen? he wondered, and had to accept that it probably was. This was not going to be easy. He was still in a deep state of shock and Randal had advised him to stay away until he had given himself time to recover. But Randal was not him. The other man could have no conception what was it was like to be him at this present moment. For how was he supposed to balance logic on the top of raging emotion? It was impossible. He was just swinging from one dark place to another with no respite in between. He had spent the whole afternoon with Randal Soames, swinging like that between a raging fury aimed entirely at Melanie and a heart-clutching sense of dismay at what he had almost tossed away today.

The curtain in a downstairs window gave a second twitch. Just before it fell back into place he caught a glimpse of Melanie's face. She had seen him. He must go in now. Had he actually been considering going away without doing so?

He didn't know, was no longer sure of anything. Half an hour ago he had been pacing his apartment; now he was here without recalling what had happened in between. He was the most controlled man he knew—prided himself on it—but control of any kind had completely deserted him. Pride, they said, usually came before a fall. Well, he was falling, had not stopped falling since he'd glanced at a piece of paper in his office and had seen the name Robert Joseph Alan Portreath typed in bold print in the middle of a blur of legal jargon.

Robert had been Melanie's father's name, but Joseph Alan belonged to him—Rafiq ben Jusef Al Alain Al-Qadim.

His throat moved on an attempt to swallow, his eyes growing glassy as he reached for the gate. It swung inwards with a creak of ageing wrought iron. As he stepped through it he caught sight of a figure through the stained-glass door and knew that Melanie was coming to open the door for him.

Don't touch the bell! Melanie prayed feverishly as she

made a last dash to get the door open before the shrill ring could fill the house and wake up Robbie.

It was like one of those nightmares where you opened the door to find yourself staring at the darkest force you could ever imagine. Big and broad and dressed entirely in black, Rafiq filled the narrow porch like a huge black shadow, blocking the light from the street behind him and taking the air from her lungs.

He believed. It was written there in every sharply angled feature, in the clench of his jaw and the muscle-locked stiffness of his big frame.

'Invite me in.'

His voice sounded like sawdust. Melanie tried to get a grip on her pounding heartbeat. 'It's late.' Like a coward she went for the easy route. 'I w-was just going to bed. W-why don't you come back tomorrow and we we'll—?'

'Invite me in, Melanie,' he repeated grimly.

'So that you can insult me again?'

'Probably.' He grimaced. 'I cannot be sure what I am going to do. I'm in shock,' he admitted.

Melanie could see it. 'All the more reason for you to come back tomorrow, when—'

His eyes gave a sudden flash. It was the only warning she got before she was being picked up by a pair of tough arms and bodily carried into the hall then into the living room.

'How dare you?' She gasped as he dropped her to her feet again.

He didn't bother to answer, instead he turned and strode back into the hallway, leaving her standing there shaking in her shoes and burning like fire down the front of her body where it had been crushed against his. She heard the front door click into its housing, heard his footsteps bringing him back this way. He stepped into the room, then closed this door also.

One look at his face here in the better light of the living room had her mentally backing away. Whatever all the hovering outside had been about, it hadn't communicated the anger she was being faced with now. He was in a rage, and a six-foot-four-inch male with a body to match his height was not what you wanted running loose in your house.

'I think y-you need to calm down a bit,' she stammered as he came towards her. 'You're in sh-shock, and you might not know w-what you're—'

'Shock,' he repeated so softly that she shivered. 'You think *this* is shock?'

'Angry, then,' she amended with a wary shrug and a gasp when the backs of her knees made contact with the arm of a chair. 'I can understand why you might feel you have the right to be. But—'

'Let us get one thing straight.' He cut across her. His mouth was thin and his eyes even narrower. 'I have the *right* to throttle the life from you for what you have done to me. But all I want from you are some acceptable answers!'

'Then back off—'

Back off? Rafiq stared down into her beautiful frightened face and blinked in complete astonishment. There was little more than an inch separating them. In fact he was standing so close she was arching her back in an effort to maintain the distance.

He was stunned. The red-hot rage had surged up out of nowhere, catching hold of him the moment he'd seen her standing at her door looking like the old Melanie, in jeans and worn-out old trainers. The years had fallen away and he'd found himself swapping new grievances for old grievances.

On a deep-throated curse he spun away from her, put a hand to the back of his neck and gripped. Behind him he could hear the uneven tug of her breathing, could feel her wariness, her fear. He closed his eyes and tried to get a hold on what was threatening to overwhelm him. He was a mess inside and the feeling was so alien that he didn't know how to deal with it.

'I apologise,' he muttered.

'It's all right,' she answered, but it was still the voice of fear.

He heard her movements as she edged warily sideways, heard the scrape of metal on metal and turned, a sense of pained horror filling him with dismay. She was standing by the fireplace and clenched in one hand was a brass poker. His eyes turned black and his stillness was suddenly electric. She believed him to be so dangerous that she armed herself against him.

'You don't need that, Melanie,' he said huskily.

He wasn't standing in her shoes, Melanie thought anxiously. He hadn't seen the look in his eyes just before he'd turned away. 'W-when you calm down I'll put it down,' she promised.

But she was shaking. Inside and out she was shaking. The way he ran those eyes over her she had a horrible feeling it would take him less than a second to disarm her if he decided to. He was big, he was strong, and he was also an expert in unarmed combat. She'd watched him in action once, in the Maitlands' all-purpose gym, when she'd gone in with a fresh stack of towels, only to find herself pulled to a complete standstill by the sight of him stripped to the waist and sparring with his brother. Sheikh Hassan had been stripped to the waist too, but she couldn't recall what he looked like. Only this man, moving with a speed and dexterous grace that belied his size and weight. He'd seen her standing there and had stopped to stare; within seconds he'd been flat on his back with his brother pinning him there. 'Such distraction is very unfair,' he'd sighed out complainingly and, as Sheikh Hassan had glanced up to see what he was talking about their positions had been smoothly reversed.

Man pitched against man, power against power, slick and smooth and so inherently masculine, with rippling muscles and the gleam of their bronzed flesh and the scent of the efforts permeating the air. She'd turned and run.

As Rafiq began walking towards her now maybe she should do the same thing, she told herself. But she couldn't run this time. This was her home. Her son lay sleeping upstairs. So she tightened her grip on the poker until her knuckles showed white, then made ready to defend herself.

His eyes were dark, his eyelashes lying thick against his cheekbones, his mouth a grim straight line. She sucked in a gulp of air as he reached out and closed a hand round the poker. With a gentle twist it was taken from her fingers.

'Never brandish point-on,' he said gravelly. 'The first thrust will tear your arm from its socket. Use it like this.' While she stood too dazed to stop him, he took hold of her hand, placed the poker back into it, angled it across her breasts, then, with a speed that set her gasping, he jerked the poker in a slashing arc towards his body. It came to stop with the point a breath away from his neck. 'This way you have a chance of doing me some damage.'

It was mad, really stupid, but her mouth began to wobble and tears suddenly filmed her eyes. 'I don't want to damage you,' she breathed shakily.

'I know.' He released his grip on the poker. 'It was my fault. I frightened you.' With that he turned and walked towards the door.

'Wh-where are you going?'

'You were right. I should not have come here tonight,' he answered grimly. 'I will go and leave you with your... safety.'

'N-no!' she cried, and wondered why. She wished she could stop trembling and tried to calm herself. 'Y-you're here now and...'

He stopped halfway across the room. Silence arrived. It pulled and it prodded. Melanie gripped the poker and tried to think of something to say that would not cause another eruption.

'Would you like a drink?' was her only inspiration. 'I can soon…'

'No—thank you,' he refused.

'Your jacket, then—let me take your jacket.' It was made of the softest kind of leather, his trousers of the smoothest suede. She swallowed thickly.

As she made to walk forward she was stopped when he turned to show her what was written in his eyes. 'I would really like to see my son.'

His son. The huskily possessive sound of his words had a creasing effect on her stomach. 'He's asleep. I don't want—'

'I was not intending to wake him, just…look upon him. Is that too much to ask?'

There was a bite to the last part. Without it she might well have given in, but the bite told her that his mood was still unpredictable. So she shook her head. 'He's a very light sleeper. The last thing he needs it to wake up and find a stranger standing over him.'

'Whose fault is it that I am a stranger?'

She ignored that. 'You need to understand a few things before we bring Robbie into this.'

'Such as the fact that you were never married to William Portreath?'

'I never said that I was,' she denied.

'You allowed me to assume it.'

'I don't recall being given the time to let you build any assumptions,' she countered coolly.

He took the criticism with a straightening of his shoulders. Melanie turned to put the poker back on its stand, but changed her mind and began stabbing at the fire log instead. Given a choice, he would rather be anywhere else than here in this room having this conversation with her, she reminded herself as wood sparks began to fly. In his eyes she was nothing, just a piece of low life he believed he had rid himself of once and for all today. Now he was being forced to backtrack, to be contrite and polite and civilised when he felt like being neither.

She made another hard stab at the fire log.

More sparks flew around the grate. 'You changed your name from Leggett to Portreath.'

'It pleased William to know that Robbie would carry on the Portreath name,' she explained.

The air was suddenly as tight at a bowstring, and Melanie knew why. He was thinking about Robbie's right to carry on *his* name. But, by the grim way he pressed his lips together, she realised he was not going to make any comment—for now at least.

Instead he stuck to his original subject. 'You call yourself *Mrs* Portreath,' he stated. 'Does this not signify a married status?'

'Why are *you* so struck by my marital status?' she countered, putting the poker back on its rest then turning to frown at him. 'I'm an unmarried mother with a son's feelings to consider,' she reminded him defensively. 'It made life simpler for Robbie if I invented a dead husband.'

'And a dead father.'

'I didn't say that,' Melanie denied. 'He knows about you. Of course he does. It would be unforgivable of me to pretend you were dead just because—'

'He knows who I am?' For such a dark-skinned man he suddenly looked ashen.

'Yes,' she confirmed. 'It was only natural that he should ask and only right that I should tell him the truth. But he—'

Rafiq's response shook her—she just didn't see it coming—so when he dropped down into one of the sofas then buried his face in his hands she was shocked.

'Rafiq…'

'No.' He shook his head. 'Leave me a moment.'

But he needed more than a moment to come to terms with what was suddenly raging inside him. His son knew about him. He knew he had a father who had never bothered to come and see him.

He couldn't make up his mind if it would have been less painful to think the boy had believed him dead!

'You have to understand. Robbie only—'

'Shut up,' he rasped, and found anger again, found strength in it, then lifted his dark head. 'I want to break your deceitful neck for keeping my son from me!' he ground out.

'You had your chance to be a father, Rafiq, and you blew it, not me.'

'When?' He was suddenly on his feet again. '*When* did you give me this chance?'

'When you threw me out of your embassy eight years ago!'

'You knew then and said nothing?'

Melanie laughed. 'You were the man who told me it was no use my saying a single word because you wouldn't believe me anyway!'

'And you could not bring yourself to stand your ground and *insist* I listen to you?'

Chin up, eyes bright, face white and body trembling, she still held her ground. 'For what purpose?' she demanded. 'You would have still called me a liar.'

A flick of a hand brought contempt back into the fight. 'You were sleeping with your step-cousin. Of course I would have questioned the boy's parentage!'

If Melanie had still had the poker in her hand she would have hit him with it. Who did he think he was, standing here trying to lay all the blame on her? 'What if I *had* come to you with your son in my arms, Rafiq?' she challenged. 'What if I'd said, Look, Rafiq, see for yourself that this child belongs to you?' She released a bitter little laugh. 'I'll tell you what you would have done. You would have taken him away from me. You would have used your filthy billions to split me from my child!'

'I would not!' He actually dared to look shocked.

Melanie wasn't impressed. 'Yes, you would,' she insisted. 'You believed I was a cheap little slut and a gold-digger who had made an utter fool out of you. You would have wanted revenge—probably still want it!' she flashed. 'But I have my own money with which to fight you now. I also have Robbie, who *loves* me, Rafiq. He loves *me*, as his mother, and he's old enough and wise enough to hate anyone who might dare to try and pull us apart!'

He went paler with every bitter word she tossed at him, until a white ring circled his taut mouth. 'If you feel like this, why have you decided to bring me into his life?'

'Because he needs you,' she whispered.

'And did not need me before?'

'No.' She shook her head. 'Before, he had William.'

CHAPTER FOUR

RAFIQ turned away as if her answer had cut him. His action
more or less said it all for Melanie. Her anger fled, leaving
her feeling weak and shaken, and she too turned away,
putting a hand up to cover her trembling mouth, and
waited for him recover from what she'd thrown at him.
Because she knew it wasn't over, not by a long way.

Neither moved nor tried to speak again. In the drumming silence Rafiq was trying to decide how he felt about
these latest revelations, and realised he was in no fit state
to attempt the problem. Or was he being a coward and
delaying the ugliness of truth?

And what was that truth? he asked himself. The truth
was that Melanie had accused him of things he couldn't
argue with. He would not have believed her son was his,
unless presented with positive evidence. He would certainly have moved heaven and earth to remove his son
from the clutches of a woman he believed unfit to rear his
child.

He still believed it, which only helped to make the situation that bit uglier.

'I think I should leave,' he heard himself murmur.

'Yes,' she agreed.

'I think we should defer the rest until another time when
we are both…calmer.'

'Yes,' she agreed again.

Yet he didn't move—he wanted to move but something
was stopping him. A need to stay? To be here where his
son was? Or was it Melanie who was holding him? He
turned to look at her, at the fall of her pale hair against
slender shoulders that were no longer straight with defi-

58

ance but hunched and heavy. Her black woollen top clung
to the gentle curves of her body and the jeans followed
the lines of her hips and thighs. She held a hand to her
mouth, he saw, which explained why her answers had
sounded muffled, and the other hand was wrapped around
her body, the fingernails trembling where they dug deep
into black wool.

He turned away again, and looked at the room for the
first time since he'd entered it. It came as a small surprise.
The décor was old-fashioned, the furniture the same,
mostly heavy dark pieces that spoke of another era, like
the patterned red carpet that covered the floor and the dark
red velvet curtain fabric that matched the upholstery covering the sofas and chairs. It was a man's kind of room,
warm and solid, with the odd female touch, such as the
jewel-coloured silk cushions heaped on the sofas and
chairs.

He liked it, which further surprised him because he was
so predisposed to dislike anything to do with Melanie right
now.

Or was it William Portreath's taste he was reluctantly
admiring? he then wondered suddenly, and felt the bitterness well up again, felt the hard cut of envy for a man
who had loved another man's child enough to present him
with his own name.

He didn't want to leave. Melanie could feel his reluctance wrapping round the room like a heavy dark cloud
that stole all the oxygen. He was still steeped in shock.
His son was here in this very house. He needed to see him,
see the truth for himself. She understood that, and wished
so much that things had worked out differently this morning, because they could have got all the fighting out of the
way then and he could have happily met Robbie and have
seen what a wonderful child they had made together. More
importantly, Robbie would have met his father and would
have known that he was no longer in danger of being left
alone in this world if anything should happen to her.

Should she say something—hold out yet another olive branch? Should she tell him that she understood how he was feeling, but that she had to protect both herself and her son?

Would he listen? Was he ready to do that now?

A log dropped in the grate and sent out a spray of crackling sparks. As it did so the Westminster mantel clock chimed the hour. Then a floorboard creaked somewhere, making Melanie turn to look at the door. Sensing her doing it, Rafiq did the same thing. It came again; the pair of them went so still they could hear their hearts beating. Melanie knew every bump and creak in this old house; she knew every draught and whistle.

'What?' Rafiq asked.

'Robbie,' she said, and started walking. 'Stay in here,' she cautioned as she opened the door. Then she disappeared, closing the door behind her without seeing that Rafiq was incapable of going anywhere.

He had frozen into a posture only his brother would recognise. But even Hassan had only seen it happen when it involved their father and his battles with death that were sometimes too close to call. The name of it was fear—fear of losing a man he loved above all else in this world—only here he was experiencing the same paralysed fear of meeting his seven-year-old son.

Would she do that? Would Melanie bring the boy down here and present them to each other without any preparation to ease the—?

Another log fell in the grate and broke him free from his stone-like stasis. He turned his head and saw the log was in danger of rolling into the hearth.

Robbie was just coming out of the bathroom when Melanie arrived on the upstairs landing. 'Okay?' she asked softly.

'Mmm,' he murmured sleepily. 'I thought I heard voices.'

'The television, probably.' Melanie smiled through the

untruth and walked with him into his bedroom, then helped to tuck him into bed.

'I had a dream tonight, but it wasn't a bad one,' he told her.

'Good.' She stroked his silk dark head.

'There was a man on a big black stallion and he stopped and said, ''Are you Robbie?'' I said, ''Yes'' and he smiled and said, ''Next time, you can ride up here with me, if you like.'''

'Well, that was nice of him.' Melanie smiled, thinking she didn't like the idea of some stranger offering her son rides.

'Mmm.' His eyes were drooping; he gave a yawn. 'He was wearing one of those white robes and had a thing on his head, like Arabs wear.'

Melanie's stomach rolled over. She wasn't one of those people who believed dreams forecast the future, and Robbie knew about his Arabian side because William had spent hours with him in his study, filling his mind with all things Arabian. No doubt there had been a picture of an Arab on horseback at some time. But for her son to have the dream tonight of all nights disturbed her more than she liked.

'Go back to sleep,' she whispered.

'You won't go anywhere, will you?'

'No, I won't go anywhere,' she softly promised. 'Except back downstairs to watch television,' she added, just in case he was expecting her to remain right here, kneeling beside his bed for the rest of the night. It had happened before and probably would again, she mused bleakly.

But not tonight, she saw as he dropped back into sleep without another murmur. She waited a few minutes longer to make sure he was fully asleep, though, taking no chances in a situation that was hazardous enough as it stood without Robbie deciding to follow her downstairs as she knew he was quite capable of doing. But eventually she rose up and left him, silently closing the bedroom door behind her—just in case voices became raised again.

Walking back into the living room required her to take a deep breath for steadiness. What she found was that Rafiq had removed his jacket to reveal a black cashmere roll-neck sweater and was squatting down in front of the fire. His body twisted when he heard her come in, eyes fiercely guarded as they shifted across the empty spaces at her sides. Tension screamed from every muscle, from every flicker of an eyelash. He was looking for Robbie.

'He got up to use the bathroom,' she explained quickly. 'Then fell asleep again almost as soon as he'd climbed back into bed.'

With a nod of his head Rafiq turned away again, but not before she'd seen a war between desire and relief taking place upon his face, and her heart gave a twist of sympathy for this man who had to be struggling with just about every emotion available to him.

It was only as she began to walk forward that she noticed he held the hearth brush and pan in his hands. She also noticed the stretch of fine wool across expanded shoulder blades and remembered what it had felt like to press against them with the flat of her palms. Heat began to pool low down in her stomach; memories that really should not be so clear and sharp after all of these years sent her eyes on a journey down the length of his spine to the leanness of his hips and the power in his spread thighs.

'A log fell onto the hearth,' he said as she came up beside him. His voice sounded rough, like gravel. He wasn't actually using the brush and pan because he was just squatting there, staring at them as if they weren't there.

Coming down beside him, Melanie took them from his loose fingers and laid them aside. 'Rafiq…I'm sorry for saying what I said before. I was angry, and—'

'You needed to say those things, and I suppose I needed to hear them.'

But he wasn't sure. She watched the firelight play with

his taut features and enrich the dark olive tones of his skin. 'Here,' she said, and dipped a hand into the pocket in her jeans, then gently slotted a photograph into one of his hands. 'I thought you might like to have this.'

It was Robbie, looking all grown-up and smart in his school uniform and wearing that familiar rather sardonic half-smile. It had occurred to her as she was coming back down the stairs that Rafiq still had no conception of how like him his son was. If she had taken him into William's study he would have seen Robbie's face laughing back at him from photos on every available surface, because that was the way William had liked it and she hadn't yet got around to moving anything—hadn't had the heart to change anything anywhere in the house.

'It was taken in school only a few weeks ago,' she explained. 'He looks so much like you that it came as a shock when I walked into your office this morning and realised just...'

Her voiced trailed away, dying on words that did not need saying because she could tell from Rafiq's reaction that he was seeing it all for himself. His eyes were fixed on the simple four-by-four portrait. She could hear the strain in his shallow breathing, feel the tension in his body and the pulsing, stinging agony of his stress.

She tried to swallow, but found it impossible. She felt the sudden need to give him some space and privacy for what was battering him, but couldn't bring herself to get up and move away. Tears thickened her throat; her chest began to feel too tight. In desperation she reached out to pick up the hearth brush and pan and began carefully gathering up fine flakes of wood ash still scattered on the grate.

It was dreadful. Say something, she wanted to beg him. Shout at me, if you like! But I need to know what you think of this beautiful child we made together. I need—

His hands came out and took back the brush and pan. As her breathy gasp filtered through the air she watched him lay them carefully aside. She didn't know what was coming—was afraid of what was coming. Especially when long lean fingers curled around her upper arms and began drawing her to her feet. She felt small suddenly, overwhelmed by his superior height and size. He was standing too close, his touch achingly gentle yet frighteningly disturbing. The heat of his breath was on her face and his thighs were touching hers. Her arms felt soft and frail beneath the controlled power in his imprisoning fingers, and her breasts were tingling at the nearness of his chest.

Wary, she lifted her eyes to his, and the breath shivered from her lips at what she saw written in the dark glitter of his eyes.

No, she wanted to protest, but the denial just wouldn't come, and it would have been too late anyway because his dark head lowered and he was kissing her, though not hard or hotly as he had this morning. Nor even because he felt driven by a simple need to make physical contact with another human being right now. He was kissing her with reverence, gently crushing her against him, gently crushing her mouth with his.

Then he released her and turned away, dark head slightly lowered, wide shoulders set. He picked up his jacket, then just walked out of the room and, seconds later, out of the house, leaving Melanie standing right where he had left her, with the warmth of his kiss still pulsing against her lips and what she'd seen in his eyes before he turned away, quietly tearing her apart.

Tears, she'd seen the hot black glint of tears in the eyes of a man who'd gone way beyond the point of being able to contain the power of what it was he had been forced to deal with today.

She had done that. With her little plots and shock strategies she had managed to reduce a proud man to tears in front of her. She had never felt so ashamed of herself.

Rafiq sat in his office staring down at the neatly processed, finely detailed document he had spent the whole night working on. He was good at this, he acknowledged with absolutely no sense of pleasure. Concentrating his talents on the detached and inanimate was most definitely his forte. Money instead of emotions. The planning and arranging of someone else's finances instead of allowing himself to lie in his bed crucifying himself with his inadequacies as a fully paid up member of the human race.

The phone on his desk began to ring, halting the urge to put his head back and close his sleep-starved eyes. It was Randal Soames. 'Are you sure you want this?' the lawyer asked him.

'Exactly as I have set it out,' he confirmed.

He sounded dubious. 'You might marry some day, have more children.'

Not this man, Rafiq thought bleakly. 'Have you spoken to Melanie?'

Swift change of subject. He could almost hear Randal thinking it. 'She isn't there. There is some kind of function on at the boy's school, I seem to recall. I'll try again later.'

The boy's school. Some kind of function. Just two more things about his son he had no knowledge of.

Oh, damn. He got up and swung away from his chair, shoved his hands into his trouser pockets, then stood staring out of the window at a cold grey day. It had now begun to pour with rain.

Safely slotted into his wallet rested a miniature image of himself at the age of seven. Similar hair, similar eyes, similar slightly rueful expression which hid the same vulnerability he had suffered at the same age. He felt as if he knew this child of his inside out, yet he could not say which school his dark red uniform represented, nor what the boy ate for breakfast each morning.

His son even had his skin shading. So where were Melanie's genes? Where was his French blood? Where was there anything in the photograph to say that his son had not been cloned on a scientist's bench instead of conceived during the act of love?

Love. He cursed the word, hated it—despised it—and felt it grinding against his every muscle like a physical torture set up to make him accept that love could beat the hell out of any man's wish to feeling nothing.

He was in love with his son, but had made no attempt to go anywhere near him. He loved his father, his brother, and Hassan's lovely wife, Leona—but differently. With them he felt safe to love; with the boy he did not. Which was why he was standing here preferring to stare at the rain than take the bull by the horns and face uncertainty.

As for Melanie...

A sigh shot from him at this other reason why he had spent the past two days simmering in his own confusion. He had loved Melanie when they had conceived their son, but he would prefer not to be reminded of it. Now, what came next? Where were they supposed to go? Into one of those awful situations he had witnessed amongst so many friends with broken relationships, where they shared the children by cool agreement—when there was nothing damn cool about a child's feelings?

A knock sounded on his door; he swung round to watch Kadir walk in the room. As his aide offered a bow of apology for intruding Rafiq caught the sparkle of raindrops on the shoulders of his neat grey jacket. 'Been out in this filthy weather, Kadir?' he quizzed.

'Yes, sir.' Rafiq received another bow. 'A note has just arrived for you,' Kadir explained, and walked forward to hold it out to him.

Rafiq looked down at it without attempting to take it, wearily wondering, What now? Because this was no formal business note. The envelope was small and square, and its sender female, by the neatly scripted way his name had been written upon it. No address or postage stamp, which said it had been hand-delivered.

'Who is it from?'

Kadir cleared his throat. 'It arrived in another envelope addressed to me. This is all I know.'

All he knew. Frowning, Rafiq pulled his hands out of his pockets and accepted the letter, then he broke the glued seal. Still frowning, he took out the single sheet of paper and read the two short sentences written upon it. 'Can I come up? I'm standing across the street.'

His heart hit against his ribcage. He swung back to the window to stare down through sheets of rain to the street. A solitary figure stood against the building opposite, sheltering from the rain beneath a big black umbrella.

Melanie. Something burst into life inside him. With a twist of his body he snatched his jacket off the back of his chair. 'Have my car waiting,' he instructed Kadir as he headed for the door—then paused as his mind made a connection. 'Don't make a habit of lying to me, Kadir,' he advised.

Then he left, with Kadir's rather heavy, 'No, sir,' hanging in the air.

The lift took him downwards; his feet took him outside. The sheeting rain drenched him in the few seconds it took him to cross the street.

Melanie only realised he was there when she saw his feet appear in front of her. The umbrella was wrenched from her fingers, and was held higher, so he could join her beneath it. She looked up and saw the strain in his face, the tiredness, the frown. 'Are you mad?' he demanded. 'Why are you standing out here?'

'I didn't want your security people throwing me off the premises,' she explained. 'But I needed to talk to you.'

By the way he flattened his mouth she assumed he'd forgotten about his instructions regarding her and his bank. Then he noticed that she was shivering so much her teeth were chattering and, taking a grim hold on her arm, he hustled her into the nearest doorway, snapped the umbrella shut and laid it aside. Then he removed his jacket and swung it around her shoulders.

'You're freezing,' he muttered. 'I cannot believe you came here dressed like this.'

She was in her designer suit again. It had seemed appropriate when she'd made the decision to come. Now she was so grateful for the added warmth of his jacket that she huddled greedily into it. 'It w-wasn't raining this much when I left home and—and I'm not thinking very clearly right now...'

'I understand the feeling,' he murmured dryly.

'Now y-you're wet too,' she continued in an agitated rush. 'Y-you should have got Kadir to—'

'Run a few more messages?' he offered when she tried to swallow her runaway tongue.

She glanced up, met his eyes, saw the sardonic gleam in them and released a sigh. 'He told you. He promised he wouldn't. I didn't want him to get into trouble for colluding with me.'

'You believed I would be angry with him?'

'It's been two days...' Two days of waiting and pacing and jumping out of her skin every time the doorbell or telephone rang. In the end she hadn't been able to take the stress any longer and had come to find him. Now she wished that she hadn't because she was feeling like a fool.

'Kadir carried out your instructions to the letter,' Rafiq inserted. 'As for the rest...I guessed.'

He'd guessed. 'Mr Omnipotent,' she muttered.

To her surprise he laughed, it was a low deep sound that brought her eyes fluttering up to his again, which were warm and dark and concentrated on her. Things began to happen she just didn't want, like a pooling of warmth deep down in her abdomen and a breathlessness that tightened her chest.

Don't look at me like that, she wanted to protest, but too many things were leaping between them, such as the son they shared, not to mention shared kisses. Intimacy, in other words; too much of it that went back too many years yet could tug on her senses as if everything, including the events leading to Robbie's conception, had happened only yesterday.

'I needed time to think,' he murmured huskily.

Husky suddenly made her clothes feel too tight. 'I know you m-must be hurt, but I h-had to protect myself.'

'From the omnipotent Arab with revenge on his mind?' He smiled as he said it, but it was a grim smile.

'I'm sorry, but, yes,' she answered honestly. 'You—'

His hand lifted up to push a stray coil of damp hair away from her temple and she responded with a tense little jerk. Beyond the shelter of the doorway, the rain pounded on the pavements. The coil of hair left a trailing raindrop behind it so his finger moved to scoop it from her cheek.

Someone dashed into the doorway, stopped to shake out their umbrella, then, with a curious glance at them both, walked into the building, leaving Melanie with the disturbing impression that she must look like a wicked woman snatching a secret assignation with her tall dark lover.

Lowering her eyes, she huddled further into his jacket. It was big on her—huge—the slippery silk lining whispering softly against the thin fabric of her suit. She was picking up the scent of his aftershave from it, subtle and spicy, tantalisingly familiar. He couldn't stand much closer to her if he tried.

Maybe Rafiq was thinking along similar lines, because he released a short sigh. Her eyes became fascinated with his slender red tie and the way it lay down the length of his white shirt, covering muscular proportions that expanded and contracted with the sigh.

Her lips began to pulse, and it scared the life out of her. Things were happening here that really should not. 'I don't think this is an appropriate place,' she said a little wildly.

'No,' he agreed, but made no move to do anything about it.

One of those silences fell; it pumped up her heartbeat and dried out her mouth. His hands began to move, sliding beneath the lapel of his navy blue jacket until the backs of his fingers came to rest against her breasts. She pulled in a sharp breath; for a fine tight nerve-singing moment she thought he was going to lower his head and kiss her.

Then she shivered as genuine cold made itself felt again, and he was setting her free to reach for the umbrella. Opening it up, he urged her beneath it, then out into the pouring rain. Her stiletto shoes danced puddles as he hurried her across the street. Expecting to be ushered into the bank, she was surprised to find herself being bundled into the back of a car. It was big and plush, with a glass partition between them and the driver, and seats made of soft black leather.

Through shivering chatters she watched Rafiq toss the umbrella onto the floor of the car, then climb in beside her. His shirt was wet, showing patches of dark skin beneath its white fabric and his black hair was soaked and slicked to his head. He leant forward to pick up a telephone, uttered some terse command in Arabic, then sat back with a sigh.

'Where are we going?' she questioned.

'Somewhere we can talk.'

'Oh.' She took a pensive glance out of the window. 'I thought the bank...'

'No,' he said, and that was all. Her top teeth pressed into her bottom lip because she wasn't sure she liked the sound of that no.

'Rafiq—'

'Randal has been trying to contact you.'

A diversion. 'Has he?'

'He said you were out at some function or other.'

'First thing this morning, yes.' She nodded. 'Robbie's school is putting on a pantomime at Christmas. They're doing *Cinderella*. There were rehearsals this morning. I—helped out.'

'Which school?'

She told him. He pressed his lips together and nodded his dark head. Melanie shifted tensely, unsure of his mood now and even more uncertain that she wanted to be sitting here in such close confines with a man she couldn't read from one second to the next.

For all she knew he could be sitting here plotting her downfall—or her seduction. Because something improper had been running through his mind back there in the doorway. It had been running through hers too, she was forced to admit. It just wasn't fair. Only this man had ever been able to toss her into this hectic state of sexual awareness just by—being there.

She frowned at the rain-spattered window. That feeling had been there from the first time her arm had brushed against his shoulder when she'd been serving him at the Maitlands' dinner table. Twenty years old, as naive as they came, she'd caught his scent, the sound of his low dark laughter and the deeply smooth voice tones as he'd spoken to the person sitting next to him, and her response had been so primitively sexual that she'd spilled the sauce onto the tablecloth.

After that had come the humiliating dressing down from Sally Maitland, then her first real contact with his hand, when Rafiq had cornered her later and tried to make light of the embarrassing incident. He'd been dressed in a dinner suit, big and dark, suave and sophisticated, with an easy grace that had belied his size and a lazily worn self-confidence that aimed to charm.

'Watch him,' Sally Maitland had warned later. 'Arab men are notoriously attracted to slender young blondes. He'll take what you are putting on offer, Melanie, then despise you for it later.'

She had been right, too. Rafiq had pursued her like a man besotted until he'd finally managed to break down her defences. He'd promised her everything: love, marriage, the whole wonderful package. But the moment he'd taken what he had really been after he'd despised her for giving it. He'd seen a tramp then, a woman willing to give it out to all and sundry once she'd acquired the taste.

He moved. She stiffened and swung her head round to send him a hard, accusing glance.

'What?' He looked shocked by it.

'Nothing.' She looked away again, hoping to goodness that eight years of abstinence had given her some defence against him, though why did she think she needed it?

Because Rafiq still desired her. It had been there when they'd met in his office two days ago, there when he'd come to her home. It had been there just now in the doorway when he'd almost given in to it and kissed her.

Three meetings, two kisses, and one still hovering on the sidelines with time on its side to give it a chance.

As for defences, they were not much use when she only had to look at him to feel that old breathless, sensual pull.

The car drew to a stop outside a block of select apartments. Life took another worrying twist when she realised where they had to be. Rafiq opened his door and braved the rain again to stride round to her side of the car and open her door.

'I don't think...'

His hand found her wrist and the jacket began to slip from her shoulders as he tugged her into the rain. As she grappled to save the jacket from falling onto the wet pavement he pulled her inside the building before she had a chance to voice a bigger protest.

A man dressed in a security uniform sat behind a desk. He stood up and smiled. 'Good morning, sir...madam,' he greeted politely. 'Dreadful weather,' he opined with a glance at their rain-soaked clothes.

Rafiq murmured a reply; Melanie offered a nervous little smile and wondered what the man must really be thinking as Rafiq pulled her into the lift.

'I don't think this is a good idea,' she protested a trifle breathlessly.

'I do,' he countered, and one glance at him told her why he did. He wasn't even trying to hide it!

A wave of answering heat put her into a panic. 'No,'

she said, and tried to twist her wrist free from his grasp so she could turn and make a diving exit before the lift doors closed. But Rafiq was one step ahead of her; with only the gentlest of tugs he brought her hard up against his body at the same time as his other hand snaked out to hit the lift button.

To the man on the desk they must have looked like two people so hungry for each other they couldn't wait until they were alone. The lift doors closed while Melanie was still trying to recover from the shock contact with Rafiq's body. Eyes like hot coals burned his intention; her blood began to race, charged by her hammering heartbeat.

'How dare you?' she choked in shrill protest. 'This is supposed to be about Robbie!'

Rafiq laughed. Maybe she was right, but he didn't think so. For two long days he had prowled through his life trying to understand what it was that was holding him back from going to meet his son. For two aching days and sleepless nights he'd swung from one reason to another without hitting upon the right one. But one look at Melanie standing in the rain and the answer had lit up in his head like a beacon. He could not deal with the problem of his son until he'd dealt with the problem of his son's mother. He wanted her—all of her. He wanted every single thing he had walked away from eight years ago. He wanted her in his life, in his bed! And the best thing about it was that he meant to have it all, without the love thing cluttering up his reasoning.

'I am going to take you in my arms and kiss you stupid,' he informed her grittily. 'I am going to strip the clothes from your body and enjoy your exquisite flesh. I will take you to my bed and avail myself of every sweet, delectable inch of you,' he rasped with husky incision. 'I am going to take you out and buy you a ring which will say that you belong to me. Then, and only then, I will take you with me to meet my son! You owe me this much, Melanie-of-the-sweet-face-and-lying-little-heart. You owe me for eight long years of bitterness, and seven years of never knowing my son!'

CHAPTER FIVE

'YOU'RE crazy,' she breathed as she strained to get away from him.

'Maybe.' He shrugged, but the look in her eyes told him she was captivated by the whole exciting agenda, and she was quivering against him like a trapped little bird, mesmerised and enthralled.

'How long has it been for you, Melanie, since a man laid his hands on your body?' he questioned darkly. 'How long since you felt the burning thrust of a man's pleasure zone driving you mindless with need?'

Her mouth was trembling, her eyes were bright, her skin pale with what might have been mistaken for fear if it hadn't been for the seductive scent of her arousal sweetening the air. He knew that scent, had picked up on it at their first meeting, and it had never failed to be there every time they'd been near each other since. Eight years had not changed it; eight years had not diminished one small part of what it could do to him.

'Sex…' He leant close to whisper. 'It is all around us. You can feel it. Stop pretending.'

'If you don't stop this I am going to start screaming!'

His response was to clasp his free hand round her nape, his eyes glittering his intention just before he lowered his dark head and took what he wanted: her mouth, her hot, dry, trembling mouth, that opened without pause to welcome him. Her fingers grappled with his shirt front; her breasts heaved against his chest. And as her beautiful thighs arched in their eagerness to make contact with his, it was Melanie who plunged into the kiss.

She groaned as his tongue caressed moist tissue. He

laughed, low and throatily deep, pulsing with dark triumph that brought her nails clawing into his neck in punishment. He didn't care. He liked those sharp nails digging into him. They let him know this could be as wild and unbridled as he wanted it to be. They made him feel alive, energised! With Serena it had been sex. With this woman it was— regeneration of every single cell he possessed!

The lift doors slid apart. Without breaking the kiss, he swung her up into his arms and carried her towards his apartment door. Opening it with the key was a struggle when he was not prepared to release her mouth, but he managed it, stepped inside, kicked the door shut behind him then, with a satisfied grunt, began walking down the hallway towards the only room that mattered right now.

His jacket slipped from her shoulders, trailed its way to the ground and was left where it fell as he walked with unerring steps into the bedroom and shut this door too. Which left only them and a giant-sized bed, standing proud with its cover of royal blue silk. No soft feathers this time, no deep eiderdown, just a firm flat mattress dressed in the perfect colour on which to lay his prize.

When he lowered her feet to the floor she was trembling so badly she could barely stand upright unaided. Her eyes were big, glazed, and the colour of the richest gold, her mouth full and red and begging for his.

'Now tell me no.' He laid the silken words down like a challenge.

She couldn't answer. When all she did was reach out a hand to steady herself, he caught it and placed it onto his chest. Her eyes flickered down to absorb the fact that she was touching hair-roughened flesh. She had done it again. Without knowing it she'd unfastened his shirt during their walk down the hall!

'Yes,' he breathed in dark confirmation, and yanked his tie loose then tossed it aside. The last shirt button came undone at his throat and the shirt fell wide open to reveal a body built to carry the world if it was ever called upon to do so.

'Oh, dear God,' she managed to breathe in shaken realisation. By then his fingers were unfastening the buttons of her jacket to reveal a fitted top she had added to the ensemble that had not been there the last time.

Protection from him, or herself? The jacket slid from her shoulders; the top slipped over her head. As she lifted those dazed eyes back up to his he kissed her, fiercely, just in case she decided to try and stop this.

But Melanie was in no fit state to stop anything. She was lost in a gripping love affair with this man's body and the power of his kiss. Every time she breathed she drowned in the scent of him; every time she moved she felt the impact of his strength. His mouth consumed her with a voracious hunger; the stroke of his hands collapsed her brain. She had no sense, no will, no desire to do anything but be here, feeling the raging torment of a need so potent it overwhelmed her. The eight years since she'd been with him like this didn't seem to matter. Her senses remembered, desired and demanded she feed them with everything.

'This is mad,' she whimpered.

He didn't answer. His hands were ridding her of her bra. The black lace drifted away from full rounded breasts with nipples already tightly distended. He touched; she groaned and simply fell against him, then fell again, into a pit packed full of sensation. Sleek bronzed skin electrified her fingers; the rasp of curling hair excited her breasts. The kiss was a seduction on its own hot merits, and as he slid down the zip of her skirt she wriggled her hips to aid its journey to the floor. The powerhouse thrust of his erection jumped as she writhed against him. His breathing was rough, his body clenched by the ferocity of his desire. But when he slid his hands beneath the final piece of black lace to tug her more firmly against him, she was the one to fall apart.

It was a complete loss of control. She cupped his face, kissed it all over, urgently, desperately touching and tasting, and forcing tight, thick sounds to rasp from his throat. He belonged to her. This man, this glorious dark-skinned giant, belonged to her. She'd believed it eight years ago and she believed it again now. Part of her might be yelling, *Fool!* but at this precise moment she didn't care.

His hands spanned her hips and lifted her up against him; her arms wound around his neck. He began carrying her again, to lower her down onto the firm cool expanse of the large bed. Warm skin slid against the smoothness of silk; long limbs stretched sensually. Her eyes caught a glimpsing impression of ivory presented on a bed of blue, with her hair a golden halo as she watched him divest himself of the rest of his clothes. She watched in fascination as he drew in tight muscles in his abdomen then unclipped his trousers; her mouth ran dry as she watched him slide down the zip. Two seconds later he was naked, and her insides were curling on a mixture of excitement and stark, staring alarm until she remembered how it felt to absorb this man into her.

Then he was lowering his big frame down right next to her, reaching out to roll her against him. Skin met skin, stealing her breath away. His mouth claimed hers and his hands began to wreak magic, shaping her breasts, her stomach, the sensitive inner flesh of her thighs. She still wore silk stockings; deft fingers removed them. She still wore panties; they drifted away next. She moved and writhed to every clever stroke of his fingers. The kiss broke apart as she gulped greedily for breath. She was lost, gazing into eyes so black they drew her into them. Loving him, needing him.

'Do we stop?'

Do we stop…? she repeated dizzily, and tried to focus for the first time. His cheekbones stood out on a face taut with passion. His mouth wore the swollen bloom of desire gone wild. His beautiful bronzed body lay half across her and a hand was gently circling her navel.

'To continue means you accept my intentions.'

Intentions? Each time he spoke she had to work hard to grasp the words. 'Do you want to stop?' Long lashes blinked him a bemused look.

He touched his tongue to her lower lip. 'No,' he said.

'Then why ask?'

He smiled an odd smile, and used that tongue to circle the full pulsing beauty of her whole mouth. 'So be it,' he said.

She mimicked the stirring manoeuvre with an impulsiveness that for some unfathomable reason flung him over the edge. Passion roared like a lion, and the whole thing became a hot and seething whirl. He closed his mouth over one of her breasts, nipped her nipple with his teeth. As she drew in a sharp breath he sucked and played and tormented, with his mouth, with his hands. Then, with the glide of long fingers down the length of her, he descended into the cloud of gold at the apex of her thighs.

Pleasure became a greedy animal. Where he touched, she yearned for more. Her fingers dug and scraped and moulded rippling, trembling, slick male muscle. The whole thing grew like a mushroom, building pleasure on pleasure, and it made it all so much more exciting to know his breathing was ragged, that his heart was thumping madly and his body throbbing with a need as acute as her own.

I shouldn't be doing this. One single brief glimpse at sanity attempted to spoil it. She released a small whimper of distress. Then he was invading the soft tissue of her femininity with the touch of a master, and the door slammed on sanity, along with her ability to control anything, because she was flying, or as near as, her fingers clutching at him as she gasped out his name and begged him never to stop.

The ragged sound of his breathing filled her ears; the heat of his breath moistened her face. He moved over her, hair-roughened thighs parting her smooth ones. A hand slid beneath her hips to bring them towards him and she felt the first probe of his entry, then felt another set of fingers coil into her hair. He lifted her head from the bed, bringing her eyes flying open. Black heat blazed a path of fire right through her—compulsive, compelling, it warned of what was to come. Then he made that single surging thrust at the same moment his mouth smothered her cry.

It was possession in its fullest meaning. He moved, and she responded with pleasure-wracked sounds he claimed for himself. Each thrust sent him deeper, each withdrawal set her quivering in pleasurable response, each slide of damp flesh became an exquisite torment that heightened everything. When he increased the rhythm she just hung on and let him conduct the whole concert, and her imagination helped him by offering up picture flashes of pale skin against dark skin, slender white limbs clinging to majestic bronze. Darkness and sunlight became one glorious entity. He drove her into its seething depths then snapped the last thread of her control with a kiss that claimed every gasp and quiver as they came together as lost-souls in a black cavern that held back everything but the pin-sharp song of ecstasy.

He was lying beside her with his chest still heaving out the last throes of his own fulfilment. A brown hand covered his eyes. Melanie didn't move—couldn't. When she eventually managed to open her eyes it was to the grey day pouring into the bedroom and the chill that was already settling on her flesh. The ivory and blue room was about as cold a place as anyone could wish to enjoy a soulless tumble upon a strange bed. The slack-limbed languid aftermath was being replaced with reality, the dawning sense of horror, the flaying sense of dismay. What had she done—what had *they* done?

She wanted to die here, she decided. She just wanted to close her eyes and die rather than face what had to come next.

The truth. The cold, dark hollowness of truth. She'd expected him to seek revenge in one form or other, but she had not expected anything like this.

'I hate you,' she whispered as her mouth began to wobble.

He stopped breathing. The hand left his face.

'You did this on purpose. You meant to shatter me.' On a flood of tears she scrambled from the bed.

'In case you may not have noticed, I shattered too,' he fed after her quietly.

'That's different.' She began picking up her clothing. Every move, every grasp of her fingers shook with the agony of her distress. 'You're a man. You're allowed to behave like that.'

'Like what?'

'Animal!' she choked, searching the floor for her panties and not seeing them anywhere. Her cheeks were hot, yet her flesh felt so cold it was almost numb. 'Y-you look at me and see a western woman. Cheap to buy and easy to have!' she threw at him in shaken bitterness. 'You did this the last time. Y-you wanted and you took, then despised me for letting you!'

'I despised you for going from my arms into the arms of your cousin.'

'*Step*-cousin!' she corrected. 'And I am not going to discuss that with you!'

'Why not?' In a single lithe movement he snaked off the bed and came to stand over her. Naked, bold, so forcefully male, she almost sank beneath the swimming tide of her own response.

'Because you had your chance to listen eight years ago and decided it wasn't worth the effort.' Clutching her clothes to her front, she began looking wildly around her. 'Now hell will freeze over before I will defend myself to you—! Where's the bathroom?'

'Wait a minute—'

'No!' She swerved away from his reaching hands.

'Don't touch me—ever again!' The breakdown into tears was gaining momentum and she needed to get out before it happened. 'I adored you,' she whispered painfully. 'You know that I did. Y-you thought it a great hoot to relieve the besotted innocent of her virginity.'

'Hoot?' he repeated. His voice shook.

She made the mistake of looking at him.

He was laughing at her! It was the final humiliation. She turned and ran for the nearest door, found herself standing in a long wide hallway with a pale wood floor and walls painted pale blue. Where to now? Which door next? she asked herself frantically. Any door, she decided, and sped across the hall's width to the nearest one, opened it, fell inside, then closed it behind her.

It was a blue and ivory bathroom. She could not believe her one bit of good luck. With fumbling fingers she pulled her skirt up over her hips and fastened the zip. No bra, she realised, no stockings nor panties. The stretchy black top covered her naked breasts. Her nipples stung as the fabric slid across them; sparks of awareness set her teeth on edge. She pulled on the jacket and tugged it ruthlessly across her front. Then she turned to leave, caught sight of herself in a mirror and was suddenly left suspended by what she saw. Her eyes were so dark she could see no hint of gold anywhere; her mouth was swollen and pulsing and red. Her hair needing brushing. She looked wild and wanton. Cheap and easy! One kiss and you fall on him, she accused that hateful face.

Now she had a son to go home to and face, knowing what she had been doing here with his father. Nausea leapt to her throat. She spun, wondering dizzily where her bag had gone. She decided it didn't matter; she could walk home if necessary—anything so long as she could get out of here!

She tugged the door open to find him standing there waiting for her. He'd pulled on a robe, a dark blue thing that covered hardly anything. A blanket of awareness attacked each sensitised erogenous zone. 'Get out of my way,' she said through clenched teeth.

'You are not going anywhere.' A big shoulder made contact with the door frame. 'We agreed terms.'

'Terms?' She blinked. Narrowed eyes held hers with a warning glint. In a vague part of her mind she remembered words being spoken. 'Accept my intentions,' and, 'So be it.' Then he'd licked her mouth and—

'Oh, dear God,' she breathed.

'You remember?' he mocked. 'Well, that makes it easier.'

'I want to go home.' She was pale now; she could actually feel her skin turning cold and thin.

'Later,' he agreed, and a hand came out. 'Don't you want to put these on?'

He held her stockings, her bra and her panties, flimsy pieces of black silk and lace threaded through long, very male fingers that gave shamelessness a whole new edge.

But Rafiq hadn't finished with her yet—not by a long way. 'I have no objection to you choosing a ring without these on, you understand.' His dark-toned voice was remorseless. 'In fact I think it would be rather excitingly decadent to know that only you and I know you wear nothing beneath that smart suit. But the stockings, maybe, to protect your legs from the cold weather?'

'Ring?' she repeated. 'You were serious about the ring?'

Big and dark, lean and hard, he wore the face of an Arabian warlord in no mood for compromise. 'I was serious about everything,' he confirmed with silken emphasis. 'My possession of your body, the ring—my son. We will greet him as a single unit, marry with him at our side, and become a family.'

A family eight years too late. Some family, Melanie thought as the whole wretched debacle came tumbling down upon her head. Her legs went weak and she turned to lean against the inner edge of the door frame. Determined not to cry, she closed her eyes and covered her mouth with a hand.

Watching her lose the will to fight him had the odd effect of tearing at the seams of his heart. On a sigh that rid him of mockery, he tossed the scraps of silk aside. 'I do not think you cheap and easy,' he uttered grimly. 'If anything I think it is I who is guilty of being both of those things,' he admitted, with just enough bite to let his bitterness show. 'But we will put the past in abeyance and speak for now. And now demands that we pool our resources, for our son's sake.'

'You haven't even met him yet, and you're planning his life for him.'

'But I *know* him,' he declared. 'I know what it feels like to have only one parent. What it can do to his head to know that the other parent does not seem to care if he lives or he dies. I have been there before him.' It was tense, tight statement of grim factuality. 'He bleeds inside. He will bleed no longer.'

'William loved him.'

If she'd meant to hurt by saying that, then she'd succeeded. Rafiq stiffened away from the door frame. 'My half-brother, Hassan, loves me without question. But he could not be the mother I never met or fill the hole in my heart left by her.'

With that he turned and walked back into the bedroom, not liking how much of himself he had just revealed and liking even less the way that Melanie followed him when he now wished to be alone.

A familiar feeling, he noted with a tense flexing of his shoulders.

'Who was she?'

The question placed a bitter taste in his mouth. 'A Frenchwoman—Parisian,' he drawled with bite. 'Very dark, very beautiful, very much out to catch herself a rich Arab with the oldest tricks known to man.' He turned to look at her and saw a different kind of beauty standing in his bedroom doorway. A soft golden beauty—but the same flawed beauty nonetheless.

Okay, he argued with himself as he moved over to the bank of wardrobes that filled one wall. So Melanie had not blackmailed him with the child they'd made together—still was not doing that, he was forced to concede since it was he who was using the blackmail here. But she had seen her chance of marrying wealth and had been prepared to forfeit her childhood sweetheart for it.

Shame that he'd had to discover her duplicity, he thought angrily. Shame he had not married her anyway on a desire to punish her for the rest of her life. At least he would have known his child then, would have seen him grow big in her womb as Hassan was seeing his child grow. He would have been there at his son's birth, and would have loved him so much he would never have needed to know those bleak, dark little moments in life when rejection could tear at the soul.

'When she discovered that my father was already married, and his wife pregnant, she was not pleased.'

'I don't blame her,' Melanie responded. 'It sounds to me as if your father deserved the blame. He was playing with her, obviously.'

'True.' A glimpse of a hard smile touched his mouth as he pulled a clean shirt from a hanger. 'He was young, he was arrogant and unforgivably self-seeking. But when my mother decided to cut her losses and have an abortion he showed a different side to his nature by talking her out of it—or should I say that his money did the talking?' he offered cynically as he placed the shirt on the bed. 'It matters not.' He shrugged. 'She died giving birth to me.'

'I'm sorry,' Melanie murmured.

'Don't be.' The clean shirt was followed by a clean dark suit, still wrapped in a tailor's suit bag. 'The deal was that she hand me over to my father the moment it was legally possible to do so.'

'And you think that decision denies her the right to have

anyone feel sorry at her passing? That's mean and shallow, Rafiq.' He froze in the act of selecting fresh underwear. 'For all you know she might have changed her mind about you. It happens all the time. How can you condemn someone who was never given the chance to offer an opinion?'

He turned on her. 'As I was offered that chance with my child?'

She blinked, then lowered guilty eyes from him. For some reason it infuriated him to see her do that! He covered the distance between them in a few angry strides, then used his hand to capture her chin and make her to look at him. 'Yes,' he hissed at what he saw there. 'We come full circle, my unforgiving Melanie. We reach the point where this truly began. You denied me my chance just as I deny my mother her chance. It makes us two of a pair, does it not?'

'I'm giving you your chance now.' Reaching up she grasped his wrist in a useless effort to pull his hand away. 'But it doesn't have to come with a ring attached to it!'

'Yes, it does,' he insisted. 'Because my son will not remain a bastard. My son will be surrounded with love on all sides! *My* son will not be put at risk of you marrying another man who can treat him as a second-class member of his family!'

Her beautiful eyes darkened in horror. 'Who did that to you?'

He let go. 'It is of no matter.' And turned away again, cursing his own stupid mouth!

'Rafiq…' She touched his arm with sympathy.

Sympathy! The bubbling black mass of old hurts came thundering up to the surface. He turned back, knew he was losing it—*knew it* and could not stop it! 'Get out!' he breathed. 'Get out of here, Melanie, while you still can!'

What she did was step closer and wrap her arms around him like a mother would—like *she* would do with his son! 'I'm sorry,' she was saying. 'I'm sorry. I didn't know…'

He gripped her arms and tried to prise her free; he

needed to put a safe distance between them or he did not know what he would do! But she held on, lifted her face, lifted eyes that understood when he did not want anyone to understand!

'I am dangerous,' he grated. It was his final warning.

She reached up and kissed him. Blackness turned molten, molten spun itself into something else. She was amazing, fearless—foolish! She had to be to still be here when anyone with eyes must know he was about to slake all this emotion in the only way he knew how!

He caught that mouth with a kiss that blazed. He picked her up and pressed her back against the wall. Her skirt rose above her hips as he parted her legs and wrapped them around him. He entered her with no preliminary at all.

Bright fireballs of sensation propelled themselves at her senses; she clung to his shoulders and his mouth. It was all so intense that she barely noticed when he ejected into her with the shuddering groans of a man lost in hell. When it was over her feet slithered like melted wax onto the hard wood flooring. Shocked and dazed, and still caught by the pulsing aftermath of her own shimmering climax, she stared blindly at his chest, where damp whorls of black hair curled around his gaping robe.

Then once again the horror of reality hit: the knowledge that she could be so primitive! She choked on a sob as a stream of Arabic flooded over her, then hoarse thick English words of apology, of remorse and self-whipping disgust and disgrace as he picked her up in his arms and carried her out of the bedroom and down the hall.

Safety came with the neatness of a sitting room, apparently. He set her down in a low soft leather armchair, then muttered something she did not catch before striding away. A doorbell rang; he must have gone to answer it because she heard the sound of voices talking, then nothing until he came to squat down beside her and offered a glass to her trembling mouth. It was brandy; it burned as she swallowed. He took a gulp himself.

'I don't know what to say to you,' he pushed out thickly.

Her lashes flickered downwards as she made herself look into his face. He was as white as the chair she was sitting on, guilt-riddled and appalled with himself.

'I'll marry you,' she whispered. 'I'll marry you.'

'Why?' He couldn't have sounded more stunned if he'd tried.

Tears filled her eyes. It was all so—*basic!* She wanted him again so very badly it burned like a wound inside! He filled her with a thousand contradictions. Anger, hurt, resentment, confusion—desire! He ran cold, then hot, was ruthlessly hard and tough, yet so very vulnerable it almost broke her heart.

And then they came—the words that really mattered. She was still in love him, even after all these years and all the heartache and pain and the sense of betrayal. She still loved him no matter what or why. Realising that hurt more than anything else did. She couldn't tell him—would *never* tell him.

'Robbie needs you,' she said.

Robbie needs you. Once again they'd arrived back at the beginning. A different beginning in an ever-confusing spiral of beginnings.

He stood up. It was a withdrawal in many ways. 'Yes,' he said. 'Of course. I will go and dress. You may safely use the bathroom to—tidy yourself before we leave.'

CHAPTER SIX

His suit was a dark blue, almost black, in colour, the fabric an exquisite weave of silk. His shirt was white, his tie blue, and the whole ensemble blended perfectly with the man he had turned himself into.

Cleanly shaven face; neatly combed hair; raven eyelashes keeping a permanent guard over his eyes, and his mouth a beautifully defined example of sombre elegance. Melanie had to bite hard into her bottom lip so as not to say a word. If he'd dressed like this to put Robbie at his ease with him then he could not have got it more wrong. Her son was more likely to stand in awe than feel at ease. Rafiq was the ice man, a man who belonged in a palace built of glass, steel and marble.

She shivered and fiddled with the ring on her finger. It was made of gold and bright, flawless sparkling diamonds. She had chosen it from a luscious selection set on a black velvet tray in the privacy of his sitting room. Between her running for cover in the bathroom and their confrontation across its threshold he had called up a top London jeweller and had had them bring a selection to his apartment.

It was money wielding its awesome power. She shivered again; he shifted tensely and sent her a sharp look that scoured the skin from the part of her profile he could see. Sitting next to each other in this car was the closest they'd been to each other since he'd fed her the brandy. No eye contact nor body contact, words spoken as if through a glass wall. Why? Because they'd delved into a dark place they knew they should never have visited. It had exposed too much of an inner core that most preferred to keep hidden away.

Now here they were, driving towards her home where another ordeal was about to be enacted. Melanie tried to swallow and found that she couldn't. From the corner of her eye she caught sight of his hand where it rested on his thigh. The long fingers moved ever so slightly, but she could almost taste the tension that forced them to make that minuscule jerk. She dared a quick glance up from beneath her lashes and almost shattered on impact with the hard profile of a cold and aloof Arabian male: his long thin nose; his curling black eyelashes hovering against the firm glossy texture of his olive-toned skin; his jaw line taut and rock-like, the set of his mouth implacable and flat. If she superimposed Arab clothes over the suit she could be looking at the Arabian prince he was in everything but name.

But that memory belonged to another time, and it did nothing for her nerves to remember it now. Daunting as he was in his western sophistication, she preferred it to that other man she had met only once, when he'd torn her apart with his contempt.

This time she managed to contain the shiver. 'Robbie might mention your father,' she heard herself say as thoughts of his ruthless Arab side led her onto other things.

The dark head turned with frightening precision; eyes too dark to read fixed on her face. 'He knows about my father?'

It was too quietly and too smoothly spoken. Melanie tried that swallow again. 'W-William liked to keep him informed ab-about your country,' she explained. 'Your father's poor health is reported in the press occasionally, and a party six months ago was given quite a lot of coverage. A thirty-year anniversary?' she prompted.

He nodded. So did she, then dragged her eyes away to look down at the ring again. 'Robbie decided that your father's ill health m-must have kept you at home with him. H-he worries about things like that, so it suited him to give you that particular reason why you didn't come to London.'

The hand resting on his thigh gave that telling minuscule twitch once more. 'Without William Portreath's money, would you ever have told me about him?'

It wasn't harsh but it was coldly accusing. 'Robbie only started asking questions about you a year ago. He never asked to see you, but if he had done I'd like to think I would have done something about it.'

'You'd like to think?' he repeated.

'I had to protect both him and myself,' she reiterated.

'From me?'

'From this!' she cried, shattering the wall between them with a spectacular eruption, blasting away all of this nice polite civility. 'Look at what you've already done, Rafiq! Even with William's money as my so-called safeguard. I've been packed up and taken over! You did it before. You packed me up and took me over, then dropped me like a brick when I didn't come up to your high expectations!'

'You are twisting the truth.'

'No, I'm not.' Trying to make the eruption subside again was impossible. The bubble had burst and she suddenly didn't know what she was doing, sitting here next to him travelling towards calamity at what felt like the speed of light. 'If Robbie can't meet those same high expectations does he get dropped?' she pushed out thickly. 'Do you truly think I believe I am doing the right thing bringing you into his life? Because I don't! You're so hard and tough and unpredictable.' She sat upright on a raw flick of tension. 'You blow hot, then icy cold. I can't tell what you're going to do next, and I'm frightened I've made a huge error of judgement here. I feel like I'm playing Russian roulette with a child's life!'

'I will not drop him!' he raked at her. 'Nor you, for that matter,' he added with a lofty promise that aimed to put all the emotion back under wraps but didn't quiet make it. 'And if you still feel this way, why am I here at all?' he demanded, and brought the whole thing toppling down again.

Melanie looked down at her tightly clenched hands, then out of the car window while her chest grew tight on words she did not want to speak.

But time was beginning to run out. 'William's death had a profound effect on Robbie,' she told him. 'He suddenly realised that without William he had only me to take care of him. So he worries that I—'

'Might die too and leave him with no one.' Rafiq took over in a deep voice so drenched in bleak understanding that she glanced sharply at him.

He was sitting there with the same carved profile, but his eyes had come alive, burning with a personal knowledge that brought into hard focus the kind of childhood he'd experienced as a motherless son—a second son and an illegitimate one at that.

'Y-you had your brother,' she reminded him.

His tight smile mocked the remark. 'Hassan is six months older than I am. Every time his mother looked at me she saw the bitter proof of her husband's infidelity while she was heavily pregnant. Do you think she didn't yearn for the day when she could toss me out of her household? In the end she died before she could achieve her dearest wish, but as a child I learned to appreciate the vulnerability of my situation.'

'I'm sorry. I didn't know.'

'How could you?' He shrugged. 'These are not the kind of memories a man usually shares with other people.'

Not even with the woman he professed to love? If he had been a bit more open with her eight years ago maybe she would have stood a chance at understanding what had made him the man he was, and dealt with the situation of Robbie differently.

'So, he worries?' Rafiq prompted.

She nodded. 'He has nightmares about it,' she confessed, and watched in thick-throated distress as he turned his head so she could see those dark knowing eyes. 'He worries himself sick if I so much as sneeze. As I've been saying from the start, he—'

'Needs me,' Rafiq finished. 'As back-up,' he added.

It sounded so very cold put like that, but— 'Yes,' she confirmed.

'And if I had not come through with this back-up?'

She looked away and did not answer. But, being the man he was, he had already worked out what her alternatives were going to be. His hand snaked out to catch her chin, then he made her to look back at him. Hard eyes glinted into her eyes. 'As far as my son and his mother are concerned I will not be walking away,' he vowed very clearly. 'So you may put away any other options, Melanie. For the ring on your finger will be joined by another, and you will not need to look elsewhere for anything—understand?'

Yes. She nodded and let her eyelashes flutter onto her cheeks so he couldn't read her thoughts. Because she was beginning to understand an awful lot of things, and none of them helped her to feel less anxious about the situation. With every word he uttered, Rafiq was revealing an affinity with his son that promised to grow into a bond like no other. Who would become the expendable link then? She would, and on realising it she began to appreciate what it meant to feel so frighteningly vulnerable.

The car pulled up outside her house. Melanie was never so relieved for an excuse to escape. She went to pull her chin free of his fingers, but he held on until she surrendered and looked back up at him. The glow in his eyes was skin-piercingly covetous. It pricked at just about every nerve-end she possessed. The sexual pull was stunning; the emotional one threatened to strip her bare. Sparks flew; her breathing snagged; for a few blind seconds she had to fight the urge to turn her mouth into those cool fingers and say something calamitous like, I still love you, Rafiq.

She wanted to run and Rafiq didn't blame her. He could

not look at her without the sexual fallout drenching the air. The cool tips of his fingers slid against skin like fine satin, the inner recesses of his mouth sprang into life with a need to taste what he could feel. A driving compulsion to lean down and take what was throbbing in the atmosphere held him motionless, because he dared not even breathe in case he gave in to its magnetic pull.

He had revealed the absolute worst of himself to her today, yet she was still sitting here looking at him through those hungry eyes. Why was that? he asked himself. She was wearing his ring and was prepared to marry him when she had to know his arguments for marriage were a bluff, and that she possessed the resources to turn her back on him if she so pleased.

Was she doing this for their son? A son who had not even looked upon his father's face and who, when he did, might well decide he didn't like what he saw! What then— what did Melanie do then?

He removed his fingers and looked away from her, and heard her feather out a shaky breath. His driver opened the door for her. She scrambled out of the car and hurried up the path to fumble the key into the lock of her front door. The black suit skimmed her slender figure; her pale hair swung around her slender nape. His heart gave a tug. It was fear. He grabbed it and crushed it down again.

It had stopped raining but the air was cold and damp. As he stepped out of the car he felt it seep into his bones and had a sudden wish to be at home, standing beneath the relentless heat of the desert sun.

But first he had a son to meet and a relationship to build. His heart gave a different kind of tug, and he grimaced as he turned to dismiss his driver. Then he swung back to look at the house into which Melanie had already disappeared. The car moved away as he walked up the path. As he walked inside the house seemed to stir, like a sleeping monster awakening from a long dark slumber as its senses picked up on the scent of threat.

Threat to whom? To Melanie or his son? Was it William Portreath's ghost Rafiq could sense stirring in the shadows, watching Rafiq infiltrate his domain so he could see for himself if he was a worthy successor? He gave himself a mental shake. He wasn't usually prone to such superstitious nonsense, he grimly mocked himself.

A sound came from the living room and he stepped into it to find Melanie on her knees in front of the fire, putting a light to the logs neatly aligned in the grate. Flames leaped to life and she was on her feet, moving round the room lighting faded old lamps, plumping faded old cushions. 'Make yourself at home,' she invited. 'I need to go and change before— The fire should be okay, and I've switched on the central heating system so the house will heat up pretty quickly.'

For a man who had never walked into any of his many homes needing to think about what kept it heated—or cool, for that matter—Rafiq viewed all this brisk domesticity through vaguely shocked eyes. She disappeared into the hallway. He listened to her light footsteps as she ran up the stairs, and heard a door open and close. A few minutes later the clock on the mantelpiece chimed the half-hour. It was instinctive when he hitched back a snowy white shirt cuff to check the time on his state-of-the-art satellite-controlled wrist-watch and grimaced when he discovered that the old wooden-cased clock was accurate almost to the second.

Three-thirty, Melanie noted. That left them with ten short minutes before Robbie arrived back from school, and she tried not to predict what was going to happen as she scrambled out of her suit and into jeans and a pale blue sweater, then brushed her hair while avoiding any contact with a mirror because—

A ball of heat rolled in her stomach, then sank to the apex at her thighs. She caught her breath, then just stood there staring at the old-fashioned roses on the wallpaper while her head decided to play her some flashbacks from the last few hours just to make the feeling worse.

Oh, she'd behaved like an absolute wanton. What must he be thinking about her?

He—Rafiq ben Jusef Al Alain Al-Qadim. She gave him his name and was immediately hit with his naked image. Big, dark, muscular and sleek, with curling black hair following the contours of his long torso from his wide chest like an arrowhead pointing the way to the enthralling eminence of his, of his—

No. She blinked the image away, eyelashes fluttering with a terrible reluctance to let the image fade, which brought a flush to her cheeks as she slid her feet into a pair of lightweight flat shoes and tried very hard to concentrate her mind on what lay ahead of them instead of what lay behind.

She came down the stairs to the sound of a car engine idling outside the front gate. A door slammed; there was a child's shout of 'See you!' and her whole body froze on a moment's stark panic of what was about to happen.

The door was on the latch. She always made sure it was left on the latch so that Robbie could let himself in. His bag arrived first, swinging in through the door to land on the polished wood floor before he propelled himself inside. His tie was flying, as usual, his shirt collar curled up towards his chin.

'Hi,' he said, seeing her standing there as he closed the door behind him.

'Hi, yourself.' Her heart dipped and dived as she made herself walk forward on legs that felt hollow. 'Have you had a nice day today?'

'We've been making Christmas cards,' he informed her as she went down on her haunches in front of him. 'Mrs Dukes is going to print lots of copies so we can send them to our friends.'

'Well, that sounds like a good idea.' She smiled, or tried

to, while anxiously straightening his shirt collar and running shaky fingers through his ruffled hair.

'What are you doing that for?' Robbie frowned at her. 'I'm going to get changed in a minute.'

'Because I have a surprise for you,' she told him, feeling her tension hit its highest point, and feeling yet more tension coming at her in waves from inside the living room. She wondered what Rafiq was thinking, feeling—*doing*!

'A surprise?' Robbie prompted.

'Yes.' She smiled and straightened, then took hold of his hand. 'A really marvellous surprise. Come and see.'

With that she led him towards the living room, heart in her mouth as she brought him to a halt in the open doorway. She felt Robbie look up, felt him stiffen, then felt her own deep sinking sensation as she looked up into Rafiq's carved face. He was still standing where she had left him in the middle of the room, with the firelight flickering behind him. The air crashed with tension. It was sheer motherly instinct that made her swing her son to stand in front of her with his back to her, her arms wrapping themselves around him so she could feel his little heart pounding like a hammer drill.

'Rafiq, th-this is Robbie.' She made that first stammering introduction.

'Robbie,' she murmured gently to her son, 'this is—'

'My daddy,' the little boy said.

No one could have predicted he was going to say that. Melanie wasn't even aware how he knew what his father looked like; Rafiq just looked shell-shocked.

'I saw you in a picture William showed to me,' Robbie enlightened them. 'You were in Egypt with a lady, but you weren't dressed like that, though.' He frowned at the smart Italian suit. 'You had Arab clothes on and the lady had on a red frilly dress.'

As her son built a host of vivid pictures in his mother's head he also began slipping through her fingers, drawn towards Rafiq as if he'd known him since birth and had simply been waiting for him to come. Through eyes gone glassy with tears and a heart almost too swollen to manage to beat, she watched Rafiq observe with bottomless black fascination as his son approached him with his head tipped back so his eyes could maintain contact with his.

Move! Melanie wanted to shout at him. Make a response! Can't you see how brave he is being, coming to you like this? As if she'd shrieked the words out loud the stiffness faded from Rafiq's body and he lowered his big frame to his son's level.

'Hello,' he murmured rustily.

'Hello,' Robbie replied gravely. Black eyes searched black eyes for a few seconds. Then Robbie made his next courageous move and lifted up a hand and offered it to his father. Rafiq took it. Melanie watched through her tears as his large hand closed around her son's tiny one.

It was the first touch, first contact. She saw Rafiq's mouth move in response to it, then saw no more as tears blurred the rest of the tableau, and the silence throbbing all around them threatened to suffocate all three.

Then Robbie spoke again. 'Can you ride a camel?'

A camel, Melanie repeated to herself numbly as she listened to Rafiq's thickened reply. 'Yes.'

'William said you would know how. William said…'

She took the coward's way out, turned and made a dash for the kitchen, where she gave her legs permission to fold and slid into a huddle on the floor in a corner. She pressed her face into her knees, covered her ears with her hands and waited in trembling agony for the emotions trampling through her to subside.

The telephone began to ring, cutting through everything like an unwelcome intruder. She leaped up, wiped her eyes with trembling fingers, and made herself answer it.

It was Sophia, ringing to tell her she had decided to stay the weekend in Manchester with friends. 'How's it going?' she asked.

'Robbie is with his father in the other room,' she announced huskily.

'So he remembered to turn up.' Sophia had called Melanie every day to check on progress and had become more hostile with every day that Rafiq hadn't put in an appearance. 'If he hurts that boy, I'll—'

'They came together like long-lost friends!' Melanie said with a choke. 'Give them both a few minutes and they will have me all trussed up and labelled as the bad guy for keeping them apart!'

'Then don't let them do it,' Sophia said firmly. 'You know why you kept Robbie a secret from him. Just keep on reminding yourself that the rat dumped you without cause, on the hearsay of some very twisted people, and then left you alone and damn near destitute to carry his can of oats!'

His can of oats. Melanie couldn't help it; she laughed. 'Thanks,' she murmured.

'Don't mention it,' Sophia dismissed. 'I can still remember what you looked like when you turned up on William's doorstep as fat as a pig and looking like the original bag lady. Homeless, loveless and still trying to get a line of communication through to that arrogant fool sitting comfortably on his billions.'

'He doesn't know that.'

'Well, *tell* him!'

'No.' The stubborn lip protruded. 'That belongs in the past and I am determined to concentrate only on the future.' She paused, then decided to get the really bad news over with. 'We—we're getting married,' she added reluctantly.

'*What—?*'

Melanie winced. 'We decided it was the best thing for everyone. Robbie needs him—even you agree with that, Sophia! And marriage seems to be the best way to give him the security he—'

'Are you mad?' her friend shrieked. 'I'm coming home,' she decided.

'No!' Melanie cried. 'Don't do that, Sophia! I know what I'm doing, I—'

'You're a babe in arms when it comes to men, is what you are, Melanie Portreath!' the other woman derided. 'Have you stopped for one minute to think what his motives are for suggesting such a wicked thing?'

Oh, yes, Melanie thought, she'd stopped to think. The word HOT lit itself up in block capitals, followed by the word SEX!

'He will rush you to his desert hideout and lock you away there while he waltzes off with your son! It's the way they do things over there! Get behind me, woman, and all that!'

'He isn't like that,' she said, agitatedly twisting the ring on her finger.

'*All* men are like that if they think they can get away with it!'

'You don't know him—'

'Neither do you! You just slept with him once—'

Twice, Melanie silently corrected, then closed her eyes and thought—three times if you counted the last feverish grappling.

'Then he took off, with your virginity etched on his belt,' Sophia was saying, with no knowledge that Melanie had just taken off to a place she knew she should not be revisiting. 'And left *you* behind with the word *slut* etched on to your blasted forehead!'

Melanie blinked. Sophia was right. She had walked around for years thinking that word was branded on her brow. She hadn't dared trust herself with another man just in case he believed it and treated her the same way that Rafiq had done.

'Do me a favour, Melanie, and don't do anything stupid until I get back,' Sophia said urgently. 'Then we will grab your lawyer and sit down to talk through all of this.'

'Okay.' It made a lot of sense—more sense than she had been making all day, for that matter. 'But don't cut short your weekend or I won't forgive you!'

The call ended with Sophia reluctantly agreeing to wait until Monday before she began her crusade to save Melanie from a fate worse than death. Melanie put the telephone back on its rest, feeling a whole lot better for having had Sophia talk stubborn strength back into her.

It lasted only as long as it took her to prepare Robbie's favourite meal of pasta with tuna then to go in search of the two of them. She found them in William's study, and the moment she stepped through the door her new-found strength collapsed like a house of cards.

The room itself said everything about the man who had spent most of his life in it. The walls were lined with books, the furniture was so old it was threadbare. The fire wasn't lit and the two high-wing-backed chairs that flanked the fireplace looked as if they had been there for centuries. There was a chill in the air because the room was so rarely used these days, but someone had closed the heavy velvet curtains across the window and had switched on the faded table-lamps.

William's big old desk stood in the window. Robbie had pulled a chair up to it to kneel on while Rafiq stood beside him. Both of them had lost their jackets, both dark heads were close as they pored over the huge map that had been spread out across the top of the desk. Robbie was using an elbow to support his chin, Rafiq the flat of a hand as he listened to his son tell him all about the Arabian state of Rahman as if he had lived most of his life there.

'William said the river here keeps the valley fertile. And the mountains have snow on them in the winter,' Robbie was explaining casually. 'He said that you can walk for six days without seeing anything but sand, and that your daddy built this huge place—here—for the camel trains to use when they need to take a rest.'

His finger was pointing knowledgeably, but Rafiq

wasn't watching it. He was watching his son. The light from the desk lamp caught both sets of features, one young and smooth and contentedly serious, the other carved like wood to represent total infatuation.

'William said you have the biggest oasis in the country. Is that true?' He looked up, big brown eyes fixing on their older matching pair.

'It belongs to my father.' Rafiq nodded. 'It is called the Al-Qadim Oasis. My—home is there.'

'Yes.' The boy looked away again, graver now, worried a little. 'William said that your daddy is poorly. Is he feeling better? Is that why you've come to visit me?'

'I came because—yes…' Rafiq paused, then answered, 'he is a little better.'

'Good.' Robbie nodded. 'William was poorly for a long time before he— Shall we look at the photographs now?'

'How about some supper first?' Melanie inserted, trying hard to keep the thickening tears from sounding in her voice.

Both looked up; both straightened. One smiled at her; the other didn't. 'Hi,' Robbie said. 'I was just telling my daddy about Rahman.'

My daddy clutched at a tender spot inside her. 'That's nice.' She tried a smile but couldn't quite pull it off. 'But it's getting late. Why don't you go and get washed and changed now? It's your favourite for supper.'

'Tuna? Oh, great!' At once he was her little boy again, all beaming smiles and bouncing energy that had him leaping from the chair to land neatly on the faded carpet. He came towards her with a jaunty little stride—then stopped, the smile fading from his face as he turned to look at Rafiq. 'You won't go while I'm upstairs, will you?' he said cautiously.

'No, I won't go,' Rafiq promised him.

'Great,' Robbie said again, then grinned widely. 'Great!' he repeated, and was running out of the room, leaving two adults with a fallout he would never understand in a million years.

The moment they were alone Rafiq turned his back on her, broad shoulders like rods as he stared down at the map. 'I will never forgive you for this,' he breathed harshly.

'Won't forgive me for what?' she took the challenge head-on.

'*This*!' he rasped, waving a hand across the spread map. 'He knows more about Rahman than I know about it! He can plot a track across the desert from one of my homes to another!' he stated harshly. 'And he has learned it all from another man!'

'William—'

'Yes, *William*!' he incised, then gave his big shoulders a shrug, as if to rid them of whatever it was that was sitting on them. 'I think it is time you told me about William Portreath,' he demanded tightly.

Tension spun through every tight syllable, bitterness and anger and—yes, Melanie realised there was a burning jealousy for the love and affection Robbie felt for William.

CHAPTER SEVEN

RAFIQ did not know what he was feeling. He tried grabbing in a lungful of air in effort to control himself, but he was way past the point of controlling anything. The last hour had been heaven and hell wrapped in one package. He had never felt such instant attachment to another human being, and all that person could talk about was William Portreath.

He turned to glare at Melanie. She was standing in the doorway looking wary and stubborn, and it was clear she did not want to have this kind of discussion with him.

'Please,' he ground out from his chest like the rattle of a pistol.

With a little jerk she swung the door almost shut behind her, her fingers still clutching at the handle and her shoulders straight and tense.

'Okay,' she agreed reluctantly. 'What is it that you want to know?

His teeth gritted at the reluctance, and his chest clenched at the rebellious expression on her beautiful face. But he had a right to know, dammit! 'Exactly what was William Portreath to you?'

'If you'd read my papers you would know what he was,' she returned. 'William was my great-uncle on my mother's side. He made his fortune travelling the world as a diamond merchant before coming back to England to retire.'

Her left hand appeared from behind her back and she glanced down at the diamond ring circling her finger. So did Rafiq, and he felt his skin prickle when he remembered the safety deposit box listed in her assets; it was packed full of diamonds that could probably kill the sparkle in the ones she wore on her finger.

'You were his only beneficiary,' he said, as if that had anything to do with all this. It didn't. He was just linking one thought with another.

'I didn't know that until he'd died,' Melanie made clear. 'In fact I did not even know of William's existence until my twenty-first birthday, when a letter arrived from Randal's firm informing me that I was William's heir and he would like to meet me,' she explained. 'So I agreed to come here to see him, and found myself faced with this crabby old eccentric.' An odd little smile softened the defiance from her mouth. 'We had a fight—'

'About what?'

'William had known since the time when my parents died that I would inherit from him. He also knew that I had been sent off to live with another obscure uncle but, because he didn't want the responsibility of a child cluttering up his reclusive life, he chose to ignore my existence until I was—old enough to be sensible, as he put it.' Her mouth took on a bitter twist now. 'But he didn't get a sensible person. He got an angry one who was heavily pregnant and with no sign of a man to make her respectable.'

Rafiq flinched. 'I can do simple arithmetic.'

'William called me a few unpleasant names that you would recognise,' she said, retaliating to his bite. 'And I called him a few names in return. I went to leave. He stood up to stop me, tripped over his walking stick and would have fallen if I hadn't grabbed him. It—it was like holding frail skin and bone in my arms,' she recalled, not seeing the way Rafiq stiffened in recognition of that sentiment. 'H-he asked me to stay,' she went on. 'He was lonely. I was—in need of a roof over my head, so I stayed.'

Her accompanying shrug said, End of story. But as far as Rafiq was concerned it was only the beginning of it.

'So you allowed William Portreath to become both father to my son and a grandfather in place of my own father!'

'Am I supposed to feel guilty for allowing William to give Robbie something no one else would?'

'Yes…' He moved restlessly. 'You should be feeling as guilty as hell.'

Melanie was not impressed. 'You can say that now,' she mocked. 'But we both know you didn't feel like that eight years ago. You just walked away.'

'I did not know I was leaving a son behind.'

'You didn't want to know.'

'How can you say that? How dare you say that when you never gave me the opportunity to make that decision?'

'A decision?' she flicked back at him, and was suddenly lurching away from the door to come and stand directly in front of him. 'You think it required a *decision* as to whether you condescended to want Robbie or not? How dare you stand here and be so conceited?' she said angrily. 'How dare you be so bloody superior that you can even put up such an argument? You threw me out without a hearing!' Her golden eyes flicked the accusation at him. 'That was your decision, Rafiq. Anything at all that came after that was *my* decision! And I did not *decide* to love Robbie. I just *do* love him. Can you possibly understand the difference?'

'Jamie,' he installed into the argument. 'As a mother you love without question, no matter who is the father of your child. But a father needs to trust he *is* the father before he can dare to love! You slept with Jamie within a week of sleeping with me.' His hand flicked out to toss that claim at her. 'You cannot possibly have known, therefore, which of us was his father until the boy was born.'

'Is this leading somewhere?' she demanded coldly.

Was it? Rafiq asked himself. 'Yes,' he hissed. 'Once you knew for sure that I was Robert's father you had a moral duty to get in touch with me.'

Nothing—he received absolutely nothing back from that

final accusation. Her rebellious eyes held his steady; her mouth remained defiantly shut. She had planted her hands on hips and was taking him on as if she was easily up to his weight in a battle. Frustration attached itself to his ribs and his fingers. He wanted to reach out with those fingers and shake her into talking—and he wanted to wrap her to his aching ribs and just kiss her senseless!

He sighed, wishing he knew what it was that was actually driving him here, but he didn't. There were so many feelings trampling around inside him that he couldn't distinguish one from the other. His gaze shifted around a room that was not dissimilar to a room his father had in Rahman. He looked at the map again and saw the years he'd been robbed of by his own blind stubbornness represented on the desk, and also in the sound of his son's voice unwittingly telling him how William Portreath had attempted to give them to the child.

It hurt. This house hurt. This room, the dead man who still lingered inside it—this woman and her refusal to admit that she owed him something for what she'd taken away!

'I need to get out of here,' he decided suddenly. It was that quick, that desperate, and he just stepped around her and walked away.

As he made for the door Melanie felt the bitterness rise up and try to strangle her. 'So you still walk away from promises you make.' She slid the words deridingly after him. 'What happened to your "united we stand" speech, Rafiq?' she taunted. 'Or the promise you gave to your son that you would still be here when he comes downstairs?'

Rigid back, rigid shoulders; he went still by the door. 'I am finding it impossible to justify that for seven years my son has been deprived of his right to know a father's love,' he said harshly. 'And that William Portreath stole something from my father that did not belong to him!'

'William didn't steal anything from anyone. I did.'

He turned to look at her. Pale but still perfect, Melanie

thought painfully. Still loftily superior, but struggling with it. 'William Portreath aided and abetted you to keep my son hidden away from me!' He stated it clearly.

Melanie pulled in some air, then made herself say what she knew she didn't want to say. 'On the day Robbie was born William begged me to tell you about our son and offered me any money I might need to fight you in court,' she confessed. 'I refused.'

His eyes narrowed. 'I don't believe you.'

'I don't care what you believe,' she returned. 'I know it is the truth. This has never had anything to do with money. It was to do with a man who could walk away from his promises and never—ever—look back! Now here you are, intending to do the same thing again. Only this time you're going to break a small boy's heart instead of a stupid young woman's!'

'You never loved me,' he said, denouncing that claim. 'It was always the money! You were always only looking for a rich man to take you out of the hole you lived in!'

'And I chose you?' Melanie gasped out. 'Think back, Rafiq, and tell me who it was that did the chasing! Because I recall you virtually laying siege to me!'

'Tactics,' he said cynically. 'You played the game perfectly.'

'No.' Melanie denied that. 'If I'd been playing the tactical game I would have made you wait for sex until the ring was safely on my finger. But not me—not this gullible fool!' A shudder of self-disgust ripped through her. 'I gave you it all—just as I gave it to you again today—and if you think I am proud of myself for that, then think again, because you have a real knack for making me despise myself!'

She turned away from his stunned expression, despising herself all the more for letting fly at him. What was she trying to do here? Bury her pride completely? She lifted a hand to cover her mouth with it, caught the glitter of a diamond and with tears suddenly burning in her eyes she wrenched the ring from her finger and stepped up to hand it back to him.

The swine took it—he *took it*! 'Now you can leave,' she whispered shakily.

Footsteps suddenly sounded on the upper landing, then came clattering down the stairs. Both stopped breathing and went perfectly still. It lasted only a couple of seconds and Rafiq was the first to recover. His eyes gave a flash like lightning—the only warning Melanie received before she was being crushed in his arms. Heat drenched her body from the burn of the kiss; tension ricocheted through her muscles as she tried to fight him. In a single smooth movement he'd caught her mouth and was lifting them both out of the way from the door as their son pushed it open. Robbie just stood there, staring at the fascinating sight of his mother kissing his newly found father.

Deliberate. The whole swift, nerve-shaking move had been a deliberate one aimed to make a particular impression on their highly impressionable son. When Rafiq finally released her mouth Melanie found herself staring at the hand she had splayed out against his snow-white shirt front. Somewhere between the grab and the kiss Rafiq had also slid the ring back onto her finger. It was now sparkling at her in much the same way as her son was sparkling.

'You were kissing my mum,' Robbie accused.

'Mmm,' Rafiq agreed. 'I like kissing her, and she likes me doing it...'

Melanie's gaze jumped from the ring to his face. Those devil-black eyes were glinting down on her with lazy triumph. Deny it if you can, that mocking glint challenged. She was breathless—helpless—literally stewing in her own foolish response. And what made it all so much worse was that Rafiq knew it. He released a low, soft, throaty laugh, caught the hand wearing the ring, then swung them both to face their small witness. 'We have been talking about what to do about us,' he informed his son smoothly. 'How would you feel about us becoming a proper family, Robert?'

Robert. Melanie blinked at the *Robert* she'd only ever heard William use. Then she blinked again at her son, who was suddenly wearing a smile that lit his whole face. 'Will you come here and live with us?' Robbie demanded in breathless excitement.

Rafiq's brief moment of stillness was Melanie's only reward for the web she was allowing herself to be wrapped in. He hadn't thought as far on as *where* they were going to live. Then he said, 'Yes. Tonight, I think. What do you think?' he deferred to his star-struck son.

'Oh, yes!' Robbie exclaimed, as if he'd just had his dearest wish granted.

'Good,' Rafiq murmured. 'Then you may show me to the room in which I am to sleep...'

'Rafiq...'

Her one burst of protest was denied by a man intent on getting his own way. Lifting the hand wearing his ring to his mouth, he kissed it and murmured, 'Hush,' then gently let her go so he could turn his full attention on Robbie. His hand was offered to his son. Watching through a daze, she saw Robbie's smaller hand disappear inside it. As the long fingers closed she felt something clutch at her heart. The pair began to move out of the room, man and boy linked by their hands and a genetic influence that was so strong it hurt.

Maybe she even groaned at the recognition, she wasn't sure, but something made Robbie stop and turn his head to look at her. 'Is something the matter?' he asked frowningly.

'No, of course not.' She smiled. 'I am just trying to decide whether to eat in the kitchen or go all posh and use the dining room.'

The diversion was an inspiration. Robbie's eyes widened in dismay. 'Not the dining room, Mum!' he protested.

'It's all big and cold in there.' His hand gave a tug at his father's hand. 'We can eat in the kitchen, can't we?'

There's your choice, big man, Melanie thought cynically. The boy, the trusting hand, the kitchen and the house. The arc of his silky black lashes curled against his high cheekbones as he looked down at his son.

'The kitchen sounds perfect,' Rafiq agreed.

'Good.' Robbie beamed. 'I knew you'd want to. William liked the kitchen the very best—and this room, of course. Come on, let's go upstairs to my room. You'll like it…'

Robbie didn't see his mother wince at his mention of William. He didn't see Rafiq's fleeting glance her way before he allowed himself to be pulled towards the stairs.

Later they sat at the scrubbed kitchen table, eating pasta turned to rubber, pretending to enjoy it. Rafiq had probably never eaten in a kitchen in his life before, Melanie mused. He had probably never eaten from anything but the best bone china, nor been forced to sleep in a draughty old bedroom.

Then she took that last thought back with an inner snatch when she recalled her bedroom at the farmhouse. It had been cold and draughty. The bed had been an ancient metal-sprung affair with a deep feather mattress and a propensity to creak when they…

She got up from the table in an agitated flurry, bringing two pairs of matching eyes shooting questions her way. She ignored them, moved to the sink with her plate, then just stood there driven into remembering the man and the bed and the way he had drawn her down upon it, his dark face wearing the intensity of what had taken him over. He had touched and tutored her, had slowly brought her to a yearning pitch at which she would rather have died than drawn back from accepting him.

But the bed—the bed had creaked and groaned like a guilty accomplice. The room had been so cold he had pulled the heavy eiderdown over them, cocooning them in warmth and the soft, heaving rush of their own sensual breathing. Flesh moving against flesh, scents stirring the senses. They'd remained there throughout a whole afternoon while her uncle and Jamie had been out in the barn, and the old farmhouse had rattled against an icy storm hitting its outer walls—while another storm beneath the eiderdown had been hot and sultry.

Someone touched her shoulder. She almost jumped in the air. It was Rafiq. She jerked away. He released a small sigh and turned her to face him.

Big; his chest was big, wide and deep and beautifully masculine. Her breasts sprang to life, tightening and tingling and sending messages down to other parts of her that droned with an ache she did not want to feel.

'Where's Robbie?' she murmured, vaguely aware that they were alone in the kitchen.

'Gone to find a video I am to watch,' her son's father replied, with just a hint of huskiness that told her he was touched by his son's desire to share everything with him. 'But I wanted to take this moment to apologise for my remarks earlier. You were right: William Portreath is not to be blamed. He was a good man. He loved my son. I can only thank him for taking care of Robert as wisely as he did. It is no wonder Robert misses him.'

She nodded, unable to speak. He believed she had been standing here thinking of their argument when in reality her thoughts had been lost in a different kind of place entirely. She ought to be ashamed of herself, but oddly she wasn't. She was hot and hungry struggling not to close the two-inch gap between his chest and the tingling tips of her eager breasts.

'Y-you can't stay here. It wouldn't be right.' She managed the sensible sentence.

'The decision has been made. I do not back down on my promises.'

'To your son.' It was bitter. 'You are cynically using him to get your own way where I am concerned.'

'To both of you,' he insisted. 'And cynical I may be, but the sooner we place this relationship on a permanent footing, the sooner we can give Robert what he needs.'

'Stop calling him Robert,' she snapped out impulsively.

'It is his name,' he insisted. 'And why are you trembling?'

Melanie almost laughed out loud at the question. 'Because I think I am going to fall into a flood of tears,' she lied, instead of telling the truth—that she was longing to fall on him like a ravenous fool!

Though the tears weren't that far away, she realised. Tears and desire. What a combination. Both ate away at self-control. She tried to move away; his hands pressed her closer. Two inches became a half an inch. Her trembling became a fine shimmer. Could he feel it? Yes he could feel it; his fingertips were moving lightly against her spine, as if to encourage it.

'Please let me go now,' she said a little desperately.

'When you look at me.'

'No.' She didn't want to look at him so she turned her face and looked at the kitchen, with its old-fashioned familiarity, and wondered why he didn't look utterly out of place in here.

'Why not?' he challenged, and his voice was like a quiet rumble, vibrating all around her, husky, sexy.

Don't give in to it, she told herself, then tipped her head back, made contact with eyes like the darkest brown velvet set between ebony lashes. They drew her in as she'd known they would. They sent messages she'd already read via a body language that was threatening to pull her apart inside.

'I didn't betray you with Jamie,' she whispered.

On a growl of anger he swooped with his mouth and captured her throbbing declaration, captured and returned it to her with the furious flick of his tongue. He didn't believe her. He didn't *want* to believe her. Because to believe meant he would have to place himself so much in the wrong that his ego wouldn't cope with what that would brand him.

Bitterness welled again, scouring out the desire that had held her in his arms so long. She broke away from the kiss, moved away from his body, and turned away from the whole tempting package being sold to her.

A man with no mercy. Sex without respect. It hurt. She was never going to repeat that denial, she promised herself grimly as she began picking up plates from the table.

'Which bedroom did you choose? I need to go and make up the bed.'

There was a silence behind her; it trickled down her spinal cord like the scrape of a fingernail warning her that danger lurked behind.

It took the form of silk-like satire. 'Our son assures me that all his friends' parents sleep in the same bed.'

She spun back to find him leaning casually against the sink with his hands resting in his pockets. He was enjoying this, she realised. 'You're joking!' she insisted.

A single eyebrow mocked her horrified look. 'I was very impressed with his forward thinking,' Rafiq answered lightly. 'He gave me a choice. His room or your room. And since his room has only one small single bed in it and yours has a very large divan, I took the advice I was being offered and agreed to share—as parents do.'

'Well, I *don't* share!' She itched to swipe that mocking smile from his face. '*Never.* Do you understand?'

'Not even when we are man and wife?'

'I've changed my mind; I don't want to marry you!' she said. 'We—we will have to come to some other arrangement about sharing Robbie.'

'Now, that is one area in which *I* don't share,' he warned.

'And I won't marry a man who feels as bitter about me as I feel about him!'

'Then we are both on a learning curve.'

'Don't talk business-speak to me!' she snapped out angrily.

He leapt on her like a cat, picked her up and sat her down on the kitchen table, braced his hands beside her legs then pushed his dark face up close. 'Would you rather I woo you into accepting me?' he purred.

She stiffened like a cardboard cut-out; if he'd said it to insult her then he had certainly achieved his aim. 'I've been wooed by you before and I would rather have a snake do it.'

'Remove that ring one more time and you will regret it,' he warned very, very succinctly.

Melanie looked down and was surprised to find her fingers trying to work the ring loose. The threatened tears came back. 'I don't want you here,' she choked.

He saw the tears, touched a finger to the corner of her eye to capture one. 'Too late,' he announced, then stepped back.

He had heard what she had been too busy to hear—their son coming towards the kitchen. She leapt from the table just as Robbie appeared to take Rafiq off to watch his video. Melanie forced herself to tidy the kitchen, then went upstairs to make up the bed in the spare bedroom. It was a cold, dark little room with a cold little bed, and she had to grit her teeth as she made it so she would not let her conscience accept that a man of Rafiq's size would never be able to sleep in it—or at least he'd freeze trying, she added as she snubbed her nose at the room and walked out.

Robbie kept the atmosphere buoyant right up until she eventually coaxed him into bed. He fell asleep blissful in the knowledge that when he awoke his daddy would still be there.

By the time Melanie trudged back down the stairs she had developed a throbbing headache and was intending to go straight to the kitchen to find some painkillers when she caught sight of Rafiq through the half-open door that led into the living room. He was standing by the fire with a hand thrust into his trouser pocket while the other held a mobile phone to his ear. He was speaking in fluent French. For a few seconds he even looked French, a smooth, sleek and dauntingly sophisticated Frenchman with the language for lovers falling from his lips.

It was not the cleverest of thoughts to have, she realised as her senses rose to the invitation to remember the lover once again. She made herself move on to the kitchen before he caught sight of her standing there looking at him like some sex-obsessed idiot. It had been that kind of day! A day packed full of old obsessions and new raging impulses. Sexual impulses; angry impulses. Her impulse to go and seek him out; his impulse to lay siege and seduce. The shocks, the grip of an old obsessive desire, the excitement in knowing they were both running out of control.

The headache got worse. She took two painkillers and set about preparing a pot of coffee. He was standing in more or less the same place when she carried the coffee tray into the room. He was still on the telephone, speaking in Spanish now, a language she recognised easily because Sophia was half-Spanish and could tumble into the language when she was angry enough to need its extra fire.

He turned his dark head as he heard the tray rattle. Their gazes clashed, and Melanie broke hers away. Five seconds later the mobile was back in his pocket.

'Coffee?' she offered politely.

'Thank you, yes,' he replied. 'Black, no sugar.'

Black with no sugar, she repeated. Like the man himself: dark and unsweetened. She poured the coffee, then handed him his cup. He accepted it with a murmured, 'Thank you.'

She looked pale and tired, Rafiq noticed, and had to smother the urge to sigh as he turned to look at the fire, taking with him the image of Melanie sitting there on faded velvet looking down at her coffee mug curled inside fingers that looked bloodless and cold. Hell, he thought in frustration, to him this whole house was cold. Even with the fire burning in the grate, the ancient central heating system only managed to take the edge of a subfreezing temperature! Despite his millions, and the loving attention he had poured into Rafiq's son, William Portreath had not poured much love into his home. It was virtually falling down around them. Everything in it came from a bygone century.

'Your requirements do not make any provision for the renovations this house clearly requires.'

Eyes like dark amber blinked at him. 'What are you talking about?'

'The papers you left with me,' he explained. 'They talk a lot about investments and trust funds but nothing about your annual expenditure or how much it is going to cost to bring this house into the twenty-first century.'

'I don't want to bring it into the twenty-first century. I like the house just as it is.'

She did? Was she lying just to go against him? 'It is cold in here, Melanie,' he said, stating the obvious. 'The walls are so cold that the wallpaper is peeling.' Not that its demise was much of a loss, he added with silent disdain. 'I, for one, see no reason why we should live like this.'

She bristled. 'Nobody is asking you to!'

He ignored that. 'I will employ someone to draw up some plans for renovation,' he announced.

Tired golden eyes began to sparkle. The mug was replaced on the tray. 'William has been gone only two months and you come in here wanting to obliterate thirty years of his life?' She rose stiffly. 'You will touch nothing,' she told him. 'It isn't yours to touch. And if you don't find that acceptable then you know what you can do!'

She was hurt; he could see it. Rafiq wanted to kick himself. Ridding himself of his cup, he offered her a deep bow. 'I have offended you,' he acknowledged. 'I apologise. It was not my intention to—'

'Y-you think I can't compare this—*home* to that super-expensive luxuriously blank space you like to live in?' she said, interrupting his apology. 'That I haven't noticed the way you've been looking on everything here with disdain? Does it offend your ego to know that your son loves this house?'

'No.' He denied that. 'I just think that it needs—'

'Well, forget it,' she said, cutting right across him a second time, and turned her stiff back towards him and walked to the door. 'You can use the room at the end of the landing. Be sure to make the fire safe before you go up. Now, goodnight.'

She'd left the room before he could speak another syllable, leaving him standing there feeling as if he'd just struck a woman for the first time in his life.

'Damn,' he muttered, and took the first step to go after her. Then on a heavy sigh changed his mind. She'd had enough for one day. He had had enough! 'Damn,' he cursed again, and turned back to the fire. It was dying fast, like the whole blasted day.

A car drew up outside the house. He listened to the sound of its door slamming shut. Another sigh and he was striding for the front door before Kadir could ring the doorbell and awaken Robert. I learn very quickly, he mused grimly as he reached out to take the suitcase from his aide.

'Thank you,' he grunted. 'I do not need to tell you that this situation is no one else's business.'

'No, sir. Of course, sir.'

He nodded, said goodnight and closed the door.

Upstairs Melanie listened to the car from the comfort of her duvet. She'd curled up beneath it after taking a shower in her *en-suite*, very ancient bathroom. Her teeth still chattered from the chills she'd given herself drying her body. She'd pulled on a knitted-cotton nightdress and was now only waiting for the duvet to infuse some warmth into her body.

Okay, she reasoned, so she knew the house needed a complete face-lift. She'd been wanting to do it for years, but William hadn't liked change. He'd been an old man who'd had a right to feel like that. And he did not deserve that some complete stranger should walk in here and start tearing his life down!

How dared he? Her throat caught on a muffled sob. How dared Rafiq believe he could just take over everything—even her bed if she let him get away with it!

The front door closed; she felt it reverberate through the floor beneath her bed. She'd heard Rafiq telling Robbie that someone was going to bring his suitcase here. Well, she hoped he'd changed his mind and had left with the delivery person! And on that final, wholly satisfying thought she closed her eyes and willed her icy feet to get warm so that she could just go to sleep. She had almost—almost—achieved both impossible feats when a curse in the darkness brought her swimmingly awake.

Suddenly the duvet was being lifted, to let the cold night air come into her warm cocoon. A short second later a body followed—a very cold, very naked body with an arm that clamped her to him and powerful limbs that curled snugly into hers.

'Oh, my God,' she gasped on a shocked little shiver. 'What do you think you are doing?'

'Getting warm,' Rafiq informed her grimly. Furious, she wriggled to get free. 'Stay still,' he gritted, close to her ear lobe.

He had to be joking! 'You could have had the decency to put some clothes on!'

'If my nakedness offends you then consider it punishment for that bed you prepared for me.'

He'd actually tried it? In a mulish kind of way Melanie was rather pleased that he had at least attempted to do the honourable thing. 'I don't want you here,' she protested nonetheless.

'The choice does not belong to you. Our son expects me to be in this bed when he wakes in the morning, and the other bed was an insult.' A hand on her shoulder turned her to face him; dark eyes glittered down into hers. 'You are a ruthless woman, Melanie Portreath,' he told her. 'Now it is my turn to be ruthless.'

And he was, in the way he wrapped himself around her, punishing her by stealing all her warmth, then punishing her again by falling fast asleep.

CHAPTER EIGHT

IT WAS a horrible weekend. There was not one single part of it that Melanie would have wanted to live through again. Daylight became an agony of hours watching her son sink himself into total hero-worship, and the nights an agony of too much intimacy with a man who clearly did not want more than to share her bed.

In his new role of father Rafiq dedicated himself to learning everything he could about his son. They talked, and they commandeered William's study, where Robbie hit Rafiq with a million questions, all of which his father answered with a considered seriousness that made Melanie's heart ache. Rafiq could do no wrong. She tried not to resent the way Robbie was turning to his father for everything. She tried to tell herself that this was what she had wanted, what she had hoped and aimed for when she had brought Rafiq into Robbie's life.

But it hurt to witness their growing closeness while she was required to contribute very little other than the odd smile or nod, or food when necessary. By the end of each day she was so exhausted playing the smiling little woman in the background that the moment Robbie was safely in bed she took herself off to bed too, leaving Rafiq to do what men like him did—use his evenings to work from the laptop computer that had arrived with his suitcase—before he came to slide into her bed, draw her in, sigh, then fall asleep.

She didn't understand him—didn't think she wanted to understand a man who could ravish her with a blind compulsion one minute then spend whole nights lying beside her and not offer one measly pass!

Their son loved the whole family scenario. In fact it made Robbie's day to run into their bedroom each morning and find both his parents wrapped snugly around each other. He couldn't be happier if he tried.

But for Melanie resentment sizzled across her senses; frustration throbbed in her loins. Had she sunk so low that she could become hooked on passion after a couple of quick sips?

Monday morning could not come quickly enough. She waved Rafiq off to work in his sharp dark business suit, and only did that because her son's hand was firmly attached to his father's. Rafiq was delivering Robbie to school, along with other children, as part of the morning school run!

I've been made redundant, she thought peevishly as she closed the front door. Daddy is the new rising star in the street and I am the fading one.

The jaded one, she corrected as her shoulders sagged wearily through lack of sleep and a whole truckload of tension. Standing there in the sudden quietness of the hallway, she actually took a moment to consider going upstairs and just crawling back beneath the duvet to sleep the rest of the day away while there was no Rafiq to spoil it for her.

But his presence was there in the bedroom, she remembered. His clothes hung with her clothes in the wardrobe; the scent of his soap permeated the adjoining bathroom.

You wanted this, she tried telling herself. You instigated the whole darn thing and, if anything, you should be pleased by how successful Robbie's introduction to his father has turned out, not standing here wilting like a wet leaf.

The light tap on the back door was a welcome diversion. Straightening her shoulders she walked into the kitchen just in time to watch Sophia step into the house.

'Hi,' Sophia murmured, and her expression could not have looked more sombre if she'd tried. In her hand she held a newspaper, which she set down on the kitchen table. 'Take a deep breath, Melanie,' she suggested, 'because you are not going to like this…'

Rafiq was sitting in his chair behind his desk in his beautifully warm centrally heated office wishing he dared close his eyes and fall asleep because for these last miserable nights he'd lain awake in that bed with Melanie and had ached.

Ached. There was no better word for it. Was he a fool? Was he going insane, playing it this coolly? Yes, he was a fool, he accepted, because all it would have taken would have been one touch and she would have been his for the taking.

But he was out to prove a point. Melanie had hit him hard with some of the things she had thrown at him. She had made him out to be selfish and fickle. She had implied he did not have it in him to stay the course. She believed he would get weary of being a father and walk away when the novelty wore off him.

She'd also told him he thought her cheap by tumbling her into bed with him at the first opportunity. Which he had done; he freely admitted it. But not for one moment had he considered her cheap! Indeed, it had cost him a very great deal because he had been so bowled over by the strength of their feelings that he wanted to do it all again and again—and again.

She had claimed he had made love to her eight years ago then had despised her afterwards. Now she was waiting for him to despise her again. So sex was out of the question until he had placed a wedding ring on her finger. If that did not show her he meant serious business, then nothing would.

So, he thought with grim impatience. He had arranged a civil wedding service. From that day on he meant to have everything: a wife, his son, and some serious passion—

preferably in a bedroom that did not send him into a paroxysm of shivers every time he stripped off his clothes.

And he had just the right place for this serious seduction. He knew the day on which it was going to happen. Now all he had to do was ring home and speak to half-brother, Hassan.

'Where have you been hiding?' his brother demanded, the moment the connection was made. 'I have been trying to contact you all weekend.'

'It cannot have been urgent or Kadir would have found me.'

'What intrigues me is why he refused to divulge to me where you were.'

'I was busy,' he said, and could almost see Hassan's grimace at his don't-go-there-tone. 'How is Father?'

He asked the usual question and he received back the reassuring answer he was looking for. 'He is well and content.'

'And Leona?'

'The same—what is this, Rafiq?' Hassan put in curiously. 'You sound—different.'

Different? He grimaced. Different did not come close to describing the changes in his life. 'Do you think it would be safe to leave them for a couple of days?'

'Yes, if I have to.' But Hassan sounded puzzled. 'Is there something wrong at the bank?'

'No, this is a—personal matter,' Rafiq answered coolly. 'I need you to do me a great favour. If you could be in London on Friday I would much appreciate it.'

'Rafiq needs a favour?' Leona repeated as she lay on the bed, letting her husband smooth oil into her swollen abdomen. 'Well, that has to be a first.'

'Not quite,' Hassan murmured. 'But it is certainly unusual for him to ask anyone for anything.'

Leona was frowning thoughtfully. 'Do you think this

business with Serena Cordero has upset him more than we thought it would?'

'Could be.' Hassan paused in his ministrations to kiss her frown away, then went back to his duties, long fingers smoothing oil over creamy white skin stretched taut across the mound that was their growing child. 'He has been acting strangely since the announcement of her marriage.' It was his turn to frown. 'I am reliably informed that he has hardly been to the bank since the newspaper article appeared and is almost impossible to track down. Nadia gets shifty if I ask questions, and so does Kadir. So I will have to go to London if only to quench my curiosity as to what it is he's up to.'

'Of course,' Leona agreed. 'But I hope you're just a bit worried about him, too.'

'Of course,' he mimicked. 'Do you want to roll over so I can rub this into your back now?'

'No, thank you.' She declined the offer. 'I am perfectly happy with what you are doing right now.'

'Witch.' He laughed, and came to lean over her, eyes like brown velvet gently mocking hers of saucy green. Late afternoon sunlight was pouring in through the grilled window, turning everything in the bedroom a burnished gold. Leona's hair shone like fire on the pillow; her porcelain skin wore a lustrous glow. She was exquisite in every way possible. 'Why did no one warn me that pregnant women were such rampant sex machines?' he murmured throatily.

'It is nature's secret weapon, aimed to keep husbands from straying to more slender delights.' She smiled.

A black eyebrow arched. 'Was that a deliberate dig at my father?'

'Like father, like son,' Leona quoted.

'Yes.' His frown returned. 'You don't think Rafiq could be planning revenge on Serena, do you?'

'I don't get the link.'

'There isn't one.' Lowering his eyes, he began gently stroking a point on her stomach where he could feel his child's heart beating steadily. Leona reached out and gently touched a fingertip to the point where his brows met across the bridge of his arrogant nose.

He glanced up, smiled, then sighed and lay back against the pillows. 'Rafiq was hit hard by a woman once before—about eight years ago,' he confided. 'She was a beautiful blonde creature with golden eyes and a mouth designed to turn a saint into a sinner. I must add that Rafiq has never been a saint. But he fell head over heels in love with this woman, then found out she was taking him for a fool.'

'Name?' Leona asked curiously.

'I cannot remember. She was as English as you are, though, and young—quite shockingly young for one filled with such calculation. She was a farmer's daughter, as I recall, and saw Rafiq as her ticket out of drudgery. He asked her to marry him then discovered she was sleeping with her step-cousin. Rafiq severed the relationship and that should have been the end of it.'

'But it wasn't?'

'No.' Hassan shook his head. 'She tried to contact him again many months later. It was the only other time that I can recall him asking me to do him a favour. She rang the London bank while I was there and Rafiq was here in Rahman, playing the nomad while still licking his wounds. She wanted to see him. When I relayed the message he asked me to meet with her to see if she was okay.'

'He still cared?'

'He was besotted.' His brother sighed out heavily. 'I have never seen him like that with a woman before or since.'

'So what did you do?'

'I had her checked out before I did anything. Discovered she was living with a man old enough to be her grandfather and, more to the point, was as heavily pregnant as you are now, my sweet.' He caught hold of her hand and kissed it. 'I arranged a meeting; she arrived expecting to see Rafiq. She tried convincing me that Rafiq was the father of her baby. So I told her what I thought Rafiq would do if she managed to convince him that this was true. She did not pursue the claim,' he concluded with grim satisfaction. 'A very nasty paternity battle through the courts was too much for her to take, apparently. She slunk off into the ether and was never heard from again.'

'But what if the child had been Rafiq's?'

'It was not,' he stated with absolute certainty. 'You know his background. If there had been the slightest possibility that he had made the woman pregnant he would have followed the prospect until he could be certain either way.'

'What did he say when you told him she was pregnant?'

'I didn't tell him,' he replied. 'I said I couldn't find her but that I'd heard she was living with some man. He never mentioned her name again.'

'Sometimes I really don't like you,' Leona informed him. 'You have a ruthless streak so wide it makes me shiver.'

'She was a woman on the make, Leona,' he said deridingly. 'People in our position meet them all the time. They see dollar signs up above our heads and latch on like limpets.'

'But still….'

'Rafiq caught her red-handed with her other lover.'

End of story. 'What a manipulating bitch,' Leona murmured, taking it personally that some woman would dare to use her beloved bother-in-law in such a way.

Rafiq had only just put the phone down when Kadir knocked at his door, then quietly let himself into the room. He was wearing the look of a man who was walking towards the gallows. Rafiq straightened in readiness, but nothing prepared him for what he was about to be hit with.

'My apologies, sir, but I think you should see this…' Carefully Kadir placed a newspaper onto the desk in front of Rafiq. With his usual efficiency his aide had folded the

English tabloid so that Rafiq needed only to glance down and see what it was Kadir was showing him.

There was Serena, smiling up at Carlos Montez. It was the same damn article, now reproduced in spiced-up English. Rafiq couldn't believe it. He shot to his feet. 'What the hell?' he muttered.

'Apparently Miss Cordero arrived in London this weekend, sir,' Kadir quietly explained. 'Her show opens at a West End theatre on Wednesday. The—er—article is by way of a promotion for this event. I thought…'

He was talking to fresh air because Rafiq was already striding across the room with the rolled-up newspaper clenched in his hand.

'H-How did you get hold of this?' Melanie asked Sophia.

'My grandmother likes to send me the Spanish newspapers to make sure I keep in touch with my roots,' Sophia explained.

Melanie nodded unhappily. 'And it says?' she prompted.

'You don't really want me to read it out to you again, Melanie,' Sophia murmured gravely. 'The point is that this paper is dated last Tuesday—which is the same day you went to see Rafiq…'

'Meaning what?' Her lips felt too cold and numb to move properly; her whole face felt very much the same.

'Meaning the guy was publicly dumped on the day you walked into his office. He was already out for someone's blood before he even saw you. Therefore I think you have to ask yourself the question whether his actions since have been motivated by this.'

'Saving face?'

'Yes.' Sophia sighed. 'To suddenly pull a wife and son out of the hat will turn the tables on Miss Cordero. It will appear as if she is the one who married on the rebound while he walked away from their relationship of over a year unscathed.'

Over a year… Melanie lowered her gaze to the two photographs printed side by side on the page. One was of the beautiful Serena Cordero standing with her handsome new husband. The other was of Rafiq standing with Serena. Her heart crashed against her ribcage, turning her insides to jelly, because the photograph was just as Robbie had described it: Rafiq wearing Arab clothes while the lady wore a red frilly dress. William had shown this photograph to her son but hadn't shown it to her. Everyone but her—including her son—seemed to know about Rafiq's beautiful long-standing Spanish mistress!

Did Rafiq love this woman? Was the luscious dark beauty what he really wanted, and now that he couldn't have her was he prepared to take anyone?

No, not just anyone, she grimly amended, but a woman who happened to come packaged with his son.

She thought about the phone call he had taken in his office when he hadn't spoken a single word. She thought about the look in his eyes as he'd listened to whoever had been on the other end of that phone, followed by the kiss before he'd coldly thrown her out.

Then she thought about the way he had found out about Robbie and had been forced to rethink his stance. Days later had come his sudden explosion of hot passion followed by nothing since.

Nothing.

She swallowed down a lump of nausea. Clearly he had tried to burn Miss Cordero out of his system and failed. She had been nothing but a substitute, and a disappointing one at that. I must have been, she thought painfully—because look at her! Black hair, black eyes and a lush-red passionate mouth looked back at her. Miss Cordero possessed the kind of sumptuous hourglass figure that most women would kill to own.

Which makes me the consolation prize.

She caught the sound of a key in the front door then. Only one person beside herself had a key to this house. Her insides became a mess of misery as she listened to

Rafiq call out her name. Sophia straightened in her chair, her eyes growing wide and dark and curious. Footsteps sounded on the polished wood floor as he strode towards the kitchen, then arrived to fill its doorway. Melanie tried focusing on his face, but all she saw was the shadowy outline of his whole dark bulk. Weakness feathered its way through the misery, because he did not fill the doorway with just his size, but with—everything. The darkness of his hair, his skin and his clothes said so much about him, and the stillness of every perfectly formed feature warned of the inner strength that so matched the outer shell.

His gaze flicked from her face to Sophia's face, then remained there. Melanie glanced at Sophia too, and was suddenly struck very hard by her friend's likeness to Serena Cordero. Another wave of nausea lodged in her throat, because he couldn't seem to take his eyes off her.

Rafiq had not expected to find Melanie with a visitor. For a moment he was struck numb by the thought that it was Serena herself, come to cause yet more trouble. Then the likeness faded and he glanced back at Melanie to find that she was looking down at the table. He saw the newspaper, felt his fingers clench around his own, and knew what Melanie was going to say before she even spoke.

'You have a mistress.'

'I *had* a mistress,' he corrected, coming further into the room as Sophia rose from her seat.

'I think I'll leave you both to it,' she murmured, and went to pick up the newspaper.

It was a gesture that did not pass by Rafiq. 'If the newspaper is yours, then I must assume you enjoy playing devil's advocate,' he drawled icily.

Sophia being Sophia, she took up the challenge in his tone. 'I don't like whatever it is you are trying to do here,' she informed him coolly.

Sparks began to fly. 'You believe I care one way or another what you like or dislike?'

The dark beauty's chin lifted, sending ripples of raven

hair flying over her shoulders. 'I don't think you care about anyone's feelings so long as you get your own way.'

'Well, I did not get my own way here,' he said, stabbing a long finger at the damning newspaper article.

It was then that he realised what it was he was stabbing at, and began to frown in confusion. While he was doing that Melanie got up and on a soft choke, rushed from the room. The urge to stop her was halted by his curiosity about this other woman.

His eyes narrowed. 'How did you get hold of this?' he demanded.

She shrugged. 'I am Spanish on my mother's side,' she explained. 'My grandmother sends me her newspapers once a week.'

'Industrious lady.'

'Very.'

'You have a point in hurting Melanie with this?'

'You are the one playing hurtful games with her feelings,' Sophia responded. 'I didn't like it from the beginning.' She let her glance fall to the newspaper. 'This tells me why I don't like it.'

And I do not like you, Rafiq thought as he looked into her face and saw a different face once again. She was so like Serena it could be the dancer standing there.

'You are on a face-saving exercise,' she dared to accuse him.

'What is your name?' he demanded.

'Sophia Elliot,' she announced, making his gaze narrow even further, because he had heard that name before. 'I am the next-door-neighbour from hell, Mr Al-Qadim,' she informed him, with a cool humour that confirmed the impression he had gained from his son that this woman was as tough as she was beautiful. 'I am also a pretty good lawyer,' she added. 'So if you are thinking of trying to bully Melanie into accepting a situation she doesn't really want, then try thinking again,' she advised. 'Because it is my belief you don't give a fig for her feelings, and Melanie and Robbie have taken enough over this last year without you using them as a method of deflecting your little embarrassment with the—'

'Name of the law firm you work for?' he cut in coolly.

She told him.

With a curt nod he stepped up to open the back door. 'You come and go via this route, I believe?'

'How did you know that?'

Because his son had been as admiringly vocal about his aunt Sophia as he was about William Portreath. 'Trouble rarely enters by conventional means, Miss Elliot,' he replied, knowing that she would work out his source later. But for now she was simply too busy bristling.

'I don't think you have the right to—'

'May I suggest that you mention my name to your employer before you begin informing me of my rights?' Rafiq drawled coolly.

'Is that a threat?' she demanded.

Rafiq's answer was a polite bow of his head meant to leave the question open to interpretation. 'Good day to you, Miss Elliot,' was all he said.

But the woman had sense, Rafiq allowed, as he watched her self-confidence begin to waver. She wasn't sure about him and therefore took the wiser route: lifting her chin and stepping through the door.

He closed it behind her, took a moment to grit his teeth. Then he was moving across the kitchen on his way to find Melanie. He located her in the bedroom, where she stood in the window gazing out on yet another cold grey frost-grained day. The room was no warmer, the woman in it was as cold as ice. Anger roared. A bloody anger aimed at Serena, at the press, Miss Elliot and anyone else who thought they could meddle in his life!

'Your cynical friend stole my thunder,' he announced very grimly.

'Don't try telling me you came back here to confess your sins.'

'It is not a sin for a single man to maintain a mistress,' he countered. 'And I was referring to...this.'

'This' arrived on the tallboy beside her left shoulder. Melanie turned to see what it was he was talking about. It might have been Sophia's Spanish newspaper, only the glaring headline shouted at her in English and the date printed on it was today's. It was one of the more down-market British tabloids.

'Now you may read the whole article for yourself,' Rafiq said cynically. 'It has been spiced up since the original Spanish version was written. But—please...' he flicked a long hand in invitation '...enjoy—if you are into this kind of trash.'

'I never read newspapers.'

He had noticed their lack of evidence about the house. 'Well, read this one,' he advised, shot back a shirt-cuff, then strode towards the door.

'Where are you going?'

'I have things to do.'

'Aren't you even going to explain about this?'

'What is there to explain?' he countered. 'Serena Cordero and I were lovers until recently. But that, and the fact that she decided to use this very public source to announce the end of that relationship, has nothing to do with you, quite frankly.'

'It does when that announcement also came on the same day that I went to see you.'

'You see this coincidence as significant?'

She folded her arms across her body again. 'You changed,' she told him. 'After you took a call on your mobile. It was her on the phone, wasn't it? That call gave you the idea of using me to save your face.'

'It crossed my mind,' he admitted. 'But if you recall, Melanie, I still threw you out.' She flinched at the reminder. He nodded in acceptance of what that flinch represented. 'And if you believe that anything I have done since then has been due to a need to *save my face*, then there is really nothing left for me to say here.' With that he turned back to the door.

'Then why did you bother to come back here now?'

'Courtesy,' he said icily. 'I believed I owed you the courtesy of an explanation for why this article appeared in the newspaper today. But since you and your—friend have already dissected the week-old version, I see I wasted my time.'

'Wasted nearly a whole week of your time,' she murmured bitterly.

He paused. 'What is that supposed to imply?'

'I am not going to marry you.'

'Why not?'

She lowered her eyes. 'You're in love with her. She's what you really want.'

He laughed; it was harsh. 'If I'd wanted to marry Serena I could have done so at any time over the last year,' he announced. 'But what interests me here is that you seem to be thinking that loving someone is a prerequisite for marriage.'

'I don't think that.' She stiffened. 'I just don't want to marry a man who is pining for someone else.'

'Pining?' he repeated.

'It's obvious.' She shrugged, then made the big mistake of glancing at the bed.

His dark gaze followed suit. One of those awful tense silences they were so good at developing began to sing in the room. Hot colour flooded her complexion; she spun back to the window, wishing the man wasn't so good at reading her like an open book!

Did she have to be so obvious? she railed at herself. Did it always—always—have to be this man who made her feel like a lovesick fool?

Sex-sick, she then corrected. God, she hated herself sometimes. 'Go, if you're going,' she snapped. Make it quick and don't come back!

'I have changed my mind.'

'Not on my account.' She tried to recover lost ground.

But she should have known by now that this man gave nothing back once he had gained it. She heard a rustle, felt a shot of alarm shoot down her backbone, spun, then just stood there staring in open dismay as the jacket to his suit hit the floor.

'Come any closer and I'll start screaming,' she warned, backing herself into the window as he began walking towards her with fingers smoothly loosening his tie.

'Scream,' he invited. 'Who will come? Your cynical friend from next door?' Reaching over her shoulder, he tugged the cord that closed the heavy curtains. The room was suddenly shrouded in darkness. A dangerous glitter burned in his eyes. 'Think of the embarrassment, Melanie, if Miss Elliot was foolish enough to come running in here only to find you begging in my arms.'

'I will never beg!' She gave an angry push at his body.

He laughed, low and deep and tauntingly. 'One kiss and you will not be able to stop yourself,' he derided. 'Do you think I have not been aware that you have hardly slept a wink in that bed because you want me so badly?'

'That's a lie.'

He kissed her. It was no lie. She dived, she fell, she almost—almost begged him. Her breathing went haywire, her senses caught alight, and she whimpered into his urgent mouth. His arms imprisoned her, but they didn't need to. She was clinging tightly.

'I hate you for doing this.'

'But, as you see, I am not pining for a lost love,' he murmured, and to punctuate his meaning he caught hold of one of her hands and placed it down his front, then caught her protesting little gasp in his mouth.

Desire pulsed with every hammering heartbeat; it bounced off the walls and back at her in wave after wave of blistering passion, battering her every sense into submission. They kissed; they lost their clothes with an urgent lack of finesse. Somehow they managed to make it to the bed; his hand grabbed the duvet and stripped it back from the mattress before he tumbled her down on it. They kissed some more; they rolled; he stretched her out and ravished her breasts, then placed a line of hot wet kisses down her front; he buried his mouth between her thighs. She almost leapt into the air in shock, then went wild, utterly wanton. Bright hot lights were propelling themselves at her eyelids; she couldn't keep still and his hands had to clamp her hips so he could sustain the torment until she lost herself completely, lost him, lost everything.

When she opened heavy eyelids she found black eyes glittering down at her, his face a smouldering cast of raw sensuality made all the more potent by triumph. 'You shouldn't have done that,' she whispered.

'Why not?' The hand he used to push the damp hair away from her face was trembling.

'Because...' she breathed. He hadn't leapt with her, and she wanted him to leap with her. It was essential that he lose touch with himself as she had, or what had he proved here except that he was the expert and she was just somebody, nobody—anybody?

So she pushed him onto his back and came to lean over him, calling upon instincts she had never used before to take him where she had just been. He lay in the darkness and let her do whatever she wanted. She kissed his shoulders, his chest, sucked deeply on the hard points of his male nipples, stroked her hands down his body when he groaned hoarsely, took her mouth on a journey that stopped at nothing. His fingers coiled into her hair and his laboured breathing drove her on. When he shifted to grasp her beneath her arms then drag her upwards for a kiss that devoured she was ready for him to finish what she had started with the deep, urgent thrust of his pelvis.

They shuddered together into a drumming ecstasy; he seduced her mouth until the very last whisper of pleasure had faded, and eventually she lay heavily upon him, limp and useless. She couldn't even draw enough energy to care that once again she had given him more of herself than she had ever wanted to.

She belonged here. It was that simple—and that sad.

'We marry as soon as possible,' he announced suddenly. Then, before she could raise so much as a gasp in protest, he switched their position and began the whole wild adventure all over again.

CHAPTER NINE

MELANIE sat in a chair beside Sophia and carefully rotated her aching shoulders. 'Can't I just wear that one?' she said hopefully.

'If you want to look like a fairy on a Christmas tree, of course you can wear that dress,' Sophia replied.

'Don't be cruel.'

'Do you want to knock his eyes out?'

'No—yes.' Melanie sighed and fiddled with a drink-starved wilting rosebud. 'I wish he wasn't so determined to make all of this fuss about a silly civil wedding.'

'I still can't understand why you are going through with it,' Sophia said with a disapproving snap.

'You've seen him with Robbie, Sophia,' Melanie reminded her. In an effort to get Sophia and Rafiq to stop sniping at her about each other she had invited Sophia round for drinks. Rafiq had been about to take Robbie to bed when she'd arrived. She had caught him holding his son in his arms, accepting the kind of love-shining hugs Melanie had witnessed many times. 'They adore each other. I couldn't stop this now even if I wanted to,' she concluded heavily.

'Do you want to?'

She hesitated a bit too long without answering.

'So you're the sacrificial lamb.' Sophia sighed.

Oh, yes, Melanie thought. I sacrifice myself every night in his arms.

Getting up, she walked back to the rail filled with frothy white dresses and began flicking restless fingers along the selection. Why did she let him get away with it? she was asking herself crossly. Had she no pride left at all?

She knew the trigger that set him off each time. It was called Serena Cordero. Plant the beautiful Spaniard's name into his head and he responded by diving into sex like a man in search of blind escape!

But you dive right in there with him, she admitted. In fact you only have to start thinking about diving in and you break out in a hot sweat.

'I'll try this one,' she said, choosing a gown at random which she passed to the hovering assistant who carried it off to the dressing room.

Sophia waited until the woman had gone out of earshot before she said tentatively, 'Melanie…have you thought about when you're married to him and things become… intimate?'

'Are you joking?' she gasped.

But, no, Sophia wasn't joking, she realised. She was actually looking like a rather anxious mother hen trying to prepare her innocent chick for what the big bad rooster did.

'I'm sorry to disillusion you about me, Sophia,' she responded. 'But what do you think we have been doing in my home all this time?'

For the first time ever she saw shock then embarrassment flood her tough friend's face. 'You mean you—'

The words dried up. Melanie laughed; it sounded strangled. She spun back to face the rail. The silence between them sizzled with the kind of images that just did not belong in this pretty shop adorned with chaste and virginal white.

'But I thought—'

'Well, don't think,' Melanie cut in on a tight little mutter. Her cheeks were hot. Sophia's cheeks were hot. What was it about people that they believed they could make assumptions about her? Rafiq believed she was a sex-hungry wanton; Sophia believed she was about as naive and dumb as a woman with a seven-year-old child could possibly be!

Maybe this was a good time for the assistant to reappear, because she helped to carry them over a very uncomfortable moment. Melanie scowled at the dresses on display and wondered what Rafiq would do if she turned up to their wedding in her best black suit?

A beautifully manicured hand appeared to one side of her. 'You are your own worst enemy, aren't you?' Sophia murmured sombrely. 'Here,' she said, 'try this…'

Sophia had pulled a misty-blue silk suit out from amongst the swathes of white. Her whole attitude altered from that moment on. She's given up on me, Melanie realised as she wriggled into the fitted blue suit. I've put myself beyond redemption.

But then I placed myself beyond that when I let him make love to me knowing he was using me to block out another woman, she acknowledged helplessly.

She bought the misty-blue suit. It looked right somehow—made her legs seem longer and her hair more golden, made her eyes glow a deeper shade.

'What do you think?'

Rafiq was standing in the hallway of Melanie's house while Ethan Hayes was still looking about him with an interested eye. 'You must already know that it has tremendous potential,' Ethan told him. 'But I don't know how you expect to modernise the whole house while still maintaining every worn-out feature.'

'There is an old man's life etched into those features,' Rafiq explained. 'Can we not give the shell an uplift, then simply put everything else back the way it is now?'

'I am an architect, not a miracle-worker,' Ethan said dryly 'The heating is useless, the fires belch smoke, the floorboards creak worryingly and the walls seem to be warning anyone that dares go near them not to remove a single picture unless you want them to fall down. All of that can be put right,' he stated. 'But the wallpaper will have to be hand-reproduced, the furniture will need to be sent away for some careful renovation, and nothing we replace will have the patina of age it wears now. I have a worrying suspicion that the deeper we look, we will find wet rot and dry rot, not to mention woodworm. You need Leona on this, not me, Rafiq,' he concluded.

'Leona is busy with other things,' Rafiq reminded him. 'I just wanted your opinion before I decided whether to go ahead.'

'It would be simpler to gut it and start from scratch,' Ethan advised. 'You only have to look at the other houses on this street to see what it can look like, given the chance.'

'I have no wish to make it look like the others.' This was his son's home, the place where Robert and Melanie had found love and security. Aesthetically it must not change. Structurally, he feared it had no choice.

'If Leona is out of action, then what if I hand the project over to my wife?' Ethan suddenly suggested.

'To your *wife*?' Rafiq couldn't hide his surprise.

Ethan turned a rueful grin on him. 'Yes, I do mean the flighty piece who spent the evening flirting with you a couple of months ago,' he confirmed lazily. 'She has hidden talents,' he confided. 'One of those talents being a very impressive track record in house renovation.'

Rafiq was momentarily diverted. In the space of just a few short weeks, earlier this year, Ethan Hayes had gone from being a serious enemy of the Al-Qadim family to being a good close friend due to falling into love with Eve, the provocative granddaughter of the Greek tycoon Theron Herakleides.

'The lovely Eve renovates old property for a living?' Rafiq could not withhold his disbelief.

'She shocked me with it too,' Ethan confessed. 'On the morning after we returned from our honeymoon, in fact, when she came to breakfast wearing overalls and put a builder's hat down on the table. She's been buying, renovating and selling on houses in London for years—as a hobby, apparently. Loves to get her fingernails chipped, has an affinity with dirt and grime. Give her a lump hammer and she will have that wall down in half an hour.'

His eyes were glowing with amusement. But beneath the amusement was a love and pride that made Rafiq want to sigh. At home in Rahman his brother was no doubt relaxing with the woman he adored with every breath that he took. And here stood Ethan Hayes so in love with his lovely, if highly provoking, wife, that he could not keep his feelings from showing on his face.

And here I stand, planning to marry a mere obsession, he mused heavily. A past obsession, a present obsession, but most importantly of all a sexual obsession. Upstairs their bedroom had become a place for hot and tumultuous orgies. Melanie had revealed a capacity to take eagerly whatever he chose to offer in that bed upstairs. But what really ravaged him was not knowing if she responded to any man in the same mind-blowing way.

He swung away so that Ethan Hayes could not see his expression. Sometimes he wished he had never come here, had never given in to the temptation that was Melanie Portreath. She turned him inside out, made him behave as he had never behaved in his life before. Which made him—what?

A man in love with his obsession? The words filtered like poison into his brain tissue, sending him on yet another restless swing that concluded with him frowning at his watch. Melanie was due back soon from the hours she donated to Robbie's school several mornings a week, helping out wherever she was required to do so. He did not want her to find him here with Ethan Hayes.

'Have you no ambition to do anything with your life?' he had asked her one evening.

'Should I be ashamed of wanting to be a full-time mother to my son?' she'd bristle indignantly by return.

'No, of course not. I just thought—'

'Well, don't think,' she'd snapped. 'I am comfortable

with who I am, but if you're not then you know what you can do.'

Leave. She never failed to let him know that the option was there for him to use if he wished to do so. He usually answered by kissing her breath away. But would she care if he did leave? Or would she heave a sigh of relief as she watched him walk away from this idea that marriage between them could work?

'I would like work to begin while the owners are away,' he said to Ethan with a calmness that belied what was going on inside his head. 'It will be less painful for those concerned if they do not have to witness the initial destruction of everything they love.'

'Who owns the house?' Ethan questioned.

'A—friend of mine.' He couldn't even say the words, My wife, as of the day after tomorrow, which angered him all the more. Was he ashamed? Was he afraid it might never happen? She was still having second thoughts despite the torrid sex; he was aware of that. Recently she had even withdrawn the sex. She had turned a cold shoulder upon him and said she had a headache.

A headache. The oldest excuse in a woman's vocabulary. He frowned, glanced at the time again but did not register it because he was remembering that she had spent yesterday out with her cynical friend, choosing something to wear for her wedding day. Ten minutes alone with Miss Elliot would have been long enough for Melanie to begin piling on the doubts.

'Then this house cannot be touched without her permission.' Ethan's voice intruded on his own dark thoughts.

The very walls seemed to move, as if William Portreath's ghost was stirring himself to warn Rafiq to be careful how much he took for granted. I take nothing for granted, he grimly told the old ghost.

'You said it is in danger of falling down,' he responded.

'Yes,' Ethan confirmed. 'But you will still need written permission from the owner to touch it, Rafiq,' he advised.

'Even my flighty wife would not dare come near it without written consent from the owner.'

'I will obtain it.' He nodded. By fair means or foul, he added silently, thinking of the trust with which Melanie signed any papers either he or Randal Soames placed in front of her.

Which was just another thing about Melanie that irritated him. The money she now possessed meant nothing. Her son and this house meant everything.

Where did he fit in?

The telephone in William's study began ringing. Since he had commandeered the room for himself, Rafiq assumed the call must be for him, and excused himself, leaving Ethan to wander the house some more while he went to lean against William's old desk and lifted the receiver to his ear.

'Yes?' he said brusquely.

There was a small silence, then a tentative-sounding voice. 'Is Melanie there?'

Rafiq froze on instant recognition of that deep country burr. 'No,' was all he could manage to utter.

'Oh...' Jamie Sangster sounded momentarily nonplussed. 'Who are you?' he then asked curiously.

'A—friend,' Rafiq gritted.

Another 'Oh' raked his eardrum, followed by, 'Will you give her a message for me, then? Tell her that Jamie will be in town on Saturday and could she give me a ring so we can arrange dinner or something to talk about her proposition?'

Rafiq replaced the receiver without replying. He then carefully removed it from its rest. Beyond the study door he could hear Ethan Hayes moving about the hallway. In William Portreath's study the only sound was the buzzing taking place inside his own head.

* * *

Melanie signed all the papers Rafiq set in front of her without bothering to look at them. She was so tired she knew she couldn't see straight to read them anyway.

'Randal tells me you have decided to set a separate fund aside,' Rafiq murmured levelly. 'Is it for anything special?'

'Is Randal supposed to pass on to you every decision I make?' She frowned.

'Taking care of your money is what you signed me up to do for you.'

Shame this relationship hadn't stayed that simple, Melanie thought heavily and got up from the desk with the grim intention of taking herself off to bed. She was exhausted beyond anything—stress and tension—tension and stress...

'So, what is the money set aside for?' Rafiq prompted an answer.

'Personal stuff,' she said.

'A million pounds of it?'

His sarcasm showed. Melanie turned to look at him. There was something different about him tonight. He'd been quiet and withdrawn, even with Robbie. And he looked paler than he usually did. Was the stress of it all getting to him also?

'I might want to go on a spending binge.' She attempted to make light of a tricky subject. 'Your know, retail therapy and all that.'

He didn't even try to smile. 'You believe you may require such therapy once married to me?'

She glanced at him, standing there in so-called casual clothes that had clearly cost the earth. 'Well, my one good suit doesn't look much next to the dozen or so suits you have hanging in my wardrobe,' she pointed out wryly.

'It will not cost a million to replenish your wardrobe.'

'I might decide I want to by loads of things—like a new car or two,' she suggested. 'Why, is there a ceiling on how much I am allowed to stash on one side?'

'No,' he answered quietly. 'But I think you have over-done it a little. Why not allow me to place, say—one hundred thousand in your account to be going on with?' he suggested. 'You need only say when you require more.'

Melanie shifted tensely; she did not want to talk about this. 'Don't talk down to me just because you know more about money than I do, Rafiq,' she told him crossly. 'If I'd wanted only one hundred thousand I would have made it only one hundred thousand.'

With that she went to leave the room.

'Where are you going?' His dark voice came after her.

'I'm tired. It's been a—long day. I want a nice soak in a warm bath, then just to fall asleep as soon as my head hits the pillow.'

'What—again?' he drawled lazily.

It was like a red rag to a bull. She whipped around to look at him. It was a terrible—terrible mistake. He was leaning against the edge of William's desk with his arms loosely folded and eyes slightly hooded by long black lashes, as usual.

Why? Because he was trying to impose another woman's image over her image. He wanted that other woman so badly that sometimes she could actually feel him ache.

'We aren't even married yet and you sound like a husband,' she lashed out. 'There has to be more to this relationship than just sex, or we are about to make a big mistake.'

The light from the desk lamp was playing across his bold dark features. She thought she saw a different kind of light glint in his eyes and stiffened her shoulders in readiness for him to throw something really nasty back at her like, Be grateful we have sex!

But he didn't say that. In fact he didn't saying or do anything but study her, and she felt herself begin to tremor, felt her inner self wanting to reach out for him with a desperation that made her want to cry. Simple eye contact and she was falling into that terrible pit. Her senses came alive, slinking terrible temptations down her quivering spine.

Then the heavy eyelids lowered even further. He began to straighten and her senses went haywire. If he starts walking, I start running, she told herself agitatedly. I don't want him to touch me—I don't! But what he did was unfold his arms and drop them to his sides before offering her one of those cold, curt formal bows he could demonstrate with such devastating effect.

'Of course,' he said. 'My apologies. Forgive my crass instincts,' he begged.

There was nothing crass about his instincts. Nothing crass about the way he could turn himself into this coldly polite, lofty giant of a stranger who contrarily made her want to be very gentle with him.

Her stomach muscles quivered; her heart began to ache. 'Rafiq…'

He turned away from the husky little murmur of his name, and picked up the papers she had just signed for him. 'I will be leaving early in the morning and will not be returning here tomorrow night. Robert knows this, but please reassure him that I will ring before his bedtime.'

All of a sudden she didn't know if she was standing on her head or her heels. Her emotions were flipping over from one thing to another; now she was experiencing stark fear.

'Y-you mean you're not coming back at all?' she managed to stammer.

He sent her a glance, a fleeting glance. 'A car will collect you on Friday morning. Please attempt not to be late.'

A car. Friday. Don't be late. She almost sank to her knees in relief. Which said it all really, didn't it? she accepted bleakly. I'm hooked. I can't bear the thought of living without him.

'Yes,' she whispered. 'Goodnight,' she said, and got herself out of there before her knees actually did give out.

Rafiq sat in the back of his chauffeur-driven car and stared out of the window at yet another cold, wet day in London.

Beside him his aide, Kadir Al-Kadir, sat quietly. He was in shock, but then who would not be to find himself hauled out of his bed at six in the morning by a man who was not happy that his plans were already beginning to fall apart?

Hassan had not made it to London. Something had come up involving important matters of state. If he had not been so stubborn and had told Hassan exactly why he wanted him here then his half-brother would have left no stone unturned in his quest to be at his side on this day. But that had not been the way he wanted to play it. Hassan had met Melanie eight years ago, during the weekend they'd spent on the Maitland estate. He knew the history of their relationship and had no kind thoughts for Melanie. Given enough time and the opportunity, he would have tried to stop the marriage today.

But he had still wanted his brother at his side on this important day for him, so he had planned Hassan's arrival to give him neither time nor space to voice his objections. As the old ones liked to say about meticulous planning, it simply begged to fall apart on you, he mused heavily.

He glanced at his watch. Thirty minutes to go. Melanie should be leaving home with their son and her cynical friend about now. 'Check what is happening with the other car,' he instructed Kadir.

The younger man located his mobile telephone. A few murmured questions later and he was putting it away again. 'The car is still awaiting its passengers, sir,' he informed him.

Rafiq nodded, slid a long finger across the tense line of his mouth and wished he hadn't asked the question. He would not do so again, he determined. Which meant he now had to endure a very tense half-hour.

'Ready?' Sophia asked.

No, Melanie thought. 'Yes,' she answered quietly.

'You look so pretty, Mummy,' Robbie told her. 'Doesn't she look pretty, Aunt Sophia?'

'Stunning,' Sophia agreed with a touch of dry cynicism. 'Now all she needs to do is smile to show she's happy about this.'

'Of course she's happy.' Robbie was jumping up and down with excitement. 'She's getting married to my daddy today.'

'Go and check if the car is still there, Robbie,' Sophia instructed. 'The innocence of youth.' She sighed as Robbie bounced out of the room and went clattering down the stairs. 'One good look at your face and he would know you are about to fall into a maidenly swoon.'

'Don't be so Gothic,' Melanie said. 'I'm fine. I just didn't sleep much last night.'

'Missed your man?'

Missed him dreadfully, she thought hollowly. Which only made the ache she was carrying around inside worse.

A telephone began ringing downstairs. 'I'll get it!' Robbie shouted.

'The big man is checking up on you,' Sophia wagered. 'He can't be certain that you are going to turn up.'

'Yes, he can. He only has to think about his son to know that I am going to be there— You look fantastic,' she put in when Sophia opened her mouth to say something Melanie knew she did not want to hear.

Her friend was wearing a dark purple suit that followed her hourglass figure to perfection. With her exotically dark colouring she made Melanie feel washed out and ordinary in her misty-blue outfit with its short straight skirt and nipped-in jacket edged with soft blue fake fur at the round neck and cuffs.

A rush of nerves suddenly washed through her, sending her heart down to her neat blue shoes. 'I don't think—'

Robbie came running down the landing 'Can we can go now—please?' he begged.

'You're not wearing something old,' Sophia murmured as they moved down the landing.

Melanie wriggled her diamond ring at her.

'Something borrowed?'

The hesitation was only slight before Melanie wriggled the self-same ring. Which said a lot as to how long she expected this marriage to last.

'Who was on the phone, Robbie?' she asked her son as they hit the downstairs hallway.

'Uncle Jamie,' he replied. 'I told him you were getting married to my daddy today and he rang off without saying goodbye.'

Melanie's footsteps stilled on the polished wood floor. But Robbie's moved him onwards to pull open the front door. Ice-cold air rushed into the house and she shivered. A man wearing a dark overcoat stood just outside, holding up a huge black umbrella. He saw Robbie and Sophia into the car and out of the pouring rain first. As Melanie stood there on the doorstep, waiting for him to return for her, she experienced the only real moment where she actually thought she was going to change her mind. Then the driver came back to offer her shelter; his smile was warm. She stepped out of the house, closing the door behind her.

Rafiq was standing with Kadir in the elegant foyer belonging to one of London's local government town halls when the entrance doors suddenly opened and his son, Melanie and her friend appeared. His son ran straight towards him. Miss Elliot became busy brushing away the few raindrops that had caught her clothes; Melanie looked at him and went perfectly still.

His heart began to pound against his ribcage; his legs suddenly felt heavy and weak. His son was talking away to him but he did not hear a single word. She was so lovely she tore at his senses, enchanting, shy and uncertain, like the younger woman he'd used to know.

'Stay here, Robert,' he instructed, and made himself

walk towards Melanie. As he came to a halt in front of her he saw her eyelashes flicker just before she looked up at him. 'So this is it,' he said with a smile that did not quite make it.

'Yes.' The single word whispered nervously from her. Her gaze drifted away. Her cheeks were pale and her fingers were trembling.

'I'm sorry we're a few minutes late,' she said in a little rush. 'The rain...'

The words became muffled by a smothering breathlessness as she picked up the aroma of his scent. He was wearing another midnight-blue suit made of a crease-free touch-temptingly smooth fabric. His shirt was so white it made his skin look darker and temptingly smooth like the suit. Her fingers twitched nervously against the little blue purse she was holding, and she kept her eyes averted in case she did something stupid like come jolting to her senses.

Was she really about to marry this tall dark beautiful man? 'W-where do we go?'

It was all she could think to say in the circumstances.

'Up the stairs.' He offered his hand to her. 'Shall we go?' he said.

There was another moment of complete stillness while Melanie stared at his hand. They never touched, unless compelled to do so by that awful sexual force. Did he know that? Was he aware that his outstretched hand was breaking new ground here? Her mouth ran dry; she tried to swallow. From the sidelines she caught sight of Sophia, watching them. Her friend too had noticed her hesitation and was probably making her own deductions as to what it meant.

The fact that Rafiq had noticed Sophia studying him showed when he turned his head to flash her a look. Sophia dared to cock a mocking eyebrow. Hostility sparked into life. Melanie responded by lifting up a hand and placing it in his. The gesture brought his gaze flashing back her way, and his fingers closed gently round hers. Warm strength enclosed icy frailty; something very dramatic began to build in the air. As he turned them towards the elegant stairway that led to an upper foyer she noticed Kadir Al-Kadir standing quietly to one side, with his dark gaze fixed on Robbie as if he could not quite believe what his eyes were telling him.

By necessity Rafiq made the polite introduction, though Melanie suspected he did not want to speak at all. He was tense; she was tense. They moved up the stairs together, with Robbie dancing behind them, his hand tucked into Sophia's, blissfully unaware of the stress-load weighing down everyone else's shoulders.

Not twenty minutes later they were walking down those same stairs again. It had all been so quick, so efficient— so impersonal. But in those few minutes she had changed her name to Al-Qadim and was now wearing a wedding band on her finger. Even more disturbing was the ring Rafiq had given her to slide on his long brown finger.

That hand now rested at the base of her spine, and remained there until they stepped outside. The rain was still bouncing off the pavements. Three cars now stood in a row at the kerb, with three black-coated men standing beside them holding black umbrellas over their heads.

With a click of his fingers Rafiq brought one man running. With a brief word of thanks he sent Kadir on his way. Next came Melanie's first shock, when the second man was brought running and she found herself being hugged by Sophia, who murmured, 'Surprise, surprise. I am taking your son off your hands until tomorrow.'

'But I don't want—'

'Not your choice any more, little sacrificial lamb,' Sophia informed her dryly, only to be replaced by Robbie, who was demanding a hug from his mother and excitedly explaining all the things he and Sophia had planned for the day, before he was ushered beneath the umbrella and hurried away.

Standing there, shell-shocked beyond speech, Melanie found herself left alone with the man she had just married, watching another car move off, which left only one—a long, low-squatting animal thing with darkened glass and a distinct air of menace about it.

The snap of Rafiq's fingers set her blinking; the return of his hand to the base of her spine had her tensing jerkily. The last black-coated man came running with an umbrella. She was directed beneath it and into the warm soft depths of black-leather car seats. Rafiq followed, the car door closed with a smooth soft thud and they were alone—really alone—encased in dark glass and hidden, even from the driver.

Silence arrived. It hummed between them. The car began moving away from the kerb. She turned to look at Rafiq and found him looking back at her. His wide shoulders hugged the upholstered corner of the car and one ankle rested easily across the other knee with a set of long fingers lightly clasping the ankle. He looked relaxed, at ease, like a lazy cat contentedly at peace. Indeed, slumberous lashes barely flickered as he studied her face. But there was nothing relaxed about those devil-dark eyes hiding behind the lashes. They glinted in a way that sent tiny hot frissons chasing down her spine.

'I can't believe you planned all of this without my knowledge,' she said, jumping nervously into speech.

'It is tradition for a newly married couple to spend this time alone.'

'This isn't a traditional marriage.' That short ceremony they had just performed mocked the very word. 'We did this for Robbie, so why shouldn't he be here with us now?'

'Robbie is perfectly happy doing what he is doing.'

Well, I'm not, Melanie thought, and with a pressing together of her lips she turned her face away. Beyond the darkened glass she could see London moving past at speed. They were crossing one of the bridges that spanned the river, she realised, and she felt those frissons chase through her again, because they didn't need to cross the river to get to her house or even his apartment.

'Where are we going?' she asked sharply.

'To a place where my sacrificial lamb can perform in complete privacy,' he murmured silkily.

CHAPTER TEN

HIS reply tugged her face around to him again. He was smiling, but it wasn't a nice smile. Obviously he had overheard Sophia and, despite appearances to the contrary, he was actually as angry as hell.

'I am nobody's sacrifice,' she objected.

'Shame,' he drawled. 'I was looking forward to watching you lay yourself out on some softly sprung, silk-covered altar, then offer yourself to me.'

His description conjured up exactly the image it had aimed to. Heat stole into her cheeks; she bristled in annoyance with it. 'Back to sex again,' she derided.

'Would you prefer it if we discussed other things?'

'Like what?' she asked warily.

'Jamie,' he inserted with velvet precision. 'Our son tells me he spoke to his *uncle* Jamie on the telephone this morning, but he rang off before he could invite him to come to our wedding.'

At last she understood where the anger was coming from. 'I never said that—'

'Our son has a very generous nature,' he cut in. 'He seems to hold a great affection for his uncle Jamie. Do you think this affection has anything to do with how close he came to having Jamie as his father instead of me?'

Melanie released a sharp gasp. 'That is a terrible thing to say!'

'But the truth.'

'You don't *know* the truth!'

'He is still in your life. That is a clear truth.'

'I don't—'

'Do not begin this marriage by lying to me,' he gritted warningly.

Melanie took a deep breath to stop herself from exploding. 'I was about to say that I don't think that is any of your business,' she said coldly.

'From now on everything that you do is my business.'

'Does that mean everything that you do is my business too?' she tossed back. 'In this country we believe in equality. So why don't you tell me all about Serena Cordero.'

'You are trying to divert me from the main issue here.'

'That is because I have nothing to say on the subject,' she declared stubbornly.

'Then let me assist,' he offered. 'I took a call from your step-cousin Jamie last week in William's study. This morning my son took another call from him. To me your step-cousin mentioned a—proposition. With Robert, he simply rang off when he discovered that you were marrying me today. Maybe if you are wise you will explain the proposition, and why this man is still so much a part of your life that my son calls him *uncle*!'

The sleeping cat had awoken. Melanie watched with increasing wariness as the long fingers slid away from his ankle and his shoulders began to tense. She lost every scrap of colour and spoke without thinking. 'Anyone would think you were jealous—'

He moved like lightning, catching hold of her nearest wrist and pulling her across the gap separating them. She landed with a thud against his shirt front; her silk skirt slithered up her thighs as he hauled her onto his lap. Her fingers clawed at his shoulders; her breath panted into his face. His eyes had turned silver; she had never seen them do that before.

'Start talking,' he gritted.

She trembled all over, but held onto this one promise she had made to herself. 'Jamie is not up for discussion between you and me.'

'He was your lover eight years ago. I will not be betrayed by you twice!'

She struggled against him. 'Let go of me. You're hurting!'

To her absolute surprise he set her free. She slithered onto the seat beside him, too shaken to notice the new expression in his eyes. 'I apologise,' he said curtly. 'I don't usually forget my own strength. Where did I hurt you?'

'My wrist.' She was rubbing it, though it didn't really hurt. It had been the fear that he was close to hurting her that had made her tell the white lie.

Careful fingers took the wrist from her; very gently he began stroking the pink area with the smooth pad of his thumb. It was a stupid thing to react so badly to, but her pulse suddenly went crazy. He felt it happen and the thumb-pad stilled; she released a strangled little sigh. The mood flipped from anger to electrified awareness so quickly that it threw her into a state of confusion.

But not him—not him. He simply accepted the change with a shrug and a grimace, then lifted the wrist to his mouth and stroked the pink area with his tongue.

'So we're back to the sex again.' It was a supposed to be a withering condemnation, but it didn't quite come out like that.

'Blame yourself,' Rafiq murmured, and in the next moment she was pulled back into his lap.

'Don't!' she protested.

'Scared?' he drawled. 'Because you know your defences will not hold through one small kiss? Or is your pulse beating so fast because you are afraid that I *won't* kiss you?'

'No.'

He tested that denial with devastating consequences: the moment her lips clung he removed his own and watched her stare at his mouth like a hungry woman. One of his hands began to stroke her silk-covered thigh, left provokingly exposed by her slippery skirt. She moved against him, breasts searching for contact with his chest, her hips pressing into the cradle of his pelvis where the thrust of his erection was making itself known.

'You don't play fair,' she groaned helplessly.

He just laughed low in his throat, then gave her back his mouth. It stayed this time, seducing with lazy dips of his tongue, while he undid the jacket buttons and removed it altogether. Beneath she wore a creamy white body. One light touch and he knew she was wearing no bra. 'Interesting,' he murmured as the hand began to follow the clinging outline of Lycra. When the waistband of her skirt stopped his progress he merely switched attention to the other hand and finished the journey via her thigh.

A single smooth slide between her thighs and he had released the tiny poppers that held the body in place.

'Oh,' she whimpered, when he discovered for himself how warm and moist she was. For the next few dizzying minutes she just hung on and let him work his seductive magic. She moved, she stretched, she curled herself around him, she moaned into his hungry mouth. He broke the kiss on a hiss of tension, caught her chin between his teeth and bit, then her throat, then her breasts, first one then the other, sucking at them through the Lycra. She clutched at his neck, his hair, the hair-roughened wrist attached to the tormenting hand. She begged, she pleaded, he growled something and came back to pester her mouth again at the precise moment she was threatening to topple headlong into the kind of orgasm that didn't belong in this situation.

'We can't do this here,' she whispered anxiously.

With a growl of impatience he pressed his body forward, taking hers with him as he reached for the in-car phone. A few husky words in Arabic and the car was sliding to a standstill. Ten seconds later, Melanie heard the thud of a car door and realised that the driver had left them alone.

Embarrassed heat flooded her cheeks. 'He will know what we're doing!'

He was way beyond the point of giving a care. His

mouth claimed hers again; his hands claimed her hips. 'Release me,' he commanded in a throat-hoarse murmur.

'I can't.'

'You can.' Capturing one of her hands, he pressed it against himself. He was trembling as badly as she was, and maybe it was those tremors that stopped any more protest. A minute later she was straddling him, her mouth devouring his hot mouth while her body slowly took him in. She had never felt so wickedly wanton, had never thought she could behave like this. She moved while he held her slender hips steady; she copied the movement with her tongue. His breathing was ragged; the car filled with the scent of heat from their bodies. As she began to rise towards the edge, her inner muscles closed so tightly around him that he had to stop kissing her to throw back his dark head and close his eyes.

Pleasure like this could never be repeated, she found herself thinking as his hands reached up to frame her face and black eyelashes lifted to capture her eyes. She drove; he let her. It was a powerful, powerful aphrodisiac. When she leapt she cried out. When he followed he pulled her face into his shoulder and held her there throughout the ragged, pulsing finish until the weakness of exhaustion made her feel boneless.

They did not speak. Not then—not later, when eventually he gently eased himself from her and set her down on the seat at his side. Clothes rustled as shaking fingers replaced them into some semblance of dignity. Melanie kept her head lowered so her hair hid her hot face. She could sense the gravity shrouding Rafiq.

Cool air hit the interior as he let down the window. A minute later the car was moving again. The window remained open, though, circulating the hot air of seduction out of the car.

They turned in through a pair of high gates and began driving down a lane between a tunnel of trees with gnarled naked branches reaching out to tangle across the gap.

The car stopped. Rafiq climbed out and came around to open her door for her. Still without daring to look at him, she arrived at his side like a cracked piece of porcelain, in danger of shattering if anyone so much as spoke.

She found herself standing in front of huge sandstone monolith with tall sash windows and an oak front door. Beyond caring what this place was, she followed Rafiq to the door, which he unlocked with a key then stepped to one side, as if to invite her to precede him. She took a single step—that was all—before he was lifting her up in his big arms.

'More tradition?' she mocked shrilly.

'For once in your life keep your mouth shut,' he grimly advised her, and stepped over the threshold with his bride. He kicked the door shut again.

She gained a vague impression of oak panelling and iron fretwork, but most of her attention was honed on his taut profile as he proceeded to carry her up a stairway that curved around a panelled wall. They walked through an archway and down a dark red-carpeted corridor, passing more oak doors on their way. When they arrived at the one he was aiming for he opened it, then walked inside.

The room was so dramatically Gothic in design that she half expected to find a headless ghost standing in one of the shadowy corners. A fire burned in the grate of a big fireplace and a tray laid for coffee waited on a low table set between two richly upholstered wine-coloured velvet chairs. But what dominated the room was the huge and heavy oak four-poster bed hung with more wine-red velvet and, of all things, a dark purple throw made of silk.

The scene for a bridal seduction was set right down to the last detail—right down to the two matching black silk robes that lay draped across the foot of the bed. Shame, she thought cynically that they had pre-empted the moment; it had certainly spoiled all of this.

Allowing her feet to slip to a thick purple carpet, Rafiq

then turned to close the door. 'Sit down—pour yourself a drink,' he invited.

She almost jumped when he spoke to her. She spun on her heel then wished she hadn't done it when she found herself looking at a man at war with himself. He was yanking his tie loose with impatient fingers; the frown on his face was a definite scowl. Heat bloomed in her cheeks; shame choked her lungs. Turning away, she felt the sting of tears in her eyes.

'I don't like what you do to me,' she breathed out painfully.

'You surprise me. I had not noticed,' he drawled.

It was derision of the crushing kind and the worst insult he could have offered her. Moving on legs that did not want to support her, Melanie went to the nearest chair and sank down.

He disappeared through a door near the bed and came back a few minutes later wearing only a long black robe. She glanced at the bed, saw that one robe was now missing. It was so glaringly obvious what he was intending to do next that she wished she had never been born.

But what made it worse was the low soft pulsing taking place between her thighs. She could still feel him there, hard and silken. She could still taste his kisses on her tongue. He took the other chair, saw she hadn't touched the coffee pot and leant forward to pour it himself.

Silently, he handed a cup to her. With lowered eyes she took it. 'Thank you,' she breathed.

He huffed out a laugh. It brought her wary gaze up to clash head-on with his harshly mocking expression. 'How can you manage to sound so prim when we both know that prim is the last thing that you are?' he threw at her.

It was like being kicked when she was already down on the floor. 'I don't know how you can sit there and speak to me like this when you only married me an hour ago,' she responded shakily.

'And was seduced by you half an hour later.'

'You started it!'

'You finished it!' he raked back. 'In the name of *Allah* I cannot believe I am even sitting here with you! You are poison to a man like me.'

'Oh.' She stood up. 'How dare you say that?'

'Your step-cousin says I can say what the hell I like to you.'

He looked hard and dark and dangerously foreign. His anger and contempt washed over her in waves. Senses that just should *not* respond to this man she was seeing stung her with their awful message.

'I n-need to use the bathroom.' She turned away dizzily.

'You need an escape.'

'I *hate* you!' she cried.

He launched to his feet. She dropped her cup and ran towards the door he had used a few minutes ago as a dark coffee stain seeped into her skirt. Slamming the door shut behind her, she expected to find herself standing in a bathroom and instead found her eyes flickering round a room full of clothes. Men's clothes, women's clothes—rails and rails of them. It took only a glance at a couple of dresses for her to realise that every female item in here was so new it still wore its label.

Bought for her? She couldn't be sure. Didn't even think she wanted to know. They were her size and that was all that she cared about, since she didn't have anything else to wear and she needed to get out of this stupid wedding outfit that made such a mockery of the word marriage— and which was impregnated with the scent of him!

With trembling fingers she stripped the suit from her body and had just removed the wretched Lycra body when the door opened. She spun, clutching that silly scrap of material to her. 'Get out!' she shrieked at him.

With his usual arrogance he ignored the instruction. Instead he tossed something at her. She had to drop the body to catch it. It was the black wrap that matched the one he was wearing. It felt like the final humiliation to have him stand there viewing her through cold opal eyes as she fumbled on the robe over her near nakedness and dragged the two pieces of black silk across her body, tightly knotted the belt.

'Tell me about Jamie,' he demanded remorselessly.

He just was not going to give up!

'Which version would you really like to hear, Rafiq?' she flashed at him. 'The one where I admit to going from your arms to his arms with no conscience? Or the one where I tell you just how fickle you were—how easy you were to dupe and how badly you let me down when you dared to believe I could play such calculating games?'

His dark face tightened, big shoulders flexing at her bitterly deriding tone. 'The truth,' he gritted. 'Just tell me the truth!'

The truth? She almost laughed, though she'd never felt less like laughing. She wasn't that sure that he could take the truth! Did she actually care any more whether his pride was up to weathering the blow she could deliver it?

No, she didn't, she realised. He had called her poison. Well, maybe it was time he discovered just how poisonous she could be. So she lifted her face and looked at him squarely.

'The truth is that you were set up,' she said. 'Uncle Thomas and Jamie always knew I would inherit from William. William actually paid my uncle money for my keep. Uncle Thomas was greedy; he wanted to get his hands on *all* of William's money. But the only way he could do that was if he kept it in the family. He encouraged a romance between Jamie and me. I refused to play. They didn't like it. Tensions in the house became pretty grim. I decided I needed to get away and started hiring myself out to the local gentry to earn some extra money so I could leave the farm. Which was how I came to meet you.' She released a short laugh which stung with mockery, for never in a hundred years would a woman like her normally have come into contact with a man like Rafiq. 'You swept me off my feet and into bed, even asked me to marry you.'

'And you saw your quick escape from drudgery?'

Her eyes widened on this darkly handsome, beautifully put together man who could harbour such a huge inferiority complex. 'If I'd known about William's money it would not have changed anything. Haven't you noticed yet that I don't have much use for the stuff?'

'Unless you want to give it away to your step-cousin.'

He was mixing the past up with the present. 'Do you want to hear the rest of this or not?' she demanded.

A muscle in his jaw clenched tightly. He gave a grim nod of his head. 'I said yes to your proposal,' she continued tightly. 'And was then left with the unhappy task of breaking the news to Uncle Thomas and Jamie. They saw their chance of getting their hands on William's money slipping away, so they decided to do something about it.'

'I saw you with him in your bedroom.' His dark eyes were glinting as if he could still see them there. 'You were standing in your bedroom window, locked in each other arms.'

'I was locked in *his* arms!' Melanie flashed out the distinction.

He didn't believe her. 'Brazen,' he gritted. 'You were kissing as if you couldn't get enough of each other!'

He was right; the kiss had been fevered. Jamie had been feverishly trying to seduce her while she had been trying to get away! 'I was young and a complete fool,' she admitted cynically. 'I actually believed that Jamie truly loved me. I was attempting to let him down gently because I believed I was hurting him!'

'In your bathrobe. It was gaping.' His eyes were black with accusation.

'It was not!' she denied, paused to think about that, then had to offer a small shrug. 'Maybe a little,' she conceded. 'Things were getting a little out of hand, and I—'

'A little?' he cut in. 'Do you believe *a little* should mean something here?'

The jeering tone of his voice straightened her backbone. She looked into his hard, condemning face and wanted to hit him! 'Well, you tell me what *you* think it means, Rafiq,' she challenged. 'Or don't I need to ask?' It was written on his face! 'Because you saw me locked in that embrace with Jamie you just had to believe that I must be enjoying it! Didn't it occur to you for one small second that I might not have had much choice in the matter?'

'So you were the victim?' His tone derided her.

'As much as you were,' she replied.

'I know your passions,' he countered gruffly.

Melanie released a hard laugh. 'I suppose I should have expected a man from your culture to think like that,' she murmured bitterly.

'Meaning?'

'Primitive!' she flashed at him. 'I let you make love to me so, in your primitive view, it therefore goes without saying that I would let any man do that same!'

'I never said that.'

'You don't need to say it when I see it written on your face every time you look at me,' she denounced. 'The day I let you into my bed I lost your respect.'

Her shrug said she no longer cared that she had. As she began to walk towards him, Rafiq stiffened in the doorway. He had never seen her look upon him with such open dislike. 'I was twenty years old,' she said as she reached him. 'I let you take something very special from me. It should have meant something to you, but it didn't or you could not have walked away.'

'Your own uncle stood beside me as I watched you with Jamie. He told me things I would have been a fool to—'

'He lied,' she stated with a cool, quiet simplicity, then brushed past him to go back into the bedroom. Rafiq turned to watch her walk across the room with her shoulders straight and her slender shape shimmering with contempt for him.

The coffee cup still lay on its side on the carpet, a dark stain seeping outwards from its rim. He stood watching as she stooped to pick up the cup then reach for a napkin to mop up the stain. The soft fall of her hair curled around her slender nape and caressed the edges of the black silk robe. He could see her profile, delicate and pure in its smooth lines, even while her lovely mouth still pursed with dislike. Something shifted inside him—not sexual this time, but more a shifting of other desires—a desire to drop his guard and let himself believe what he knew deep down inside was the damning truth.

Because if what she had told him was the truth then it damned him and not Melanie. Because she was right and he had been fickle, easy to dupe. Most damning of all, he had let her down in the worst way a man could let down the woman he professed to love.

Primitive. He almost laughed. For primitive hardly covered the way he had behaved—if she was telling him the truth. At home in Rahman women might not enjoy the same equal rights as their western counterparts, but they did have the right to defend themselves when accused of a crime. He had denied Melanie even this basic right.

And in so doing he had forfeited the love she'd used to feel for him—and seven years of his son's life. Which left him with what? he had to ask himself. A marriage filled with bitterness and resentment? A wife who would never be a real wife to him unless he could accept her truth and put the past behind him?

Patiently pressing the napkin into the coffee stain, Melanie could feel his silence with every pulse of her heartbeat. She could sense his battle with every frail breath that she took. He had a choice; they both knew it. He must believe her or not believe her. She had no proof she could pull like a rabbit from a magic hat.

There were words, of course—lots more words. Were they worth uttering?

'They knew what time you were coming to collect me that evening.' She gave the words a chance. 'By the time you pulled into the farmyard the whole scene had been set so perfectly that I didn't really stand a chance. When I was allowed to turn and see you standing there, you were already turning away. I caught the next train to London...'

She paused in what she was doing and let the next ugly scene play inside the privacy of her own head. By the way he moved over, to stand frowning out of the window, so did Rafiq, she suspected.

'When I arrived back at the farm Uncle Thomas and Jamie were having this big row and I heard enough to know how neatly we had been set up. Jamie admitted his part in it before I walked out of there for good. He felt guilt...' Because I was so distraught. She did not say it out loud.

'Where did you go?' He sounded husky.

'To stay with friends in Winchester,' she answered, her fingers pressing at the wet patch again. 'I managed to get a job there, working in a factory. But they laid me off when it became obvious that I was pregnant. So I came up to London to try you again...'

'Hassan told me you had been trying to contact me,' he inserted. 'I was at home in Rahman. I asked Hassan to meet with you but you had not left a contact number. He did attempt to find you but was unsuccessful...'

Sitting back on her heels, Melanie looked up at his tall dark shape standing by the deep purple curtains, and felt something painful slice across her chest. So his brother hadn't even told him he'd spoken to her.

Neat, she thought ruefully. Tidy and slick.

'He merely said that he had heard you were living with another man.'

Pressing her trembling lips together, she refused to say

anything. There was enough bitterness flying around this room without her adding his brother into the mix.

He moved, shifting his tense frame to look at her. 'What happened to Jamie?'

'He left home too, went up north. I didn't hear from him again until his father died.' She stood up; her fingers were sticky and covered in fine fibres from the carpet. 'He's married now, has two beautiful children and a lovely wife he adores. He works with her father on a farm in Cumbria and would have been perfectly content to live the rest of his life milking cows for a living if the recent foot-and-mouth epidemic hadn't devastated the herd.'

'So he came to you for help?'

'Financial help.' Melanie nodded. 'They want to go organic, but it takes time to clear the land of chemicals, disease and…whatever else.' She shrugged. 'They still have to live while they are achieving all this. Then they have to restock their herd. They want to specialise, so I am investing half a million pounds into their project.'

'With no real hope of any return,' Rafiq added, 'because you still care for him.'

'Of course I still care for him!' she cried. 'He was sorry for what he'd done. What use is there in bearing grudges? He is my only living relative besides Robbie!'

'Not a blood relative.'

'Does that matter? Who are you to criticise?'

'I have a father and a half-brother.'

'Would you turn your back on your brother's wife if she came to you for help?'

No, he wouldn't. She could see that in the sudden frown on his face.

'We have wandered from the subject,' he said tensely.

'I've finished with the subject,' she replied. 'You believed what your eyes told you, and as far as you were concerned I did not warrant a single word in my defence. I gave birth to your son and with William's help brought him up. When I thought it would be safe to do it I introduced you to your son, and ended up—here.' She glanced around the Gothic bedroom. 'Married to a man who can't even look at me without seeing a slut.'

'I do not think you are a slut.'

'Poison, then.'

He released a harsh sigh. 'I was angry when I said that.'

'So was I. But do you want to know something really funny, Rafiq?' She lifted cool gold eyes to him. 'I really thought that you cared about me. Right up until you placed this ring on my finger I thought that, deep inside, beneath the rock you would call a heart, you still cared enough to want to make a success out of this marriage. But now?' She turned away. 'I think we've both made a terrible mistake.'

He didn't protest it, which more or less said the rest for her. 'Where is the bathroom?' she asked, holding up her sticky fingers.

He turned to open a door she hadn't noticed on the other side of the four-poster bed. And with her expression as closed as she could make it she walked past him into a rather startlingly decadent oak-panelled room with a huge free-standing bath tub overhung by a big brass shower head and a purple silk curtain that would circle the whole thing when closed. The rest of the fittings were antique porcelain. She walked over to the pedestal-mounted wash-basin, then stood grimacing at her fingers before reaching for the taps.

Another pair of hands beat her to it. She was suddenly surrounded by Rafiq. Her body stiffened, her mouth ran dry. Water gushed into white porcelain, swirling around its curving bowl before spiralling its way down the drain. He took her hands and began to gently wash them.

Move back, she wanted to say, but found she couldn't. It just wasn't fair that after everything they'd just said he could *still* affect her like this!

'Mistakes, even terrible mistakes, can be rectified. You proved this yourself when you came to tell me about the wonderful child we had made. If I made a similar terrible mistake eight years ago then you must, in all fairness, give me the opportunity to make it up to you.'

Grave words, reasonable words, words that pulsated with the promise of a different kind. 'I can do this for myself.' She tried to defer offering an answer.

'But when I do it you know there is more to the chore than a simple washing of hands.'

Oh, dear God, he was oh, so right. She closed her eyes and tried very hard to stop a sigh of pleasure from developing. But, as with everything else about this extraordinary man, whether it be with anger or hate or sensuality, he moved her so deeply she really did not stand a chance.

His mouth found the pulse just below her ear lobe and his thumbs gently circled her wet palms. She was lost and she knew it. On a helpless groan she turned to capture his ready mouth. It was, she supposed, already written that they would drown their problems in the long deep warmth of the kiss.

A telephone started ringing somewhere. No one answered it. Was there anyone else here? Melanie tried to ignore it, wanted to stay just where she was in this man's arms, with his kiss filling her up from the inside.

The telephone went on and on until, on a rasping sigh of impatience, he broke away, muttered a curse and an apology, then went to answer it. The nearest land-line extension was downstairs in the study. As he strode into that room Rafiq made a mental note to get some extra extensions put into the house.

He knew so little about its minor details, having only taken possession of it yesterday. He had wanted somewhere special to bring them while William's town house was being attended to. He had viewed many properties, but this house he had liked on sight—had seen Melanie and his son fitting into it with ease. The master bedroom up there had seemed the perfect place to take a bride on her wedding night. Though now he had pre-empted that idea by a few hours, he mused grimly, as he stretched across the big dark antique oak desk to lift up the telephone.

'This had better be good, Kadir,' he barked at the only person who knew this telephone number.

What Kadir had to say to him set him cursing. By the time he put down the phone he was different man. He strode up the stairs and back into the bedroom to find Melanie standing by the bed—waiting for him.

For a moment, a short sweet tantalising moment, he considered forgetting everything except what this beautiful woman and the bed were offering him. Then reality hit.

'Get dressed again,' he instructed grimly. 'We must leave immediately.

CHAPTER ELEVEN

'WHY—what's happened?' Melanie demanded. He could see from her eyes that she was already thinking of their son and conjuring up some terrible accident.

'No, not Robert.' He quickly squashed that anxiety, though the one threatening to strike at him was almost as bad. 'Kadir has just received a call from my father,' he explained.

'He's taken ill again?'

He gave a shake of his head. 'It is such a rare occurrence for my father to speak to anyone outside his family that on hearing his voice Kadir went to pieces and told him about you and Robert and our marriage today.'

'You mean, he didn't know?'

'No,' he answered. 'No one in my family knows,' he added as he walked towards the bathroom. 'Now my father is shocked and angry. We have to go to him.'

There was a strangled gasp he recognised as anger. 'What were you intending to do—keep Robbie and me a dark secret for the rest of our lives?'

He paused in his stride. 'I am not quite that ruthless,' he countered grimly. 'But our marriage and the fact that we have a seven-year-old son is something I preferred to tell my father to his face. It is—complicated.' That seemed to be the word to describe the situation.

Not for Melanie, it seemed. 'Explain complicated,' she commanded, following him as he moved on into the bathroom.

His mouth flattened. He did not want to say this! 'He knew about our relationship eight years ago and is therefore against you before he even sets his eyes on you.'

172

She did not say a word, but simply turned and walked away. In a mood that hung somewhere between fury and frustration, Rafiq closed the door, shrugged off his robe and stepped beneath the shower.

By the time they met up again Rafiq knew hostilities were back with a vengeance. They met on the landing. Melanie had clearly used another room to dress and was now wearing a suit from the selection he had bought for her. It was long and slinky, in a shade of rich moss-green that did wonderful things for her sparking eyes.

By the way she pursed her beautiful mouth as she ran her gaze over him he did not impress, he noted heavily. 'It is expected of me.' He felt compelled to defend the long white tunic, dark red top-robe and chequered *gut rah* which was covering his head.

It was only when she walked down the stairs without saying a word that he remembered another time she had seen him dressed like this: he had been throwing her out of his life. A silent curse rattled around inside him. Once again he considered leaving his father to wait while he seduced this woman of his into a sweeter temper.

But shocks were bad for his father's health. Rafiq would never forgive himself if the old sheikh took a turn for the worse while Rafiq was lost in the act of lovemaking.

As they stepped outside the car was waiting with its engine running. As soon as they were on their way he offered his mobile phone to Melanie. 'Ring your friend,' he said, 'and warn her that we are coming to collect Robert.'

Without comment she made the connection with Sophia's mobile phone. 'We have to go to Rahman,' she explained. 'Can you have Robbie ready to travel by the time we arrive to pick him up?'

Whatever her friend said to her, Melanie's expression was rueful. 'No. But you had better prepare him for a bit of a shock. His father has turned himself into an Arab, so if he knows beforehand he might not find himself looking at a total stranger.'

With that, she gave him back his phone.

'Was that necessary?' he asked.

She turned an icy stare on him. 'Yes,' she said.

He released a sigh. 'It was not my intention for this to happen.'

'Keep your excuses,' she told him. 'And just so that you know,' she added, 'I am coming with you only because I have made that decision. Your father deserves to meet his grandson. But let one person look upon him like a leper, Rafiq, just one—!'

'And you will do what?' he questioned curiously.

'I am relying on Rahman's reputation for being a free and equal society,' she said. 'If I don't like what we meet there then Robbie and I are coming home to England.'

'With or without me?'

'Without.'

He sighed and said nothing more. For what could he say other than to offer yet another apology? But he suspected it would not be enough for a woman looking at her ruined wedding day.

The rest of the journey was achieved in silence. The meeting with his son did not take place with shock but with awe. 'Will I have to dress like that?' Robbie asked dubiously.

'Not unless you want to,' Rafiq answered smoothly, while Sophia Elliot looked on in complete silence. No mocking tilt to a sleek black eyebrow, no glowering frown of disapproval.

They made their farewells and within the hour were boarding the Al-Qadim private jet to Rahman.

Within the next hour, his son was fast asleep in one of the cabins and Melanie was curled up on a soft cream leather sofa, clearly unimpressed by her luxury surroundings.

Rafiq decided that he had taken enough of her cold

shoulder. Picking her up as she was, he sat himself down and placed her on his lap, then lifted up a hand to remove his headgear and toss it aside. 'There—is that better?' Dark eyes mockingly quizzed her. 'Can you bring yourself to look at me now?'

What he didn't expect from his bit of sarcasm were the tears that filled her lovely eyes.

'You're ashamed of me,' she said.

'No,' he denied.

'If I had let you do it you would have brought Robbie with you and left me behind in London.'

'No.' He denied that too.

'You ruined my wedding day.'

'I will make it up to you.'

'You—'

It was no use carrying this conversation any further. So he kissed her. Why not? She needed kissing. So he kissed her until the tears went away. And kissed her some more until she slowly relaxed into a quiet slumber on his lap. He waved away the attendants when they walked down the cabin, and did not bother to move her to a bed because...he liked to have her just where she was.

Which meant...what? he asked himself as the air miles flew by them.

Hell, he knew what it meant. He had known it for a long time. A week—eight years—it mattered little how long he had known it.

They came in to land at dawn, circling around the perimeter of a great modern city which glinted in the early-morning sun. From the jet they transferred to a small Cessna, drawing curious glances from dark-eyed Arabs as they moved from plane to plane.

Rafiq flew them himself, leaving Melanie and Robbie to drink in the dramatic landscape panning out beneath them, with its silver thread of a river winding through a lush valley surrounded by high, lurking dunes and miles of sand. It took only twenty minutes before they were landing again. A four-wheel drive waited to receive them. Rafiq placed himself behind the wheel of this, and began driving them over tarmac towards a sandstone fortress backed by the fertile oasis of Al-Qadim.

Melanie knew all of this because Robbie had maintained a running commentary throughout both the short flight and this short drive towards his father's home. The child's grasp of this part of his heritage was so intense that even Rafiq allowed himself a couple of grimaces as he listened to him. But other than grimaces he offered nothing; his expression was sombre, the harsh lines of his profile telling her that he was lost in grim places of his own.

A pair of thick wooden gates swung inwards as they approached them, then closed behind them as they passed through into a beautiful courtyard laid with tropical plants and sparkling fountains. They came to a stop in front of a rich blue dome suspended on sandstone pillars. Rafiq got out of the car and strode round to the other side to open the other door. In silence he offered Melanie his hand to assist her to alight. Robbie scrambled out of his own accord, then stood gazing about him with dark eyes that greedily drank in every detail they could.

Then his father was quietly calling him to heel, and the small boy came with his dark head still twisting in frowning curiosity. 'Are we going to live here now?' he asked.

'No, we will continue to live in London,' his father assured him. 'And come here to visit during the school holidays, if you like.'

Nodding his head in approval, Robbie cleared the small frown from his brow, and walked happily beside his father into a vast entrance hall with a beautiful lapis-blue and white domed ceiling and pale sand marble covering the floor.

The first person Melanie saw was Sheikh Hassan Al-Qadim, and her heart slithered to her stomach. Dressed like Rafiq, he was standing straight and still beside a beautiful creature with dark red hair and perfect porcelain skin.

She was quite heavily pregnant beneath the slender white tunic she was wearing.

Both of them fixed their eyes on Robbie. Both looked shocked, if not dismayed. Melanie's fingers twitched within Rafiq's. He glanced down at her and she glanced upwards, the anxiety in her eyes making his grim mouth flatten as he looked away again.

Sheikh Hassan was looking at her now. One glimpse at his expression and Melanie knew what he was going to say. Her heart leapt from her stomach to lodge in her throat. He took a step towards her. 'Miss Leggett,' he murmured deeply, 'I must beg—'

'Mrs Portreath,' she corrected, leaping on anything just to silence him. His dark eyes narrowed and sharpened. With a minuscule shake of her head she tried to relay a message to him.

'Al-Qadim,' Rafiq corrected both of them. 'We married yesterday as you no doubt know by now, Hassan.'

'Of course. Rafiq, if you had only explained why you wanted me to be in London I would have been there. You know that.' Sheikh Hassan begged his understanding, taking the diversion Rafiq had unwittingly offered to him.

But Melanie could see he was not happy about remaining silent over their last meeting. As the two brothers greeted with an embrace and words spoken in Arabic those dark eyes so like Rafiq's remained fixed upon her over his brother's shoulder. She looked away, found herself gazing at the other woman, who had witnessed the exchange and was now looking very concerned.

She stepped forward with a smile, though. 'Welcome to our family,' she greeted warmly, and surprised Melanie by brushing a kiss to each of her cheeks. 'My name is Leona and I am married to Rafiq's brother,' she explained. 'Our child is due in two months—just in case you did not like to ask me. And this...' she turned to smile at Robbie '...has to be the most handsome Al-Qadim of the three.'

It was all very light, very eager to please, but Melanie

could sense the other woman's tension and she could see it repeated in Sheikh Hassan. She could feel it pulsing in Rafiq. When she added her own tension into it all the vast hall almost sparked with it.

'My name is Robert Portreath,' Robbie corrected with a faintly puzzled frown. The business of names was going to take some explaining later, Melanie realised as she watched Leona Al-Qadim dip down to his level to offer Robbie her hand.

'Then, I am very pleased to meet you, Robert Portreath,' she said gravely.

'You're English?' he said.

'Like your mother.' She nodded.

'You have very pretty hair and eyes.'

'And that,' Leona murmured sagely as she straightened, 'is most definitely the Al-Qadim charm. Hello, Rafiq,' she added gently.

'My lady,' he returned with a sweeping bow that held Melanie transfixed in surprise—until she realised she was seeing some kind of in-joke being enacted here, because both pairs of eyes were warm with amusement.

Then Rafiq was introducing his son to Sheikh Hassan, who bent to shake Robbie's hand very formally. When he straightened his eyes made that fleeting contact with Melanie's again.

It was Robbie who broke this next moment of tension. 'Where is my new grandfather?' he wanted to know.

All pleasure—forced or otherwise—instantly dropped away from everyone. Rafiq looked to his brother; his brother gave a reply. 'He is in his rooms,' his said quietly. 'He knows you have arrived.'

'Is he still ill?'

'Ah,' Hassan grimaced. 'His health is just fine; it is his temper that is threatening to fail him.'

It was automatic for Melanie to reach for Robbie, protecting her son being her paramount need. Rafiq noted the gesture and his expression hardened. 'You used to be famed for your diplomacy, Hassan,' he drawled.

'My apologies.' Hassan offered Melanie the kind of half-bow she was used to receiving from him. 'I was referring to our father's impatience at us keeping him waiting.'

It was a slick recovery, but a lie nonetheless. Rafiq saw Melanie's giveaway expression, went to claim Robbie's hand, then slipped his other hand back around her waist. She looked up at him, eyes anxiously searching his for reassurance.

He tried to give it with a small smile. But with his brother and Leona watching them Melanie knew there was little more he could do. They began to walk down a wide corridor between pale blue walls on sand-coloured floors. No one spoke. Even Robbie had picked up on the tension and was quiet.

They entered a room that might have been William's study in a lot of ways, though it was bigger and lighter and many degrees warmer. In the middle of the room, reclining on a divan, lay an old man whose fragile state tugged at Melanie's heart. That he was seriously ill was obvious; that he was resigned to that illness was written in his face. He lifted himself as they came towards him, though, sliding his thin body up a high bank of pillows and fixing his eyes on Robbie.

Rafiq went down on one knee to embrace his father. The old man's fingers held Rafiq's face as they spoke in low and husky Arabic. What bowled Melanie over most was the wave of love she could feel coming from the two men. It filled the room, tripped her heartbeat, while she waited for them to remember she and Robbie were here. Then Rafiq was turning and beckoning to Robbie. Tears glazed her eyes as she watched her brave son step into the curve of his father's arm.

An arm settled across her own shoulders. It belonged to Leona Al-Qadim.

'This is your grandfather, Robert,' Rafiq was explaining.

'Does he speak English?' the boy whispered.

'Yes,' the old sheikh answered for himself. 'I speak many languages. Come…will you take my hand?'

It was an old hand, a gnarled hand. Robbie placed his own hand into it without hesitation and allowed himself to be drawn towards the divan. As he did so he slipped free from Rafiq's comforting arm and, without needing any prompting, began to talk.

It was his way. Melanie knew that; Rafiq had come to know it. 'William said that you've been sick. Are you doing to die like William? I like your room; it's nice. Can you play chess? William played chess with me. Have you read *all* of these books?'

The old sheikh answered each separate question. He fell in love as they all watched. As the questions flowed so did Robbie's small figure flow into a sitting position on the divan, then he curled until he was almost on the old sheikh's lap. He was used to old men; he had grown up with one of the very best. To her son there was no fear in age and wrinkles. Melanie had always been aware that Robbie missed William, but she had not realised just how much until she saw how naturally he had drawn close to his grandfather.

Tears blanked out the old man's image. Rafiq was standing straight and still. Leona's fingers smoothed one of her shoulders, and somewhere behind her she was aware of Sheikh Hassan's silent observation.

'You have a beautiful son, Melanie,' Leona said softly.

The sound of her voice broke the loaded atmosphere. The old sheikh lifted his eyes and looked directly at her. 'You denied us all.'

It was a quiet and level accusation, designed to make its point without alarming her son. Rafiq stiffened his body. Melanie didn't know what to say. The sheikh was right: she had denied them. The guilt of that was going to live with her for a long time.

'She did not,' a sober voice inserted. 'I am afraid it is I who must take the blame for that.'

Rafiq turned to stare at his brother. Leona's fingers pressed gently into Melanie's arm.

'I'm going to take Melanie away now,' she informed all of them. 'Robert, would you like to come?'

It was not the voice of choice; little boys recognised these things. He scrambled down from his grandfather's divan and obediently walked with the women from the room.

'Don't shake so,' Leona murmured softly. 'My father-in-law is a good man. He just doesn't know the truth.'

'Neither does Rafiq,' Melanie said. 'I didn't want him to.'

'It is the way with these Al-Qadim men that they do not live well with itchy consciences. Hassan was honour-bound to tell Rafiq what he had done eight years ago from the moment he recognised your name.'

Leona led them up a wide staircase lined with pale cedar doors set into deep stone arches. It was a beautiful suite of rooms, wide, light and airy, in the coolest shades of pale aquamarine and ivory, with fretwork doors flung open to a balcony and the soft morning breeze.

A tiny dark-haired creature appeared from an adjoining room. She smiled at Robbie and held out her hand to him. 'Would you like to come and explore?' she invited.

Robbie looked at his mother; his mother looked at Leona Al-Qadim. 'This is Nina,' she explained. 'She is a trained nanny. Robert, if you want to go with Nina, I promise you will have great fun.'

The boy went without any more encouragement. As he walked away Melanie could hear him throwing out questions again. 'Are there camels here? Will I be able to touch one? Has my daddy got one I can see?'

'His daddy must be very proud of him,' Leona said gently.

'He didn't mention him to any of you,' Melanie pointed

out, and walked over to the open windows to gaze out on the kind of view she'd only expected to see on the television screen.

'Rafiq is an—unusual man,' Leona answered. 'He is a brilliant mathematician, incredibly loyal to the few people he loves, but he is a law unto himself and always has been. And his private life is generally sacrosanct.'

'Serena Cordero didn't think so.'

'Ah, Serena Cordero should be eternally grateful to you that you came along when you did.' Leona smiled. 'From what I can glean out of Hassan, Rafiq cancelled the rolling cheque that supported her dance tour, and which she was so fond of; then a few days ago he reinstated it. Said bitterness warped the mind, or some such clever phrase. We suspect this change of heart happened because you were busy turning him inside out. Though you will have to ask the big man himself, because he won't tell us anything.'

'So you speculate.'

'Yes.' Leona admitted it. 'We feel we have to. We worry about him, you see.' She released a sigh. 'I know you might laugh at this, but beneath that big tough exterior Rafiq is vulnerable to hurt.'

But Melanie didn't laugh. She shifted restlessly.

'You would have to know about the circumstances of his birth to understand this, his childhood living here in this palace as very much the resented second son of the old sheikh,' Leona continued, unaware that she was confiding in one who already knew these things. 'He is proud—too proud sometimes—and wary about letting anyone get too close to him. But from what Hassan has told me he took one look at you eight years ago and fell in love so totally that when you—'

'Accuse me of betrayal and I will walk right out of here,' Melanie cut in.

'Take note of that,' another deeper voice advised. They turned together to find Rafiq standing in the open door. There was a smile on his lips but his eyes were narrowed, and though he was attempting to look at ease Melanie could sense the tension in him, the anger that they were standing here talking about him like this.

'You're cross,' Leona murmured. She knew him well, Melanie noted. 'I was only trying to help Melanie to understand why we—'

'Then let me help you to understand,' Rafiq smoothly cut in. 'My wife did not betray anyone. But your husband may require your help to convince him that he did not do something very similar.'

'You've upset him.' Leona sighed.

'I forgave him,' Rafiq returned.

'Well, that only makes it worse!' she cried. 'You know what he's like; he will prowl around now, seething with frustration!'

Rafiq offered her one of those bows. 'Then may I suggest to my lady that she goes and joins him as he prowls?'

He was dismissing her, even holding the door open at the ready. Melanie decided she did not understand these people as she watched Leona Al-Qadim stroll up to Rafiq, smile and kiss him on the cheek before she left the room.

'That wasn't very nice of you,' she remarked as he closed the door.

'Leona is beautiful, charming and an absolute delight to be around, but she knows I dislike people meddling with my life.' With that the red-chequered *gut rah* was dragged from his head and tossed aside. 'As for you...' He strode forward, sending her spine erect and at the ready. 'You lied to me.'

'I did not lie!' she denied.

'By omission you did.'

'If your brother had kept silent there would have been no reason for you to know!'

'That you came looking for me while heavily pregnant with my son? That you took the risk of yet more cruel rejection because you cared enough to try again? That you had to sit there listening to him scare you with the kind of scenario that would make any mother's blood go cold?'

'He loves you. He was protecting you. I understand that now.'

'You understand nothing,' he denounced. 'I asked him to check if you were all right. I trusted him to do that small thing for me!'

'I was all right.'

'Well, I wasn't!' he rasped. 'I was out there—' he flung a hand out towards the sand-dunes she could see rising above miles of lush fruit groves '—pining for you!'

Pining? Melanie blinked. He spun his back to her on a tight hiss of a sigh. 'When Hassan told me you wanted to see me I did not dare go to London in case I fell at your feet,' he went on. 'But I needed to know that you were okay. I *hoped* that by some miracle you were going to tell him some magical reason that would make everything okay. I sat out there...' the hand flicked again '...waiting like a fool for the call that would send me to London on the next plane. What I got was a call telling me he couldn't find you but he had heard that you were living with a man.'

'I'm sorry,' Melanie murmured. 'I didn't—'

'Don't touch me,' he grated.

For a moment she froze in dismay. Then with a sigh she did the opposite, and walked around in front of him so she could wrap him in her arms. His heart was pounding, the great chest trembling as he fought a battle with himself.

He had lost, she thought. He had lost the battle. His arms came around her. 'I don't know what I am supposed to say to you, Melanie,' he muttered. 'You make me realise what a fool I was eight years ago. You make me face the high price I paid for my own pompous pride. You make me see that I have been treating you without honour from the moment I met you, and have done it all from a superior stance that deserves nothing but your contempt.'

'I don't hold you in contempt,' she denied.

'Then you should.'

'Because you believed what you were carefully primed to see?'

'Your uncle said some wicked things about you that day,' he said heavily. 'He poured out his poison and I, like a fool, drank it down, when any other fool would have known you were not the person he was describing to me.'

'If it had been you in that window with another woman and your brother pouring poison into me, I would have believed,' she admitted.

'Hassan did poison you.'

'He frightened me off for your sake. And he did it out of love, not avarice. There is a difference.'

'A forgivable difference?'

'You forgave him,' she pointed out.

'I forgave *him*,' he agreed. But not himself, Melanie defined from his tone. 'Tell me what you want from this marriage, Melanie,' he demanded. 'Tell me what the hell I can do to put some of this right for you.'

Lifting her chin, she looked up at him, saw glinting black eyes and harshly etched angles burnished bronze by the morning sun. 'I would like you to make love to me without thinking that you only do it because you feel utterly compelled to,' she told him softly. 'I would like to lie in your arms afterwards and know that you really want me there. I would like to look into your eyes and see tenderness sometimes, not just anger or passion.'

'You want me to love you.' He smiled oddly.

'I want you to *care*,' she amended.

'Take the love,' he advised. 'For it has always been there.' He grimaced, then released a long sigh and framed her face with his hands. 'Eight years ago I fell in love with the scent of your skin as you leant over my shoulder. I fell in love with the heat that coloured your lovely cheeks whenever I caught you looking at me. I wanted every part of you, every minute of your time, every kiss, every smile…' He kissed her. It was so tender it brought tears to her eyes. 'If you want my heart on a platter, Melanie, you can have it,' he offered huskily. 'I could not forget you—did not want to forget you. It was a lonely—lonely state of mind.'

There was nothing she could find to say in answer to that. Instinct—only instinct could respond. Her arms lifted to his shoulders and she pressed her mouth to the warm brown skin at his throat. 'I love you, Rafiq,' she softly confided. 'But you have to believe it if this marriage is going to stand a chance.'

'I believe,' he murmured. 'How can I not believe when you are still here in my arms after everything I have put you through?'

But he didn't sound happy. On a small sigh she lifted her eyes and parted her lips to speak again—only he stopped her. 'No,' he denied. 'Don't say any more. It tears me apart when we talk about those things we cannot alter. Just answer me one last question. Can we put the past behind us and start again?'

'Of course we can.' She smiled at him.

The smile turned his heart over. The shine in her eyes warmed him right through. Lifting her up against him, he caught her mouth with his and refused to let it go as he walked with her across pale blue marble and through a door on the other side of the room. The door closed behind them; he released her mouth only long enough to lock it.

'What about Robbie?' the mother in her questioned. 'He might come looking for us.'

He was already carrying her across to a huge divan bed that stood on a raised dais. 'Not while he has my father waiting to pore over maps of Rahman with him,' Rafiq lazily replied. 'And this is the beginning of our honeymoon.'

'I quite liked the Gothic setting,' Melanie said as he laid her down on a sea of dark red satin.

'Next time,' he promised.

'Why? How many honeymoons are we going to have?'

'A lifetime of them.'

He wasn't joking. Two months later they were back in England, locked away inside their Gothic mansion. Melanie was lazing in the bath when Rafiq strode into the room and announced, 'Hassan and Leona are the proud parents of a baby boy. Both mother and child are very well.'

'Oh, do you think we should fly back?' Melanie suggested anxiously. 'It seems wrong for you and I to be enjoying ourselves here when we might be needed there.'

'No,' Rafiq replied adamantly. 'Our son is with his new best friend—my father, Hassan and Leona are in twelfth heaven with their own son, and you and I, my darling, are on our second honeymoon here while Ethan Hayes and his crazy wife make William's house fit to live in.'

'You really should have told me about that,' Melanie chided as he strode towards the tub. 'I had a right to be consulted before you dared to touch anything in my house.'

'But the house does not belong to you,' Rafiq informed her as he removed his clothes. 'William left it to our son—though you saw fit not to tell me that. So I asked Robert's permission to renovate. He was delighted to give it. Unlike you,' he mocked her, 'our son had the good sense to know the house was in danger of falling down.'

'It wasn't that bad!' Melanie protested. 'And I thought Robbie loved it exactly as it was!'

'No, he has better taste—as I do,' he added arrogantly, referring to his good taste in wives.

With that, he stepped into the tub and slid himself into the water at the opposite end from Melanie. A hand reached up to pull a cord, which drew the purple silk curtain around them.

Candlelight flickered from hidden places. Silhouettes moved and came together...

BELOVED SHEIKH

by
Alexandra Sellers

Alexandra Sellers is the author of over thirty novels and a feline language text published in 1997 and still selling. Born and raised in Canada, Alexandra first came to London as a drama student. Now she lives near Hampstead Heath with her husband, Nick. They share housekeeping with Monsieur, who jumped through the window one day and announced, as cats do, that he was moving in. What she would miss most on a desert island is shared laughter. Readers can write to Alexandra at PO Box 9449, London NW3 2WH, UK.

This book is dedicated to my niece Jessica
Sellers Stones, the rarest of creatures – a poet

Rafi's Inheritance
The Sword of Rostam

---

*To Prince Rafi's lot fell the Kingdom of East Bar-
akat, a land of richly varied landscape, extending
from marshlands at the seacoast, through the broad
desert with its ancient remnants of civilisations long
dead, to the broad flowing river called Happiness,
and into the mountains, where his palace lay.*

*To him also was given the great Sword of Rostam.
This fabulously jewelled and inscribed sword had,
according to the ancient story, once been the battle
sword of the great hero Rostam. Since that time, any
King of Barakat who drew the sword in anger signalled to his people and to the enemy against whom
he drew it that there should be no respite from battle
until one or the other was vanquished. Once the*

Sword of Rostam was drawn, negotiation was no longer possible.

Therefore a king must be very certain of his ground before drawing the Sword of Rostam.

There was once a king of ancient and noble lineage who ruled over a land that had been blessed by God. This land, Barakat, lying on the route of one of the old Silk Roads, had for centuries received the cultural influences of many different worlds. Its geography, too, was diverse: it bordered the sea; then the desert, sometimes bleak with its ancient ruins, sometimes golden and studded with oases, stretched inland for many miles, before meeting the foothills of snow-capped mountains that captured the rain clouds and forced them to deliver their burden in the rich valleys. It was a land of magic and plenty and a rich and diverse heritage.

But it was also a land of tribal rivalries and not infrequent skirmishes. Because the king had the ancient blood of the Quraishi kings in his veins, no one challenged his right to the throne, but many of the tribal chieftains whom he ruled were in constant jealousy over their lands and rights against the others.

One day, the king of this land fell in love with a foreign woman. Promising her that he would never take another wife, he married her and made her his queen. This beloved wife gave him two handsome sons. The king loved them as his own right hand. Crown Prince Zaid and his brother were all that he could wish for in his sons—handsome, noble, brave warriors, and popular with his people. As they attained the age of majority, the sheikh could look forward to his own death without fear for his country, for if anything should happen to the Crown Prince, his brother Aziz would step into his shoes and be equally popular with the people and equally strong among the tribes.

Then one day, tragedy struck the sheikh and his wife.

Both their sons were killed in the same accident. Now his own death became the great enemy to the old man, for with it, he knew, would come certain civil war as the tribal chieftains vied for supremacy.

His beloved wife understood all his fears, but she was by now too old to hope to give him another heir. One day, when all the rituals of mourning were complete, the queen said to her husband, ''According to the law, you are entitled to four wives. Take, therefore, my husband, three new wives, that God may bless one of them with a son to inherit your throne.''

The sheikh thanked her for releasing him from his promise. A few weeks later, on the same day so that none should afterwards claim supremacy, the sheikh married three beautiful young women, and that night, virile even in his old age, he visited each wife in turn, no one save himself knowing in which order he visited them. To each wife he promised that if she gave him a son, her son would inherit the throne of Barakat.

The sheikh was more virile than he knew. Each of his new wives conceived, and gave birth, nine months later, to a lusty son. And each was jealous for her own son's inheritance. From that moment the sheikh's life became a burden to him, for each of his new young wives had different reasons for believing that her own son should be named the rightful heir to the throne.

The Princess Goldar, whose exotically hooded green eyes she had bequeathed to her son, Omar, based her claim on the fact that she herself was a descendant of the ancient royal family of her own homeland, Parvan.

The Princess Nargis, mother of Rafi and descended from the old Mughal emperors of India, had in addition given birth two days before the other two wives, thus making her son the firstborn.

The Princess Noor, mother of Karim, claimed the inheritance for her son by right of blood—she alone of the wives was an Arab of noble descent, like the sheikh himself. Who but her son to rule the desert tribesmen?

The sheikh hoped that his sons would solve his dilemma for him, that one would prove more princely than the others. But as they grew to manhood, he saw that each of them was, in his own way, worthy of the throne, that each had the nobility the people would look for in their king, and talents that would benefit the kingdom were he to rule.

When his sons were eighteen years old, the sheikh knew that he was facing death. As he lay dying, he saw each of his young wives in turn. To each of them again he promised that her son would inherit. Then he saw his three sons together, and on them he laid his last command. Then, last of all, he saw the wife and companion of his life, with whom he had seen such happiness and such sorrow. To her willing care he committed his young wives and their sons, with the assistance of his vizier Nizam al Mulk, whom he appointed Regent jointly with her.

When he died the old sheikh's will was revealed: the kingdom was to be divided into three principalities. Each of his sons inherited one principality and its palace. In addition, they each inherited one of the ancient Signs of Kingship.

It was the will of their father that they should consult the Grand Vizier Nizam al Mulk for as long as he lived, and appoint another mutual Grand Vizier upon his death, so that none would have partisan advice in the last resort.

Their father's last command had been this: that his sons should never take up arms against each other or any of their descendants, and that his sons and their descendants should always come to each other's aid in times of trouble. The sheikh's dying curse would be upon the head of any who violated this command, and upon his descendants for seven generations.

So the three princes grew to maturity under the eye of the old queen and the vizier, who did their best to prepare the princes for the future. When they reached the age of *twenty-five, they came into their inheritance. Then each prince took his own Sign of Kingship and departed to his own palace and his own kingdom, where they lived in peace and accord with one another, as their father had commanded.*

One

A horseman, his companions lined on either side, his black charger beneath him, galloped across the desert under the morning sun, while the wind scorched his face and lungs, and his horse's tail streamed out behind. His companions, in high spirits with the impromptu race, laughed and called, their voices ringing on the air as they urged their mounts on.

Some distance ahead of them, beyond a harsh rocky outcrop enclosing a few date palms, stood the fallen white stone pillars of an ancient ruin, encircled by the low green roofs of tents. But it was not towards this settlement that they headed. The goal of the race was the rocky outcrop and its sparkling waterfall and pools. The rider on the black broke from the rank with a cry, surged ahead of the others and passed through a narrow defile in the rock walls, one arm and his horse's tail high in the air to signal his triumph.

His companions followed closely, but the gap was torturous and some were obliged to check their mounts as others passed in. Three who were hot behind were in time to see their leader halt his snorting mount abruptly and give a smothered cry. Then they, too, pulled up in amazement.

To see a woman in the desert is not entirely unexpected, of course. To see a half-naked, perfectly formed beauty of delicate stature standing under the waterfall of their favourite resting place, her curling black hair streaming down around her shoulders and back as she raised her face and arms to the cool torrent, was like something out of the ancient tales.

Still unconscious of their presence, for no doubt the sound of their hooves had been smothered by the thunder of water in her ears, the girl lazily moved out of the stream of water, opened her eyes, and saw them. Her eyes and mouth opened wide for a moment of startled stillness as she stared at the dark, handsome horsemen all around her.

There was silence. Then the girl stepped a little away from the waterfall on the rock ledge and said gravely, *"Salaam aleikum."*

Her accent was foreign, and so was her cool, haughty dignity, the faint air of challenge. The leader gazed speechlessly. She was lovely as a gazelle, the water drying on her skin as he watched, leaving it soft and glowing, her mouth the perfect bow of the ancient paintings that adorned his palace, her wet hair a wild mane of curls that the paintings also showed. Her breasts were high and rounded, her hips slim but very female. Her bathing suit was a soft colour that matched her lightly browned skin. Her legs were slender and curved, her bare feet sure on the smooth wet rock.

His brain stupidly told him that she was one of the Peri of the old tales. In a moment she would disappear.

Around him his men flicked him glances and waited for their lord to speak. Her dark eyes, too, were upon him. Her eyes had been drawn to him from the first, and she seemed to realize that he was their leader.

He gazed steadily at her. When the silence stretched too long he saw alarm kindle behind her gaze, and then, still speechless, he saw decision there and watched aghast as she turned and agilely began to climb the dangerous rock face beside the falling water. It was not a long way up to that other small pool above. In a moment, just as in the tales of Peris, she had indeed disappeared.

Around him, his men began to talk and exclaim. The leader shook himself as if from a dream. He realized that, from the moment of their entering the place, no more than a minute or two had passed. In so short a space of time, his world had changed.

"What the heck is happening out there?" Gordon asked. Most of the team were already sitting around the long lunch table by the time he arrived, stepping under the long green canvas roof with relief and pulling off the hat that was an absolute necessity for anyone working under the blazing sun.

"Haven't you heard?" squealed Lena, delighted to have someone to pass the news on to, since she herself had been one of the last to hear. "That's the tent of the sultan himself going up."

Gordon blinked, but whether it was from his eyes' difficulty in acclimatizing to the shadow or from astonishment was impossible to say.

"We've all been invited to dinner tonight, the whole team," Ryan, the site director, informed him. "Those are his minions out there preparing for the feast."

Gordon strode to the edge of the canvas shelter and gazed out over the desert to where the circular red-and-blue tent was going up. "It looks the size of a football stadium," he observed mildly. "How many of us does he think there are?"

Gordon was English and it was a point of honour with him never to show excitement. Zara had seen the facade crack only once—when the first clear evidence was found that they really were at the site of ancient Iskandiyar, that all his educated guesswork had paid off at last. This would be the crown of his long career as an archaeologist. They had all stood around cheering and jumping for joy then, and Gordon had joined in. No mere feast laid on by the Prince of East Barakat would evoke such a response in him, though.

"He asked for exact numbers," Zara said now, "but who knows how many of his own court will be in attendance?"

Someone said, "What's the point of it all? Why is he doing it?"

"To welcome us to his country, according to his messenger."

"We've been in his country for three months."

"The wheels of princes grind slowly."

"I suppose it's possible that someone finally gave him the message I sent telling him that we had found the gates that confirm that this is ancient Iskandiyar," said Gordon. "Maybe he figures it's time to check up on us in case we're about to find treasure."

"He's as rich as a sheikh already," said Warren.

"He *is* a sheikh," Lena pointed out in her scratchy, breathless voice. "He's not married, either," she went on. She was completely unaware of the non sequitur, and when the shout of laughter went up she looked around.

"Why are you all laughing? He really isn't, I heard it on the radio. Don't you remember when that woman was kidnapped by the sheikh of West Barakat awhile ago when that guy stole something from him?" Of course they all remembered, they had talked of nothing else for days. "Then she ended up engaged to him. They said then that his two brothers weren't married."

Lena sighed, making them all laugh again. She blinked at the grinning faces around her and shrugged good-humouredly. "All right, what did I say this time?"

"Nothing, Lena, it's just that you're so obviously hoping that this one will kidnap *you,*" Zara told her kindly.

"Oh, am I that obvious? Well, a girl can dream, can't she?"

Zara shuddered involuntarily. She still hadn't told the others about her experience at the wadi. Partly because she knew she would get blamed: they had all been warned that there were bandits in the desert and they should never venture off the dig unaccompanied. But there was more to her reluctance to talk about the incident than that.

She had felt so exposed when the bandit chief—she supposed he must have been that—had stared at her. It was as if her whole being had stopped for a moment while he had entered like a conqueror and taken possession. Even now she wasn't sure what had given her the strength to break out of the prison of his gaze and climb the rock face. Or why he had let her escape.

She had been terrified that when she got to the other side of the outcrop he and his men would be waiting there, and when he was not she had run, slipping and gasping, sobbing with exertion, all the way to the camp, not looking back, but with every cell of her body listening for the sound of hooves.

She knew that Lena was a fool to fantasize about being kidnapped—it must be a dreadful, hellish experience, and if that *had* been the bandit's impulse she was glad he hadn't acted on it. And yet there was a part of her that was sorry to think she would never see him again...sorry that...

"Listen, that reminds me," she said now, still unwilling, but knowing it had to be confessed. "I think I ran into that bandit and his men."

That got their attention. Some of them choked on their coffee, and everyone's eyes were on her. "Where?" two or three demanded at once.

"I went to the wadi early a couple of days ago," she said softly.

"By yourself?" said Gordon. "Zara, that was very unwise."

"Yes, well, I won't do it again. They galloped in while I was standing under the waterfall. I didn't hear a thing. I opened my eyes and there they all were, on horseback, snorting and stamping.''

"The bandits were snorting and stamping?''

They laughed lightly, but this was serious and no one was pretending it wasn't. "Did they see you? How did you get away?''

Zara swallowed. She was not sure why she was so reluctant to tell them the details. "I went up over the rocks and ran like hell.''

"If they'd seen you they could have caught up with you, on horseback,'' someone said. "They must not have seen you.''

Zara said nothing, got up and wandered over to the fridge to get a cold drink, then leaned against it, drinking and staring out over the site, leaving the rest of the team to talk over this latest development.

She was amazingly lucky to be on this dig, which was now certain to make archaeological history. The fourth- and third-century B.C. city called Iskandiyar had been mentioned by several classical authors. Its whereabouts had puzzled modern archaeologists, though, because it was described as being on the banks of the river which now bore the name Sa'adat, Happiness. For more than a century travellers had searched in vain for some sign of it. Such an important city should have left extensive ruins.

Some had even suggested that the classical writers were confused, or inaccurate...but Gordon had never doubted them. Gordon had researched Iskandiyar throughout his career, and one day had stumbled on a much later reference to the fact that, "in her lifetime Queen Halimah of Barakat built bridges and tunnels and many public buildings. She changed the course of rivers, even the mighty River Sa'adat, when it suited her...''

That was the clue he needed. If the course of the river had been changed eighteen hundred years after the city had been built, then it followed that the city's ruins would no longer be on the banks of the river.

By good luck and good timing, Zara was taking Gordon's classes during the time that he found a possible site in the desert south of the river, and by even better chance she had graduated by the time his funding was in place. And best of all, he had offered her a place on the team.

Until they had uncovered the massive marble lion from the sands of time, there could be certainty only in their hearts. But the classical authors had described Iskandiyar's "Lion Gates," and now it was proven almost beyond doubt. This was a city founded by Alexander the Great on his victorious Eastern march more than two thousand, three hundred years ago. Not long after his conquest here, he would weep because there were no more worlds to conquer.

And now here she was, finding history and making it at the same time. Zara gazed out at the white pillars that shone so harshly in the fierce sun. She wondered sometimes about Alexander's tears on that occasion. Had there been a hollow inside him that he could ignore as long as he kept on the move, kept fighting, kept conquering all he met and saw? Was it a lack in his own life rather than the lack of new worlds that had made him weep?

Zara wasn't thirty-three, the age by which Alexander had conquered the then known world, and although to be associated with such exciting success was a wonderful piece of luck for someone so young, she still had plenty of worlds left to conquer. But sometimes she had the urge to weep, because in unguarded moments her life seemed empty. She didn't understand why. It was as if she had a voice inside telling her she had missed something, had left something out, as though there was something else she should have done or be doing.

She loved her work. She had always loved history, right from the moment she had understood what history was. She enjoyed the mental exercise of trying to understand old ways, the things that had motivated cultures long disappeared. As a child she had been taken on a class field trip to a new archaeological dig on a site in downtown Toronto, and she could still remember her thrilled amazement when she realized that history could be touched, smelt, dug up out of the ground. From that moment she had known what she wanted to do with her life.

Nothing at all stood in her way. She got the marks, she was accepted at the University of Toronto, and Gordon had recognized her commitment and taken her under his wing, as he had several promising students before her, who now had reputations of their own in the field. She couldn't have asked for a better start to her professional career than to work under a man of Gordon's calibre on a find of such importance.

Her personal life was comfortable. She had had an easy, fairly happy childhood, and had come through the teenage years with only a couple of years of tears and slamming doors and impossible parents before things had righted themselves. Zara dated only casually, and kept things light. Of course one day she hoped to fall in love, but she was in no hurry.

And yet…like Alexander, she wanted to weep.

Why? What was missing from her life? What did she want?

For no reason at all, she was suddenly remembering the piercing eyes of the bandit chief as he stared at her on that morning a few days before. There had been another world in his eyes, a world far from her own neat, comfortable existence. That dark, hungry gaze had promised her a passion, a way of living she had never even dreamed of…till now.

For a moment she thought of what it would have meant if he had come after her…swung her up on his horse and ridden away with her. They said he might try to take a hostage, but he had not looked at her like a man who sees a potential hostage. Zara shivered at the memory of how he had looked at her.

She had run harder, faster than she had ever run in her life to escape him. Her heart had never beaten so hard. She closed her eyes, shutting out the glare of the sun on the desert, but the bandit's eyes were still with her.

Two

The preparations at the sheikh's tent went on all afternoon. Helicopters flew in, disgorging lines of people carrying food and supplies, and took them away again; men came and went in Jeeps and on horseback. Except for a moment when it seemed as if the half-erected tent would blow away in a sudden breeze, no shouting was heard, there was no running. Everything was done with an orderly calm and neatness that, as Lena said, made the archaeological team feel "sort of like a low-budget film."

One thing the women were all agreed upon, and that was the necessity of dressing in their best for the feast. By common consent everyone downed tools early to take time to prepare. One of the volunteers produced an iron and asked if she could plug it into the generator lead. The other women fell on this with cries of delight.

"How wonderful! Whatever made you think of it, Jess?"

"I didn't. My mom packed for me. I told her I'd never use it, but she insisted."

"I kiss your mother. Please thank her from all of us in your next letter!"

"I don't have an ironing board, though."

"A towel! All we need is a towel on one of the tables…"

The men went away scratching their heads.

There were lineups for the shower and for the iron, and a lot of excited repartee as people dashed to and fro. Fortunately nearly everyone had something suitable to wear, since everyone had expected to be sampling the city nightlife of the Barakat Emirates some time or other during their stay. But some—the lucky ones—had what Gordon called "the full monty." Including Gordon himself, who stunned everyone when he appeared just before time in white tie and tails and polished shoes.

"Can't let the side down," he said by way of explanation when the others fell back in amazement at this vision of British Establishment eccentricity.

"Gee, Gordon," Lena said in stunned tones, "it's just like one of those films—you wearing all that in the desert and all."

Blonde Lena herself got the prize for feminine magnificence in a low-cut, blush pink dress under a matching gauzy pink georgette coat embroidered in the Eastern fashion with lots of silver thread.

But it was Zara who really stopped them in their tracks. Small and slender, wearing a beautifully simple, high-necked, long-sleeved white dress in heavy raw silk that hung straight and smooth to her bare brown feet in delicate gold sandals, her curling cloak of hair spilling over her shoulders and down her back, one gold bangle at her wrist, she was a vision. Lena eyed her with mock dismay.

"I dunno, you kinda make me feel overdone," she observed plaintively. But a chorus of voices assured her that many men preferred the obvious, and large numbers of those who did were Oriental potentates.

"And me," said one male voice. Greg moved to her side and mock-ferociously put an arm around her, leering down into her cleavage. "Any Oriental potentate is going to have to get past me first."

"That'll take about a minute," another man observed.

Lena giggled and rolled her eyes. "Oh, Greg, as if I'd look at you if the prince wanted me!"

"Right, are we all here?" said Gordon's dry voice above the nervous, excited banter. "Before we start, may I just remind you all that we will very likely be sitting on cushions on the floor, and that it is considered rude in this part of the world to direct the soles of your feet at anyone. So don't think you can lie stretched out with your ankles crossed and feet pointing towards the prince. You sit with your feet tucked under you, one way or another. In addition—" He gave them several more pointers and then consulted his watch and said, "Right. Time we were off."

And in a column of twos and threes they left the dining enclosure and began to move across the sand in the direction of what they were still laugingly calling the sultan's tent.

They had barely set out when they saw lights, and a moment later they were greeted by a party of servants with flaming torches and a man dressed in peacock blue magnificence who bowed and introduced himself as Arif ur-Rashid, Cup Companion to the Prince.

"Very flattering," Gordon muttered into Zara's ear. "By tradition the further the king or his emissary comes to meet his guests, the higher the honour. We've been met effectively at our own doorstep. Very nice indeed. I think we can look forward to a substantial feast. Pearls in the bottom of our wine goblets and told to keep them sort of thing."

Zara gurgled into laughter. She was one of the few who recognized when Gordon was joking, and his eyes glinted approvingly down at her.

But it wasn't quite so much of a joke as he had imagined. All the archaeological team gasped with awe when they passed through the doors into the tent.

It was like entering Aladdin's cave. Everything glowed

with richness and warmth. The colours were deep and luxurious—emerald, ruby, sapphire, turquoise. Every inch of walls, floor and ceiling was hung and draped with carpets, tapestries, or beautifully dyed cloth, and the furniture—of walnut, mahogany and other unknown, fabulously grained woods—had such a deep polish it seemed as if it would shine "even if no fire touched it."

All the light came from naked flame, or flame under delicately painted or cut crystal globes that sent light shimmering around the room like a thousand flung diamonds. And all around them were handsome men in exotic dress introducing themselves as the Cup Companions of the prince. The team felt as if they had stepped back centuries in time, straight into the pages of the *Arabian Nights*.

One of the Companions had visited the dig earlier in the afternoon, and had been introduced to every member of the team by Gordon, and now they were all greeted by name. For several minutes they made conversation.

Then the heavy sound of a helicopter was heard close by. There was an expectant pause, during which the team found it impossible to chat normally. All of them were surreptitiously watching the entrance. Suddenly a group of men erupted into the room, talking and laughing, and bringing a vital and very appealing energy with them. As one man, the Companions in the room turned and bowed.

The new arrivals were all just as exotically and colourfully dressed as the Companions, and the brilliance of the prince himself was breathtakingly unmistakable.

His long, high-necked jacket was cream silk and seemed to be studded with pinpoints of green light from elbow to wrist and around the collar. His flowing Eastern trousers were deep green. Diagonally across his breast he wore a cloth-of-gold sash, and a double rope of absolutely magnificent pearls at least a yard long was looped and draped over his chest, and fixed at one shoulder with a ruby the size of an egg. He had a lustrous black moustache and thick, waving black hair, which, like the heads of all his

Companions, was bare. His fingers were clustered with a king's ransom in gold and stones.

He put up one arrogant hand in a gesture that in any other man would look, Zara thought, ridiculously theatrical, but in him seemed perfectly natural and engaging. Smiling broadly, he recited something in Arabic, and then said in English, "It is very kind of you all to come to my poor table. May so propitious an occasion be blessed."

The efforts of the team to think of some suitable response would have made Zara laugh if she hadn't been similarly dumbstruck herself.

Prince Rafi recognized Gordon in the throng and strode to his side to greet the director, where Arif joined him. The prince chatted briefly to Gordon and then Arif introduced Maeve, then followed the prince slowly through the room, introducing him to each member of the team. The prince tilted his head solicitously to each and shook their hands, exchanging a few words before moving on.

He made his way around the room and at last appeared at Zara's side. Now she was aware of two things not quite so obvious from a distance—a heady yet elusive scent of sandalwood or myrrh or something similar, and the powerful physical aura of the man. He was not tall, but he exuded power.

"Miss Zara Blake, Your Highness," said Arif, and a well-shaped, graceful hand was extended to her. Aware that she was blushing, Zara flicked her eyes to his face as she put her hand into his. "Miss Blake, His Serene Highness Sayed Hajji Rafi Jehangir ibn Daud ibn Hassan al Quraishi."

The name rolled off his tongue like poetry.

"Miss Blake, it is a very great pleasure," said the prince in a tiger's fur voice, with such emphasis she almost believed him.

"How do you do, Your Highness," Zara murmured, finding that, whatever her democratic principles, her head seemed to bow of its own accord. Dimly she supposed that was the definition of true royalty—when you couldn't help bowing.

"I hope your stay in my country will be long and fruitful," he said.

Zara looked up again, but found that she could not meet his dark eyes for long. She blushed even more warmly, though she had hardly blushed in her life. "Your Highness is very kind," she murmured.

She expected him to move on then—he had only exchanged a few words with each of the others—but to her surprise he asked, "Your name is Zara?" He pronounced it with a little explosion of air on the first vowel. *Zahra.*

"Yes."

"This is a very beautiful name. In my language it means both *flower* and *splendour, beauty.*" Without saying it, he managed to imply that she was well named.

"Ah…oh."

"Are your parents perhaps Arabic speakers?"

"No…my father's background is French and my mother—" she shrugged and tried to smile "—just plain Canadian. Sort of mixed."

Zara was amazed to find herself so stumbling and confused. It was not at all like her, and she was furious with herself. He was a prince only by the luck of birth, and his compliments were no more significant than anyone else's! There was no reason to start blushing like a fifteen-year-old. A glance around the room showed her that the others had noticed his interest. Passionately she wished he would move on to the next team member.

He did not. She looked at him again in time to intercept the tiniest flick of his long black lashes to Arif ur-Rashid.

The Companion nodded, raised his mellifluous voice slightly for attention, and said, "Here in Barakat, ladies and gentlemen, we do not follow the Western custom of preliminary drinks and hors d'oeuvres while standing. You are invited now to sit at the prince's table."

The wall behind Zara suddenly opened, and only then

did she notice the big wooden arch she had been standing in front of, revealed as a doorway as servants lifted the heavy draperies that had closed it.

Prince Rafi lifted his arm. "Allow me to escort you, Zara."

At the sound of her name on his lips, Zara stiffened a little. Okay, this had gone far enough, and it was going to stop right here, before she found herself ensconced in the harem.

"Thank you, Rafi," she said coolly, and put her hand on his arm.

He smiled into her eyes and drooped his eyelids with pleasure, tilting his head in acknowledgement. Zara gasped a little. She was a fool to play games in so different a culture. She had no idea what message she had just sent him. For all she knew she had already said yes to a post-prandial romp.

And, she recollected somewhat belatedly, she had more than herself to think of. The whole future of the dig was under this man's sole sway. He could wave one graceful, masculine hand and the desert would be clear of them to-morrow.

The archaeological team filed after them through the arched doorway and into the dining room, where they stopped amazed, cries of astonishment soft on their lips, and feeling just a little, Zara thought, like barbarians seeing civilisation for the first time. Among them, the Companions moved with polished grace, inviting them individually to sit.

Prince Rafi led her all the length of the room while Zara gazed in unaffected delight at the spectacle before them. Dozens—hundreds!—of multicoloured silk and tapestry cushions lay massed around the long, low rectangular table that stood about six inches off the ground. It shone with cut crystal and painted porcelain, silver and old gold. Down the centre of the table and all around the walls could be seen the flicker of numerous flames under the most artistically painted glass globes. Against one wall there was a large fountain—she couldn't believe it, but it was a real marble fountain, and the sound of the softly splashing water was better than music. All along the opposite wall, panels had been rolled up to allow the gentle night breeze to cool them, and the moon and the stars and the desert to form part of the decor. Zara had never seen anything to equal it in her life.

"It's very beautiful," she said quietly, and Prince Rafi smiled.

"I am very happy to please you, Zara." He led her to the farther end of the table. The smell of cooking food rose deliciously on the air.

Prince Rafi stopped and guided her to a place. He stood beside her, and with a curious sinking elation she understood that she had been chosen to sit beside him during the meal. A Companion was on his other side, and next to the Companion was Gordon. All around, the others were finding their places, and in a moment it became clear that every second or third place was taken by one of the Cup Companions.

Prince Rafi raised his arms and gestured them to sit. Zara settled herself among the most comfortable cushions she had ever sat on in her life, and tucked her feet neatly beside her. She turned to find that Arif ur-Rashid was on her other side.

Music started playing. Several musicians with stringed and other instruments—some of which she had never seen before—had come in and settled in a corner and were playing a soft accompaniment to the coming meal.

Arif clapped his hands, and a small army of white-clad boys and girls appeared, each boy carrying a pitcher, each girl a basin, all in silver chased with gold. They approached the table and knelt by the diners. One girl knelt between Prince Rafi and Zara, and, balancing the basin on her knee, offered the prince a bar of soap. He spoke a few gentle words, and she blushed and turned to Zara, offering her the bar. Grateful that Gordon had warned them of the ritual, she took the offered bar and washed her hands lightly under the flow of water that the boy produced from the pitcher.

When Zara had finished, the girl reached to take the soap from her, but her hand fell back as Prince Rafi's own hand stretched across the basin. Her heart beating hard with unaccustomed confusion, Zara slipped the perfumed soap into his hand. His dark hand closed firmly on the slender white bar, and Zara's mouth opened, gasping for more oxygen than seemed to be available. She watched transfixed as he stroked the bar of soap into a lather between his hands, then, as if without volition, felt her gaze drawn upwards to his face.

He was watching her, a half smile in his dark eyes. Slowly, lazily, he set the soap in the basin and held his hands under the stream the boy carefully poured. The scent of rosewater mingled with the other subtle scents assailing her nostrils.

''The towel is offered you, Miss Blake,'' said the prince, and she blinked and smiled at the worried girl who was holding the soft oblong of fabric up for her.

''Thank you,'' she said. She dried her hands and watched as the prince did the same. Then the boy and girl moved away to join the phalanx of water bearers, who all bowed and then filed neatly out of the room.

Almost immediately another group of servants filed in, bringing with them this time the welcome, delicious odour of food. Within the next few minutes a feast appeared. Some dishes were placed on the table, some were carried around and offered to the guests. The beautiful silver and gold goblets were filled with water and wine and exotic juices.

After the bustle had died down, Prince Rafi lifted his gold cup. ''I extend to all members of the archaeological team my congratulations on the important historical site which you have discovered and will no doubt in the years to come excavate, to enrich the knowledge of my country's and the world's ancient history. In particular, I commend Mr. Gordon Rhett, whom I know well from those occasions when he visited and wrote to me in his enthusiasm for this project.''

He turned and saluted Gordon with his glass, and everybody drank.

''But now is not the time for speeches. The pleasures of the mind are offered when the pleasures of the flesh have been satisfied.'' He invited them all to eat and drink, but Zara could hardly take in the words. When he said those words, ''the pleasures of the flesh,'' it was as if his body sparked with electricity so strong she received a shock from it. She was covered in gooseflesh.

She thought, *I'm helpless already. If he really does want me, I won't be able to refuse.*

Three

It became clearer and clearer as the evening wore on that Prince Rafi had eyes only for Zara. Whether he was speaking to the whole room, or to an individual, or listening or silent, there was a kind of glow around the two, apparent to almost everyone in the room. Several times, as if hardly realizing it, the prince would break off what he was saying to lean over and encourage Zara to try the most delicious tidbit on the platter that was being offered, or to signal the cupbearers to refill her glass, or to ask her with an intimate smile whether she liked some flavour.

When the whole roast sheep came in, he regaled them all with the story of the time his father had, according to custom, made the grand gesture of giving one of the sheep's eyes to his most honoured guest—the British Ambassador. He mimicked the British Ambassador's false expressions of gratitude.

He was a magical storyteller, with the knack of making

people laugh. "Did he have to eat it in front of everyone?" Zara asked.

Prince Rafi turned lazily approving eyes upon her, which shocked her system as if with an unexpected touch. "My stepmother, my father's first and most beloved wife, was then a new bride. She was sitting on the other side of the Ambassador. Just after the sheep's eye was served to him, my stepmother had the misfortune to knock over her water glass. The ambassador certainly put something into his mouth and ate it with great enjoyment. But it was rumoured that my stepmother afterwards berated my father and made him swear never again to offer sheep's eyes to a foreign guest."

They were all laughing. Rafi watched in admiration how Zara's neck arched, her eyes brimming over with mischief and merriment, her black lustrous curls falling just so with the tilt of her elegant head.

"My stepmother was a foreigner herself," he said then. "She understood the ways of foreigners, and she gave my father much good advice. She was of great assistance to him in his rule. He always said so." He paused. "They were much in love, all their lives."

He said this gazing right at Zara. The laughter died in her, and heat crept visibly up her cheeks. She was beginning to be a little angry now. Making eyes at her was one thing. This was getting ridiculous. She was starting to feel like an idiot.

She returned his look coolly. "It didn't stop him taking other wives, though, did it? She was not, after all, your own mother."

Instead of chilling him, this comment had the effect of making his eyes spark with interest, as if she had betrayed jealousy and he counted that a point in his favour. "Ah, you do not know my father's tragic story!" Rafi exclaimed. He looked around at the musicians. "Where is Motreb? Ask him to come forth."

A man in curious dress entered carrying yet another unfamiliar stringed instrument not unlike a banjo. "Motreb, I ask you to sing for my friends the song of my father's love," cried Prince Rafi.

He leaned to Haroun on his left and murmured a word in his ear, and when the singer-storyteller settled himself to sing the song of the great king who fell in love with a bewitching foreigner, the Companion got up and stood beside him. Between the plaintive lines, Motreb paused, playing his instrument, while Haroun translated the story of King Daud.

"'And will you take no wife but me? You cannot swear to this, quoth she.'"

Zara, who had never heard the story, was entranced, both by the tale itself and by the haunting ululating melody of the singer's voice.

"'I will. I swear. No wife but thee…'"

Then she heard the story of how King Daud had married the stranger and to the great joy of his people, had made her his queen. And how thirty years of happy marriage and two sons followed, giving no warning before disaster struck in the shape of a fatal air crash. The king and queen mourned long.

"'We have lost our beloved sons, my husband. And though with all my heart I would give you more, I am old…your promise, too, made in the sweet blossom of youth, is old. I say it is no more. It has died with our sons. Take therefore, my husband, three young wives, and get a son for your kingdom, that this land may remain what men call Blessed.'"

Zara's eyes burned as the tragic voice sobbed out the story. Somewhere on her right she heard a sniff, Lena probably, which made her own control slip. She dropped her head, surreptitiously pulling a tissue out of her bag with one hand, and dabbed her eyes.

Her free hand was taken in a firm but gentle hold, and her eyes flew to Prince Rafi. He drew her hand up, gave her a long, slow, dark and sexy look, and kissed her knuckles once, twice. Not a simple pressure of the mouth, either, but a dragging pressure from parted lips, his eyes half closed, as if he wanted to eat her. Her body seemed to melt in spite of all her determination to be unaffected. Her heart had been knocked from its moorings and lay kicking helplessly in her breast.

After that, she had trouble swallowing. Never had she experienced so public or so determined a seduction. When the song was over, Prince Rafi himself poured wine into a silver goblet for the singer, who drained it to find a large pearl at the bottom as his reward. He bowed and retired, and there was a pause in the entertainments and the buzz of conversation arose.

The song was followed by stories from one or two Companions, then by gymnastic young performers, then by a very artful belly dancer in the most bewitching costume Zara had ever seen, then by another song. All the artists seemed to be paid with jewels or gold, in scenes straight from the *Arabian Nights*.

Meanwhile, the food came in a never-ending supply. And so did the approving looks from Prince Rafi's dark eyes. Zara's heart seemed to kick into a new, higher, faster rhythm with each look.

He was staggeringly charismatic—handsome, virile, with a smile women probably jumped off cliffs for. But he was also a desert chieftain, however rich, and her own inner response to his admiration frightened her. A girl should have some resistance if she was going to be propositioned, and Zara felt she had no more resistance than a kitten.

When the last empty tray had been carried away, small silver salvers laden with soft Turkish delight in powdered sugar began to make the rounds, and there seemed to be general movement among the guests, led by the Companions. But when Zara tried to get up, Prince Rafi's firm hand was on her arm. And she was too much of a coward to resist the implied command.

After a few moments, Prince Rafi made a signal to the

Companion named Ayman, who had changed his seat and was now lounging on the cushions beside Lena, to the obvious displeasure of Arif. With a nod to his prince and then to Lena, the Companion got to his feet and left the room.

"It was a tradition among my forebears to give robes of honour to those who had performed some signal service," Prince Rafi began. "Since each of you contributes to the overall achievement of proving not only that the great Iskandar, whom you call Alexander, visited this land, but also uncovering the city that he himself founded, it is my pleasure to reward each of you with the traditional robe of honour. Even so would Alexander have been presented with a robe by my own predecessor."

At that moment, Ayman returned, leading a train of the boys and girls who had been the water bearers at the start of the evening. Each youth was the bearer this time of a neat cube of folded cloth, all of different colours, in stripes or swirls or solids, glittering with gold and silver threads. Each knelt at the side of one member of the team and offered the robe.

There were loud squeals of surprised and appreciative delight from all the women, but the men, too, were clearly very pleased. People began jumping to their feet to unfold the robes and try them on.

A pretty girl, gazing in deep admiration at Zara, knelt beside her, her arms full of glittering cloth. Zara thanked her. The child flicked a glance at Prince Rafi, who nodded approvingly. To Zara's surprise, the girl smiled affectionately at the prince, who winked at her, before bowing and departing.

"Who are these servant children?" Zara asked.

Prince Rafi laughed. "They are not servants! They are young courtiers. They are the younger sisters and brothers of my Companions, or my own cousins...all are educated at the palace. As well as academic subjects and languages, they learn the rules of hospitality."

All around, people were on their feet, trying on and admiring their robes. "Oh, my!" Zara exclaimed breathlessly, as she began to examine her own gift. It seemed to be made of spun gold, and embroidered with fabulous designs in red and green. She had never seen anything so rich and lustrous outside of a medieval painting. "But it's *beautiful!*" she whispered helplessly. "I can't possibly…"

Not far away, Gordon was standing up to model his own very rich robe. Hearing her cry, he glanced down and gave her an admonitory look, which she interpreted as meaning that it would be a grave insult to refuse a robe of honour. If she insulted the prince, the dig might be history. She knew they were hoping to convince the prince to contribute the funding they would need to keep it going beyond this season.

"It's very beautiful," she murmured, drawing her feet under her haunches and struggling to stand gracefully amid the cushions. But her foot was on the hem of her dress and before she knew what was happening she had fallen straight onto Prince Rafi.

His arms quickly caught her, and his eyes closed as her long black hair spilled over him. The robe of honour tumbled from Zara's hands and was splayed out around them, glittering in the lamp flame like something magical, a thing of inestimable value.

Prince Rafi inhaled, his eyes closing, and murmured in her ear, "The perfume of your hair would drive a man mad. I have dreamed of you, waking and sleeping."

As a tableau it ranked with the most beautiful miniature paintings in the prince's own extensive collection. Even the Companions were not proof against it. Everyone in the room was frozen in some posture, half with their arms in their robes. All eyes were on them. If she were not so covered with embarrassment, she could have laughed at the picture of so many startled, curious, gawking faces.

But it was her own reaction that was the danger. Zara felt molten, like the golden robe, electrified by the man's touch, his whispered words.

"I—I'm so sorry," she stammered, struggling from his grasp to her feet. "I don't know what made me so clumsy."

"Do you not?" he smiled. He solicitously helped her to gain her feet.

"Ah...well..." She hardly knew what she was saying. Trying for calm, for the ordinary—so far as anything in this remarkable evening could be called ordinary—Zara lifted the robe and put it on.

It was breathtakingly beautiful, utterly rich and luxurious. It fanned out at the back in a broad curving sweep to the floor, while in front it was cut shorter, the hem just skimming her toes. "Thank you," she whispered.

Trying to give her breathing room, Gordon sat down and said to Prince Rafi, "I think I should tell you that one of our team saw a group of mounted bandits the other morning. There seemed to be quite a number of them, and I'm afraid our security may not be sufficient."

Prince Rafi's head straightened with surprise. "Bandits!" he exclaimed. "So near! We do not often see Jalal on our side of the river. His headquarters is in my brother's land. Where, exactly, were they seen?"

"At the wadi. Members of the team go there to relax away from the heat whenever they get a chance. Everyone has been warned not to go off the site alone, but I'm afraid the waterfall there is very tempting."

"At the waterfall?" Rafi repeated, in a different voice. He turned his head towards Zara, who had sat down to listen. "When, and how many?"

Zara smiled. "It was three days ago. I didn't stop to count their numbers. I just took one look and ran! But I think there were ten or twelve, anyway. All on the most magnificent horses."

He was watching her intently. "Were you frightened?"

"Terrified," she agreed without emphasis.

"Their captain—did you see him?"

"I think so," Zara told him, repressing a shiver at the memory of the bandit chief's gaze and her own reaction to it. Not much different from the response Prince Rafi raised in her. Maybe she had a weakness. "There certainly was one man with an air of command."

"And he—did he see you?"

That passionate black gaze rose up in her mind's eye, and, pressing her lips together, Zara only nodded.

"But you were not taken? Twelve men and you escaped?"

"I don't think he—they tried. I am sure if they had ridden out of the enclosure and around—well, on horseback they could have caught up with me before I got back to the tents." Her mouth was dry, she didn't know why. Something she had noticed but which hadn't filtered through to her conscious mind was making her uneasy.

"Then he is a fool," said Prince Rafi. "When a man sees what he wants, should he not take pains to achieve it instantly?"

Zara smiled. "Maybe he didn't see what he wanted," she said, and shivered, knowing it was a lie. The bandit chief had wanted her. There must be something about her that appealed to the Arab temperament, too.

A marriage made in heaven, then, she told herself dryly.

"What man would not have wanted you, so beautiful under the fall of water, your limbs bare and your skin so silken? He must have been jealous even of the eyes of his companions for the fact that they also saw the vision. If he did not pursue you across the sand and catch you up on his horse then, it can only be because he had other plans to obtain you. Did not King Khosrow fall madly in love with Shirin when he caught sight of her bathing? And he stopped at nothing to gain her."

It was the naked passion in his eyes, more than anything else, that told her the truth. He had been veiling it from her all evening, letting her see only a portion of what was there. But now she saw again the black flame of complete and determined need burn up behind his gaze.

Her hand snapping to her open mouth, Zara gasped, an

electric sound that caused conversation everywhere to stop.
Her hand slowly lowered, while her eyes gazed helplessly
into his. Take away the white keffiyeh that had enwrapped
the bandit's head and chin…

"A man would do all in his power," Prince Rafi promised her softly.

"It was you!" she whispered.

His black eyes fixed hers, letting her read the truth. That
was the reason, then, for the prince's sudden interest in the
team, for this dinner…she saw it all. That was why he had
singled her out.

His Serene Highness Sayed Hajji Rafi Jehangir ibn Daud
ibn Hassan al Quraishi was the man at the wadi she had
thought the bandit chief.

Four

Zara succeeded in tearing her eyes away from the prince's at last, and glanced up to see that the gaze of every member of the archaeological team was rivetted on her. The Companions, more socially skilled, pretended not to notice, and were making light conversation to their inattentive neighbours.

She really couldn't think. She needed air, and solitude.

"Excuse me," she said. Struggling to her feet again, the coat billowing and glowing behind her, Zara walked down the length of the room, past little clusters of people who tried to cover their fascination with chatter but could not help following her with their eyes.

Outside, the full moon glowed on the broad desert, its sweeping dunes, the tents of the archaeological team in the distance, and closer, the outcrop where the tall palms that surrounded the pool and waterfall were just visible above the rocks.

Pressing her hands to her hot cheeks, the robe billowing

behind her, Zara moved towards it. There was a narrow defile in the rocks from this direction, dark now with moon-shadow, but she knew her way through. Soon she was inside, listening to the rushing sound of the falling water.

It was Gordon's theory that this was the original course of the river, before Queen Halimah, in one of her public projects, had diverted it, and that an underground stream remained as testimony, forced to the surface here by some geological fault, to form the delicious waterfall and its pools before disappearing underground again.

She was walking where Alexander the Great had probably once walked. Zara sank down on the rocks by the pool and dipped one hand in, leaning over to press the cool water to her cheeks.

The moon was strong, casting black shadows under the walls of rock, but she sat in full moonlight, and it glistened on the water, on her hair, and on her golden robe.

It was two thousand, three hundred and thirty years since Alexander had come here with his armies, but humankind had not changed very much. Men were still consumed by jealousies and passions…and sex was still like this river…try to divert it, and its power went underground, to force its way up at any weak spot…

She did not know what to do about Prince Rafi. That there was a powerful attraction between them she couldn't, wouldn't try to deny. She had felt it for him when she thought him a bandit, and finding him a king had certainly not lessened its force.

But she was a stranger in a strange land, a woman desired by a king. She had no idea what dangers awaited her if she gave in to what she felt, what he wanted. She spoke only a little of the language, knew not nearly enough about the country and its culture. Her knowledge of the area was all of the distant past, and she wasn't sure that the autocratic powers and ways of the ancient kings whose names she knew had altogether passed into history.

Suppose she gave in to him, for one night, or one week,

or…what would it mean, in the end? Did kings let women go after they had loved them, or did they guard them jealously in their harems, not wanting them, but not willing that any other man should ever have the power of being compared with the king as a lover?

Ridiculous. She was sure that was ridiculous. But what was not ridiculous was the fear she felt. The thought of letting him make love to her frightened her. No man had ever made her so nervous.

She heard a clinking sound, and something that sounded like a horse blowing. In sudden alarm, Zara lifted her head.

She was beautiful, a white dress and a flowing golden robe, and her black curling hair another robe over her shoulders and back, like the descriptions by the poets. Her face a painting, the eyebrows darkly curving, the mouth a perfect bow. The mountain tribes had their tales of the Peri, the race of Other, whose tiny beautiful women enticed men and disappeared, but this was the desert. Behind her the moon shimmered on the rustling water.

This was the one. There could not be another.

"Who's there?" Zara called, trying to keep any sign of nerves from her voice, realizing she had been a fool to come wandering out here on her own. "Who is it?"

Suddenly the place seemed eerie, full of danger. Zara shivered and got to her feet. What a fool she was! What if Prince Rafi followed her out here? What if he had construed her movements as an invitation?

She heard a footfall. The waterfall disguised everything, but she thought it came from the passage. It was Prince Rafi. She knew it, and panic filled her blood with the urgent command to flee. She ran light as wind towards the sheltering rocks. Damn the moonlight! It caught in the glittering robe and would betray her whereabouts even in the darkest shadows.

Zara turned her head this way and that, peering through the gloom, trying to remember the layout of the place. There was a niche somewhere, a place to hide, but the shadows were very black. There was no time to think. She flung herself into the unknown.

Then she shrieked as the black horse reared up in front of her. Out of the shadows a body bent down and dark hands reached for her. The prince! *My God, is he mad?* she thought, in the moment before the strong hands grasped her, the powerful arms lifted her, and she felt the horse beneath her thighs and her face was smothered against his chest.

She clung to him for safety, there was nothing else to do. He had already spurred the horse to a wild gallop, and to fall now might kill her. Her heart pounded deafeningly in her ears. In the tiny part of her mind that remained cool, she had time to think, *I didn't scream. I suppose that counts as an invitation in this part of the world.*

She couldn't scream now—she was pressed into his chest, almost smothered. She smelled the odour of male sweat and desert and horse in the all-encompassing burnous he was wearing over his clothes, and the hairs lifted primitively on the back of her neck.

The smell was not right. He had been sandalwood and myrrh, and another scent, all his own, that was missing now.

In the same moment she heard a curse resonate in the chest under her cheek, and the horse veered wildly and half reared, throwing her harder against him. For a moment, one arm loosed her and he wrestled with the reins, and Zara lifted her head and saw a man flung to the ground by the horse's powerful forequarters as they rode past.

In the moonlight the colour of his coat seemed purple, but he was impossible to mistake. Prince Rafi leapt to his feet and gave chase as she watched, but the horseman had goaded his horse into a violent gallop and in seconds he was left far behind.

She screamed then, loud and long, but it was too late. All around her stretched the glow of moonlight on the wide, bleak, empty desert. Fear was nearly overwhelming. She gasped and choked, but before she could scream again the strong hand came up and pressed her face into the stifling folds of the burnous.

She was afraid of falling off the horse as it made its headlong plunge down a cliff of sand, but the suffocating hold was too firm. The sickness of terror was in her throat and she wondered which would be worse—what the bandit had in mind for her, or being crippled or killed under the sharp hooves.

She must get calm. She gained nothing by thinking of what lay ahead. She had to plan. She had already missed a crucial opportunity. If she had not believed it was Prince Rafi on the horse, she might have…but it was no use thinking of that, either. She should think of escape now.

"If you struggle I will tie you over the saddle," the man grunted as she stirred. "If you scream I will knock you on the head." Shivers of terror chased up and down her spine at the threat in his voice. He sounded like a man who said what he meant, who would stop at nothing.

"I can't breathe!" she cried, and he must have some humanity, she thought, because he let her turn her face into the air.

He kept one hand over her mouth, her head pressed back against him. Zara impatiently forced her stupid mind to think. There must be something she could do! They would follow her. Prince Rafi, Gordon—they were sure to chase the bandit. They might already be in the helicopter. And there were the Land Rovers, too.

He had thought of the same thing, she realized, for after a time she could not measure they left the sand and entered an area of stony ground they had been galloping at an angle to for some time, and here he turned the horse so sharply that it was almost facing back on its own path. He had ridden away from the camp towards the east, but now she thought they were headed west north west. How long would it take the searchers to give up on the easterly direction and search other possibilities?

Far to the left now on the clear desert air they heard the sound of the helicopter beating the air. Her head was pressed firmly back against the bandit's chest, but she could just see the light in the distance that told her the helicopter had a searchlight. If only she could leave some sign, some signal of the way they had gone! Something that would shine in the searchlight...her sandals were gold.

She still had both her sandals on. It seemed impossible, after all that had happened. There was a little strap between each toe, fanning out to a lacy pattern over her instep. She had never realized before how firmly they held.

Slowly, trying not to think of what she was doing lest the bandit pick up the thought, Zara worked one sandal off her foot and kicked it free. She didn't look back, didn't try to see how it had fallen. It might be days before it was found, if ever. A few miles later she let the second sandal drop.

The helicopter was going the wrong way, carefully following the horse's first easterly direction. The sound grew faint. Her captor's firm hold on her slackened. "They will not hear you now, if you scream," he told her. But the horse's pace continued.

Her hip felt bruised and she shifted to a more comfortable position. The golden robe was billowing in the wind. She pulled at it, amazed to find that she was still wearing that, too. "Where are you taking me?" she asked. Her throat was hoarse.

"To my camp."

"Isn't your camp on the other side of the river?"

He glanced down at her, the moonlight full on his face, and did not answer. She caught her breath on a gasp.

"You look like Prince Rafi!" she whispered.

The man laughed, flinging his head back. "Do I so?"

Fear chased up and down her spine. "Who are you?"

"Have not you been told tales of me? I am Jalal the Bandit, grandson of the great Selim."

"Who—" Zara began, but he interrupted her.

"Do not waste your breath with asking questions. I will answer nothing and we have a long, hard way to go."

He hadn't been exaggerating. Zara had lost track of time. She had rarely been on a horse for longer than an hour, and she was sitting sidesaddle, one hip thrust higher than the other in a posture that became increasingly uncomfortable as the time passed. She was glad when numbness set in, but even that was painful.

"I must blindfold you now."

She surfaced from the daze she had sunk into, and wondered how long they had been riding. The horse was covered in lather, and obviously miserable, but doing his best for his master.

Jalal lifted an arm and pulled the large keffiyeh from his head. "Wrap this around your head and eyes."

They must be near some landmark that she would be able to identify. She prayed that this meant that he intended to keep her alive—for otherwise why bother about what she saw?—and sobbed once with the relief of a fear she hadn't been letting herself feel.

She cast one last glance around her, trying to memorize the scene, imprint it on her mind, as she reached to take the cloth and wrap her face in it. Ahead there was a mound of rock, made huge with shadow. She thought she heard the sound of running water in the distance, but the desert was full of moonshadows that made it hard to distinguish features.

A buffet of wind caught them then, and her golden robe suddenly snapped and billowed out behind her…. Zara thought, *It's the one certain marker I could leave*—if she could drop it without his noticing. If they found it, Prince Rafi would recognize it, she was certain. He would know that she had passed this way…*if anyone, nomad or trader, ever passes this way,* she told herself ruthlessly. *And if the wind hasn't buried it, and if the nomad takes it to his prince…* but she had to try *something.* If she gave up hope now she was lost.

Under cover of wrapping her head, Zara released one arm from the beautiful robe. Now it was held on only by one arm. She finished wrapping the scarf around her eyes. Then blindly, inch by inch, working by touch alone, she drew the robe into a bundle in her lap.

The horse, very tired now, struggled on for minutes while she nearly suffocated with fear behind the constricting cloth. At last it was reined to a very slow walk. Zara tensed for action. She sensed an echo, their approach to something large. They were about to enter some place. Pulling her arm from the robe, she screamed and began to struggle.

She was no match for the bandit's strength, and her rebellion lasted hardly more than a second. But the robe was now loose in her hands. "Bend down, it is low," he ordered curtly, pushing her flat against the horse's neck and bending over her. This was her last chance. Lying over the horse's neck, Zara dragged the crushed robe from under her and flung it away. A moment later the sounds told her that they were entering something like a cave.

"Cover your face," he ordered again.

Behind them, the golden cloth glittered for a moment in the moonlight as it fell to the desert floor.

Rafi ran all the way to the helicopter and pulled futilely at the door before he realized that Ammar had locked it. Precautions against Jalal, he reflected grimly, but this would give the bandit a head start he would probably never lose. Rafi ran back towards the tent, calling for the Companions. But the party was noisy, drowning his cry as it had drowned the sound of the horse and Zara's scream.

By the time he had reached the tent again, he knew too much time had passed. The bandit could be heading anywhere, and in darkness his trail would not be easy to follow.

At last Rafi was close enough for his cries to be heard, and the party was silenced. There were shouts, and the Companions came spilling out of the tent on the alert. All the archaeological team followed, calling questions.

Rafi curbed his impatience to be gone, told them what had occurred, and gave orders for some to take the land vehicles in a search that would be virtually useless. Even if they could find the trail, the land vehicles would not be able to follow everywhere a horse led.

"He galloped east till he was out of sight," he said. "But he is not a fool. He might be headed anywhere." Seconds later he set off running across the sand back towards the helicopter, with Arif and Ammar silently pacing him.

"What a fool to have set no guard tonight!" he berated himself as they flung themselves into the cockpit and Ammar started the rotors slowly beating.

"Shall we go to his camp, or follow his trail?" demanded Arif as they lifted off.

"Follow his trail," said Rafi briefly, straining to see against the deep moonshadows on the desert.

"His camp is still on the other side of the river, is it not?" Ammar said, as he flicked on the landing light. All three peered out, but this was not a military helicopter and it was not a powerful searchlight. "He can only get across if he goes to the bridge. Why not meet him there, Lord?"

"We do not know that he means to take her to his camp. A man who has plotted to take a hostage for so long may have chosen another place to keep them," said Rafi, his jaw clenched. "Radio Haroun to drive to the bridge." He did not want to think of what conditions Zara might be kept in, or for how long, if they did not catch Jalal tonight.

The air was strangely damp, and the sound of the horse's hooves echoed. They were moving slightly downhill. Zara strained her ears, trying to take in every detail of what she heard, in case it might later prove useful. Was it a cave? If so, it was a very large one, and she was sure they had not been riding towards the mountains. An underground cavern? The thought that it might be her prison made her shiver. The horse seemed to pick its way in darkness.

After a long time measured only by the beating of her terror, the dampness lifted and their path went uphill again. Then the horse whickered softly, and there was a voice.

Her captor called out, and the voice answered, and now through her makeshift blindfold she saw the glow of light. The horse stopped, and her captor called soft commands, and she was lifted from the horse and carried.

She didn't scream or struggle. Better to give them no excuse, she thought. Not that they would need one.

Rafi cursed himself. He would never buy a civilian helicopter again. There was no infrared, no night search capability besides the feeble landing light. And the whole desert to search. They radioed the nearest military camp to scramble a couple of Sikorskys, but Rafi knew in his heart the task was now impossible. They had given him time to get to cover. Jalal was not such a fool as to go on riding through the desert with a captive woman all night long.

And even if he did, he was not the only rider in the desert. They might stop half a dozen riders abroad on legitimate—and illegitimate—business on a night of full moon like tonight.

But he searched, all the same. Once they reached the hard ground he saw the extent of the task, for the man might have gone anywhere from here and left no trace. There were thousands of trails across the desert.

At dawn, ordering the search to continue, he returned to the palace and went alone to his study. He sat in thought, but thinking would not change anything. Prince Jalal's ransom demand would come soon enough. Before that, if possible, his brothers must be warned.

"Ah, he chooses well, Prince Rafi!" said the bandit, his teeth very white against his dark beard.

They had set her on her feet by a roaring fire. Her heart-beat was stifling her. "He has not chosen me for anything," Zara said. "I am a member of a Canadian archaeological team and believe me, the Canadian government—"

He laughed. "We heard that Prince Rafi had followed in the steps of Khosrow and fallen in love with a woman bathing. Do not deny that it is you. I saw you with a robe of such value that only he could have given it to you. And I saw your beauty. By moonlight I thought you a Peri. By firelight also your beauty enchants."

She was in a strange compound, that seemed to be sur-rounded by rocks and ancient ruins. But the fire blinded her. She could not see much beyond it. There were people in the distance moving to and fro, as if going about their regular business. Where could she be?

"He gave everyone on the team a robe," she said dis-missively. Zara felt sick at heart. He looked so like Prince Rafi! How could such a startling resemblance be coinci-dence? What did it mean? "We have found the lost city of Alexander. Prince Rafi has no personal interest in me at all."

The dark face closed. "If it is true, that is a pity for you."

Five

FROM JALAL IBN AZIZ TO HIS SERENE HIGHNESS RAFI IBN DAUD: I HAVE YOUR WOMAN. NO HARM WILL COME TO HER IF YOU AND YOUR BROTHERS OMAR AND KARIM AGREE TO MEET WITH ME AND HEAR MY DEMANDS.

"**T**he fault is all mine!" Rafi said. Prince Karim and Prince Omar had arrived for a council of war. "In the first place, I should have had guards posted."

"True enough," said Omar dispassionately. "Why didn't you?"

"Because I was besotted by black curls, like the excellent Khosrow," Rafi said.

Karim nodded. "We heard. You came back from a ride and put the whole palace on alert for a grand feast in the desert. It was said you had seen a woman bathing in the Wadi Sahra and lost your mind. Your cooks worked flat out for three days."

"Word travels, doesn't it?" Rafi said.

"When a prince loses his marbles there's always someone with access to a phone."

"Well, I don't deny it. I've found her, and now because of me she's in danger. Worse. If I hadn't—and if we hadn't disagreed with you, Omar, about how dangerous Jalal would become, we might have dealt with him ages ago."

"We'll deal with him now," Omar said.

They had agreed that the tribes would see it as a sign of weakness if they submitted to Jalal's demands.

"I admit I was hoping to plan my wedding before undertaking a desert campaign. But Jalal comes first now," Omar added.

"Do we know where he's taken her?"

"I've got half the army out scouring the desert for any sign, but one thing is certain—he's on this side of the river. He didn't cross the Dar al Jenoub bridge—we had that closed off before he had any chance of reaching it. And now with your men monitoring the other bridges...and there have been no unscheduled aircraft flights anywhere in the area."

"So he had a place chosen in East Barakat."

"And until my men stumble on it, there's only one way to find out where that is," Rafi said.

His brothers looked at him expectantly. "Send someone to infiltrate Jalal's camp to listen for clues. Someone there knows where she's being held."

Karim and Omar nodded silently. "Yeah, sounds good," said Karim after a moment. "Who will you send?"

"Myself," said Rafi.

FROM HIS SERENE HIGHNESS SAYED HAJJI RAFI JEHANGIR IBN DAUD IBN HASSAN AL QURAISHI, PRINCE OF EAST BARAKAT, TO THE BANDIT JALAL: WE OFFER NOTHING AND ACCEDE TO NO DEMANDS. WE URGE YOU TO GIVE UP YOUR HOSTAGE INSTANTLY. REMEMBER THE SWORD OF ROSTAM. WE URGE YOU TO AVOID THE

CATASTROPHE WHICH WILL SURELY ENSUE IF YOU PER-
SIST IN YOUR PATH. WE URGE YOU TO AVOID THE FATE
OF THE SWORD OF ROSTAM. RELEASE YOUR HOSTAGE.

Zara lifted the battered tin pot for the third time in five
minutes and confirmed that there was still no water in it.

If there was one thing solitary confinement taught you,
it was how irrational the human mind really was. There
was no water in the pot, and there wouldn't be any until
the woman came and brought some, but she was thirsty and
could not control the urge to check. It did not help that by
her reckoning—which might or might not be accurate, since
she had no watch—the old woman was late. She came
every day, once during the morning and once in the late
afternoon, to bring the modicum of water and food Zara
was allowed and to empty her latrine. Other than that she
was left entirely alone.

The woman spoke no English or French, and Zara's
handful of Arabic words hadn't been designed with the
needs of a hostage in mind.

She was irritable because it was so hard to keep her mind
off her physical discomfort. She was lying in a disintegrating room of an ancient ruin that appeared to be the
camp of Jalal the bandit and his far from merry men. She
had been wearing the same dress for three days. The dress
had been white: there was nothing to disguise her filthy
state. That was worse than the intermittent hunger and
thirst. The dirt was a constant. Her hair was matted. The
thick walls of her prison had been designed to stay cool
during the summer heat, but still she sweated in the after-
noons. Although she mercifully could not smell herself, no
doubt she stank.

Her prison cell was doorless and empty, with collapsing
walls, and the once-beautiful tile floor was faded and broken, and gritty with desert sand that had been blowing into
the ruin for centuries. They had given her a camel blanket
to serve as both mattress and covering.

Worst of all, she was chained by the ankle to a bolt in the wall which, for all that it looked as if it had been there since Noah, was absolutely immovable. She had a range of a few feet, enough to take her from her blanket to her latrine—a tin pail mercifully covered with a thick wooden lid—in the only corner she could reach.

At least her nose and ears had not been removed, which had been standard practice for the enemies of the state under Darius, King of the Medes and Persians, in the time before Alexander came to conquer these lands. "Him I punished well," was the way Darius had recorded such events. She wondered how Jalal the bandit would record her incarceration for history, given the chance.

Two thousand five hundred years ago. She supposed she wasn't anything like as miserable as those poor rebels against the great usurper Darius had been—or even many more recent hostages—but she was uncomfortable enough.

Alexander the Great had been appalled by the Eastern treatment of prisoners. History suggested that he had been met by a group of Greek craftsmen and artisans—prisoners, who had all suffered amputations of whatever part of their anatomy was not relevant to their art, in order to prevent their escape. In those days, she supposed, potters were the lucky ones—their craft had needed both feet and hands. But painters, silversmiths, or mosaic workers would have lost their feet. Some sources said it was in revenge for these atrocities that Alexander had burned the great, magnificent palace of Persepolis, but Zara had never quite believed it....

God, if he started cutting off bits of her! It had been said that Mohammad had only countenanced such barbarity because he knew it would be useless to try to ban it completely. But fourteen hundred years later it was still the treatment of choice for some...was Jalal one of them?

Alexander. Why couldn't she entertain herself with stories of Alexander instead of frightening herself with possibilities? She moved restlessly, trying to control her thoughts, and the chain on her ankle clanked. Zara laughed, but without much real mirth. Impossible to escape from her thoughts.

She heard no warning. There was simply no one in the doorway one minute and a man standing there the next. His face was covered; he was swathed in a burnous and keffi-yeh. Zara gasped in fear and struggled to her feet, her back against the broken stone wall. She cowered for a moment as the chain dragged painfully at her ankle and reminded her how helpless she was, then stiffened her courage and straightened her back.

She had tried not to imagine this moment, tried not to think that it must come. "Women will attend you," the bandit had told her grandly. "Have no fear for your virtue while you are in my protection!" She had tried not to believe that, either, knowing if she did it would only be worse if it happened. When.

"*Alhamdolillah!* Can it be you?" cried the man in a fierce whisper, and launched himself at her. He wrapped his arms around her, and she felt sickness rise in her throat, choking her. Pushing at him, she drew her head back, gasped for air to scream. But he was quick. One slim dark hand, fine and hard as steel, smothered the cry.

"Do not cry out!" he pleaded in English. "It is I!"

His other hand pulled down his scarf. Jalal the bandit himself, she thought bitterly, blinked, then stared. Smiling reassuringly, he took his hand from her mouth.

"*Prince Rafi!*" she whispered, aghast. Oh, worse, much worse than she had imagined! If she were a prisoner of the prince himself...now it all fell into place.

"I am a fool to have frightened you," he murmured. His arm still behind her back, tight across her waist, he lifted the other to stroke her hair from her face with melting tenderness. "But I was overwhelmed at seeing you. We did not think you could be here. Thank God I have found you! Are you well? How has he treated you?"

"Get away from me," Zara hissed, and fought against

his grip. "Do you think I'm a fool to be taken in by a trick like this?"

Releasing her instantly, His Serene Highness drew himself up in frowning amazement. "I am party to no trick. What is it you believe?"

"The man who kidnapped me is not Jalal the bandit," she said. "You should have chosen a conspirator who looked a little less like you, Your Highness! Who is he, really—one of your brothers? Am I supposed to faint into your arms with relief and gratitude at being rescued? Or doesn't my reaction matter too much?"

Prince Rafi eyed her with concern, then began to paw at his voluminous burnous. "I have water," he said gently, his voice still scarcely above a whisper. He pulled out a canteen. "And a little food. You are perhaps delirious with want after three days."

Furiously she knocked his hand aside. "Do you imagine I'll take anything at all from your hands? How *dare* you do this to me? Let me go!"

"*Khanum?*" called a voice from the passage. Prince Rafi froze.

"If they take me, we are lost," he whispered, lifting a finger to her lips, then whirled, glancing swiftly around, saw and slipped agilely through a gaping crack in the wall to the room beyond.

His reaction was so basic. Suddenly she was convinced. His life depended on her not giving away his presence here. Zara sank down onto her haunches and picked up the empty water pot. "I need water!" she cried in the same tone she had used to the prince, banging the pot on the ground for good measure. "How dare you leave me to starve?"

The frightened old woman slipped in through the doorway and murmured incomprehensible apologies. Zara gazed balefully at her. "Water!" she commanded. "*Ma'!*" She had learned the word quickly.

"*Ma',*" the old woman agreed, smiling and gesturing, and lifted the small earthenware jug she was carrying. Between her clothing, her sun-scored skin and the jug, she was a timeless figure. Probably she hadn't changed much since Alexander was here, Zara thought, watching the water trickle invitingly into her little pot. There was never enough water in the jug the woman brought, and she never seemed to understand Zara's attempts to convince her to carry a bigger one. Perhaps Jalal had given orders to limit what she got.

Zara snatched up the pot and drank thirstily, and the woman obligingly refilled it again with the last of what she had. That, Zara knew, had to last her the next twelve hours or so. The old woman reached into a pocket of her robe and pulled out a cake, which she placed in Zara's hungry hand with another smile and muttered word.

"*Shokran.* Thank you," Zara said, between bites, and the woman bowed, nodding, picked up the latrine bucket, and was gone.

Her chain did not allow her to reach the wall through which he had gone. "Are you still there?" Zara whispered between bites. Now she was desperate to know he had not gone and left her alone.

Prince Rafi slipped back into her cell and stood waiting in silence as she wolfed down the strange little cake. It tasted like a cross between wheat and potatoes, flavoured with unknown spices.

"It doesn't compare to a meal in your tent," she said dryly when she had finished, a little embarrassed to have shown such hunger in front of another human being. "But it's better than starving."

"Much better," he agreed gently, and suddenly she was no longer embarrassed. "I am sorry that you suffer for the troubles of my country. We should have dealt with this vandal long ago. My brother Omar said so, and we did not listen. It is my fault that you are here, and I will get you out."

He stepped to the door and looked through while Zara tried not to drink more of the water in the pot. "You are not guarded? Jalal must be very sure of his perimeter defences to mount no internal guard on this ruin."

Zara shook her head, though he had his back to her. "No, only that woman comes—usually twice a day." She took another tiny sip. "Otherwise I haven't seen anyone." Suddenly remembering, she gasped and said, "She'll be back in a minute with my…with the bucket. You should hide."

He obediently turned back and went through the wall, and a moment later she heard the old woman's step.

He was back with her again soon after the old woman left. He pulled out his canteen again, unscrewed the cap, and offered it to her without a word. Taking it with a little murmur of gratitude, Zara drank her fill for the first time in three days, and gave a long sigh of relief. Her hand was wet, and not to waste a drop, she wiped it across her dusty face. It was sharply, deliciously cooling.

"Oh, that is so good!" she said.

He was pulling something from another pocket and she watched him like a hungry cat. "Dried dates," he said. "Desert food."

After three days without sugar in any form, she found them surprisingly sweet. "Thank you!" she said, her voice cracking. "Thank you so much for coming!"

Tears of gratitude, hot as acid, burned her eyes. She saw how terrible a punishment solitary was…to be cut off from all human interaction had shaken her to the core. She had not understood how deeply she was affected till this moment. She hungered to touch him, to be held and comforted, to be reassured that she was a valued member of the human race. It was as hard to fight as the need for water.

He did not wait for her to ask. When she ate another date and began to cry in earnest over its precious sweetness, he cradled her in his arms, pressing her head to his shoulder. "Cry, my dear one," he soothed her. "Cry first, and then we will discuss the future."

She could not resist, but stood sobbing against him, while

a wave swept her—the release of pent-up fear and anguish that she had not allowed herself to feel before.

He felt the sobs tear at her, her struggles to keep them silent. He did not know what suffering her tears covered. Imprisonment, of course, that was natural enough, but…she had said no one came, no one hurt her, she had seen no one save the old woman. And yet…

"If he has hurt you, Beloved, believe that you shall be avenged ten times over," he promised, choking back sorrow and rage.

If she had been harmed, nothing would prevent Rafi from spilling the bandit's lifeblood, every ounce, into the sand of the desert he pretended to own. He would make her his wife and his queen regardless—nothing could prevent that except her own wish…but he would kill the bandit first, without mercy; he would cut his heart from his breast and hurl it to the dogs, if she had been hurt.

The rush of relief was terrible to him—as primitive as birth and death—when she shook her head resolutely against his breast. "No. He said he wouldn't, and I haven't seen a man since I got here. That was why I thought you…" she whispered through her tears, and broke off to sob again. "Please don't kill him on my behalf."

"Beloved, I cannot swear to spare this bandit's life," Rafi said. "But his death will not be laid at your door."

He stroked her hair tenderly, and murmured soothing words to her in his own tongue, the soft music of which she found comforting. Her sobs subsided quickly; she was resilient, and she drew back and smiled up at him.

"Now," he said. "We must talk. Every moment is precious. Sit, and tell me all that you know. Tell me first how you were brought here. We did not think to find you here. We thought you still on the other side of the river."

She stared at him. "What do you mean? What side of the river am I on?"

He helped her to sit, and pulled up his burnous to reveal desert boots, jeans, and a hip holster, from which he pulled a gun. Then he sat beside her, leaning against the ancient wall, and drew her against his shoulder with his left arm while he cradled the gun in his right and watched the door.

"We are in my brother Omar's territory, Central Barakat. You were not aware of being brought across the river?"

"No! Are you sure? Oh, sorry, how stupid! Of course you're sure. But I think I'd have realized."

"Were you drugged at any time?"

"Never—well, not so far as I know. Anyway, not while he had me on the horse, and he brought me straight here, we didn't make any stops. I thought it was going to kill the horse."

"How long did you ride?"

"Hours. I lost track."

He watched her. "You travelled for hours and you arrived at this place without crossing the river?"

Zara nodded. "After a long time he made me blindfold myself, and then I thought he was taking me into an underground cavern, or something. It was very damp. There was water dripping, and I could hear wind roaring at a distance. I was terrified he was going to tie me up deep underground. But then there was light, and voices, and we were here. By that time it was almost dawn, but I was put in this room before I saw much. Is this his headquarters? I thought he must have moved them."

He was frowning with thought, and nodded absently. "How can this be?" After a moment, his brow cleared. "What can you remember of where you were before you were forced to put on the blindfold?"

"I—oh! I almost forgot! I dropped...threw down that beautiful gold robe you gave me, just before we went inside, I think. I hoped it was, but maybe we were already in the cave.... I thought the helicopter searchlight might pick up the glitter. I'm sorry, was it very valuable?"

"It will never be more valuable than as a marker. We must send out parties to search for it, and solve this mystery."

"My sandals too. I did think I saw one of those big piles of rock in the distance when he blindfolded me, and I thought I heard running water," Zara contributed, as her memory came back. "But I couldn't tell whether we went towards it or not after I was blindfolded."

Still thinking, taking it in, Rafi nodded. "What else, my beloved? What other clues have you? For I must go. Time is passing."

She said doubtfully, "Do you know that you and Jalal look alike?"

"No, though you said it a moment ago. Is it a strong likeness?"

He turned and his black eyes fixed hers, reminding her, and doubt crept over her again. She had only his word for anything—only his word that she was on the Central Barakat side of the river. Didn't captors try to disorientate their captives in order to break them down mentally?

He understood directly what she was thinking, as if the thoughts were in his own head. Rafi shook his head at the great mystery. Had not his father often spoken of knowing his beloved wife's thoughts?

"Do not mistrust me," he urged her softly. "A moment of doubt at a critical moment and all may be lost. You can, and you must, trust me absolutely, now and forever. I am your husband. You are my wife. There can be no room between us for doubt."

Six

She felt the silence enter her soul. "What are you talking about?" she asked in a level voice.

Rafi drew back a little to look at her more closely, there in the circle of his arm. "You have not felt it? You do not yet know?" he asked.

She looked at him wordlessly. She was sure of nothing. She was so disorientated—could this all be part of a good-cop bad-cop routine? Was he going to try to convince her that she had amnesia or something?

He smiled into her suspicious, doubting eyes. "I knew it in the moment that I looked at you. My father also knew like this, in one blow, when he saw my stepmother for the first time. He saw his fate. It has been so for me. Of course you do not feel it now, here in a prison—your mind is too full of other things. But you almost felt it that night, as you sat beside me—I know that the knowledge was close to you then. Is it not so?"

With all her might, Zara resisted. She had to look away

from his dark, entrancing, love-certain eyes. "If it was true that you loved me, you would not take advantage of this situation."

She felt it go through him like a little shock. "You are right," he said. Gently he lifted his arm and took it away, and she felt her loss so keenly her eyes burned. She bit her lip on the retraction that almost burst from her. She was certain of nothing, and she was vulnerable. Very vulnerable.

"Now," he said, in a more businesslike tone.

"How did you get in here?" Zara pressed. "Aren't there armed guards?"

Rafi nodded. "We stopped the truck of a man from the village who brings in supplies. We thought he might know where you were being kept, but he swore he had not been asked to take his vegetables and meat anywhere save here." He shrugged. "We took his brother hostage, and I came inside in place of the brother."

"Why?"

"Why? To find news of you. I hoped to hear talk of where you were being kept. We did not dream that you were here." Rafi paused. "He is a fool to have brought you here. When I heard one of the women call to another that she would soon take the prisoner food and water, I did not dare to hope it could be you."

His voice was soothing her, making it difficult for her to concentrate. Zara shook her head, trying to clear it. It was so hard to keep her suspicions high, and yet she was sure she should. She had no idea whether it was plausible or not. At the dig they were supplied by such an arrangement as the prince described, by one of the local villagers in his battered truck...but what did that prove? Perhaps only that Prince Rafi knew his story would be convincing.

Before she could decide what to answer, he was on his feet. "My brothers are waiting for me in the desert, where they hold the villager hostage. I must leave with the truck. Do not lose hope. We will free you before long."

She struggled to her feet, and, without meaning to, wailed, "You're *leaving?*"

Of course he could not resist the tone of despair and longing. He bent and swiftly kissed her mouth. "I swear to return," he whispered.

It was their first kiss, and each felt the sudden fire of the connection. Rafi smiled, his teeth looking very white in the gloom, and restored his gun to the holster. He picked up her hand, and bent to kiss it. "I will come to you soon, my beloved."

Rafi moved quickly through the empty rooms of the fortress ravaged by time and Genghis Khan and crept through the shadows till he was close to where the now nearly empty truck stood. To his dismay, all the buying was finished. There was only one woman still standing with the driver. He strode out into the open, where he began a tuneless whistling as he slung an empty crate onto the pile of empties on the truck bed. He was surprised at the amount of food that had been offloaded. Jalal's band of rebels must be bigger than any of them had guessed.

The villager threw him a look of mingled fear and relief, set down the glass of mint tea with a word of thanks to the woman who had offered it, and signalled to him to get into the truck. Rafi wordlessly climbed into the cab.

"Is your stomach very bad?" cried the old woman to him. He had used his sick stomach as an excuse to ask for a toilet. But he had been gone a long time. Too long.

He was afraid to say too much in the desert accent. "Thank you, Mother," he said, shaking his head.

"You should have some mint tea, that will settle a sick stomach," she cried.

"Next time," he muttered, smiling.

The vegetable supplier slammed the truck noisily into gear and turned towards the gate.

"I told her my brother was sick with the same thing, that I had asked you my cousin to help but you were no better, with a stomach like a woman's. I drank four cups of tea, as a preventative. I thought you would never come back," he said, in frightened irritation.

He did not know who his passenger was, nor the partners who held his own brother hostage, but he had seen the bandit Jalal many times, and his passenger's likeness to him behind the keffiyeh was not reassuring. If he was on the wrong side of an internecine struggle, it would go badly for him and his family when whatever was coming was over—and a man who was on both sides was sure of only one thing: being on the wrong side.

Both men sighed with relief as the guard at the gate waved the truck through without incident.

"The tunnel. The tunnel of Queen Halimah," breathed Omar. "Is it possible?" They sat in silence for a moment, absorbing the thought. "It would explain why my siege of the place never had any effect. They could bring anything they wanted in through the tunnel."

"I've always thought that story was a myth," said Karim. "Every old ruin of a public works is attributed to Queen Halimah."

Rafi said, "Just because she's become a legend doesn't mean there isn't some truth to the stories. Zara wasn't taken across a bridge. She's on the other side of the river. How else did he get her there?"

Karim shrugged apologetically. "A woman who has just been taken hostage isn't necessarily in the best frame of mind for making acute observations."

"You're speaking from experience, of course," Omar returned. Karim flushed.

"There is nothing wrong with Zara's mental capacity," Rafi said quickly. "She said she wasn't taken across a bridge and I believe her. Anyway, the alternative requires not only that she was hallucinating, but that our soldiers screwed up at the bridges. The alternative is simpler. I think he's found a tunnel."

Omar said quietly, "I agree. Look at the archaeological dig. Your archaeologist is the first one to take the old stories about the change in the river's course seriously, and as a result he found the lost city of Iskandiyar." Omar lit a black cigarette and drew on it thoughtfully. "And there's a direct connection, isn't there? Because the story suggests that the course of the river was changed in order to build a tunnel under it. Queen Halimah had a tunnel built and then moved the river to flow over it, isn't that the archaeologist's idea?"

Rafi, who had heard it all at impassioned length from Gordon at the time of giving permission for the dig, nodded. "That's about it."

"We need to consult him on this. He must have done aerial photography of the whole area when he was looking for Iskandiyar," Omar continued. "Maybe they'll show something."

"We also have Zara's help," Rafi said, and told them about the golden robe. "I want to get the men to work searching for that robe."

His brothers stared at him. "It'll be covered with sand, if not blown away entirely," Karim said. "It's been four days."

"They'll find it somewhere," Rafi insisted quietly. "Don't give up till they have."

Omar frowned. "What are you going to be doing meanwhile?"

"I'm going back into Jalal's camp."

There was a startled silence. Omar squinted at him through the smoke. "You can't do it," he began.

Karim jumped in. "You're crazy, Rafi! What good will it do if you're taken prisoner, too?"

"I don't intend to be taken prisoner. She's being kept in an isolated part of the ruined fortress and there are plenty of places to hide."

"I still think we should just roll up with tanks and smash through the main gate," Karim said.

"She is chained to a wall in a ruin. Even artillery fire could bring the place down on her head. Mortar certainly would," Rafi told him. "I am going to get her free before we make any attempt to storm the place, and that is not open to discussion."

Karim turned to Omar. "He's crazy. Don't you think he's crazy? We can't let him do it."

The cigarette dropped to the sand, and Omar's boot absently crushed it in. He looked at Karim and shrugged. "It's his woman, Karim. What would you be saying right now if it were Caroline?"

Karim started to say something, stopped, thought for a moment, and shook his head in resignation.

"There's no time to argue. We've got to get organized. I want to go back in with some equipment and supplies. We have to work out how to get me in there. And we have to make contingency plans, and work out a signalling system, because once in I may not get out again," said Rafi.

She lived in perpetual shadow. The light in her prison was diffused, creeping in through the cracks between the stones, spilling in from the passage outside, with more or less intensity, depending on the time of day. Zara lay and watched the sunlight retreat through the door and down the passage, until she was in the near darkness that she knew would last till morning. Sometimes the firelight reached her, but more usually it appeared only as flickering shadows.

She was being swept by feelings over which she seemed to have no control. Sometimes she loved Rafi so fiercely it hurt. From these deep feelings of trust and longing she would be swept to feelings of terrible doubt. Everything he had said and done came under the review of a hard, frightened little voice in her: how was it Jalal and he looked so much alike? And why was he ignorant of that fact....? And how had he found her cell? He had said he heard two women talking about taking her water, but Rafi had arrived *before* the old woman with the water.

Those and a thousand other doubts tormented her, like flies buzzing around her head. And there was no reality check in a place like this. She had nothing but her own mind, and her mind at the moment was a sea of chaos with hardly a spar in sight.

Would he come back, or was it a trick?

If he did come back, should she trust him?

At last she wrapped herself in the dirty blanket and fell asleep on her hard bed to dream confused dreams. She awoke, as usual, in the night. Hunger and thirst and discomfort disturbed her sleep, but now she felt that something had awakened her. She sat up, leaning against the wall, and listened for a moment, but there was only silence.

"Rafi?" she whispered.

Suddenly there was the sound of an explosion, and the passage wall outside her cell glowed a faint red for a moment. Then there was the crackle of gunfire, and she heard shouts and calls, and more gunfire. Explosions, and the sounds of galloping horses, the high ululating cry of raiders.

For several minutes, her heart beating crazily with fear and uncertainty, Zara sat listening to the sounds of attack. Nameless terrors rushed through her head: if everyone who knew she was here was killed, would she be left to starve and die? Who were the attackers? What if they found her? How would she be treated? As a freed hostage, or as a spoil of war?

It was over quickly. The horse hooves faded into the distance, the last shots were fired, the uncomprehending screams of women were silenced, the random flickering light changed to utter darkness. A man shouted incomprehensibly for a few minutes and then all was silent.

Zara stood waiting. All she could hear now was her own anguished heartbeat. Wild thoughts occurred to her like cuts from an invisible whip. What had happened? Were they alive or dead out there? Suppose it had been a chemical attack? She was so powerless here, chained to the wall like a dog, to be forgotten or remembered at someone's whim...should she call out or remain silent? What was safer?

She saw the glimmer of a distant light reflected on the wall of the passage outside the door. She watched it without breathing. She had never seen a light there at night before; no one ever came to her cell during the hours of darkness, but somehow she knew that this was the light of a lantern approaching her.

Footsteps, and then the lantern was in the doorway, held high. She saw the dark eyes, and almost cried his name aloud. She bit it back for a split second, and then noticed the beard.

"You are well?" said Jalal the bandit.

Her breath hissed between her teeth. Thank God she had not called Rafi's name! Her heart had never beat so wildly in her life. Sick fear invaded her. What was he going to do? She needed a delaying tactic, needed to get him talking...

"What happened?" she asked.

His eyes glittered as they raked her, seeking the answer to some question. "A small harassing campaign—it is nothing. A few men from one of the desert tribes, perhaps, looking for easy pickings, hoping to find our guards asleep. Or perhaps not."

She stared at him.

"Perhaps it was your lover, the prince. He may have hoped to judge our strength and readiness from our response to such a raid. What do you think?"

"Or maybe he planted a bomb inside the camp. Maybe it will go off when you least expect it." She stood wrapped in her blanket, her eyes wide in the lantern light. He was reminded suddenly of a small, trapped animal, delicate, beautiful, but capable of very fierce resistance if attacked.

"Do not be afraid of me," he said suddenly. "You are in no danger here. My men obey me."

"Then why are you keeping me?" she managed to ask over the lump of terror in her throat.

Jalal grinned, showing his teeth like a fierce wild animal that smiles as a warning. "You are the bait in my trap to draw the princes of Barakat. They will come to me—of this you may be sure."

"They'll come and kill you, I'm sure of that."

He smiled and shook his head. "They cannot kill me. They know it."

His confidence could only be braggadocio. If she could keep him talking about the magic that made him invincible.... "Really?" she asked in bright curiosity, as if they were at a cocktail party. "Why not? What makes you invincible?"

He grinned again. "Ask your lover, Prince Rafi, the next time you see him! He will tell you! You have food, water?"

Taken aback by the sudden question, Zara nodded dumbly.

"It is good." To her amazement he bowed and swept out.

It was useless to lie down. She was wide awake with nerves. She sat waiting for her eyes to grow accustomed to the darkness again, thinking. She wished he had left her the lantern. The night was friendlier when you had light.

As if the thought gave rise to a hallucination, she saw the flickering glow of a light, not from the passage, but from that gap in the wall opposite that led to a room beyond.

"He never thought you would be able to respond to his parting advice so quickly as this," Prince Rafi murmured, sticking his head and the candle through the wall and smiling at her, "but since I'm here, you may as well take advantage of my presence, don't you think?"

Seven

"**P**rince Rafi!" she whispered, and threw herself towards him. The chain around her ankle pulled her up short so that she fell forward, but he dropped the candle and swooped to catch her in his arms. Relief overwhelmed her.

The candle lay burning in the dust as his mouth found hers. Zara trembled as his passion enclosed her. Her heart yearned towards him, she felt both tears and laughter in her blood, and the complete conviction that she had come home at last.

His mouth was cool and warm at the same time, his tongue delicious, his hold both tender and ruthless, his body accommodating hers like the softest bed, and yet so strongly muscled. When their mouths parted she lay in his arms, and felt his lips tremble along her throat, her cheek, her forehead, her hair, felt her own response to the loving touch swamp her, drown her, move her almost unbearably to tears and joy.

"Beloved," he was murmuring. "My beloved."

The candle flame gave a last flicker in the dust and went out. This broke through the spell, and she reluctantly drew away. She was so vulnerable here, both mentally and physically. Between one moment and the next, she had become desperate for his company, his touch, considered him her saviour.... She knew such things happened in situations like this. Hostages fell in love with their captors. Judgement got lost.

Her emotions were so near the surface—she had never before experienced anything like what she felt now around Prince Rafi. It frightened her, because what else could it be but the peculiar madness of being held hostage?

He didn't attempt to keep his hold on her, but bent and snatched up the candle while the glow of the wick still announced its whereabouts. Zara heard the click of a lighter, and then the candle flame flared up again.

"Oh, how lovely to have light!" she exclaimed involuntarily. "It's so beautiful, candlelight!" And again, the softness of it, the tenderness of that fragile flame in a dark world brought her close to tears.

He stood before her, holding the candle up and looking at her by its light, much as the bandit had done, and with the same dark, flashing eyes. But for all that, there was a world of difference in his gaze. She would never mistake them for more than a fleeting moment. "Come," he murmured. "Let us sit."

She allowed him to guide her to where her blanket lay crumpled, and stood passively holding the candle while he folded it and placed it neatly on the ground. They sat and Rafi carefully spilled a little wax and fixed the candle on the ground between them.

"Now," he said.

Questions tumbled over themselves in her mind. "You came back," she said wonderingly. "How did you do it? Was that your men who made the attack tonight?"

"Not my men, but my brothers, and my Cup Companions, and theirs."

"Your brothers? All three of you?" she repeated. "But what if you'd all been killed?"

He shook his head. "We did not think it likely. In any case, most of the noise and light was caused by fireworks." He tapped the stone wall they were leaning against with one knuckle. "This structure is not so sturdy that we could risk real mortar. We fired some mortar out into the desert as if we had bad aim, then my brothers rode up with the Companions firing and making as much noise as possible, and I slipped in as the guards all moved to counter the assault they expected. Instead of attacking, they rode past."

He was so clean. He smelled of soap and aftershave. Zara inhaled the delightful odour of him, and was abruptly aware of her own condition.

"I'm very dirty," she said. "I know I smell horrible, and my hair is so matted—I wish I had a comb, even!"

Rafi looked into her eyes and said, "Your smell is intoxication to me, and your hair a bed of delight." She shivered with longing.

"But since you are unhappy..." Rafi leaned a little to one side and slipped his hand into the pocket of his black jeans, which he wore with a loose white shirt and the same enveloping white keffiyeh around his head that Jalal and his men wore. He was dressed like one of them.

What he pulled out was a small velvet box. He offered it to her on his palm.

Zara frowned wonderingly. "But what is it?"

"It is for you," he only said. "Take it."

She took the box, marvelling at the velvet's smoothness to the touch after days of feeling the rough blanket, and grit and hard stone.

It was a ring. A ring to dream of, a ring to die for. A huge deep green cabochon-cut emerald encircled by gleaming, glittering diamonds, rubies, sapphires. It caught the candle's glow, magnifying and intensifying it, so that she seemed to look through the ring into a starry sky.

"Ohhhh," breathed Zara. She could find no words. "How beautiful." She raised her eyes to his. "But—"

Rafi lifted his hand to stop the words on her lips. "This is a wishing ring," he said. "No more, no less. Rub the ring, and make a wish, and it will give you your desire."

She smiled, caught like a child by the promise of magic. "Really? Whatever I ask for? Suppose I ask to be free?"

"Some wishes take longer than others, but all are granted," Rafi assured her. "Put it on, and make a wish."

It was large, fitting her middle finger, where it made her hand look as if it belonged to some Eastern potentate's favourite. "What will happen when I rub it? Will a genie appear?"

"The genie is already here." He bowed. "Rub the ring, my lady, close your eyes tight, and name your wish."

She laughed aloud, for the first time in days, and instantly choked it back, reminded of her surroundings. Laughter carried like no other sound. Her heart soared. "All right!" she said, closing her eyes to concentrate and carefully rubbing the ring. "I wish I had a comb!"

Rafi raised his arms in the air, waving his hands, and said, "Abracadabra! You may open your eyes, my lady!"

On his palm lay a neat, wide-toothed comb. Zara gasped with delight and reached for it. "You have one! How did you know?"

"But the ring is magic, lady," he said, his eyes flashing with love and humour. "I of myself know nothing. Shall I comb your hair for you?"

Entranced by the look in his eyes, she passed the comb back to him. Rafi took it, picked up a lock of her matted hair, and began tenderly working the comb through it.

"Madam, shall the genie tell you a story while he combs your hair?"

Zara sighed, feeling his hands in her hair, feeling how the shock of his touch travelled to her scalp and over her skin. How her prison had been transformed! Just in this

moment, she thought, if freedom meant she would not see
him again, she would not change places with anyone.

"Oh, yes, tell me a story!"

"Turn your back, so that I can reach, please," he said.
She turned, and crossed her legs under her, pulling the slit
skirt of the once-white dress up around her hips and knees.

Behind her, his voice began, "Once upon a time, long
ago, there lived a great king. Mahmoud of Ghazna was his
name. This king had a beautiful Turkish slave, Ayaz. Ayaz
was a faithful and very beloved slave, whose hair was a
special glory. It was long, and curling, and tumbled down
the slave's back like a thousand black narcissus blooms,
and it seemed that even the candlelight was ensnared in the
fragrant net of curls."

His voice was hypnotic, and his hands worked through
her curls as he spoke, so that Zara was uncertain whether
it was present or past that he spoke of. His touch caused
tremors to ripple over her body—shivery, delicious little
tremors that put her in a kind of trance.

"The slave was forbidden to the king, and the king knew
it and strove to live by the law. But one night, the king
drank more than usual, and in the gentle haze he looked
and saw the black hair, ringlet upon ringlet, 'in every ringlet a thousand hearts and under every lock a hundred thousand souls,' and desire filled him. He felt his approach to
danger, and cried out to the slave, 'Your hair leads me
astray from the path of virtue! Cut it off so that it will cease
to tempt me!' and he handed Ayaz a knife.

"Ayaz, as perfect in obedience as in beauty, picked up
the knife and merely asked, 'How short shall I cut it, Lord?'

"'Cut off half of it,' said the poor king.

"And instantly the slave lifted the ends of those magnificent curls onto the roots, put the knife into the fold, and
cut. The king praised such devotion, drank more wine, and
fell asleep.

"But in the morning!" Rafi went on, still working his
deft way through the tangles of her hair. "When the slave

appeared to the king for the first time, shorn of those beautiful locks, how the king was miserable, and angry with himself and all the world for what he had commanded to be done. He sank into a gloom, getting up and sitting down again and approachable by no one.

"Then his Cup Companions and his courtiers began to worry, for a king who is unhappy with himself may be a risk to others. So they wondered among themselves what could be done to bring the king back into his own good graces. At last, they went to the great poet Unsuri. 'Compose a poem that will pacify the king, and recite it to him,' they begged.

"And so Unsuri went in to the king, who said to him, 'Well, say something about this.' And being a great poet, Unsuri immediately composed a poem."

"What was the poem?"

He recited it to her in a haunting, rhythmic voice not unlike the sounds made by Motreb on the night of the feast.

"That sounds magical," she said with a smile. "I feel better, and I don't even know what it means!"

"It has been attempted by several translators over the past nine hundred years. Literally, it means, 'It may be a crime to have cut a few of the curls of such an idol of beauty, but what's the point of this restless gloom? Instead you should call for wine and wassail, and be of good cheer. A cypress is most decorative when it has been trimmed!'"

Zara wrinkled her nose a little in disappointment. He was quick to catch it. "Yes, the poem in the original is more than its meaning. A modern poet has done it better justice. Shall I recite that?"

She nodded.

He began to recite with a more pronounced rhythm than she was used to hearing in English. It was seductive.

"whisper of ambergris through the cut of beauty
against the curve of spine, deep swathe and coal
his eyes in faint of length and glow

on a nape of hyacinth and honey
unravelling knots swallowed sweet and long
holding too much in the billow

although scissor slips of shame find an unsettled dawn,
watch, and call for wine,
as the strong green cypress winds radiant

clipped only this morning.''

His voice was rich, deep, taking the poem personally.
She felt his eyes on her own neck, on the billow of her
hair, and every word was charged.

When he finished they sat in silence, while Rafi drew the
comb long and straight through her untangled hair.

''That's...lovely,'' she breathed at last. She liked poetry,
but she'd never once met a man who would so unselfcon-
sciously recite it. Or admit to sharing a poet's feeling.

''Yes,'' he said, and he meant more than the poem.

''So, do you want me to cut my hair off?'' she said with
a smile, fighting to loosen the grip of the dangerous mood.

Rafi dropped the comb and laughed. ''Never!'' He drew
his hands down through the full length of her hair from
crown to below her waist, and lifted it to fall in a glittering
wave in the candlelight.

Zara swung around to face him, and took the comb as
he offered it to her. She drew it through her hair for the
pleasure of feeling how neat it was again, her head tilting
so that her face was half hidden from him. ''Doesn't it
tempt you from the path of virtue?''

He sat up and took her wrist, stopping the hypnotic,
rhythmic motion. ''Your hair tempts me, yes. It incites me
to desire, with many other things about you. But you are
not a slave, and you are not forbidden to me. It is marriage
that I think of. You know this. I have said it.''

She dropped her head further, veiling her face completely, and made no answer. There was a moment's si-

lence. Against his hand she felt his heartbeat and her own, two separate strands, and listened while they merged for a few powerful synchronous beats, then parted again, like the different threads of a melody.

They sat for a long, silent moment, both of them listening to the music of their hearts. Then Zara yawned, but whether from nerves or fatigue she didn't know. One of the worst torments of her imprisonment was not being able to sleep soundly, but in Rafi's presence she was miles from feeling sleepy.

"It is time you slept," he said.

"Is it very late?" she asked.

"Very," he agreed. "Nearly three."

She was surprised. She had thought it around midnight. She felt that she could have sat talking to him for hours yet. But she knew he would have to leave the camp again before dawn.

"How are you going to get out again?"

Rafi smiled. "I will get out again when I take you with me. This requires a plan, which it has not been possible to make without knowing more about the setup here. First I must locate the tunnel that connects this camp to the other side of the river. Then when we have worked out a plan, I will communicate it to my brothers."

She stared. "You—what are you saying? You can't *stay* here!"

"Why not?"

"Because…well, it's obvious! They'll catch you!"

He smiled. "You will learn to have more faith in your husband than this."

Zara fell silent. There were a million responses to this, but she could not find the one that fit.

"But we will not plan yet. Make another wish on your wishing ring," Rafi commanded, "and then we shall sleep."

"Really?"

"What do you most wish for?"

"A toothbrush!" she said.

Rafi inclined his head. "It shall be done, lady. And what else?"

She blinked and smiled her perplexity at him.

"Do not you wish for a softer bed?" he asked.

Zara's face abruptly lost its smile. "What? How can you possibly—"

"But have you not understood that I am your genie? Do you wish for a softer bed?"

She looked at him out of the corner of her eyes. "Ye-es," she said slowly.

"Then close your eyes, rub the magic ring and make a wish. Do not open them again until I tell you to do so."

A bubble of laughter escaped her. How astonishing to think that she should laugh in such a place! Oh, he changed everything! And if he really meant to stay...

Zara closed her eyes, lifted her hand, and ritually rubbed her ring. "I wish I had a softer bed," she chanted. She heard Rafi get up from her side and step across the room. When she peeked he had disappeared, she thought through the hole in the wall. She closed her eyes again.

"You may open your eyes now."

He was standing there with a roll of something. Zara gaped at him. First holding out to her a small package, he proceeded to spread the roll out on the floor against the wall. It was a sheet of foam rubber, two inches deep, about two feet by six, grey like the stones behind the decorative tiles that had once covered the floor completely.

"I don't believe it!" she breathed. "And this—!" In her hand was a little plastic package containing a tiny tooth-brush and tube of toothpaste, of the kind you found in hotels. "You really are a genie! How did—where..." The words died on her lips.

"But it is magic, my lady. You must not question the workings of magic."

He folded the blanket in two and spread it on the little

mattress. Obediently, at his command, Zara slipped between the two folds and lay down.

"Oh, what luxury! Oh, how wonderful not to feel every
bone in my body!" She propped herself up on one elbow.
"But where are you going to sleep?"

"Next door. It is risking too much to stay with you—
we have seen tonight that someone may come at any time."

"What if someone goes into that room?"

"The doorway is a pile of rubble. Tomorrow I will build
it higher. Tonight I will watch. I am well armed and there
are men waiting for my signal in the desert. Sleep in the
knowledge that you are safe, my beloved."

He crouched by her as she lay down again, picked up
the candle and stood looking down, the tenderest of smiles
in his eyes.

She was a hostage in the heart of a rebel's fortress, but
she had never felt so safe, so cherished, so protected, in her
life. Zara smiled up at the prince, and suddenly sleepiness
crept over her. She breathed deeply, her eyes closing.

"Goodnight, sweet prince," she whispered.

She watched under drowsy, contented eyelids as the light
moved away through the crack in the wall and into the next
room. She watched a few minutes until it was extinguished.

She drew her hand up superstitiously and rubbed the
ring. "Please keep him safe," she whispered. A moment
later, still holding the ring, she was asleep.

Eight

There was a hole high up in the wall, a hole that let in one fat ray of sunlight for a few minutes every morning. Although the walls were porous, it was the only direct sunlight Zara saw, and after the first day she had moved her bed so that the beam would play on her face in the morning and wake her. Even this brief dose of sunlight was better than nothing.

Last night, Rafi had placed her new mattress in a slightly different position, and when she awoke the sunbeam was playing with the dust a few inches from her eyes. She smiled in lazy pleasure, for the moment not remembering anything, only watching the dance of the dust motes in the warm sunlight.

She had slept well. She remembered Prince Rafi first, and then where she was. With a sudden motion, she lifted her hand and saw that the ring was really there, on her middle finger. Zara smiled, stretching out her hand in the sunlight, turning the ring so that the stones caught the light and sparkled. It was exotically beautiful, and a stone that size must be worth a king's ransom.

Zara stretched and sat up, calling Prince Rafi's name in a whisper, and then a low murmur, but he did not answer. Her heart kicked nervously. Where was he? Where could he be?

But she was quick to take advantage of his absence to use the toilet. Afterwards she reached for the little dipper that held her drinking water. She always tried to save one mouthful for the mornings, to allow her to rinse her dust-dry mouth when she woke. This morning she used it to brush her teeth, and sighed for the wonder of such a simple pleasure as cleanliness.

Then she sat down on her blessedly soft bed in her ray of sunlight again and played with it until the sun climbed higher and it disappeared. That was her entertainment for the day. Usually nothing now would happen until the old woman came with her water and food.

The old woman! Zara looked down at the foam mattress. It was grey, practically invisible in the poor light, but she had no idea how sharp the old woman's eyes were. Quickly she got up and spread the blanket so that it covered the mattress as far as possible. The blanket wasn't as long as the foam, but spread on the bias, corner to corner, it covered much of it. When the woman came Zara would sit on the end that was visible.

She took off her ring, hiding it under the blanket, and settled to wait. It had been the same every day. She sat and tried to entertain herself with anything she could remember—the plot of old films, fairy tales, history, Iskandiyar, her own memories. Tried to keep the knowledge of her plight and her fears out of her mind.

Today, she found, she had an additional worry. It was not her usual nature to be nervous, it was part of the torment of imprisonment—but she was growing more and more afraid. Where was Prince Rafi? What if he had gone out for a reconnoitre or something and been caught? What would they do to him? Would Jalal recognize him? Suppose they killed him before they realized?

The old woman came at last with water and another bit of food, and Zara watched her carefully for any signs that might tell her something had occurred. But she seemed exactly like her usual self. When the woman returned for the second time with the empty pail, Zara got her attention, then put two hands up under her tilted head and mimed sleeping.

"Boom! Boom!" she said, waving her hands to indicate an explosion, opening wide eyes to indicate the sleeper's surprise.

The old woman nodded her head vigorously. "Boom!" she agreed, showing how she herself had come bolt upright in her bed. She waved her hands and made rushing noises to indicate how people had run hither and yon, and made a comment that Zara of course could not understand.

Encouraged by this willingness to communicate, Zara shot herself in the chest with her fingers and died, then lifted her hands and eyebrows to indicate a question.

The old woman shook her head. No deaths. Some hurt in the arm, or the leg, but not seriously, she indicated. Zara held up her hands in surrender, and the woman shook her head. No prisoners either.

None at all?

None.

Then the woman did a remarkable thing. She stretched out her hands to Zara, and shook her head in sad resignation, then clapped her palms together, muttering something that even across the language barrier Zara knew could be nothing other than "Poor child!"

So the woman did not approve. Zara shrugged, as if to say, What can we poor women do? The woman mirrored her shrug, and then they smiled at each other.

"Why do we do it?" Zara asked in English. "Why do we let them run the world in this ridiculous, violent way?

Bang! Bang!'' She pointed her hands like six-guns, shooting wildly at anything.

The old woman shook her head in resigned agreement, speaking in her own language. "War, always war! Never peace!" she cried, and Zara, recognizing the word *Salaamat,* understood.

So two women stood in a dusty prison and discovered understanding and agreement across the barrier of language and the arbitrary divisions of race, nationhood, creed, and politics, and knew in their hearts that, whatever surrounded them, they were not enemies.

And then one, the warder, picked up her water jug and went out, unwillingly leaving the other, her prisoner, chained like an animal to the wall.

Rafi returned soon after, whistling softly to announce his presence, and then climbing through the wall from the next room.

Zara heaved a sigh of relief. "Oh, thank God! I was getting so worried! Where have you been?"

He smiled at her in a way that turned her bones to water. "Have you been worried for me, Beloved?"

She could not imagine the term on the lips of any other man. Her eyes fell and she nodded, half-smiling.

"Do not worry. I will be safe because I must. Nothing will happen to prevent me taking you from this place."

The sweet silence of lovers fell between them. "Have you made a wish while I was away?"

She had wished for his safety, in the foolish weakness of human superstition. She did not say so, but he shook his head patiently, as if he guessed. "Wish only for yourself while you are here. What do you wish for?"

She was almost beginning to believe he could do anything, even here in the enemy camp. "A bar of soap and a cool bath," she challenged him, half believing that two Companions would march through the door with a marble tub filled with bubbles.

"Your wish is my command," intoned the genie, and slipped back through the wall. A second later he reappeared with a large pail of water. He set it down, disappeared again, and when he returned he held a facecloth and a bar of—

"Soap!" she cried, in a hoarse, happy whisper. He passed it to her and she put it to her nose, sniffing luxuriously. It was delicately, deliciously scented with almonds and patchouli. "Oh, where on earth did you find *this?*"

"It is the magic of the ring," said the genie. "There is no towel to dry you, but the air will serve as your towel. Shall the genie bathe you, Madame?"

She glinted a smile at him. "I suppose that means there's no point wishing for something to scrub my back with?"

He lifted his hands. "But no. It means that I am the back scrubber."

She didn't know why she let him do it. Prince Rafi approached her, turned her so that her back was to him, and deliberately lifted her hair aside and began to pull down the zipper of her dress.

It was a long zipper, extending from her neck all the way to below her waist. She heard the little cry of its passage and her skin shivered with expectation. She should stop him, should push him away, should order him out while she bathed...but she did not.

When the once-white fabric fell down around her hips, Rafi caught it and lifted it up over her head. He tossed it on her mattress without turning his eyes from her.

She was small, and perfectly formed for him, but he knew that already. She stood in the briefest of briefs, her only garment save for the black hair that fell down her back and over one shoulder like a veil.

She saw his breath catch in his chest, but he said nothing.

His eyes fell to the chain that encircled her ankle, and her own gaze followed. She could not take off her briefs over that. Yet she felt his hands in the elastic of the waist, and held her breath.

The high whisper of the tearing fabric was echoed by Zara's own indrawn breath as Rafi held the two ends of the torn silk and his muscles contracted with the effort not to touch her skin. After a moment, impersonal as a servant, he pulled the briefs down her free leg, inviting her to step out of them.

He straightened and stood looking at her again, her high beautiful breasts, sloping hips, graceful limbs, with eyes so dark with passion and control she had to part her lips to breathe.

He said in an ordinary voice, "When I take you to my palace, as I shall do as soon as I have you free, then you will have a real bath," and she was grateful for his restraint. He bent to the pail of water, dropped in the facecloth, and began to rub it with soap.

"Do you have all the modern conveniences in the palace?"

He laughed, throwing his head back, very masculine and hearty for a second until he remembered and choked it off. "In the West, of course, baths are a modern innovation. In my palace, the *hamam* has been an essential for many centuries, my beloved."

Zara blushed with embarrassment. "Pardon my cultural arrogance," she said. "I do know better."

He started with her face. Carefully, meticulously, he washed her forehead, ears, eyes, cheeks, chin, lips, neck, throat; gently rinsed and wiped them.

"Shall I describe the bath that you shall enjoy as my queen?" Rafi asked in the middle of this.

How could she protest that she would not be his queen?

He took her assent for granted. "The queen's bath chamber is quite new, only about a hundred and twenty years old. My ancestor added a large wing to the summer palace when he took a new young wife who pleased him so much that the other wives became jealous. Her name was Hala, and this part of the palace is still called Hala's wing. By tradition it belongs to the chief wife. My stepmother used it all her life, whenever we went there.''

Her shoulders, her arms, underarms, breasts and back…his touch was thrilling and hypnotic at the same time. She went into a trance of shivery yet sleepy pleasure.

''The queen's bath is a suite of rooms about ten times the size of your present chamber, my lady, and built all of the rarest marble. In some parts it is inlaid with designs in many colours. It was the work of a very fine mosaic artist, the greatest of his day. There you will see Shirin depicted bathing in a stream, and Khosrow watching her. In a long line around the walls are all his horses and men and elephants caparisoned in the most beautiful of colours, for he was on the hunt when he saw her.''

He scrubbed her hands, each finger separately, then drew her down to rinse them in the blessedly cool water. She wondered how he had gotten it, but she didn't want to speak for fear of breaking the spell. Her skin seemed to be breathing again for the first time in days, and between the luxury of that and the sensation of his electric touch, she was in heaven.

''There are other scenes, too, from tales that pleased my ancestor's young wife. Some are on the ceiling, to beguile the queen's eye while she is being massaged by the attendant, some on the walls, some on the floor of the bathing pools. History suggests that my ancestor and his young wife enjoyed bathing together. Perhaps you and I, too, will bathe there. Then I will tell you the stories that the pictures illustrate.''

He washed her stomach, abdomen, buttocks. ''Your attendants will wash your body and hair, and massage you and rub rich emollient oils into your skin. Your genie has not brought any of these oils with him, my lady, because if you had all you wished here, what would tempt you to visit the palace? So some pleasures must be delayed for the sake of your lover.''

"Just the smell of this soap is heaven, at the moment," she said.

With careful deliberation, he was washing her sex. He was gentler than she could have dreamed, his touch human and personal but not sexual—and yet not denying her sexuality, either, or his own.

"When you have been massaged with the sweet-smelling oils of the *hamam*, my love, and I am beside you, your body lazy with luxury, how will you be able to resist me? If I take you then and kiss you, how will you say no to me? It would not be possible."

His voice was as sensuous as his touch. Zara's eyes were half closing where she stood, her skin rippled by wave after wave of shivery anticipation.

She thought he was waiting for something from her, but her brain was too slow now.

"No?" she asked weakly.

He smiled, as if he had had all the answer he wanted. If his touch had such power as this over her, she would be his in the end. She must be his.

"Put your foot in the pail," he commanded, and crouched down to draw the water up to her thigh with the cloth as he rubbed her, with long hypnotic strokes from thigh to shin. She rested her hand on his shoulder and lifted her foot while he scrubbed the accumulated dirt and dust from it, then she shook it dry, put it gingerly down onto the gritty floor again, and put the other foot into the water. This time she was immune to the clank of her chain.

It was blissful to immerse even just her foot in the cooling water, magic to feel so clean. But it was Rafi's touch that made her heart beat hard, his caring expertise that pulled her lips into a soft smile.

"I never expected to have my feet washed by a king," she said. "Isn't this a little out of character for you?"

He glanced up at her. "But a king is born to service."

"He is?"

"He serves his people. That is his duty. If—when you

marry me, you too will face this duty. My stepmother was a great queen. She did many things to improve the lot of the people. You will be like her. You *are* like her.''

"But I'm an archaeologist!''

"And may an archaeologist not serve the people? Perhaps we will build an important museum. Or turn the site of Iskandiyar, when you are finished there, into a tourist attraction, which will bring work to the people of the desert.''

Zara was silent with surprise. "You've been thinking about it a lot,'' she said weakly.

"How can a man think of marrying a woman without thinking how their future will be? And how can a king give his people a queen without thinking of their welfare in his choice?''

"You have a lot of duties,'' she observed. "Any others I should know about?''

He smiled up at her from his position at her feet. "Every man serves his wife in the matter of physical pleasures. That also is a duty.''

"Is your life all duty, then?''

He kissed her on the side of the knee. "God is merciful to us. Some pleasures it pleases Him to call duty.''

She had never felt the side of the knee as an erogenous zone before. That and the promise in his voice made her nerves sing. She laughed softly. "Are you seriously telling me God calls sexual pleasure a duty?''

Rafi looked up at her in surprise. "But of course! Do you doubt it? Are Western men such fools? The Prophet— may his name be praised!—instructed his followers not to climb on their wives like a mule, and get off again leaving her unfulfilled. 'Send a messenger first,' he said, and when they asked him what messenger, he told them, 'A kiss, a caress.' What is it you say in English?—'A word to the wise is sufficient.'''

He was finished now, and sat there on his heels, smiling up at her. "How do you feel, my lady?''

"Very, very clean. And pampered. Thank you."

As he had said, the air had already dried her skin. "I suppose I have to get dressed again," she said ruefully, glancing down at the filthy dress with reluctance.

He shook his head in bewilderment. "But mistress," the genie protested, "have you not learned yet to use your ring?"

Zara's eyes widened with astonishment. "You—do you mean it? Really? Clean clothes?"

He shrugged. "Wish and see."

"All right." She lifted her hand and rubbed the ring, closing her eyes. She felt him silently leave her side as she did so. "I wish for clean clothes," she murmured.

She opened her eyes. The bucket, soap and cloth and her clothes were gone, and she was alone in the room. For a moment of shocking vulnerability, she thought, panicked, *What if Jalal came to see me now?* And she realized how protected Rafi's presence made her feel.

But she had no more than time to think it before Rafi was slipping back through the wall. In his hand he carried a little pile of folded white fabric. He offered it to her. On top was a neat little pair of cotton briefs, and she heaved a sigh of delight. The little puzzle of how to get them past her shackle was quickly solved—she sat and put the shackled foot through one leg, then forced the fabric up her ankle inside and past the iron. Then she could slip the other foot through and draw them up around her hips. There was nothing sexy or lacy about them, they were comfortable, well-fitting. Just what she needed.

"Oh, that feels so much better!" she exclaimed. "What else?"

She lifted up next a pair of loose white cotton pants of ingenious wrap-around design that allowed her to fold them up around her legs and tie them at the waist. Last of all came a tunic. Only when she had put it all on did she truly appreciate what he had done—the tunic reproduced the high neck and long sleeves of her dress in cool airy cotton, and the pant legs were so loose and floppy that they looked like a skirt with slits up the sides.

"But—it's almost the exact pattern of my dress!" she exclaimed. "The old woman will never see the difference in this light!" Even Jalal would probably not notice. He had seen her only in darkness, by moonlight, lamplight, firelight. "How—where did you find such a thing?"

Prince Rafi looked at her.

"Zara, I am king." He spoke gently, but she suddenly felt his power like an aura emanating from him.

Nervously, she grinned. "So you wave your hand and some minion does your bidding?"

His eyes were black suddenly. "If *you* will do my bidding when the time comes, that will be enough for me."

Nine

That night he lay with her on the narrow bed, wrapping her in his arms as they talked. She thought how strange it was that she should feel so safe in such surroundings. Not since her toddler days, when being carried on her father's shoulders, had she felt such a sense of perfect protection in the teeth of danger.

"I would like to hear you tell a story now," Rafi said.

"You're big on the idea of storytelling."

"It is an ancient and honoured tradition with my people."

Zara certainly felt she preferred this personal storytelling to television herself. "All right. What shall I tell you?" she mused.

She had not meant it as a real question, she was running over the ancient Greek tales in her head, but he took her at her word.

"Tell me about your life," he begged gently. "Let us

learn to know each other, and make up for all the time we have not spent together.''

"Oh! Where shall I start?"

"Start with the night that your father made love to your mother,'' he said, with a warm voice that traced like silk velvet on her being. ''And take me from there through everything that led to your being here in my arms tonight. I want to know every detail.''

She laughed a little. No man before had ever shown such a deep interest in her. Men usually asked her about herself only as a nod to duty in between talking about themselves. ''That would take a lifetime!''

"A lifetime is exactly the time we will have," Rafi pointed out reasonably.

She found there was no answer she could make to that. ''What do you really want to know?''

"Everything. I have said.''

She wondered how long it would be before he started snoring. ''Well, the way I heard it, my parents had been living together for a few years when they started to think about children.''

"What are your parents' names?'' he asked.

So he really did want full detail. ''My mother's name is Maddy and my father's Brandon. So Maddy and Brandon talked it over and decided they were ready for the next step. My mother was on the pill, so she stopped taking it, and then they waited for six months for her system to normalize, and they counted dates and charted her fertility. And it wasn't exact, there was a five-day period when they should make love every day.''

"But of course,'' Rafi interjected, as if everyone in the world made love every day.

"*So*...the first big day—night, I guess—came, and they had champagne—please don't ask me what brand it was!—and a candlelight dinner and drank to the future and how their lives were going to change and then they got undressed and they made wonderful love. And then they were lying there afterwards, my mother told me, and they both kind of stiffened, and panic set in. And they turned to each other and said, you know—oh God, what are we doing? We're not ready for this! We can't be parents yet!''

Rafi was chuckling lightly beside her.

''So they agreed the time wasn't really quite right and they should wait and think about it a bit longer before taking any further steps.''

''How human your parents sound. So how did you manage, given such a hurdle?''

She smiled. ''Well, it was already too late. I was already there.''

''Excellent.'' He nuzzled her neck gently. ''I am glad you were so quick to see your window of opportunity. How would I have managed the rest of my life if you had been stargazing at that moment?''

His certainty was so enticing. Zara fell silent with wishing.

After a few moments he prompted her. ''So you proved from the start to be a determined soul.''

''That's what my mother always said. Whenever I was difficult as a child, she would say, 'Don't you blame me! No one forced you to come here! You wanted to come, too!' ''

He lay back laughing. ''What an extraordinary woman she must be! Maddy.'' He tasted the name. ''I'm looking forward to meeting her.''

His confidence was infectious. When he spoke like that, as if all this were going to pass and their lives return to normal…as if it was a foregone conclusion that they would overcome everything and get married…her heart was always lighter. Zara laughed too.

''What is it?''

''Oh, just the thought of my mother's face when I tell her the Prince of East Barakat wants to meet her,'' Zara explained lamely.

''But you are an extraordinary woman. Your mother has

known all her life that you will do remarkable things, hasn't she? Why should it surprise her that a prince should fall in love with you?''

That seemed unanswerable, so she asked him what he had done while absent from the room that day.

"I searched for the entrance to the tunnel," he said.

She clutched him. "You—you *searched?* What—how?"

"Do not fear for me, Zara," he said. "I am a man blessed by fortune, it has always been so. Today I observed the site from within this fortress. I am working to create passages for myself through the parts of it that are abandoned and empty. Already I can move through five or six rooms that way—" He indicated the hole into the next room. "The building is built in a square around a very large courtyard, a typical pattern for many centuries here. Most of the citizens seem to live not in the fortress, but in simple structures in the courtyard. It is a communal life.

"I am sure that there is no entrance to the tunnel within the courtyard. That means it is either within the ruins or outside the fortress altogether. Do you remember anything that would give us a clue?"

She remembered the downhill travel, and the uphill, she remembered the dampness leaving the air…but how long had it been before she heard the voices, saw the light?

"It wasn't very long after we came up that I was lifted down from his horse…but would they build a tunnel to open right inside the fortress? Wouldn't that be risky?"

"I agree, but do you think it perhaps depends on the period when these things were built?"

She saw immediately what he meant. "Yes, of course— whether they knew the tunnel opening was there when they built the fortress or whether it had already been buried. In that case it would be sheer chance that they chose this site. Otherwise—"

"What do you think the period of building might be?"

He was appealing to her expert knowledge. She had examined what she could of the walls, but without a larger view of the place it was extremely difficult.

"You told me the tunnel was attributed to Queen Halimah," Zara began.

He nodded. "I did, and it is, but many old structures are attributed to her which could not possibly be her work. She is renowned in our history for her public works, and naturally in centuries gone by, when people stumbled upon some forgotten bridge or building, they believed it was her doing. But it is not necessarily always the case."

"So the tunnel could be any age?"

"We know nothing about the tunnel except what you have experienced of it, and the brief historical mention that guesses it was built by my ancestress. In the time of that writer it was already old and fallen into disuse. Ibn Qalam wrote in the seventeenth century."

"And what about this fortress?"

He shrugged and smiled. "Archaeology is not one of my subjects. At the Sorbonne, I studied politics and statecraft. Not very useful in any occupation."

Zara was momentarily sidetracked. "You were at the Sorbonne?"

"I was, for my undergraduate degree."

"I did my Year Abroad at the Sorbonne! When were you there?"

Of course they had missed each other by several years, but suddenly Prince Rafi did not seem so much a stranger. She had imagined him a man locked completely within his own culture, with no understanding of her background except perhaps through his stepmother...but Zara began to think that she herself was far more culture-bound than he was.

"You speak French, too, then?"

"I do. Why does this surprise you?"

"Oh—it's just—I wish I spoke Arabic. But I've only got about five words."

"You said *Salaam aleikum* very beautifully in the morning at the wadi. And you will learn the rest," Rafi said. "You will have private tutors, and we will by no means always speak English to each other."

She bit her lip. "Rafi, you keep talking as if—" She broke off.

"As if?" he prompted.

"Well, as if I've agreed to—"

"To marry me? Yes, I speak like this, Beloved. But I will not press you so long as we remain here. I know you can give me no answer now. But I believe, I know that when this is over, and you breathe the air of freedom, you will come on a visit to me…then, then I will convince you. I will make you love me. You will see."

She could not argue with that. At the moment she felt so confused, her thinking so disturbed by her imprisonment, that she could hardly imagine getting back her stability again. She found it difficult to imagine her release. Even after a few days her horizons seemed to have shrunk to these four pathetic walls.

They talked again, about her childhood. Rafi pressed her for detail, the sort of minute detail with which she had never previously examined her life. He wanted to know friends' names, and what clothes she had been wearing during an incident she was describing, and whether she liked her playmates' mothers or the teachers she named.

Zara stretched her mind, trying to remember, and suddenly, after a long time, something changed—she was *seeing* it. Her life was there before her in the darkened room. It was no longer an effort. She remembered details she hadn't thought of since the day they happened.

It had been a pretty conventional life, and yet, like every life, it was a tapestry. She began to see and understand things she had not seen before, to make connections between elements that had before seemed unconnected.

To find the pattern in the tapestry.

"I haven't thought of that for years!" she would exclaim, remembering an incident that she now could see as in some way character forming. Her grandfather's interest in history—she had forgotten those visits to his study as a very young child, shortly before he died, where he would tell her stories about the ancient world.

"He was a writer, he wrote fiction about ancient Greece and things like that—he had been in a wheelchair ever since the war. I'm sure he told me once that he would have liked to go out to the ground where history had happened rather than get it all from books. I don't think I knew then that he was talking about an actual occupation…but he meant he'd have liked to be an archaeologist. He must have! And here I am…"

Rafi listened closely, he questioned gently, he was silent when she was silent in thought…she had never been given such deep attention in her life. She had never met anyone who was such a good listener.

He left when she began to fall asleep. The last thing she remembered was his kiss on her forehead, and then she was dreaming.

She dreamed she was falling in love with Rafi.

The next day the genie brought her a small metal file from his cache of magic. Zara, thrilled, excited, grateful almost to the point of tears, immediately set to work on the heavy padlock that held the chain that bound her. But they quickly discovered that it made a distinctive, carrying, high-pitched noise which Rafi could hear at a distance of several rooms.

"It will be safe to work on it for only a few minutes at a time," Rafi advised thoughtfully. "And in case someone comes, we must find a good hiding place for it within your reach. It will be risky. Do you want to do it?"

She couldn't bear inactivity when there was something she could be doing to gain her freedom. "Yes," she said. "Anyway, what's the point of finding the tunnel if I can't go out through it?"

"We will bring men through it to attack," he said. But

it was true that it would be a great deal safer to free Zara first, and she would weather imprisonment better if she were actively aiding her own escape through the tedious days.

They examined the stones near her by the light of his candle, and found a narrow crack not far from where her chain was embedded, in the seam where the wall met the floor. It was quite long, and wide enough to take the file. It wasn't very deep, either, she discovered by gingerly poking around with it, but she could slide the file in on a slant and it was almost perfectly hidden.

They agreed she would work on the padlock for a few minutes twice each day, after the old woman had visited her, to reduce the risk of someone coming on her unexpectedly.

Zara suddenly felt real again. She was human. She could do things that mattered.

That afternoon, when he came to bring some purloined fruit for her lunch, the genie brought her another pail of water, and she had another sponge bath and washed her hair.

As she sat combing it out, feeling blissfully cool and clean, Rafi said, "I have to try to get a message to my brothers soon. I will do it under cover of darkness. You will be here alone. You should have light if possible. I know you will worry until I return. But I am afraid someone will see the light and come to investigate."

"Oh," Zara said in a small voice, because he was right. Waiting would be far easier if she had a candle. Darkness made her feel so helpless, but they had agreed that the candle should be used only in emergencies.

"Perhaps if you ask the old woman for a candle when she comes next, she will take pity on you."

"Oh! Yes, she might, Rafi, she seems very—concerned for me."

"I will teach you the Arabic for candle. It is *shama'a.*"

"Shama'a," Zara said. When he nodded she repeated it two or three times.

He smiled that smile of approval that always melted her. "You see how quickly you will learn to speak to my people," he said. "It is a beautiful language, too, that you will enjoy learning—intricate and precise."

"Precise," she repeated smilingly. "Yes, I've heard there are about twenty words for *camel.*"

"And do not you in English have as many words for *dog?*"

She lifted an eyebrow. "We do? Pooch and dog, that's all I know."

"And hound, bitch, pup, cur, mutt, canine, mongrel. And also shepherd, terrier, basset, beagle…dozens of breed names. Am I not right?"

"Oh," was all she could say to that. Sometimes she felt as if every time he opened his mouth, Rafi gave her some new experience, showed her some barrier in her thinking. She was being stretched in a way that she had not felt at university. There everything she learned somehow fit into her already known image of the world, or broadened it only in easy, predictable ways. Rafi was constantly showing her things that did not fit, so that she had to change her image— or step outside it—to accommodate them.

Soon it was close to the time that the old woman might be expected. Rafi wanted to use the last of the sunlight in any case, for his explorations. At night he used a flashlight, but there was danger in that.

When she was left alone, Zara fretted. Now that there was something productive she could do, she was desperate for the old woman to come and go so that she could begin on the padlock.

So eager was she, she almost forgot about asking for the candle. It wasn't till the old woman returned for the second time with her empty pail that she smiled and said pleadingly, *"Shama'a?"*

"Ahhh!" exclaimed the old woman, with a jumble of

words that Zara knew expressed surprise at her coming up with the word. A short speech followed, accompanied by a clap of her hands and a pitying tone of voice that seemed to be saying no, it would not be possible. *He* would refuse.

She didn't let the old woman finish. *"Shama'a?"* she begged again.

Between sign language and murmurs the old woman signalled—but a light! What was the good of a candle without something to light it with?

Zara's heart sank. Why hadn't they thought of this? Oh, what fools they were! She could have kept Rafi's lighter and shown it—how would the woman guess that it had not been in her pocket from the start? But now…

She lifted her hands in resignation and smiled woefully, giving in to the old woman's argument.

The old woman leaned down, her wrinkled brown hand stretching to Zara's cheek, and muttered again. *Poor child! Poor child!* her tone suggested. With a lingering, sorrowful glance, she went out.

Fighting impatience, Zara counted to a hundred, then made a dive for her precious metal file. She began the ritual they had agreed upon—filing hard for a few seconds, and then a pause to listen. Filing again. Rub dirt into the shiny wound she was making in the metal, so that it would be less noticeable if anyone checked. She could keep it up for no more than a few minutes.

Impatient as she was, Zara knew how important it was to be careful. It would be worse than foolish to risk the whole enterprise by being over-eager now. So she filed, listened, rubbed, filed.

It was while she was rubbing dirt onto the metal for what she had decided was the last time that she suddenly heard the sounds of someone approaching in the passageway. Sitting straight with a start, Zara snatched up the file and slipped it hastily into the little crack they had found for it.

She was a little too hasty. Or maybe they should have checked out the hole more thoroughly. Because instead of

finding its previous resting place on stone, the file slipped
from her fingers. She heard the unmistakable sound of it
falling flat on the stones under the floor, several inches out
of the reach of her fingers.

Ten

It was the old woman, coming jubilantly and triumphantly in, holding aloft a candle and a cigarette lighter in either hand. Zara was biting her lip against tears—but she knew she had to react with gratitude to what was evidently a coup.

"Thank you, *shokran jazilan!*" she murmured over and over, as the old woman squatted down beside her and showed her the wonderful technology by which the cheap plastic lighter worked. There was only a tiny amount of fuel left in it, Zara saw. She wondered whether Jalal had given permission, or whether the old woman had done this in secret.

"*Shokran jazilan!*" she kept saying, bending her head to hide her distress. "*Shokran, shokran!*"

The old woman put her hand under Zara's chin and lifted it. Tears she could not control slipped down her cheeks. "Aiiiii!" wailed the woman on a long falling note. She wiped the tears with a gentle, work-roughened forefinger, and murmured cajolingly.

She thought Zara was crying in gratitude for the candle. Zara smiled and blinked back the tears as the woman consoled her. *It's all right, poor little one. There, there. It's all right.*

She allowed herself to be consoled. But when the old woman had left her alone again, she lit the candle with trembling urgency, impatiently brushed away her tears and tried to see down the crack where the file had fallen.

Her fingers would not go in past the knuckle, and she could feel nothing but air. Zara tried to pry away bits of mortar with her fingers, but considering what a ruin she was inhabiting, it was infuriatingly firm.

The candle was short. She knew Rafi had more, but still it was stupid to waste it. So she gave up on the hopeless task and lay down, watching the sun set by means of the diminishing light in the passage, waiting for Rafi to return. She hoped he would come back after his search and before he tried to get the message to his brothers. Surely he wouldn't make any attempt till the camp was settled for the night? It would be a long wait if he did not come....

She was already deeply dependent on him. Her emotions were volatile and far too near the surface now, and Rafi was her refuge and her strength. She felt a deep need of him, a yearning for him...but she wasn't herself. She didn't need a master's in psychology to understand that the powerful feelings she had for him might be the result of her isolation.

Yet she felt that her dream was true, that she was falling deeply in love with him, that he was the one she had been waiting for, that whenever and wherever she had met him, she would have felt it.

When she had first met him, she had thought him a bandit, and even then she had felt the pull, argued this side of her. Surely that showed that they were, as Rafi insisted, naturally drawn to each other?

She began to dream a little. If she did not love him, it would be a terrible mistake to marry him, she knew. To come to a strange country for the rest of her life, to make such a huge change—to take on the massive responsibility of being queen to a people—all that would be intolerable without a deep and abiding bond.

If she *did* love him, she was sure he would be a wonderful husband. He was brave, he was honourable, with a nobility of nature as well as being noble by birth. He was so thoughtful of her, so protective, and he listened to her in a way she wasn't used to. She was sure that wasn't common. And he had such a rich imagination, and a sense of humour…how could any woman choose better?

Zara thought of the ring, and drew it to her lips in the fading light. It caught a last glimmer from somewhere, and sparkled once, like a beacon of promise. Just before sleep she kissed it, rubbing it with her lips, and wished…

They came to her as she lay in her high white bed between silken sheets. *His Highness desires her presence,* she heard them whisper. *He commands it.*

We hear and obey, said other voices.

She felt their hands on her skin as she slept, delicate, gently lifting the silken sheets and drawing them back, carefully lifting her body. She awoke then. *What is it?* she asked drowsily.

Madame, he has asked for thee. He awaits thee. We are come to take thee to the baths.

A shiver of delight ran through her body. *He has asked for me?*

In her was the knowledge that she was newly entered to the harem, that she had arrived only today, and when the Sultan of All the Worlds had accepted her as a gift, he had cast an interested eye over her veiled form as she stepped from the litter that brought her and made her obeisance in the huge Throne Room…

He has, Madame. The bath is ready.

They led her through a bewildering series of rooms and then through a door and into the great *hamam*. In the centre the male slaves, their powerfully muscled arms and strong chests gleaming with oil, awaited her.

They surrounded her and carefully began to disrobe her. Her clothes were white, and they stripped off layer after layer until she was naked under their admiring gaze. She saw them exchange glances under lowered eyelids.

He will be pleased with thee, Mistress, they said.

She only smiled, and allowed herself to be led down into the warm water.

She dived and swam deep. On the walls and floor of the bath were images of men and women that made her gasp. She found that she could breathe underwater, and stayed there, watching the images.

They seemed to move with the flow of the water past her eyes. Handsome black-eyed men, beautiful women with hair like her own, long, flowing curls…they kissed and toyed with each other, and smiled and flicked lazy glances of desire.

She felt heat in her belly, and thought of the Sultan of All the Worlds, who had summoned her the very night of her arrival, and the heat increased.

They bathed her with soaps of a most delicious softness, like cream on her creamy skin. They washed her hair, and rinsed her carefully, and they drew her from the bath.

She lay on a bed of velvet, and a thousand hands massaged and stroked her. Perfume was rubbed deep into her skin, so that she became the perfume. The heat in her belly moved to her loins, and then to all parts of her—skin, hair, lips, eyes—under their caresses, and she thought of nothing but the man for whom they prepared her, and what he would demand of her, and how willingly she would give it.

She could not remember his face, for she had scarcely dared to glance up at it, but he had excited her. Thrilled her. His voice when he whispered to a courtier his approval;

his hand as he negligently signalled that she should be taken to the harem...she had melted with desire for him even then, and had wondered how long before he thought of her again. Whether he would ever think of her, ever send for her...

The slaves stroked every part of her, scenting her skin, making her a perfect offering to the one who was called the Sultan of All the Worlds. With careful assiduity and melting softness, they tinted her skin with palest cream. They outlined her eyes with blackest black, and her fingertips and toes with a deeper pink. Then they dyed her lips, her nipples—and even her tender, hidden bud—with sweetest pink.

They dressed her in cloth of silver. A tiny jacket that barely covered her breasts, so that the fullness of the two globes just showed beneath. A pair of trousers of thinnest gauze, full and flowing from below her waist to her feet, gathered in at her ankles. All her stomach and abdomen left naked.

Not only her stomach and abdomen. The pants were not stitched between her legs. The seam was open. *Show him this only at the last,* they advised her. *He will be well pleased with the trick. It is new.*

They argued about stones. *Ruby, emerald, sapphire,* murmured different voices. Ruby won. Ruby to match her lips, that had been red without the dye.

So they placed a large jewel in her navel, that glinted rose in the lights as she moved. They placed jewels also in her ears, her nose, on her fingers and toes, and sprinkled through the curls of her hair. They locked a jewelled belt to sway around her hips.

They stood back to admire. *Beautiful,* they agreed, with soft whispers. *Lady, you will be fortunate. When you are elevated to position, remember us, who helped you there.*

She promised. *Each of you shall have one petition answered if it is as you say,* she vowed.

They draped a cloth of ruby-spangled silver over her hair and face. *Now,* they said.

Another door opened. They led her through rooms and halls of steadily increasing beauty and magnificence. She heard music from a distance. Gold and jewels glinted from the walls. Lamps glowed behind carved wooden screens, casting magic shadows. She was terrified and thrilled together. The music played in the same rhythm as her pounding heartbeat, building long and slow to a distant but inevitable crescendo.

And then she was there, in the Sultan's own private rooms. The hangings were lushly ornate. There were paintings of men and women in intimate embrace on the walls, that sent shivers of desire through her. There was light and shadow and perfume and incense.

She was melting. They opened the one she knew was the last door, and then she entered alone. The room was dark, shadowed, huge. Through a high arched window, far away, she saw the full moon and the stars in a midnight sky. Beside it, at the far end of the room, was a bed, draped with beautiful cloths.

She knew that he was there, on the bed.

At a signal, the music started again. Seductive, demanding music.

She saw a pale hand in the shadows of the bed.

Dance for me, said a voice. His voice.

The music already urged her to dance. Her arms rose of their own accord, and she understood that she was a dancer of great skill. She began to move, with the tiniest movements of her hips, her face still hidden from him.

The floor was cool under her feet. They were the only part of her not afire with desire, with wishing. Her hips increased their movement, her arms swaying like dancing serpents in accompaniment. The jewel in her navel glinted and glowed with each flexion of perfect muscle. Those in her ears, her nose, on her fingers and toes, and in her jewelled belt sent wild shafts of coloured light all around the walls.

She danced, and each step, each movement made her more faint, more intoxicated. She smiled behind the silvery veil that still hid her face from him, and as the dance went on she began to toy with the veil, and with the promise of unveiling her face and hair for his delectation.

She sensed his attention. She had caught him—he wanted to see what woman was in that lush body, behind that spangled gauze. She dropped it first to show her eyes, holding the gauzy fabric still in front of her lower face, and sent dark glances of passion towards the shadows of the bed.

At last, as the music reached a crescendo, she whirled and spun, and lifted the veil above her head to trail behind her in the air. She heard the intake of breath from the shadows of the bed and stopped as the music stopped.

Then there was silence.

Approach, said the beloved voice.

Fearlessly, and yet full of trepidation, she stepped forward till she stood at the end of the huge, canopied bed. Still he was in shadow.

Come further, he commanded, and she entered the shadows to be with him.

They were in a world apart, the world of shadows. He was bare chested, barefoot, wearing gold trousers, and wore a gold turban with a rich green jewel.

He held a glass of intoxicating liquid, which he offered to her. There were sweetmeats. At his bidding, she ate and drank, and her wild intoxication increased.

Still she did not see his face. He ate, and placed tender morsels of food between her lips. They struck her tongue with shooting flavours that seemed to enter her being. *Delicious,* she said gratefully.

Yes, said he, but he meant—her.

At last, at long awaited last, his hands were upon her.

She felt his touch on the underside of her exposed breast, and murmured softly of hunger.

His fingers found her breast, the nipple. He stroked it while her throat helplessly moaned its quiet delirium. *You see how it will be,* he told her. *You love me without knowing it.*

Yes, she said. *I knew it when I saw you.* The fire in her was already wilder than anything she had ever felt. Her limbs burned with icy hot hunger for his touch. He stroked her—breasts, stomach, abdomen.

They know how to please me, he said, *and yet I have never been so pleased with a woman.*

Nor I, with a Sultan, she murmured, and he laughed.

Only then did she understand her danger. If he had not laughed…

But he had no choice. His touch drugged her, and drugged him. They were made for each other's delight. *Give me your lips,* he said.

She offered up the pink-dyed flesh, and he devoured it. His tongue entered her mouth, inviting her to do the same in return, and then when she did, he gnawed at it with hungry intensity.

His hand strayed along her arms, over her abdomen. *Are you a Peri, that you affect me so?* he asked.

She only smiled, and he thought that it was true. *This…how is this fastened?* he asked, of the silver cloth that hid her breasts from his eyes and mouth.

So, she said with a smile, opening the fastenings for him. Her breasts were revealed, white and pink, and his shadowed eyes were frighteningly black with interest. *I tell thee, there has never been a woman like thee,* he said.

His hands touched and stroked her full breasts, and she moaned. *There has never been a woman I would please so,* he said. *Give me your rosebud lips.*

They kissed. Her heart sang, her body shook with pleasure. His hand moved hungrily between her legs, and then he found the secret.

What is this? he demanded, one hand with firm command spreading her legs for his gaze as she lay on soft pillows. Obediently she spread her legs, and then the treasure was revealed. His breath hissed between his teeth.

What jewel is this? he asked, the silver cloth parting to reveal the pink-dyed hungry bud. *No, not jewel, but delicious fruit.*

His dark head bent over her, and she felt the burning, spiralling heat of his tongue where the silver cloth granted him access. *No woman has ever moved me like this,* he breathed, and of its own accord, her body arched and jerked with the pleasure of his hot breath, his heated tongue. *Again,* he said, and his face lowered between her thighs.

She exploded then, melting with heat and sweetness. She cried with a deep, primitive, hunger-sated, still-hungry voice, and he felt the wildness sweep through him.

Who art thou? he demanded.

I love you, she said, and of its own accord, her hand reached for him, for the hard, hungry centre of his being, for the ramrod sex that her body demanded should make part of her own being.

Is it so? he cried. *Then open thyself to me, for I am hungered with thee.*

She spread her legs. He rose up above her, strong and hard yet melting gold, over her body of white and pink and silver. He thrust into her, between the folds of spangled silver, into the path of pink, and she gasped with the sensation that flowed through her.

"Rafi!" she cried then, seeing his face for the first time.

"Zara!" he replied. He tried to say more, but he was swept with feeling, and with the need to thrust and pound his way inside the cavern of his yearning.

Zara felt total confusion, mingled with the most delicious sensations she had ever experienced. Her body shook with simultaneous hunger and fulfilment.

"Rafi!" she cried again. "What is it?"

It is love, said the Sultan of All the Worlds.

And she shook and trembled with the pleasure he gave her, and knew that it was so.

Rafi returned very late. He had had great difficulty in signalling. Jalal's guards were too watchful.

"They have a military precision, though they look like a bunch of ruffians," he told Zara. "They murmur the password very quietly. I heard it last time, but tonight I could not get close enough and had to wait. My brothers have news."

"What?" she asked excitedly. She had been sleeping, but had woken up when he merely put his head through the hole in the wall. Now they sat by candlelight, talking softly.

"We will find out tomorrow. Tomorrow the foodstuffs are due for delivery again by Mustafa. One of my Companions will come in with him in place of his brother. We agreed on this as a fail-safe."

They were leaning against the wall, side by side. Zara yawned, and Rafi put his arm around her and pulled her to rest on his shoulder.

"It is late. I did not mean to wake you. Lie down now and get some sleep."

"I'm glad I woke up. I'm not really sleepy now. I have to tell you what I did with the file," she said, and then sadly confessed.

He listened to the tale of woe, and her self-blame for not having asked the old woman for a candle on her first trip, and on several other points.

"Don't you think we could get it out again if we had a stick with something sticky on the end of it?" she finished.

Then he smiled and said, "Do not grieve over this thing. If it is God's will, we will find a way to retrieve the file. But let us wait until tomorrow. Let me speak to my Companion and learn what my brothers are planning."

She had done her crying; it wasn't hard to do as he said. "All right."

They sat in silence, and she thought of her dreams, and of what it meant to learn that she loved him, and feel the truth of it. Unconsciously she sighed.

He was always quick to sense her feelings. "Tell me, Beloved," he said.

"I'll have a lot to learn if I marry you, won't I?"

"Does it frighten you?"

"Yes, a little. I'd be a fool if it didn't, wouldn't I?"

He was silent, his black eyes grave. His hold tightened around her. "We are young, Zara. You are twenty-five, I am thirty. Whatever happens to us, we have a lot to learn. You are not a woman who will give up learning new things. The question is not *whether,* but *what* we choose to learn. Whether you marry me or not, the future is full of new things, of surprises, of truths, of experiences that you have so far not dreamed of. You are a woman who travels far in the search of knowledge. You will never in any case settle down—will you?—and be pleased to think that you know it all.

"The culture of my people will be no more difficult for you to learn than the ancient world of Alexander. It will, even, be easier. Whereas now you seek answers from stone, I will be there at every step to answer your questions. And I assure you, I am not at all like stone. When you ask me questions, I will answer. Just as, when you touch me, my blood will always run."

Eleven

When her ray of sun awoke them the next morning they were still wrapped in each other's arms. Rafi yawned and kissed her lightly. "Is this not pleasant, to wake up with each other? Does it feel to you like something you can spend the rest of your life doing?"

But before she could answer, he abruptly remembered where they were. He smothered an exclamation and murmured, "I should not have fallen asleep here. The old woman or Jalal might have come in—it will be very dangerous for both of us if my presence is discovered."

He left her soon afterwards, because during the morning bustle of the encampment he could risk walking around without too much danger. Everyone came and went, and he was just another figure in a white keffiyeh.

Zara performed her morning rituals when he was gone. She always had enough water to drink now, for there was a well in the courtyard and Rafi had managed to steal a pail which he kept next door, full of water. So she could rinse her face and hands and brush her teeth every morning, and comb the dust out of her hair with a wet comb.

Then she sat down to wait. This was the hardest part now of her imprisonment—the sheer mind-numbing boredom of having nothing to do. She had not wished on the ring for a book to read or a deck of cards, but she certainly did wish she had something to keep her mind occupied. It was too easy to slip into fear and negative thinking.

But she could at least think about her dream. She spent an hour seeing it all again, the palace ruins, the slaves, her costumes...the eyes of the Sultan of All the Worlds.

She thought, too, about what Rafi had said about waking up beside him. It was true—her heart had been singing when she awoke to find him there. It had a feeling of rightness. He did not seem a relative stranger, but someone she knew well...and would come to know better.

When he returned, slipping through the wall, he was muttering softly, "Ow, ow, ow!" and making a curious mewling sound. Zara leapt to her feet, her heart racing.

"Rafi, what is it?" she hissed hoarsely. "What's wrong?"

His shirt was bulging strangely on one side of his waist, and he had his hand clutched there. Through her mind flashed the image of a gunshot wound and a makeshift bandage. But the bandage seemed to be moving quite vigorously. Zara stared in confusion.

"Your genie returns, lady!" Rafi cried. "And none too soon—I might have screamed and given myself away! *Ow,* you little monster, don't you know when you have a benefactor?" he demanded, grabbing at the bulge in his shirt and pulling it away from him. With the other he was unbuttoning the shirt. He reached gingerly in.

His hand came out full of writhing fur, claws and whiskers. And a little pink mouth that mewed its fury at him.

"A *kitten!*" Zara cried. "Oh, Rafi! How did you—"

"Careful!" he warned her. "It's got claws like needles."

She was laughing almost uncontrollably. Rafi held the

tiny little creature in one hand, well away, and all four paws were wildly clawing, trying to get to his hand. It was an image of David and Goliath—the desert warrior defeated by a few ounces of grey and white fur.

"Go ahead and laugh," he said plaintively. He set the kitten down on the floor, where it immediately scampered to a fold of her blanket and crept under. Rafi eyed it balefully as he began to pull at his shirt. "I'll have to wash the blood off me, because I will become identifiable if I have a bloodstained shirt. I thought kittens were supposed to be gentle things. Who started that myth, or is this one just a monster?"

"Well, naturally she thinks you're a danger," Zara explained placatingly. "How is she to know your noble nature when you haven't been properly introduced?"

"She seems to know yours."

The kitten had turned around under the fold of blanket and was now blinking out at the world. Zara, crouching before her, carefully extended a finger, and the kitten sniffed it curiously.

"She's got a very pretty face. Where did you find her?"

"There are half a dozen who hang around the communal cooking area, waiting for the scraps that the women throw them. They all seem to be from one litter, and I didn't think anyone would notice if one went missing. If it's found here of course you can pretend it wandered in."

He took his shirt off, and Zara stood to examine his battle wounds. They were surprisingly extensive. Not deep, but there was a network of tiny lines all around one half of his waist and lower chest, along which blood was starting to seep in little teardrops. "Goodness, how long was she inside your shirt?"

"Only a few minutes. Another minute and I'd have had to release her, though," he joked.

Zara nodded, feeling suddenly sober. "Maybe that's what I should have done to Jalal. Bitten and scratched till he let me go."

He put his hand on her cheek, his eyes serious. "It would have been very dangerous. You were on a galloping horse, and he was in no mood to relinquish a hostage so valuable. You might have been badly hurt, if not killed."

The blood was starting to drip now. "I have no cloth or anything!" Zara said. "I'll just have to wipe it off with water and my bare hands."

She damped her hands by pouring a little water from her drinking pot over them, then ran them over his side and stomach, two or three times, rinsing off the blood. His body was very firm with muscle, his chest broad and covered with dark curling hair, his waist narrow, his arms strong...with her hands flat against his flesh, Zara paused, and the touch between them was suddenly electric.

She was afraid to look up into his face. She stood frozen there, while sensation zinged from her fingertips and palms and shot trembling along her arms and into her body.

Too late, she lifted her hands away from that dangerous touch. But the electricity did not stop when the connection was broken. Rafi lifted his hands and, her head bent, she saw how those strong but elegant fingers grasped her upper arms. "Zara," he whispered hoarsely.

She raised her head, expecting his kiss. Wanting it. Not wanting to think about what it meant, but only wanting that full, strong mouth, the taste of it on her tongue.

He said, "Zara, if I touch you the way I want to touch you now, I will lose control. It is not safe here. I want to kiss you, I want...but if I do, it will not, it cannot stop with a kiss. I know myself, I know you...I know how much I want from you and want to give you. I have never felt desire like this for any woman. If I make love to you, I will—I have known it from the moment I saw you at the waterfall—I will be lost.

"So I will not kiss you now, Zara. Not when there is such desire between us. When my brothers and I have taken you safely out of your prison, then...then." He nodded. "I tell you this because a woman likes to know that a man desires as well as loves her. But I must hide my desire both from you and from myself, so long as we are in this place.''

Her blood was champagne. The bubbles ran through her system, making her light with joyous laughter and aching desire. Never had any man's expressed desire so enchanted her, so thrilled her. Her blood rushed to and fro in her, for the sheer joy of the exercise.

''All right,'' she said, an irrepressible smile teasing her mouth. She wondered when a man had ever before in her experience put his own sexual need second to her needs. Never, probably. Sexual desire and selfishness, in her experience, seemed to go together.

A woman didn't have to be in prison to appreciate such a man. Any woman in the world, she thought, would love him.

The kitten did not at all like being bathed, but Zara had no intention of adding fleas to her expanding family. So it was soaped and rinsed thoroughly in the pail of water, and then dried—on a square torn from Zara's once-beautiful white silk dress, whose existence she had suddenly remembered. Then, notwithstanding the tiny claws, she sat down and by the light of Rafi's flashlight—which it seemed safe to use during the day—ruthlessly checked the kitten for fleas.

A little surprisingly, she did not find any. Zara set the still-indignant kitten down on a fresh square of the white silk, where it immediately began to groom itself.

Rafi, meanwhile, had gone, after removing all evidence of the kitten's ablutions except for the flashlight. He also left behind a few morsels of meat which he had picked up along with the cat.

When the kitten was fully recovered, Zara amused herself by feeding it the little tidbits of meat. It ate greedily. It was thin, but not starving, and now that the dust of the place had been thoroughly cleaned from its fur, it looked as healthy as any other kitten. It was very pretty and confiding, and quickly forgave and forgot the bathing episode. It explored the little cell, but one hiss from Zara was enough to convince it not to go out into the passage. Then it returned to the little square of white on her bed, settled itself against her thigh, licked a paw, and promptly fell asleep.

Zara didn't think that she had ever in her life been so delighted with the company of a fellow creature. Just watching the kitten sleep made her heart lighter.

The flashlight was still beside her. Rafi had left while she was examining the kitten, reminding her to hide the light if the old woman came in his absence. Zara began tucking it out of sight under the blanket, when a thought crossed her mind, and instead she knelt down beside the crack in the floor where the file had fallen and shone the light into the aperture.

It was the kitten who saved her. Zara heard an exclamation from the passage and surfaced with shock to realize that she had been trying to see down into the hole for minutes, totally lost to her surroundings. Meanwhile, the kitten had awakened refreshed and had ventured into the passage at a critical moment. When the kitten and the old woman spied each other, the old woman cried out, and the kitten made a dash for the haven of Zara's bed.

Zara had time only to bury the flashlight under her blanket, turn her ring in towards her palm, a move that was second nature to her now, and sit on the exposed edge of her mattress before the old woman came in exclaiming.

Now how did the kitten find its way in here?

"*Mash'allah,*" Zara responded. *It must have been God's will.*

God looks after his little ones. Here, my little one, here is food and drink for you.

Zara accepted the flat bread rolled around a succulent piece of meat with noises of gratitude. She did not often get meat, and she missed it. But she bit a tiny piece off first and offered it to the fascinated kitten.

Ya Allah! You don't mean to feed the animal from your own mouth?

But it is my friend. I cannot let it starve.

The old woman shook her head. *I will bring you a little food for it. Do not give it your own, you are too hungry.* How easy it was to communicate ideas around such a subject as a kitten. The mixture of sign language, body language and vocal outbursts was clear to each.

And a little bowl for water, Zara begged.

Nodding, cackling, delighted with their ability to communicate, the old woman poured out water for Zara, picked up the latrine and left. *I'll come right back.*

She returned a few minutes later with a broken saucer and a little gristly meat and fat. The sight of this made Zara understand how carefully the old woman had chosen the delectable meat in her own sandwich. She watched as the old woman bent down to stroke the kitten's head, then patted Zara's cheek.

The kitten is as pretty as you. Jalal says Prince Rafi loves you. You are so lovely, it is no surprise.

When the old woman left, Zara played with the kitten, waiting for Rafi's return. She tore a strip from the piece of white silk she had used to make its bed, and laughed at its antics trying to catch the strip, able to forget herself and where she was more completely than she could have imagined possible a few days ago.

When Rafi returned at last, she was lying on her back, the kitten standing on her chest pawing at her lips as she blew air and made little noises, laughing in helpless amusement in between.

He stood on the other side of the wall for a moment, watching in appreciation. Her beautiful hair was splayed out beneath her, her legs in a posture of graceful abandon, her attention entirely on the kitten. Just so might the favourite of the harem have toyed with a kitten, in decades and centuries past.

But the moment he stepped through the wall, she grabbed

the kitten and swung herself up to a sitting position and full attention. "Is everything all right?"

"It is very well." He was carrying a thin stick of what glowed, even behind a badly scratched surface, like marble. He sat down, laying this gently on the floor beside him.

"Did your Companion come in?"

"Arif has been here and is safely gone. He brought the message from my brother. They had much to tell me." Rafi smiled. "The first is that, thanks to your ingenuity, Zara, they have found the tunnel."

She squealed and choked the sound back, her hands flying to her mouth in happy astonishment. "They did? How?"

"At night, in helicopters. Your robe of honour reflected the spotlight. They marked the place and returned in the morning. Not fifty yards away from where your robe was lying, a pile of rocks like any other in the desert disguises the entrance. Jalal of course has no suspicion that we know of the existence of the tunnel. By great good fortune the outcrop is hidden from the view of this fortress by a much larger pile nearby, but they are being very careful nevertheless not to have any activity in the immediate area, in case he is surveilling them."

She was almost speechless with gratitude and relief. "Oh, oh thank God! Oh, Rafi, how wonderful! Have they come all the way through it? Does it lead into this camp?"

"The exploration must be done with great caution. Jalal must certainly have guards inside the tunnel—he would be a fool if he did not, and he is not a fool. We dare not signal to Jalal that it has been found—he might take…" Rafi broke off. "Take steps. He might even destroy the tunnel."

The archaeologist in her leapt to the surface. "Oh, God, don't let him do that! I want to explore it when this is over! It must be a fascinating piece of history."

He smiled at her enthusiasm. "Yes, let us hope we avoid destroying something that has lasted so long."

"What will your brothers do?"

"In three days there is a celebration here—it is an old custom among the desert tribes. I have heard conversations among the women about the feast. We will use the opportunity. I must locate the entrance to the tunnel at this side. If it is as we imagine, you can be taken through the tunnel to safety before the attack begins. That will be the safest way."

Her heart thumped with nervous anticipation.

"How will—how will it happen?"

He wrapped an arm around her. "Tonight," he said, "I will tell you another story from the Book of Kingly Wisdom. And then you will guess yourself, Beloved. It is one of the reasons why princes were encouraged to read such books. So that in difficult moments they might remember the tricks of their ancestors.

"But first we must see about retrieving the file. With this." Grinning, he reached into his pocket and pulled out a familiar-looking packet. It was white and printed with Arabic lettering in pink, but it was nevertheless unmistakable. It was open, but there were three or four sticks of gum in it. "Never again will I complain about my Companion Arif's gum-chewing propensities. He had this in his pocket."

Much later, Rafi returned from another exploration with some fruit, and a little meat for the kitten. The kitten ate ravenously and then fell asleep where it was, exhausted by its day of entertaining the prisoner.

Rafi, too, was exhausted. He had spent vain hours in another search for the tunnel. She could see he was a little dispirited by his failure. But her news would cheer him up. She let him settle and sink his teeth into a ripe piece of fruit, and then, like a conjuror, produced her exhibit.

Rafi sat up, astonished, the fruit forgotten, a grin splitting his face. "The file!" he exclaimed, wrapping his arms around her. "Zara! You did it!"

"Thank Mr. Wrigley, not me."

He sat back and gazed at her. "Who is Mr. Wrigley?"

"The man who invented chewing gum, I think!" she told him with a grin. They laughed.

"But this is excellent!" He picked up the stick of marble and examined the little pad of chewing gum still adhering to one end. "It took you a long time?"

She blew air up over her face. "Long enough." She nodded. "If I hadn't had the other Mr. Wriggly to amuse me in between I think I'd have screamed." Before he could ask, she said, "That's the kitten's new name. Mr. Wriggly."

Rafi grinned, and felt his disappointment over his own day lift in the presence of her good humour. They ate the fruit laughing and chatting, and flirting at each other with their eyes in a way that made their blood race pleasantly.

Then Zara declared, "It's time for my story now," and Rafi blew out the candle and they lay down together.

"Is this another story about King Mahmoud?" Zara asked.

"It is," Rafi explained. She realized how pleasant his voice was. She would probably enjoy a telephone book recital from him. "One day an old woman came to his Hall of Justice and complained because in a certain area of the kingdom, where she lived, they were troubled by a ruthless band of bandits."

"Oh!"

"Mahmoud asked her where this place was, and when she told him the name of it, he said, 'We don't really have much control over that region.' But the old woman said to him, 'I am a homeowner, and I control my house and garden. Are you a king, and you say do not have control over your own territory?'

"Mahmoud was shamed, and he asked her for details. She said that the bandits lived in a stronghold in the mountains and were very wild. They controlled all the caravan routes and regularly robbed the caravans and all the honest people who lived around. She herself had lost money and possessions to the bandits and she felt that as it was Mahmoud's fault for not keeping law and order, he ought to repay her.''

"Is this the same king whose courtiers were terrified because he had a hangover?" Zara demanded.

He touched her nose. "Ah, but a king must always let a subject speak unpleasant truths."

"Must he?"

"Of course. Now, do not interrupt the story. Mahmoud promised the old woman that he would establish law in the area and wipe out the bandits. And he thought for awhile, and then he sent out a proclamation saying that a caravan protected by the king's troop would be going into that area, and all those who had business there could join it.

"There were many merchants who had feared to go into the area because of the bandits, and at this summons they all began to assemble. And before very long a hugely rich caravan was ready to set off.

"On the night before the departure, Mahmoud called one of his troop leaders to him, and gave him certain instructions. And the next day, the caravan set off. It was an enormous caravan, with hundreds of camels laden with all manner of the richest goods. It proceeded for days and weeks, and at last arrived in the area where the bandits held sway.

"And one day the residents of the place where they camped came out to them and told the merchants and the soldiers that a huge group of bandits was hiding at a certain point that the caravan would reach on the following day, ready to ambush the caravan.

"The merchants became very nervous at this, and some talked of turning back, but the leader of Mahmoud's men talked to them, saying that their lives would not be in danger because it was the soldiers' duty to take the risk to themselves. And he told them that Mahmoud had a plan that would wipe out the bandits, and that if they followed his instructions all would be well.

"So the merchants agreed to go on. Now among the

camels that made up Mahmoud's part of the caravan were ten camels loaded with apples. And that night, the Leader of the King's Troop had all the baskets of apples brought into his tent. Then he took out of his wallet the bottle of poison which King Mahmoud had given him, and a needle, and he carefully dipped the needle into the poison and then into each of the apples. Then he had the apples all loaded back onto the camels.

"The next morning, he called several of his men together and instructed them what to do. Then he said to the merchants, 'In a few hours we will reach the place where the robbers lie in ambush. When they attack, all the merchants should flee to safe ground. As for me and my men, we will put up a token resistance only. When you see me wheel my mount and gallop off, all of you follow me. We will regroup and in an hour will attack again.

"So they proceeded on to the ambush, and everyone did as instructed. The merchants fled as soon as the bandits came out of the bushes, and the soldiers fought a little. Meanwhile, soldiers who had received special instructions from the leader cut the ropes on the loads of the ten camels, so that apples spilled onto the ground in all directions.

"And, seeing that it was done, the leader gave the signal and led the retreat.

"The bandits, seeing nothing unusual in their flight, since the bandits themselves were a huge band, began to check their booty. And seeing the apples rolling on the ground, many of them picked them up and ate them.

"So when the troops and merchants returned to the scene, they found the bandits sick and dying everywhere, with only a few capable of fighting. And the leader sent a message to the local amir, instructing him to invade the bandit headquarters and finish off whoever was there.

"And so that is how law and order was accomplished in the place called Dair Gachin."

Zara lay silent for awhile when he had finished. Then she cleared her throat and spoke. "Is that what you're going to do? Poison everyone in the camp?"

Twelve

She was thinking of the old woman who had been so kind to her, and wondered if her own freedom could be worth so many lives.

But then, it wasn't just her life at stake. Like the bandits of Dair Gachin, Jalal had been making trouble for a long time in the Emirates.

"We will not use poison, of course. This camp is full of women and children and other non-combatants. But we can modify the plan. My brothers will try to smuggle in to me some powerful narcotic, and with luck we can put many of them to sleep before we attack. They will also bring in fruit that has been drugged."

She heaved a deep sigh of relief, not realizing how she had communicated her fears to him.

Rafi was silent. "One day, I hope, you will trust me better than this. Do you believe I could allow the unnecessary deaths of so many innocents, Zara?" he asked after a long pause.

"I didn't know." She shifted uncomfortably. "Terrible things do happen, don't they?"

"But this would be massacre. What could justify the massacre of so many of my brother's people? My people, for my brother's people are also my people. Am I such a barbarian in your eyes? What have I done to make you think so?"

She said, "How was I to know? Isn't Jalal a terrible villain? Isn't he a murderer and worse? And aren't all his people implicated with him?"

"No. What has given you this idea? His grandfather was the great bandit Selim. In his day he dominated a part of this desert almost as ferociously as the bandits of Dair Gachin I told you about. But he had no son. He died soon after his grandson came. For twenty five years—most of my life—there was no trouble in the desert.

"Just around the time that we succeeded to our inheritance, his grandson—Jalal—began to cause trouble. He made ridiculous claims for a kingdom carved out of a part of each of the three emirates. He demanded to meet with us to show us the justice of his claims. But his activity at the moment is confined to setting up his camp here, gathering followers to his cause. My brother once laid siege to this fortress, but withdrew without casualties.

"We have known for a long time that he was waiting to get a hostage. Omar discourages tourism in this area, but still, there were opportunities which Jalal did not take. He did not want just any hostage, it seemed. One of us. Not long ago he tried to take my brother Omar's children."

"Are his claims just?"

"Of course they are not. How could they be?"

"What claims did he make? Didn't he even have a pretext?" Zara asked, a little mystified.

"I don't know what his claims may be. We refused to meet with him."

Not believing her ears, Zara struggled out of Rafi's arms and sat up. She stared down at him in the darkness, seeing

nothing but the liquid of his eyes in a glimmer of errant
moonbeam. "Are you seriously telling me you've got all
this trouble with this guy and *you haven't even talked to
him?*"

"Zara, my forebears have ruled in this land for hundreds
of years. His grandfather was a bandit. What can there be
to talk about? If he thinks he has a right to rule because
his grandfather was a marauder like the bandits of Dair
Gachin, he is mistaken."

"But how do you know what he thinks? You didn't even
talk to him!" she exclaimed. "You call that diplomacy?"

She could hear by his voice that he was keeping a lid on
irritation. "No, I do not call it diplomacy. I do not use
diplomacy with bandits. I call this protecting what is my
own from those who would steal it. What benefit could
there be to me or to my people from negotiations with a
bandit?"

"Well, okay, but what's the downside to you and your
people from just listening to him?"

"To meet with a man like this is to make the world think
he has some right on his side. He has none."

"Why do you care what the world thinks?" she pointed
out.

"We trade with the world. If the nations of the West
begin to put pressure on me and my brothers to give in to
his demands—what could we do?"

"Couldn't you meet with him informally, secretly?"

"We discussed it. We believed that such action on our
part would only fuel his determination."

"I thought you said your brother Omar disagreed with
that."

"My brother Omar was of the opinion that we should
attack quickly and arrest Jalal and his deputies, and disperse
his followers. Karim and I did not agree that a pre-emptive
strike of this kind was necessary. We see now that we were
wrong—and Omar now says that his plan was too extreme,
born of bitterness. So you see it is not easy. But Omar was

certainly right to this extent—Jalal causes disaffection among the desert tribes. We must deal with him.''

"How?"

He took a deep breath. "I am not a man who leaps on violence as an alternative, Zara. I and my brothers have the determination to end this situation without violence if possible. We do not want to start by killing. If the answer were merely to kill Jalal and his followers, that would not be difficult to achieve—but violence only opens the door on more violence. Our country now is as blessed as its name. We do not want to go the way of so many others.''

"Oh,'' she said, with a small shamed smile. The smile hid a kind of joy for what she had learned about him.

"The difficulty in this situation is how to free you *without* a killing. If he had harmed you in any way—then I would cut him down without remorse. But within his own lights, he has treated you as well as a prisoner can be treated. Is it so?''

She nodded. When she thought of the vast difference between what her lot as hostage might have been and what it was—Jalal's behaviour could practically be called noble. "If you're so determined not to start violence, why won't you take it one step further and talk to him?''

"I have told you why not. Talking is not a solution to every problem, Zara. Perhaps you think so, but sometimes it is not the answer.''

"That's just a way of saying I don't understand.''

"Are you so sure that you do understand? It is not a simple issue, and you—''

"And I'm a simple girl?''

"Do not put words in my mouth! I was going to say, you are not very familiar with the history of this problem. How could you be?''

"What you mean is, you don't want to consider a viewpoint not your own.''

"No, that is not what I mean,'' he returned irritably, sitting up himself. He groped in the darkness for a moment, and lit the candle. His eyes flashed in the little glow. "I mean that I have considered this viewpoint—we all did, long ago—and it has too many drawbacks."

"The only thing it has against it is your fear of legitimizing a claim that for all you know may be legitimate to begin with. If the claim is not legitimate, I don't see how listening to it would give it any legitimacy. And if it is legitimate, shouldn't you—"

"I have told you. It is not possible for his claim to have any legitimacy whatsoever."

"Are you telling me there is no conceivable circumstance whereby he might have justice on his side?"

"None whatsoever."

"Then why do you think others will believe it? What are you afraid of?"

"I am not afraid of his claims! I am afraid of his causing diplomatic problems for us that will affect our trade status! Can you understand what a problem it would be for us to refuse to give him sovereignty if the powerful nations threatened our trade? We are not part of OPEC! We are vulnerable to such pressure! I am trying to build roads and houses for my people! There are villages without electricity! My people can be educated in the arts and sciences here, but for technology we still send many abroad! This technological education is critical to our future! Do you ask me to threaten all this by listening to a desert bandit with not enough sense even to...to...to eat green leafy vegetables?"

The ludicrousness of this, delivered as it was in a furious undervoice, struck both of them in the same moment.

"Eat green leafy vegetables?" Zara repeated in a shaky voice, and they suddenly erupted into gusts of laughter and fell into each other's arms and down onto their narrow bed.

The noise of their laughter had to be suppressed, a fact they both instantly remembered. They lay quivering, trying to contain it, while little snickers kept breaking out. Zara pressed her mouth against Rafi's shoulder, and he felt the heat of her breath through the cloth of his shirt and against his skin. Fire erupted in his chest; his body grew hard against her thigh.

"Zara!" he whispered warningly. His hand on her arm tightened, as if to push away from her, or perhaps not.

Zara had also been suppressing more than she knew. Passion seemed to come from nowhere, overwhelming, engulfing her. Suddenly, foolishly, she didn't care about safety, secrecy, life or death. Her blood whispered that the closeness of danger only meant she should take her chance while she had it. That she should snatch at the cup of life while it was so close to her lips…

Of its own accord, her slender hand cupped his dark head. She lifted her upper body on her elbow and smiled down at him, trembling, yearning for him, for his beautiful, flashing dark eyes, for his firm, passionate mouth, for the love and need she saw reflected in both.

"Rafi," she whispered, and bent her head, her hair falling around him like a perfumed cloud, till her sweet, cherry-ripe mouth touched his.

He lifted his hands to stroke her head, he opened his mouth to accept her kiss, both of them drowning in desire. "Sweet," he breathed, "sweet, how I love you."

His mouth was delicious as the fruit they had just shared, sending spirals of delight through her. His hands were strong, thrilling her with his firm possessiveness, his powerful desire. He stroked her cheek, her hair, her back, as his mouth drank in the taste of her.

She was trembling with a feeling that was stronger than anything she had ever felt—a yearning from the deepest part of her self. "Rafi!" she whispered, lifting her mouth. They were in, not a cell, but a magic world bounded only by the edge of candlelight and the black curtain of her hair. There was nothing for her but here, and now.

For him, too. But when he lifted himself, and she turned in his arms to lie beneath him, her chain clanked. It was a loud, unfriendly sound, and she winced as the shackle

chafed her sore skin. It was only a moment's discomfort—
even as she winced she was already holding up her mouth
to be kissed again.

But for Rafi, it was the summons of reason. He closed
his eyes briefly, then opened them again to see her parted,
willing, flame-shadowed lips so close to his; he took a deep,
long, sobering breath, willing his blood to still its storm.

She was smiling at him from passion-darkened eyes. She
was his, he knew it. In this moment it was whatever he
wished. His desire swelled in him for a moment, telling
him that he might never find her so willing again, and he
struggled before he won.

When he knew he had conquered himself, he bent to
plant a light kiss, no more, on those passionately parted
lips. "Zara, this is too dangerous," he said softly. "I dare
not risk it. We must wait."

"Ohhh," she wailed softly, a whisper of complaint. She
lifted a hand to his head, but he caught it and brought it to
his lips.

"You are my treasure. Not this way, Beloved. Not with
you chained to a wall. Shall we give him such a victory?—
that to remember the first time we loved, we must remember this prison and fear and a bandit? That we stole our
pleasure in a moment, not taking time, not making discoveries, but snatching at whatever we could reach?"

He was right. She knew, too, that she must not put more
of a burden on him by protesting. She must bring her share
of self-discipline.

She nodded her agreement and struggled to sit up beside
him. "All right," she said.

"We will not regret waiting." His dark eyes promised
much more than he said aloud. "Our patience will be rewarded."

The torment in her blood slowly died. Sanity returned.
The storm passed over them, bringing peace in its wake.
She was hugely grateful to him then. He was more than
right. What would she have thought of him later, if he had

been capable of making love to her for the first time in such conditions?

FROM JALAL IBN AZIZ TO SHEIKH RAFI: I AM IN NO FEAR OF THE SWORD OF ROSTAM OR ANY OTHER. THE SWORD OF JUSTICE IS IN MY OWN HAND. I HAVE STATED MY TERMS. THERE IS NO POSSIBILITY OF COMPROMISE.

Around the camp on three sides and on the far side of the river the military presence was growing, a fact that could easily be seen from the bandit's headquarters. Rows of sand-coloured tents had sprouted like curiously regular dunes. Men moved back and forth. Helicopters came and went and regularly overflew the stronghold in a show of power.

But they were powerless, and all knew it. No mortars could be fired, no bomb dropped, without danger of bringing down the ancient stronghold and killing the hostage.

The bandit's determination to take no hostage but the right one now proved his intelligent foresight. Unless a risk was taken with the hostage's life no conclusion could be forced.

They would take no risk with Rafi's future queen.

There was one press tent. The Barakat Emirates were always news in the West; people liked to keep track of the three handsome princes. Karim and Omar cursed the press presence—one leak, one false report might cost the lives of Zara and Rafi and throw them all into a bloody battle which no one wanted—but they had to put up with it. The press of the world must be seen to be allowed to cover the story.

Omar and Karim had to stand before the press corps on a regular basis, too, briefing them with lies that would protect the mission. Mostly they repeated the same ones over in new words.

The press wasn't happy. They needed some new tidbit

every day to keep the story hot. A waiting game was not
a story. They began to ask when and if the princes meant
to take action. They could see no reason to wait—unless
there was something they hadn't been told. They wanted—
although they never admitted it aloud—they wanted the
killing to start. Some blood to show the folks back home.

One or two negative stories about the princes were filed.
Mostly these were based on the fact that restrictions had
been placed on the movements of the press corps, such
restrictions being called "anti-democratic." But some began to question the princes' "readiness for battle" and suggested there might be a little question of cowardice influ-
encing their continued waiting. One or two stories
suggested that, although each of the princes had served in
the military and was commander in chief of his own armed
forces, none had ever engaged in an actual campaign.

This last was certainly untrue. At other times Prince
Omar's personal sacrifice and bravery during the Parvan-
Kaljukistan war on the side of his cousin Prince Kavian
Durran had been noted in Western papers—but what was
one little misreporting of fact when audience was at stake?
So the princes' "failure of nerve" looked like being next
up on the agenda. It was only one or two stories so far, but
there was nothing the media loved so much as the destruction of heroes they themselves had previously created.

The princes were too involved in their plans to pay much
attention to the foreign media coverage, but it did not go
unremarked everywhere. Before the trend could gain momentum, a helicopter arrived and, to the delight of the press
and the amazement and disapproval of Karim and Omar,
disgorged Caroline Langley and Jana Stewart—looking
desert chic and lovely, and full of smiles for the mainly
male press corps.

Not just smiles. Several cases of chilled champagne were
also offloaded from the helicopter, and a couple of palace
servants and trays and glasses, and the press corps was
invited to toast the engagements and future happiness of

these gorgeous Western women who had captured the hearts of princes.

The stories filed that day were all about the beautiful blonde American fiancée of Prince Karim, the beautiful red-headed Scots fiancée of Prince Omar, their plans for a double wedding, which had been delayed by the current crisis, and the champagne on ice they had so thoughtfully brought to the desert campaign....

"What are you doing here?" the princes demanded, when all four were alone together at last.

"Saving you from a public relations disaster," Caroline replied sweetly. "None of those reporters has had alcohol for days! What do you think you're doing?"

Omar almost shouted, "My brother is inside Jalal's camp with his future wife! I have better things to think about than the alcoholic consumption of the press corps!"

"Maybe you do, but somebody had to think about it," Caroline informed her grim-faced future brother-in-law. "We've arranged for supplies to be flown in on a regular basis. Now, we're going to arrange to take the journalists off to do photo shoots of the palaces. And we'll feed them there, and bring them back in a much better mood than they collectively are at the moment."

"They need stories," Jana pointed out firmly before further protests could be lodged. "And you need breathing room. So we're buying you time."

There was one hard-headed, tough and desert-seasoned woman campaigner among the press corps. However much alcohol she might get under her belt, Jana and Caroline were pretty sure that *she* would not be sidetracked by pretty fiancées and palaces.

The woman smelled something. She had already been caught in the no-go area making for the rocky outcrop where the tunnel entrance was hidden. The princes had been very careful not to mark the area as special in any way, and a lot of totally unnecessary Jeep activity went on

in the desert to cover the necessary visits to the tunnel—
but a nose is a nose, and the reporter had one.

If she found the tunnel or even speculated on its existence, a great advantage would be thrown away. Jalal would
certainly close the tunnel, by one means or another, if he
knew they knew of its existence.

On advice from Jana and Caroline, Omar secretly took
this woman aside and promised her an exclusive when it
was over. The price was laying off until they had the hostage safe.

The coming holiday was, they knew, their best chance.
All their efforts were concentrated on that. On the last trip
in with Mustafa, Arif had prevented him taking in all the
fruit the women had asked for. Then Mustafa had promised
faithfully to go in again with the missing supplies on the
very day of the festival.

Men were now engaged in doctoring that fruit with the
drug. There was also a bag of the drug set aside to be given
to Rafi. If they could get this to Rafi during the delivery,
he might be able to put it into the vat of beans that was
part of the traditional fare of the holiday.

That side of the plan was as prepared as possible. The
exploration of the tunnel was more complicated. It might
be as much as two miles long, and there was no way of
knowing how many of Jalal's men might be lurking within.
It would be more than dangerous—it would be foolhardy
to go into it with a light, and virtually impossible to go
without one. The probability of discovery was very high,
and they could not afford to give away their knowledge of
the tunnel by killing a guard.

But unless Rafi discovered for certain that the tunnel actually debouched into the stronghold, they could not simply
hope to send a squad of men through the tunnel at the
critical moment. What if they emerged into the desert outside the walls?

The tunnel might be a huge advantage, or it might be
worthless. If the drug worked, they could land helicopters

into the compound, but this was an operation that needed ground support.

Rafi had until tomorrow. If he was unable to locate the tunnel entrance in time to inform Arif when he went in with the supply truck, someone would go into the tunnel with an infrared viewer and a tranquillizer gun a few hours before the assault on the place and, with luck, report back. Rafi had timed the shifts of the guards in the compound, and they would make the attempt just as a shift began. That would mean that, with a little luck, anyone they knocked out in the tunnel would not be missed before the assault was made.

But for now it was all waiting.

Thirteen

Early the next afternoon, the old woman entered the prisoner's cell to find her flushed and trembling, her face and hair soaked with sweat, being racked every few moments by dry heaves.

Ah, poor child! What ails thee?

Panting, the prisoner put her hand to her chest. *My heart.*

The old woman dropped to her knees on the floor and laid her ear against the child's chest. Her heartbeat was fast, very fast. She was hot and sweating hard. Gasping for air.

She gently soothed the child's forehead. *Here, drink this water I have brought you.*

The prisoner gratefully drank. Then she mimed a needle going into her arm. *Medicine. I need drugs. Jalal. Tell Jalal.*

If you rest, child, you will feel better soon. And I will bring you...

Drugs! I must have drugs or I will die! Tell Jalal. Bring Jalal. English. English.

The old woman rose to her feet, wailing softly to herself. She set the water within the prisoner's reach, and the little plate of savoury cakes and bits of lamb she had so carefully chosen from the feast food. Then, calling reassuringly that she would bring Jalal, she rushed from the room.

She brushed past the guards and into Jalal's apartments. "Where is he? Where is Jalal?" she demanded of the men lounging there, playing backgammon. They sat up, murmuring in surprise, but before anyone could answer her demand, Jalal himself strode in from the next room.

"What is it?"

"She is dying, the prisoner! Her heart races like a hunted gazelle's. She is asking for you. She says she will die without medicines. She must be released at once!"

"Calm yourself. Young women do not die of heart attacks so easily."

"Go and see her! I insist that you go and listen to what she says! If she dies, you are ruined! We are all ruined!"

Jalal and the old woman stared at each other measuringly. At last he nodded. "Yes, you are right. I will talk to her, find out what the danger is."

He strode out the doors and across the compound. The heat was already intense. Canopies were being erected by a happy group of men and boys all around the perimeter of the open square. They called greetings to him and he nodded and waved as he ducked under the doorway to the passage leading to the prisoner's cell.

"Thank you for coming," she whispered. Her face was covered in sweat, her breathing erratic. Jalal cursed under his breath and knelt by her.

"What has happened?" he asked. He lifted her wrist and felt her pulse. Well over a hundred. Perhaps a hundred and fifty. Jalal sighed. Would fate never support his cause?

"My heart. I—I have a congenital heart defect. Do you know what that is?"

He frowned at her. "Of course I know what—"

Jalal broke off. He blinked rapidly at her, and then gently

bent forward. "I—you—" he murmured. His head sank onto her breast, gently, like a child's seeking comfort.

Zara held her breath as his weight became heavier against her. His hand let go her wrist, and his arm sprawled. His legs unfolded till he was lying flat across her, trapping her arms. "Jalal!" she murmured urgently. "Jalal!"

The bandit did not answer. She shook him again, then struggled to draw her hand out from under him and lifted his eyelid. She saw the white of his eye.

"Unconscious," she said more loudly, raising her eyes as Rafi came up behind. In his hand was a small gun, which he shoved down the waist of his pants. Black, like Jalal's. He bent and lifted the bandit's body off her. It sprawled onto the floor.

"How are you?" he asked anxiously.

Already her breathing was returning to normal. "I'm fine. Don't waste time on me. A half hour of aerobics won't kill me. Can you get his keffiyeh off?"

Perhaps to mark the festive day, Jalal was wearing a green-and-white patterned keffiyeh on his head. With Zara's help, Rafi now pulled it off. He paused, looking into the unconscious face of his enemy.

"My God!" he exclaimed. The resemblance was remarkable.

"Yes, it gives me the shivers," Zara agreed.

In a moment he had wrapped his own head in the borrowed keffiyeh. "Oh, you really are like him!" she exclaimed.

"Good," he said shortly. He pulled the gun from his belt and handed it to her. "Keep that. If he stirs at all, shoot him again. Aim for the chest area, it gives you the biggest target. You have eleven more pellets, but *insh'Allah* you won't need them all."

"How long—?" she began, taking the gun calmly and weighing it in her hand.

"No one is certain. These things are still experimental

for humans; I am told the results vary greatly. Perhaps two or three hours. Perhaps much less. Be on your guard.''

''What are you going to do?''

''First I will check Jalal's private apartments to see if the tunnel entrance is there. Then I will meet Arif when he comes in with the supplies truck and give him what information I have discovered.'' He pulled a folded piece of paper from his pants pocket to double check it. It was a map showing where he thought the tunnel must be, and where Zara's cell was.

''Do you have your copy of the map?'' he asked.

She nodded, indicating the corner of the mattress where she had placed it.

''I can pass it to Arif without talking to him if necessary, and I will watch where he puts the drug. Then, if all goes well, I will put the drug into the beans. Then I will return here.''

It sounded desperately dangerous, but Zara bit her lip and made no protest. ''And then?''

''You are almost free. A few more minutes and the padlock is broken. Do that while I am away. If the old woman comes, you will have to shoot her, too. You are certain of what to do if I do not return?''

They had plotted and planned late into the night. They had discussed the probabilities and made their best guesses, drawn their maps and made half a dozen contingency plans.

''Yes,'' she said.

He waited, but she said no more. She would not weep or wring her hands or worry anxiously about failure. He bent and saluted her lips with his.

''You are a brave woman,'' he said. A moment later he was gone, leaving her with the unconscious body of his near twin. Setting the gun down close by, Zara picked up the metal file and bent to her task.

''*Salaam aleikum!*'' *Peace be upon thee.*

''*Waleikum salaam,*'' Rafi replied. *And upon thee, peace.*

He raised his hand as he had secretly watched Jalal do, and it occurred to him that the gesture was not unlike his own natural gesture.

He strode across the square towards Jalal's private apartments. Although the perimeter was well guarded, only one place *within* the fortress had a guard—Jalal's own rooms. Two men were on twenty-four-hour guard outside the doors, which lay in the east wing. All that half of the wing was, he thought, otherwise uninhabited.

To a casual observer the two guardsmen might have looked like a formality, like the beaver-hatted guards at Buckingham Palace. But Rafi also had guardsmen in his palace. He knew the difference between those whose duty was a ritual and those whose duty was to guard. These men were always alert. No one ever got near the leader's quarters without being challenged.

Yet he had also seen Jalal himself wandering quite freely in the compound among his people. So his rooms were not guarded because of fears of attempted assassination.

Put all these facts together and there was reason to think that Jalal was keeping the tunnel secret by living over the entrance.

He did not dare to risk his disguise with Jalal's closest companions, who all came and went freely to the private apartments. But there was another area, further along, where men came and went, and Rafi was almost sure that the guards also kept close watch on that entrance. With a casual lifted arm, he strode under the crumbling arches and on towards the heavy wooden door.

Inside, he saw a large, long space supported here and there by pillars. The gloom was relieved by the light of a lantern, beside which sat two men smoking and playing backgammon. They looked up at his entrance. He approached the light quickly so that they would see his face and rely on that for identification rather than his voice. When they saw their leader, they got to their feet in some alarm.

"Shall I saddle Gavrosh, Lord? No one informed us."

A stable! Rafi's heart tightened. That was a reason for the coming and going that he had not thought of. What a miscalculation!

Well, he must risk everything. "Who is on guard in the tunnel?" He spoke raspingly, and coughed as if to clear his throat.

And both men turned as one and glanced into the darkness at the other end of the long pillared room. Rafi closed his eyes with relief. Not wrong after all. The intelligence of the bandit, to disguise his tunnel with his stables!

"Jehan, Ahmad, and Zahir, Lord."

He nodded as if the information meant something, and as his eyes grew accustomed to the gloom he moved slowly down the room towards the total darkness at the end. "What time do they change shift?" His voice was still rough.

He realized he had already begun to enter the tunnel. The floor was sloping down. The darkness was the maw of it. He stood looking blindly in, but it was not the kind of darkness that the eyes grow accustomed to. Too black. He turned around, his eyebrows raised.

His guards shook themselves, recovering from their surprise. "In—at four o'clock, Lord, as usual."

Rafi nodded, and strode towards the door. "Tell Zahir to report to me when he comes up."

"Shall I call him now, Lord?"

His leader turned eyes of surprised disdain on him, and the man bowed jerkily in apology. "I will tell him, Lord, when he comes up."

Rafi went out. In the gloom under the arched overhang, he paused to make notes for his brothers on the back of the map. Then he strolled casually out into the midst of the preparations. He nodded and spoke a word of encouragement here and there, exactly as he would have done for his own people.

He paused by the huge vat sitting over a fire in one

corner, where two or three women stood chatting and stirring. He sniffed the bean stew, and asked for a taste. One of the women lifted a large wooden spoon from the mixture and offered it to him, and he bent and tasted it. He smacked his lips and said it was delicious, and they looked at him, gratified, but shaking their heads. It was not ready yet! In another hour, if their Lord cared to eat a portion, they would not be ashamed then to have their efforts judged, but now—! They clapped their hands and shook their heads.

He laughed, swore that it was already clear that it would be irresistible, promised that he would eat two bowlsful. "Be sure that you give a bowl to all the guards who have the misfortune to be on duty today," he commanded. "Let it not be said that they missed *all* the pleasures of the day."

The women nodded and promised that it would be done. "We will feed them first!" one promised.

"Excellent," he said, and passed on.

He kept his chin covered by the keffiyeh as far as possible, so that his deficiencies in the area of beard would not be noted. His moustache was as full as Jalal's.

Before long he was rewarded by the sounds of shouting, and the main gates were laboriously opened to let in the battered delivery truck, loaded with crates of fruit. Sitting beside Mustafa, the driver, wrapped in a heavy keffiyeh, he was annoyed but not surprised to detect the eyes of his brother Karim.

It was pure foolhardiness. If Jalal were to trap them both inside the walls, what choice would Omar have but to negotiate with the bandit? But Rafi understood the impulse. He lifted his hands in regal greeting and called a welcome to the deliverymen. *Noblesse oblige,* and anyway, it was a holiday.

Karim's eyes widened briefly, and then, taking his cue from Mustafa, he bowed respectfully to Jalal the bandit. Of course Mustafa and all his village supported the bandit, whether from actual political conviction or the simple understanding that it would be safer for them to pretend to do so.

With a casual eye, Rafi paused to examine the fruit they were offloading, picking up an apple and leaving in its place a piece of paper that instantly disappeared into Karim's hand. "Is this your finest fruit?" he asked.

"The very best we ship," Mustafa assured him, nodding like a puppet. He was terrified that the stranger's presence in his truck would be noticed by the bandit and then both he and his brother would undoubtedly be killed, himself by Jalal and his brother by those who held him hostage. It was a hard life.

Karim said significantly, "Excellent fruit, Lord! Everyone will want to eat it! Delicious, and even better than what was ordered! These grapes, too, are worthy of eating!" He lifted a basket and offered it.

The leader deigned to pluck a grape and taste it. "Excellent! Delicious!" he exclaimed jovially. From across the courtyard the old woman was eying him in amazement.

"What about our guest, my son? Is she well? How did you leave her?" she cried.

My son. Rafi swallowed. Could it be? Women did use the term to young men not related to them...but the tone of voice was not that of an old woman to her leader. He might fool Jalal's people, but if the old woman was truly the bandit's mother—she would not be fooled at close range, nor by the hoarseness of his voice.

In the bottom of the basket of grapes, he knew, was the supply of the drug intended for the stew. The old woman stood gazing at him, waiting for an answer. He glanced at Karim, and saw the knowledge of his danger reflected in his brother's eyes.

Fourteen

The brothers glanced at each other in the full knowledge that it was possible they would both be dead in the next few minutes. Both pairs of eyes glinted with humour and the excitement of danger.

Karim held up the basket of grapes. "Have no fear, Umm Jalal!" he cried. *Mother of Jalal.* It was the way of the desert tribes to call mothers by such an honorific, but if he had supposed wrong... "Even now our leader was asking for the best fruit to take to the sick guest! And I happen to have a beautiful basket of grapes! Your son takes care of all who fall within his shadow, does he not?"

With a large gesture he passed the basket to Jalal, who took them with a nod and turned towards the entrance leading to the passage to Zara's cell. "Now, Mother," he heard Karim's voice behind him. "See what excellencies we have brought for the celebrations today! Are these not fine apples? All the way from the orchards in the hills! Is all in hand for your feast?"

Rafi hurried to the cell. There he found Zara sitting with the kitten in her lap, the gun in her hand, and Jalal's body stretched out neatly on the floor. She jumped up when he appeared in the doorway. "Oh, thank God it's you! Did it all go—"

He interrupted her, putting his fingers to her lips. "We must hurry. We may have only a few minutes and I have to get him hidden."

Zara sobered instantly. "I can help you carry him. I've filed through the padlock."

He put down the basket. "Excellent. Take his feet."

It took them several minutes, and, healthy as she was, she was small, and she was panting when they had finally carried Jalal through to the next room. They quickly returned to her own cell, where Rafi lifted the grapes from the basket, snatched up the plastic bag underneath, and restored the grapes.

"The old woman may come in. If she does, keep her here as long as possible," he said, stuffing the bag of whitish powder into his shirt "The grapes have been brought by Jalal to make you feel better, but he left again immediately. Do you have something with which to tie your shackle on so that she will not notice?"

Zara wordlessly held up a strip of the white dress, carefully dirtied on the floor to make it less visible.

"I will try to let you know when I get back next door. Try and keep her till then if you can. It will be difficult because no doubt she has much to do for the feast. Hide the gun within reach. Don't shoot her with it to keep her here—let her go—but only if there is some other difficulty, such as Jalal awakening. She is Jalal's mother. All right?"

"Good luck," she said with a smile. Underneath she was terrified. The old woman was Jalal's mother? If she saw Rafi at close quarters—or even at a distance! Zara knew she herself could never be mistaken in the identity of the two men now. How much more must that apply to Jalal's own mother! It must not happen.

He disappeared back through the hole in the wall and she was alone. Her heart beating with fear, Zara turned to the business of fixing her shackle on again. The kitten thought it was a game, and did its best to prevent her by biting her fingers and clawing at the ribbon it was used to thinking a toy. But she managed at last.

Then she got up again and did a little quick exercise to boost her pulse rate, keeping a constant eye on the door. The shackle tore at her ankle, and she allowed the tears to come. When she was sweating more than before, she lay down.

So the old woman found her.

How are you now, little one?

"*Shokran,*" Zara said, raising herself on an elbow and smiling through her tears. She didn't want the woman so panicked she would dash off to find her son. *Thank you. A little better.*

The old woman felt her forehead. Still sweaty, but not so much as before, and it was a hot day. She put her head to the prisoner's chest.

Your heart still beats hard.

Zara smiled. She wanted to say, your son is not a big man, but heavy enough, nevertheless. *I am much better. See the grapes that Jalal brought me. Sit and share them with me, please. I am sad.*

Rafi used his pathways through the empty fortress rooms to work his way around to the corner where the bean stew was cooking. There he sat and waited for the moment when the vat would be left unattended. He was wearing his own white keffiyeh now, well wrapped around his head. He did not want to be noticed, and in Jalal's green headgear he would be.

He was relieved to see that the delivery truck had gone. It was a pity he had not spoken to Karim, but all was there in the note. The map, the number of men in the tunnel and above, the timing of the shift. And at the bottom, the words, *Let the first man in bring the Sword of Rostam.*

While he waited, he fitted the bag of soporific inside his shirtsleeve, with the open end rolled up in his cuff at the elbow. All he had to do, he hoped, was pull the plastic free and hold his arm downwards and the drug would pour out.

He could not risk this with anyone watching, but although it was clear that the stew needed little attention now, the women stood around the vat gossiping. He hid in the shadows listening. Over the past few days he had picked up information about the camp in just this way. But now their gossiping made him impatient.

Slowly people began to spill out of the various huts and rooms, dressed in finery. Suddenly one of the women standing over the vat realized that time was passing. "We must go and prepare ourselves for the celebrations!" she cried, and within a minute, all were gone.

The stew was momentarily deserted. Rafi did not wait. He emerged from the shadows and slipped under the canopy that sheltered the vat from the sun. Its rays were reduced in intensity now; it was lower in the sky. This corner of the yard was already full of shadows.

He leaned over the vat for a moment, a man curious about the traditional dish, stirred it as if absently, and then was gone.

Zara was trying, with her dress fabric, to fashion a little sling in which to take out Mr. Wriggly when the time came. Going into the next room to check on Jalal, she had noticed the remnants of her dress and carried it back with her. She tore the top of the dress off, and tied the two sleeves together to form a long strap. She was hoping that she could somehow tie the kitten snugly into the bodice—and as long as she left his head out, perhaps he wouldn't struggle too wildly. And by slinging it over her shoulder or neck, she would leave her hands free.

But exactly when to try to tie him into it would be the

problem. If she did it too soon, he would go crazy all tied up. If she left it too late…there would be no time if he struggled.

It was so difficult to tell how long Jalal would sleep. He had not stirred, but she shot him with the tranquillizer gun again anyway. The timing of the enterprise was all dependent. Rafi had to wait until people started to show the effects of eating the drug, then signal his brothers.

They were going to attack tonight whether the drug worked or not. There would never be a better time. But if the drug had not worked they were expecting bloodshed.

The worst of it was that the plan kept being modified in the light of events. Rafi had to be constantly thinking on his feet. Having found the tunnel entrance, he had told her he thought that during the party there might be a way to take Zara out by way of the tunnel before the attack started. For that, though, she would need a disguise. He could take her through a deserted part of the fortress some of the way, but still there would be twenty yards or more to cover in the open.

He was looking for a possible disguise now, while also waiting for the bean dish to be served and eaten. But all the women were wearing their beaded headscarves and embroidered tunics at the party. Zara would be noticed if she went out in someone's ordinary clothes. Most of the women had only one or two sets of clothes, and were recognized at a distance by what they wore. He was cursing himself for not having foreseen the need for a disguise.

The sun was low in the sky, Zara could tell. Should she tie the kitten into the bag now? Surely one way or the other, Rafi would be coming for her very soon? If only she had asked for a little of the drug to give to the kitten!

She heard a noise behind her and turned to greet him. What she saw instead was the barrel of an automatic pointing straight at her eye. ''Get up,'' said Jalal softly. ''Make no noise. I will not hesitate to kill you.''

* * *

They were dropping like flies, Rafi saw with satisfaction. Lying under the canopies, one after the other they set down the bowl of beans, yawned and stretched out for a nap. The guards, too.

He was watching from the roof. When he was satisfied that the effects would be widespread, he turned and gave the signal. It was quick, but repeated until he got the answering code. It came quickly.

Now he had to get down to Zara's cell, on the opposite side of the central square. He took the fastest way, around the roof to a staircase. From there it was a dangerous climb down a broken-down, almost impassable stairwell.

He saw them emerge below him, Zara with her hands tied behind her, Jalal forcing her to run, holding her up, when she stumbled, cruelly, with the bonds that held her wrists. They were zigzagging under and between the arches heading towards the tunnel.

Standing on the roof, Rafi pulled his gun from its holster and fired into the air. "Jalal!" he screamed.

Behind a pillar, the bandit turned his head, saw his enemy high above. He pulled Zara around to put her between them, and began dragging her backwards. He saluted Rafi, the gun barrel just touching his forehead. "Another time!" he cried. "I have pressing business."

He had no clear shot and he knew he wouldn't get one. Cursing, Rafi shoved the gun back on his hip and began the wild precipitous descent down the half-destroyed stairwell. By the time he had reached the ground there was no sign of them. He ran across the courtyard towards the tunnel. All around him men and women lay snoring. Some tried to get up, staggered and fell.

His brothers must have sent the troops down the tunnel long ago. They would have been in position, waiting for the signal. Jalal would never get out with her, it was impossible.

Yet still he ran.

He heard the sound of hoofbeats, and the next moment

a large black horse charged straight for him, knocking him down, sending his gun flying. On its back was Jalal, with Zara slung over the horse in front of him, face down. It was an exact replay of the first time he and Jalal had met. He vowed the bandit would pay for it.

Rafi dived for his gun, and chased the horse on foot, but the bandit knew his stronghold better than Rafi could. By the time Rafi had him in his sights, Jalal had opened a small door inset into the main gate and was bending low over the horse to go through. With a curse, Rafi aimed at the horse.

His gun jammed, damaged somehow by its fall. In a few seconds Jalal was galloping off over the desert, now glowing pink in the setting sun.

Rafi ran back towards the stable and the tunnel entrance. Surely there was more than one horse in the bandit's stable! Even on the thought, he heard the sound of horses. He entered the stable again to see, emerging from the tunnel at a near gallop, his Companions, in twos and threes, mounted on their horses.

First was Arif, leading Rafi's own black, Raksh.

"Lord!" he cried, dismounting as the others pulled up. "We heard the shot and knew that stealth was unnecessary. What's toward?"

"They are asleep, all save Jalal himself. He has taken Zara and galloped into the desert," Rafi shouted, as he mounted into the saddle. "Who follows?"

"A platoon of foot, on the run. The way has been lighted, the guards subdued. We will go with you, Lord, to bring her back!" the Companions cried.

On Rafi's saddle hung the Sword of Rostam, not in its ceremonial, but in its battle scabbard. Rafi pulled the strap over his head, settled the sword on his hip, and urged his mount into a gallop.

The Companions followed him, out into the square, around, and then through the gate and out into the desert. Ahead of them, his horse's fine black tail streaming in the wind as he urged it across the broken desert, Rafi drew the gleaming scimitar from its scabbard.

"Ya Rostam!" he cried.

It was the traditional battle cry of his forebears when they drew the Sword of Rostam against an enemy.

"Ya Rostam!" they answered. Then, as one man, the Companions of Sayed Hajji Rafi Jehangir ibn Daud ibn Hassan al Quraishi lifted their heads and opened their throats in the high yodelling cry of their warrior ancestors.

They galloped at full tilt, following their prince, crying their bloodchilling battle cry to the vengeful winds. Now it was a battle to the death.

Fifteen

Trucks and Jeeps were rolling ponderously across the desert from the highway to the south to surround the fortress. Jalal spurred his mount towards the cluster of villages a few miles to the north. The people there supported him, would receive him and hide the hostage.

He glanced back over his shoulder. A troop of horse burst from the gates and spread out across the red desert. He cursed the sun for not setting faster. A few more minutes and he would have been lost in the shadows. As it was, he cast a huge shadow. They were already coming after him.

His horse was hampered by the double burden. He would never make the villages. Jalal changed direction and made towards the biggest rocky outcrop within reach.

Zara was spending most of her energy on trying to keep conscious. Folded over the horse as she was, its sweating odour choking her, her stomach being jolted unmercifully, in terror of slipping off under the deadly hooves, she was so sick with nausea and fear that she could feel the constant drag of a faint. She was sure that would be fatal. Jalal was gripping her with one rough hand on her bound wrists, but still it needed all the effort of her stomach muscles to cling on.

She could not see where they were going, her view restricted to the tirelessly galloping hooves and desert floor. When she lifted her head her hair fell in her eyes, she could see nothing. Her last sight of Rafi had been as he was sent sprawling almost underfoot by Jalal's kick. She had seen his gun go flying, but nothing more, and he was frozen there in her mind's eye, in the act of falling, the gun on the air, dust everywhere, like some horrible photograph of war.

The sound of the horse's hooves was too close to her ears, but she thought she heard helicopters behind them, and the strangely melodious howling of animals, like the coyotes at night when she went camping in Algonquin Park. She had always loved that plaintive, lonely sound, and it comforted her now, without reason.

The horse stopped with a jerk that was so unexpected and so final she fell. But Jalal had already dismounted in time to catch her, and before she knew it she was running wildly up a rocky incline, forced to leap a chasm that terrified her, dragged further. Her bare feet were cut and bleeding, she saw, but she strangely felt no pain. Her arms, too, were mercifully numb. Her clothes were torn in several places, and stained with dirt and blood, but she had no idea where the blood came from. She didn't care. If she was going to get out of this alive, she had to keep her mind clear and watch for opportunity.

He dragged and pushed her up and up. Her ascent was difficult at all times, because her bound arms meant she had poor balance, but it was worst when he dragged her backwards, clasping her arm or sometimes her bound wrists.

Suddenly, below on the desert floor, she saw the horsemen and learned that that wild comforting cry came from their throats. One of them gazed upwards for a moment, a curving sword held high in his hand. It glowed blood red in the setting sun, and she shivered in primitive horror before she understood.

"Rafi!" she screamed.

She watched as he methodically sheathed the sword and then dismounted from his snorting, stamping horse. Then he ran towards the thrust of rock that the desert had sometime, long ago, spewed up. Jalal's gun exploded near her ear and the bullet pinged off the rocky slope below, but Rafi had already disappeared from view.

Jalal dragged her more quickly then. She thought he was heading for some known place, and wondered what it was.

"You can't possibly win this," she said breathlessly. "Why don't you give up now? If you do, Rafi will talk to you about your claim, I'm sure he will."

"I am sure he will, too," came his dry voice. "When he realizes that you are my hostage and will be so until we meet—he and his brothers and I."

On the desert floor, Rafi briefly directed his Companions to try to scale the rocks at a variety of places around the perimeter, then turned to make the ascent himself. Arif stopped him. "You have no gun, Lord! Take mine!" he said, thrusting his own revolver into Rafi's holster. "The bullets in your holster are the wrong calibre," he said then. "Take my holster, too."

Rafi impatiently shook his head. "No time for that. How many bullets in the gun?"

It was an automatic. "Nine," said Arif.

Rafi nodded. "I hope to need only one."

"Lord—" But the prince had already begun the climb. Arif waited till he had mounted a few yards and then followed.

Zara understood Jalal's choice as soon as they arrived at the place. They were within a couple of yards of the summit, a large plateau that seemed to fall away steeply on all sides except that of their approach.

At the last he led her up a steep incline and edged through a narrow passage between two high sheets of rock that admitted only one. Immediately they were faced with another chasm, three feet wide, not very deep, but sharply precipitous. Anyone falling down it would break ankles at least. For someone hurled down with their arms bound, death was more likely.

He made her leap it. She screamed in terror as she went, but somehow they both made it to the other side. There, they landed on a small shelf. It was perhaps a couple of yards square in the centre, quickly tapering to the merest toe hold at each end. There was a man-sized niche in the rock leading up to the plateau, and now Jalal stood inside it. He was protected on three sides. In front of him, he held Zara, facing the passage which was the only angle of approach. At her feet, a few feet away, was the chasm. One push would send her staggering helplessly over the edge.

She was panting with exertion and terror. If Rafi came through that little defile, he was an unmissable target. And if he was following them, he would come through. "Rafi!" she screamed, "no closer!"

She cringed, expecting a blow from the gun on her head, but he merely growled, "Shut up! He must come and he knows it."

"Don't kill him," she pleaded. "Please don't kill him."

Jalal looked down and their eyes met. "Don't kill *him?*"

"Please, please."

"He chooses his bride well, at any rate," Jalal said.

"I am his bride," she said urgently. "I am going to marry him. Let me go, and I will convince him to talk to you. He will give you a hearing if I ask him to do it."

He laughed. "You are a woman who should be believed when she says she can make a man do a thing," he observed mildly. "But I prefer my own way. I petitioned and was not heard. Now I beg for the princes' favour no longer. Now I dictate.''

''Please let me go. If you don't, you know there will be blood shed. Someone will get hurt. He told me that they are determined not to shed blood. But if you do this—please, it's so dangerous.''

''My people lie dead, and you say they were determined to hurt no one?'' Jalal laughed. ''Their determination did not last long!''

''But they're not dead, they're asleep!'' she cried. ''It's a drug!''

He stared at her, frowning.

''Why do you think *you're* alive? He could have killed you more easily—instead he shot you with a tranquillizer gun! If he had killed you we wouldn't be here now. I'd be safe, and you'd be dead.''

''My people are not dead?''

''I swear it. I swear it on my life.''

There was tense silence for a time she could not count. Then they heard the scraping of boot on rock. ''Rafi, no!'' she screamed again. ''Go back!''

Jalal snorted, and called out, ''Your woman imagines you to be a coward, Rafi, Prince of the Realm! Are you so?''

Zara gasped as Rafi stepped negligently into perfect target range between the two upright shafts of rock. ''I am here, Jalal grandson of Selim the Bandit,'' he said. ''What now?''

The light was fading; blood red shadows were everywhere. Zara felt the metal of the gun brush her forehead, and Jalal's grasp on her bound hands tightened.

''Throw your gun down,'' Jalal ordered.

As if it meant nothing, Rafi lifted the gun from his holster and tossed it into the rocky ravine at his feet.

''And what now, Jalal the Bandit? *Bien aimée, tu m'entends,*'' Rafi spoke the first phrases clearly, drawled them almost, then added the next sentence in a quick mutter she almost didn't catch.

Beloved, you hear me. He was speaking to her in French.

"How many of my people are dead, Rafi son of Daud?" Jalal asked.

"We killed none, Jalal son of Aziz. Three in the tunnel were wounded, but not mortally. All that you saw on the ground were drugged. They will recover without ill effects."

Zara felt him relax and knew that he had accepted it. She heaved a sigh of relief.

"Let her go, and we will talk," Rafi said.

"I will not let her go, but I will not kill her, either. I want a helicopter immediately, to land on the rock above my head. One pilot only inside."

Rafi laughed. "A helicopter! Where will you go? There will be no escape, Jalal. *Watch his gun hand.*"

Again the quick phrase added in French. She looked from one to the other. In the deepening gloom, their physical resemblance was even more remarkable.

"There is no escape for you either, Prince of the Realm! We will deal together sooner or later, you and your brothers and I!"

"We will never deal together unless you give her to me now. Take her from here and you lose everything," Rafi said firmly.

"I will give her up after we have negotiated. Do you think I will pass her to you on the basis of your word? What good is your word to me? You and your brothers have violated all other bonds, why should your word be good?"

"You may trust me in this. We will talk with you, but you must first give her up. *When his aim wavers I will jump.* Let her come to me now, and we will all go back to the palace and we can discuss whatever you wish. *Prepare.* If not, what can your destiny be but a prison cell?"

"If you speak to the hostage in French again I will throw her over the edge," Jalal said coldly.

Rafi's eyebrows went up in surprise. "Ah, we heard that you were an educated man. Did you go abroad to study?"

"You know well the answer to that."

I know? Rafi frowned, at a loss for a moment.

"It grows darker. You have not summoned the helicopter. Do you have a mobile phone, a walkie-talkie?"

Rafi lifted his hands. "Neither. What can I do? Perhaps we should wait till morning."

She felt Jalal's amused laugh. "Your loyal Companions are all around you, no doubt. Summon the nearest and pass on the message. If there is no helicopter waiting above me before the sun sets, I will shoot this beauty and throw her over the edge. It would be a loss. She pleaded for your life, not her own. How many women will you find of such character? You choose, Prince of the Realm."

"And what then? Do you think we would ever talk to a murderer about his claims to a heritage?"

"Summon me the helicopter before the sun sets or watch her die. Or perhaps, see her live a cripple. You have perhaps three minutes, perhaps four."

He was steely. Zara could feel the determination in him, and was afraid.

Rafi raised his voice. "Arif!"

"Lord!" came the faint cry behind him.

"You are in contact with my brothers?"

"I am, Lord."

"Tell them to send a helicopter. To the top of the rock above our heads. The pilot only inside."

There was a pause, a murmur. Then, "It is done, Lord."

In the distance the sound of an engine changed. One of the helicopters hovering over the fortress had changed course. In the shadows, Rafi dislodged a piece of the loose rock under his hand.

"Well, then, bandit. Your helicopter comes. What next?"

"You know already, Prince. She goes with me. If you wish to see her again, you know the way."

The helicopter must have been closer than they knew, flying low to the ground, the sound diminished by the wall of rock. Suddenly, with a loud roar, it roared up and appeared almost directly overhead. Jalal glanced up, no more, but for the first time the gun was not pressed against her temple. Quick as lightning, Zara opened her mouth and with all her strength bit into his wrist.

He cried out in surprise and looked at her. In the next moment, Rafi leapt onto the ledge and smashed the rock down on Jalal's fingers. The gun went flying down into the ravine. Feeling herself released, Zara dropped to her knees before he could take another hold on her, and crawled sideways out from between the two men. She saw the last blood red glitter of the sun on the blade of the Sword of Rostam as its deadly beauty whipped from its sheath.

"I warned you it would be a fight to the death, Jalal grandson of Selim," Rafi said, placing the sword against his enemy's neck, flattening him against rock.

"Don't kill him, Rafi!" she whispered helplessly.

Jalal stood straight and looked him in the eye. He smiled. "So be it, then, Rafi son of Daud. But beware your father's curse if you kill your brother's son."

Sixteen

Zara stretched and yawned luxuriously as the door opened softly and a woman in a white polo shirt and green pants entered. She crossed to the table, paused and leaned over Zara. "Oh, good, you're awake. Did you have a lovely massage?"

"Lovely," Zara agreed.

"Ready for your facial?"

"Mmmm."

The woman, a beautician named Maria, moved some wheeled trays around and then seated herself at Zara's head.

"Same as yesterday, or something new again?"

Zara smiled. "Something new again."

"How about a cucumber mask?"

"Sounds divine."

"I met Sheikh Rafi a few minutes ago. He just arrived. He asked how you're feeling today, and I told him barring a few abrasions you're pretty much back to your old self. He's expecting you for dinner, did you know?''

"Yes, I got the summons earlier." Zara smiled.

"He's incredibly dishy, isn't he?"

Dishy, she knew, was the English for *gorgeous.* "Incredibly."

"Don't you feel lucky?"

Zara laughed delightedly. "Yes, I feel amazingly, fabulously lucky that such a wonderful man wants to marry me, of course I do! I've seen him in better and in worse, and there is no one in the world like him. In the universe, probably. And on top of everything else, he lives in a palace! I keep hoping I won't wake up!''

"Well, don't talk anymore, and I'll do my best to make sure you're as beautiful as can be tonight. It won't be hard. Adilah is doing her bit, too. She has some of the loveliest costumes I've ever seen in my life for you to try on. She was showing them to me. They really know how to live out here, don't they?"

It had all been just as Rafi had promised, right down to the portrayals of Shirin and Khosrow on the walls of the bath. She had been pummelled, pampered and cosseted, her wounds had been doctored, her hair expertly trimmed, her nails manicured. She had swum and lazed in the sun. She had been fed the most delicious foods. She had gone for walks in the mountains. She had even been taken through her paces by a fitness trainer.

She had discovered the lifestyle of the idle rich, and pretty fabulous it was.

It had lasted four days so far, during which she recuperated in the palace, while Rafi and his brothers had talks with Jalal in the capital, Barakat al Barakat. Except for the staff, she had been alone. Then Caroline Langley and Jana Stewart, introducing themselves as "the other two fiancées," had flown in to visit her. They had stayed one night and most of a day and had departed again only this morning.

This morning…after Rafi sent word that he would be home and hoped to see her over dinner. Zara had heard from excited staff that he had sent orders to the kitchen for a magnificent meal for two.

Zara was nervous, excited, terrified, happy. She had never looked forward to a man's arrival with such nervous delight, such hungry anticipation, such longing, such… bridal jitters. When she thought of him, she seemed to step into a river of flowing sensuality, of rich loving need, that poured over and through her, leaving her helpless.

She loved him. It was hard for her now to remember that time—only days ago!—when she had worried that the feelings she had for him might be a result of her solitary confinement and unstable emotions. She had no doubts now. When she had stood at the precipice and thought that Jalal might kill him…everything had been clear as a running brook. She had known then that her life could never be other than bleak if Rafi died. That something so wonderful and precious as her future with Rafi must not be allowed to disappear before she had even had a chance to know it.

He had not died. Instead he had discovered a relative he didn't know he had—and now, after sorting out Jalal's future, he was coming home. To her.

"Stop smiling, you'll crack your mask," Maria implored her. "It's just drying nicely." Rafi had flown in an entire team from a top English spa hotel for two weeks, no doubt at huge cost, and they were all enjoying their stay in the palace enormously. Zara had given them the freedom of the swimming pool and tennis courts, and often they joined her there along with the archaeological team, who had also come to spend a day and a night having facials and massages. They had all quickly become friendly.

They were all envious, of course—who could help envying such fabulous luck? But no one wished her anything but good. She was friendly and easy, and everybody could see why Rafi had chosen her—she had something special, the spa team agreed with Zara's old friends. Something more than just the petite, perfect build, the wonderful hair, the gorgeous, warm eyes, the mesmerizing smile... Zara was the kind of enchanting woman who *should* be a princess.

"Everybody's saying there's going to be a triple wedding ceremony, all three of the princes at once. Is that true?" Maria asked, forgetting that she had forbidden Zara to speak.

The three fiancées had discussed it, but a lot depended on things like security; they were all aware it might not be viable. But it would be an occasion if they could do it, all right! Zara parted her lips the merest quarter of an inch and then spoke without moving a muscle. "Not sure," she said. "Hear ut Ravi says tonight."

"Well, I think it would be absolutely fabulous if you did! I gave them both facials yesterday, and they're terrific, aren't they? Did you know them from before?"

She carefully laid a warm cloth over the mask, and Zara could feel it instantly softening. "No, it was the first time."

Half an hour later she got up from the table feeling relaxed and just a little like a finely tuned, well-oiled machine, and rinsed off with a shower. Then she went to her "apartments," where her personal maid, Adilah, awaited her. Adilah was still thrilled with her sudden promotion up the palace ranks, and was learning English as fast as she could.

On the bed and couches of Zara's half-acre bedroom she had spread out several exotic, beautiful outfits for Zara to choose from, each outfit coordinated with its own pair of sandals, shoes or slippers. Zara felt she had done nothing but smile for four days, and as she stood and looked around her own private Aladdin's Cave, the smile pulled her mouth again.

Lustrous silks, spangled gauzes, jewelled belts...a bright rainbow of colours so glowing it was as if a candle secretly flamed behind everything. In fact, that was how her life felt—as if a candle had been set inside a simple glass vase, and suddenly it was revealed as intricately cut and decorated, glowing and glittering like a precious jewel.

With Adilah's help, she chose a lustrous *shalwar kamees* in a delicate transparent silk of midnight blue underlaid with glowingly soft grey silk satin and spangled with tiny silver stones, with a low scoop neckline and flowing skirted tunic over trousers of the same fabric. A long spangled gauzy midnight-sky scarf for her neck, and delicate mules with a one-inch heel, in the softest leather she had ever touched, also in deep blue, for her feet.

"Lovely, lovely!" murmured Adilah, as she stood back to admire her handiwork. She had been practising her English with the spa team. "Absolutely smashing, Madame."

Zara examined herself in the mirror. Her hair was shining and healthy, spreading in its curling mass over her shoulders and down her back to her waist. Her face glowed with expensive, subtle cosmetics, her eyes sparkling, her mouth a warm peach.

She had no earrings or jewellery of her own, of course. She had come here like the beggarmaid, with nothing. Whatever jewellery she had been wearing on the night of the kidnapping had been long since lost. She could not remember what it had been, anyway. The emerald wishing ring was on her right hand, and as for the left—well, if Rafi wanted to do something about that, she would need nothing more. She thought he would do that tonight.

Dinner was to be served in the dining room of her own apartments, and she went there a few minutes before time to check the arrangements. It was enchanting. She examined the table and the flowers, but all was perfection, and she moved out to the fountained court. She was somewhere in the centre of the palace, she knew, but in the courtyard you were aware of nothing but mountains. The sun was setting off to the south, the full moon already visible in the sky above the high peaks to the north and east, the air clear, cool and fresh and smelling of perfume, and just a little, unless it was her imagination, of the snow still capping the peaks high above her.

The fountain in the centre spilled water in an endless rippling music. All around the perimeter, bordering the roofed walkway like a medieval cloister, were perfect arches, decorated in painted blue mosaic tiles. At every arch there was some flowering plant.

Her enchanted castle. She heard a sound and turned, and the prince entered the Enchanted Castle.

He too was dressed in the Eastern style, a green silk tunic embroidered from the cuffs to the elbows and on the high collar with magnificent gold thread and jewels, loose flowing trousers. He had shaved off his new beard, but his flowing moustache still curled over his upper lip. He reminded her of the night of his feast in the desert, that seemed so long ago.

She stood beside the fountain gazing at him with love and longing, a smile pulling irresistibly at the corners of her mouth.

Rafi did not smile. He stood for a moment looking at her, too moved to smile. She was his, he knew it without her having to speak the words. She would not be here, she would not be smiling, she would not be dressed in this way, if her answer were no. He had spent the last four days torn between wishing and fearing to come to her, finding it nearly impossible to concentrate on the negotiations, until his brothers had sent him away. Even Jalal had agreed that it was useless to talk until Rafi had had his answer from his Beloved.

Birds were singing evensong. The moon was growing brighter as the sun died in the west. The sky darkened and stars came out to match those that spangled in her eyes and on her dress. His heart leapt from him and went to her, and he knew he would never have it back again.

He followed his heart across the space between them, and stood gazing into her steady eyes. He knew everything about her, and yet not enough. He would spend his life in the discovery of her magic, her beauty, her generosity, her nobility.

His hand touched hers, and they trembled. He lifted it and drew it onto his other palm, lowered his head to kiss it. His thick dark hair fell forward, and she saw it trembling with the power of his feeling. She knew she had never met a man of such honour, such truth, such bravery, such generosity of spirit. She had never loved before with all of her being. Helpless to express her knowing, she bent her own head and kissed his.

He felt the kiss on his hair as if it connected him to the deepest river of being, and then they raised their heads and their lips met at last, and the river ran through them, a rich, wild torrent.

"Beloved," he said.

"I love you, Rafi," she said, marvelling at the layers of meaning those words now had, beyond all ordinary understanding, knowing he understood.

"I will love you all my days. I will take no wife but you," he said.

He did not ask her, because he knew. And for her, too, that was as it should be. How could there be doubts or questions between them, when they knew everything with a touch?

"I will take no husband but you," she said.

They walked in the garden, while the moon climbed the sky and the stars burned brighter and the sky darkened to black. The birds finished their song, and a flower wantonly released her perfume as if the night air itself were her lover. They spoke and were silent, touched and did not touch, and it was all the same because they were enclosed in love.

Inside, behind the glass, soft lamps were lighted, and figures moved around the table, preparing for their meal. At last they went in.

The two servants turned and bowed.

Rafi took Zara's hand in his. "Hanifah, Hayat," he said,

calling each by name, and they bowed again. "I know you for true believers," the prince said.

The women bowed again. "It is so, Lord."

"Bear witness that I take your mistress as my wife," he said, and then he turned and smiled at Zara and repeated the words in English.

The women stood shy and speechless, smiling but overawed by their magnificent master and their beautiful mistress, now their queen.

Rafi spoke again. "We are husband and wife now," he said. "Whatever ceremony we choose to have later for the sake of my people and yours—between you and me and God, we are married here and now. This is the tradition and the law. We are one already. We declare it before two persons. Do you accept this?"

Tears burned her eyes. "Yes, I accept it," she said.

He turned again to Hanifah and Hayat and spoke a few words, and they bowed and left the room. Rafi led her to a low couch and seated her on it, and only then did she see the flat boxes on the little carved table nearby.

"I asked Adilah what you had chosen to wear tonight," he said by way of explanation, opening the first box. It was large, thick and square, and inside, on creamy satin, lay a magnificent collar of pearls and sapphires, like nothing she had seen before.

"Ohhh, Rafi!" she breathed helplessly.

He picked it up and slipped it around her neck. Five equal rows of pearls snugly encircled her neck, with one massive sapphire in the centre, and beneath, three more giant sapphires, linked by delicately worked platinum entwining smaller sapphires and pearls, fanned out over her upper chest. The other boxes revealed matching drop earrings and a staggering bangle bracelet studded with sapphires all around its circumference.

Zara stood and went to a mirrored pillar to admire.

"I've never worn anything so beautiful," she breathed.

"They have never been worn by anyone so beautiful,"

he returned. "They have been the property of the women of my family for many generations, but I think the jeweller was thinking of you as he crafted them."

They made her brown eyes appear black. Nothing had ever done that before. Zara closed her eyes and shook her head a little. She turned her back on the mirrored pillar and faced him. "This isn't a dream, is it?"

He rose and crossed to her. "Does it feel unreal to you, Beloved? It feels very, very real to me."

She smiled and shook her head. "Not unreal. But as though...as though I've been taken on a magic carpet to a place where—" she struggled to explain "—where my life never expected to be. And now that it's there, everything has changed."

He was smiling at her. "Yes, like Prince Tanbal and the magic horse. I will tell you the story one day. Then you will see that the best life is one that offers you a ride on a magic carpet to unknown places—if you accept the ride."

She moved closer to him and he put his arms around her. "Will you tell me that story tonight?"

"Tonight? No. Tonight I will tell you other things, Beloved."

"What things?"

"The love that I have longed to tell you since that day when I saw you in the waterfall," he said simply. She closed her eyes as feeling swamped her. Her heart seemed to be pouring with light, love, joy too wonderful to speak.

"I love you," she moaned helplessly.

"I love you. I want you now to choose a ring, as is traditional for Westerners. Come."

He led her back to the sofa and when they were seated again, he opened the last box, a huge flat box with the name Van Cleef & Arpels embossed in the velvet. Inside were about twenty-five magnificent rings.

She swallowed in amazement. "You just have a whole boxful of engagement rings?" she whispered.

Rafi laughed lightly. "The jeweller has sent these for you

to make your choice. In the future you will learn many of the rituals of me and my people, but I follow this Western ritual as testament that I and perhaps my people, too, will also learn some of your own customs. I know in your country a woman likes to receive an engagement ring. If these are not enough to choose from, they will quickly send more.''

Well, she had seen things like this in elegant windows, of course, but she had not ever dreamed of having such a tray placed before her with the instruction to choose among them. Choose a ring to treasure for all the rest of her life as a symbol of the moment when she knew she loved and was loved.

The wonderful stones danced and melted before her eyes. They were arranged in rows—the diamonds, the rubies, the sapphires, the emeralds—all so cunningly crafted, so enticingly beautiful, how could she choose…? There was a huge heart-shaped ruby embedded amongst close-set diamonds in a wide curving band, and she smiled, catching sight of it.

"Oh, how—it's breathtaking!" she whispered, her fingers just touching it.

His darker, fine-boned hand came down and firmly lifted the ring from its velvety bed. "This one?" he murmured, as if the choice appealed to him, too.

He lifted her hand in his and slipped the ring over her knuckle and down to a firm home at the base. Of course during all the various massages and treatments someone had sized her finger, she realized with a smile.

"It's beautiful," she said again, wondering again at the levels of meaning an ordinary word could have, all unknown to those who had not experienced its true depths. "A heart-shaped ruby, though! People will say it's…''

"People will say we're in love," he said. And he kissed her, and the choice was made.

At last they made their way to the table, and the feast was brought in.

When they had talked of all and everything for awhile, and taken some of each luscious dish the chef had cooked to perfection, she remembered his mission of the past few days, and her confinement, and the bandit.

"Tell me about Jalal," she said then. "Who is he? What happened? What did you decide?"

"You know that Jalal is the grandson of Selim. His mother—the woman who looked after you during your imprisonment—is Selim's daughter." Rafi took a breath, and spoke more slowly. "His father, however, was my brother Aziz, who was killed the year before we were born." Zara's lips parted in astonishment, and forgetting his story, he broke off to draw her hand to his lips.

"Please go on, this is as good as King Mahmoud any day!"

"Aziz fell in love with the bandit's daughter and was afraid to tell my father. But when she told him she was pregnant he promised to tell my father and seek permission to marry her. He was killed two days later."

"Oh, how—!" She thought again of that moment when she was afraid Jalal would kill Rafi, her anguish at the thought of losing him before they began. She broke off, closed her eyes and shook her head.

"Then what?"

"It is difficult to be sure what happened next. Jalal's mother told her father. She was lucky not to be killed outright for shaming the family, but old Selim was not a bandit for nothing. He understood the supreme importance of the baby his daughter was carrying. He married her to an old man to protect her name and so she was able to give birth and remain with the tribe. And her father made his plans. But whatever they were, they were disrupted first by the birth of my father's three new sons, and then by the bandit's own death. Her old husband also died. So she was left alone with her child."

"And then?"

"And then one day, this woman—her name is Nusaybah—got her courage up, made her way to the palace, and insisted on talking to someone. She says she talked to an old man close to the king—it sounds like Nizam al Mulk, my father's Grand Vizier, but at this distance in time, it's impossible to be sure. She was sworn to secrecy, which included an embargo on telling her son the truth.

"She and her child were given a place to live with their wants supplied, and she says that from that time Jalal's education was supervised and paid for. She herself was also taught to read. But she never met the old man again. Documents would come informing her of what was planned for her son, and off he would go to school or college or the armed forces."

"My God, is it possible?"

"We believe it. They are testing our DNA at the moment, but we do not doubt what he and his mother tell us. There is too much evidence."

"But then—why didn't he just tell you? Why all the mystery?"

"He believed we knew."

"He believed you *knew?*"

"Two or three times my brother Omar had the chance to kill him. He did not do so. Once in the desert he even laid siege to the fortress for three weeks without a shot being fired. Jalal saw this as evidence that Omar was unwilling to risk my father's curse."

"And that wasn't the reason?"

"No. Or not as far as Omar knows. Who knows what may be hidden in the deep layers of the mind? But Omar was not long back from the war in Parvan then. Although he started out with ruthless determination, he said when he got to the fortress siege he could not stand to take part in any more bloodshed and eventually lifted the siege. Jalal of course was meanwhile bringing in supplies through the tunnel.

"Omar has no explanation for why he did not pull the trigger on two other occasions when he had Jalal in his

sights. Perhaps because Jalal resembles me. Perhaps not."
He shrugged. "Is there a deeper meaning behind such
things?"

Zara's eyebrows moved together in thought. "Did your
father's curse include Jalal, then?"

"We did not understand it so at the time, of course. But
his words were—if any of my sons takes up arms against
any brother or any of his brother's descendants, the curse
will be upon his head. At the time we thought there were
only three of us."

"Your father must have known. Why didn't he acknowledge him formally?"

Rafi shrugged and smiled. "Perhaps we will never know
the answer to this. But there are some obvious possibilities.

"Jalal's birth was not legitimate, and in any case, he
could only be at best fourth in line to the throne, because
his father Aziz had died without ascending the throne. But
in those early days the memory of the sheikh's first two
sons was warm in the hearts of the people. Some might
have wished to overlook Jalal's illegitimacy and hear my
father name him heir. And my father already had three heirs
and problems enough. This might have caused factions and
rivalries...in any case, there was no possibility of certainty
then. DNA testing did not exist, blood tests were inconclu-
sive. I think my father did what was best."

"But—"

"Yes. The real mystery is why, having done it, he never
told us." Again Rafi shrugged. "For this there is no obvious explanation. If one thing could be certain in all this,
it was that Nusaybah would sooner or later break the embargo and tell her son his true parentage. She did this not
long after we came into our full inheritance. Jalal sent pe-
titions to us under the name Jalal ibn Aziz—Jalal son of
Aziz—thinking we knew his name. When we ignored
him..."

Hanifah entered with a tray of iced sorbet and tiny gold
cups of Turkish coffee. Zara surfaced like a dog from water,

shaking her head to clear it. As always when Rafi told her a story, she had lost track of time and surroundings.

"And what have you all decided to do for him?" She took a tiny spoonful of the lemony ice, a sip of coffee.

"We decided nothing. My mind was not on the task. They were united in closing the discussions and sending me back to my bride," he said softly, with a smile that would have melted her had she been stone. But she was not stone, she was flesh and blood and spirit, and so it set her on fire with love and longing.

"And now, my Beloved, this is our wedding night," he said, and rose to his feet before her.

Seventeen

He led her at last to the bedroom, where the doors were open onto the courtyard and soft mountain breezes stirred the white gauze drapes that created a haven around the big bed, a room within the room. Inside they were safe, enclosed, private. A fan turned gently, high above. Lamps were softly alight on low tables, the bed turned down and ready.

She stood facing him, too moved to speak. Love like this told you all the secrets of the universe, yet you were apparently tongue-tied in the presence of the Lover. In those long tedious nights in Jalal's fortress, Rafi had told her stories of the Lover and the Beloved, and now he would tell her the best story of all.

His hands clasped her head, tilting it as he gazed into her black eyes. He bent and kissed her, and the explosion of sensation along her skin made her gasp. She whimpered her longing and felt his arms tighten around her.

When he lifted his mouth, he was shaking. He had always known it would be as much as he could stand, to hold her and make her his own. He took a deep breath to steady himself, lifting his hands first to one ear, and then the other, and removed her earrings. He kissed each earlobe and set the earrings down.

With a smile she pulled her narcissus-bloom hair to one side and turned her back. He bent to bury his face in those perfumed curls. "How many nights I have dreamed of this," he whispered passionately, sending shivers and thrills of matching desire through her. Oh, when you truly loved, how everything was changed! All charged with joy.

He removed her necklace and kissed the neck left bare by its removal. Then her cheek, her ear, her throat, and so turned her to face him again. He kissed her face, and everywhere electricity leapt between her skin and his lips, shocking and igniting them both.

His mouth passionately covered hers, his arms embraced her, her arms enwrapped his head. His hands stroked her, pressed her, flicked her, licked her, burned her as if he were flame and she…the phoenix, burned and renewed with each touch.

He found the tab of her zipper and drew it down the length of her back, his hand hungrily tracing the skin beneath all the way down. He leaned away from her and pulled the tunic down to reveal her breasts and her arms, and it fell to the floor around her feet. He found the fastening of the trousers, and they slipped down her silken legs, and she stood in a creamy silk thing like the bathing suit she had worn when he had first seen her and known his fate.

He closed his eyes. "Your beauty would strike down mountains," he breathed. Then he lifted her bodily out of the silky pile of her clothes and slippers, an arm behind her back and under her knees, and stared down at her with eyes so hungry she was fainting.

"What if I had done this that day?" he asked. "What if I had climbed up to you in the waterfall and kissed you

then, as I wished to do? What if I had lifted you and set
you down—''

He set her down on the bed and lay beside her. His hand
traced the line of the top of the little camisole, sending
shivers of longing through them both. "What would you
have done?"

She remembered the shock she had felt, seeing him
astride his beautiful horse, virile and unbelievably handsome, and staring at her with those hungry black
eyes...there had been men with him, but if he had been
alone, if he had come upon her there...

"I thought you were a bandit," she whispered.

"Yes, you thought I was a bandit! I saw fear in your
eyes, but something else, too. I wished my Companions at
the ends of the earth that morning! I said to myself, if I
were alone, she would not say no to me. She would have
run only to be chased and captured. She would have said
yes in the end. Was it true?"

The way she was feeling now, the way she had felt every
time he touched her...how could she have gone on saying
no if he had touched her, pleaded with her? She smiled at
the thought, the smile glinting up at him under her lashes,
and his body leapt against hers.

"You were mine even then. Even believing I was a dangerous bandit—say it!"

"I was yours the first moment I looked at you," she
whispered.

His mouth kissed hers with desperate hunger, and when
she arched against him it lifted and found her breast
through the warm silk, found the nipple, the soft underarm,
and so upwards to her shoulder. He pulled one thin strap
of her camisole out of the way of his kisses while his hand
cupped her hip, her back, moved down her thigh.

He stood then, and threw off his own clothes, revealing
the powerful chest, the slender waist, the muscled thighs
and lastly...his strong, hungry sex.

She moaned helplessly and looked away.

"One day we will go back to the waterfall," he said, stretching out beside her on the wide, luxurious bed and beginning to stroke her again. "You will stand in it, all unknowing, and I will ride up on Raksh, and see you there. And I will climb up to you and enter—" he swallowed, helpless now with the desire and passion that stormed between them "—the water, and if you run away I will catch you and bring you back as I wished to do that day, and then I will undress you, so—"

With wildly trembling hands now, he lifted her upper body against his and began to draw the pale silk from the warmer, creamier silk of her skin, all the way down her long body. His breath brushed her throat, even that touch too much for her senses, so that she moaned and whimpered with hunger, need…and just a little with the fear of so much passion between them.

He closed his eyes as the action of his hands revealed her body to him. He had undressed her once before, but then, then he had put an iron guard on his wishes and his blood. Now there was nothing between what he wanted and what was right, now these two things were the same.

His passion was merciless. His hand stroked her breasts, her body. His mouth and tongue followed, he felt the heat of her mouth against his own skin, and then there was no boundary between him and her, there was only heat and honey and melting into one another. There was joy and passion and tenderness and a terrible terrible longing like the thirst of lifetimes assuaged.

He lay looking down at her, her face of unimagined beauty—yet he had dreamed of it—and thought that to lie in the lap of the Beloved, to sip the flower's nectar, like the hummingbird, to burn like a moth on the candle's flame—this was the end of all seeking.

He thought so, even as the other seeking burned up in him, and he lifted himself and pushed there again, to that place where longing ceased, and then again, and again….

She moaned with the unimagined pleasure of each stroke

reaching its limit in her, knocking at some door within, demanding an opening, an answer. She wandered fainting through rooms of bright colour, past trees laden with fruit, tasting wine and honey. Sensation poured across all the senses, confusing them, so that she drank gold and silver light and heard honey and smelled heat, and saw Rafi's face in the centre of all, passionate, anguished, his eyes drunk with love.

"This is love," she said, making the momentous discovery.

"It is love," he echoed, and each knew that love was the melting together of all the senses, of reason, feeling, dreams, everything, to find paradise.

Deep, deep in her being, a door opened then, onto a world so magic she cried her surprise and joy from everything she was. He heard the cry, and then he, too, was released to enter that world.

For impossibly long, awe-filled moments of joy and sorrow, creation and destruction, night and day, being and not being, they experienced the great and terrible knowing that is Union. They smiled and wept, and cried out and were silent, and knew and did not know, and were and were not, Love.

Epilogue

"**W**ell, Marta, this is getting to be a habit," said Barry.

Marta smiled broadly into camera two. "Yes, indeed, Barry! It's been quite a year for the Barakat Emirates! The princes, it seems, have the knack of pulling absolute triumph out of the jaws of disaster!"

"But losing your chance with all three of the princes in one day, Marta, that must be hard."

"They might have spared a thought for all the women in the world they were going to disappoint, all getting married on the same day! But you know, there's hope. I've been taking a good look at some of those—what are they called?—Cup Companions to the princes, that's sort of like the Order of the Garter or something, I understand, and they're a pretty handsome crew."

Barry lifted his hand to the earphone. Just then the screen was filled with the image of a massive arched portico magnificently decorated in the painted blue tiles and calligraphic inscriptions of another century.

"Andrea, you're there?" said Barry's voice.

The camera panned down to the reporter, standing under the arch beside one of the beautiful columns.

"Yes, I'm here, Barry, outside the wonderful palace of Queen Halimah, here in Barakat al Barakat, the capital of the Emirates, where the weddings are about to take place. The princes chose the palace so that people of all faiths could attend the ceremony. Just before the ceremony starts we'll take you to the view inside the great Hall of Justice. According to tradition, it's the largest Hall of Justice ever built by any monarch anywhere. And apparently it's just about big enough to fit in all the guests who have clamoured to come here today from all around the world.

"As you've seen over the past hour that they've been arriving, we have numerous heads of state, and representatives of royal families, crowned and uncrowned, as well as a massive representation of the aristocracy and the ordinary folk of all three Emirates, and lots of the world's idle rich. Of course huge delegations from the families of the brides. There are Barakati artists, writers and poets, many of whom will feel moved to record their impressions of the event, and even a few lowly representatives of the press.

"They are all seated, and the ceremony is about to begin. We're told that the ceremony will draw on both the Barakati and the Western traditions in a unique service used only on this occasion, because, as it says here, let me get this right..." She lifted a paper and read, "'Because, although God may be worshipped in many different ways and in numerous different guises, and his message has been brought by a variety of prophets, He is always and ever One.'"

"I like that," said Marta. "No wonder the place is called Blessed."

"I hear we'll be going to the ceremony in about a minute, Andrea. Anything to add before we go?" Barry intervened.

"Just a few statistics—the three princes have chosen three very different wives, although all are native English speakers. Caroline Langley, Prince Karim's bride, as we all remember, is an American, and she's a blonde. She was born into old money, but when her family lost its wealth, she turned to selling clothes in a designer boutique. Jana Stewart is British—a Celt, she insists, and with the red hair to prove it. She's Prince Omar's choice. She was born to the purple, but turned her back on privilege to become a teacher in an underprivileged area of London. And Zara Blake, the hostage whom Prince Rafi rescued and then proposed to, is a black-haired Canadian with a little bit of everything in her heritage. She's an archaeologist with the team that discovered the lost city of Iskandiyar not so long ago in East Barakat. That's how she and Prince Rafi—"

"We're going inside, Andrea," Marta interrupted, "where the ceremony is about to start. We'll get back to you."

As the massive doors opened, an expectant hush fell over the congregation. There was a pause several heartbeats long, and then the magnificent Princes of Barakat entered the great Hall of Justice through the massive doorway, three abreast.

Those who were watching took a breath. With natural dramatic flair, the princes paused for a moment. Their costumes were magnificent, but no more than was matched by their own regal bearing and proud nobility. Pearls, precious gems, silk and gold embroidery adorned their masculinity like a second skin, so naturally did it become them.

All three smiled and flicked glances among themselves when they saw the throng who had come to help them celebrate their weddings. The Hall of Justice, that had once teemed with those seeking redress, was a long hall divided into three by two rows of intricately decorated pillars. Each of the three sections now had an aisle created between the temporary seats, running from the massive doors at the end

of the room all the way to the raised dais at the other end,
where the princes stood.

Except for those three aisles, the hall was jammed with
people. Rows and rows of chairs seemed to run into infinity.

The princes smiled and nodded, then proceeded solemnly
to the centre of the dais, where the priest awaited them at
the long altar which had been set up underneath a beaten
gold canopy. Behind them, through the doors, came all
thirty-six of their Cup Companions. Usually the Companions drew lots at ceremonial occasions, but this time none
would be denied his rightful part in the proceedings.

"Have you ever seen so much masculine splendour all
in one place?" Marta murmured to the viewers in an awed
hush, as the Companions lined up along the edge of the
podium, spacing themselves to fill the whole width of the
hall. Then, at a signal, they moved in unison down the steps
to stand facing the congregation.

The Companions were almost as magnificent as the
princes they served. Each wore a richly coloured turban and
a ceremonial sword, and around his neck a jewel on a pearl
rope, the symbol of their high office.

There was music playing somewhere, but it was impossible to be certain what instruments were played. Flutes,
perhaps, and rebecks, and tambourines.

Two Companions from each group detached themselves
and strode in pairs down each of the three aisles to the
great entrances at the other end of the hall.

There was another long hush of expectation, and then the
three pairs of doors were opened. Through each of them,
with measured steps, came one of the three brides, Jana
Stewart for Prince Omar, Caroline Langley for Prince
Karim, and Zara Blake for Prince Rafi.

All wore the traditional Western white, but each dress
was individual, and each bride had chosen a different colour for her flowers.

The first that the cameras picked up wore a dress that

was closest to the Eastern *shalwar kamees*. It bore a high neck, was open in a V at the front, had long full sleeves buttoned tightly at the wrist, and fell to mid-calf. Underneath were the flowing trousers in the same white on white brocaded silk. On her feet she wore delicately strapped shoes with heels. She carried ruby red and white roses in her bouquet, with a thousand tiny red and white rosebuds threaded all through her luscious dark hair, as though each curl held a flower.

"Princess Zara," murmured Marta, to any member of the television audience who might happen to have spent the past month in a coma.

The second bride wore a long, slim, elegant outfit, with sleeves to the elbow, unwaisted. A gored coat, with a stiff high-standing lace ruffle running behind her neck and down into the cutaway bodice to give her outfit an Elizabethan air, was open over a matching shift beneath. She carried a white-and-green bouquet, deep-coloured ivy and the white hawthorn of her homeland falling from her waist to the floor in thick, fertile profusion. Her tawny hair was crowned with a wreath of ivy.

"And Princess Jana."

The third bride was veiled. She wore a romantic dress, flounce upon flounce of silk lace over a thick crinoline, and above, a smooth snug bodice and tiny sleeves. She carried a spilling bouquet of blue flowers of different varieties and hues, and the veil that hid her face trailed several yards behind her.

"And Princess Caroline," murmured Marta.

As if the world didn't already know.

Behind each bride came her attendants. Like their grooms, each bride had twelve. Each had chosen to be attended by a mix of ages, from three to thirty. Some carried bouquets, some overflowing baskets, but the message of female youth and beauty was there. They spilled behind their own bride with little rhyme or pattern, wearing her colour, ruby, green, blue, in a span of shades and tones.

The congregation smiled and shook their heads in amazed delight.

It was a long walk to the altar. The Companions who had opened the doors closed them again and followed the brides and their attendants back to the front of the hall. When they got there, all the bridesmaids stopped at the lowest level, in front of the handsome Cup Companions.

Each one went to a different Companion, except for one tiny stalwart beauty with long golden curls and a blue dress who climbed determinedly up the steps behind Caroline Langley and followed her all the way to the altar. Looking down, Caroline smiled approvingly through her veil and then had eyes only for Prince Karim, waiting there for her.

Lena, dressed in shot rose silk, accompanied Zara. And Jana's young sister, dressed in forest green, smiled tremulously as she followed Jana to where dark-eyed Omar waited.

"The princes drew lots to establish the order of their vows," Marta informed her audience, though the same information had already been aired many times in the papers and on television in the run-up to this moment. "No one except themselves will know what that order is until we see it happen. And now, from this moment until the service is over, there is to be no commentary."

All the commentators dutifully fell silent as the service began. It was a mixture of hymns and readings, sermons and songs, music and dance. The vows of each bride and groom were taken in turn. Young bridesmaids yawned and dropped their flower baskets, the older women in the congregation wept a few tears, the Companions exchanged warm dark looks with the older bridesmaids.

In short, as is fitting at a wedding, everyone did pretty much as nature dictated.

And then it was over. Bells rang, music played, and the Princes of Barakat embraced their new brides.

"Prince Rafi of East Barakat, as we all know, was married some time ago," Marta reminded her viewers. "For him and Princess Zara this was really more like a blessing. But the others waited for the official moment. There's Princess Caroline, without her veil now, of course. Blue flowers in her hair, as well, I see.''

The congregation was on its feet now. All the brides and grooms were still in the Hall of Justice, as were the Companions and attendants. This was as planned. ''They'll move to the Throne Room now, where the reception is being held,'' Barry informed all those who had not heard the details before.

''Yes, there are Prince Omar and Princess Jana looking over their shoulders…they're leading the way down the central aisle, and then it will be out into the sunshine, where they'll greet the waiting crowds, and the whole party will cross the courtyard…yes, there go Princes Rafi and Karim and their new princesses…the sunshine is spilling into the room through the doors.…

''What a fabulous day!'' said the announcer.

*　*　*　*　*

THE SHEIKH'S REWARD

by
Lucy Gordon

Lucy Gordon cut her writing teeth on magazine journalism, interviewing many of the world's most interesting men, including Warren Beatty, Richard Chamberlain, Sir Roger Moore, Sir Alec Guinness, and Sir John Gielgud. She also camped out with lions in Africa, and had many other unusual experiences which have often provided the background for her books.

She is married to a Venetian, whom she met while on holiday in Venice. They got engaged within two days.

Two of her books have won the Romance Writers of America's RITA® award, *Song of the Lorelei* in 1990, and *His Brother's Child* in 1998 in the Best Traditional Romance category. You can visit her website at www.lucy-gordon.com

Don't miss Lucy Gordon's latest novel,
***One Summer in Italy*, out now from**
Mills & Boon Romance™!

CHAPTER ONE

HE WAS a prince to his fingertips. Tall, black-haired, his head set at a proud angle, Prince Ali Ben Saleem, Sheikh of the principality of Kamar, drew everyone's gaze as he walked into the casino.

It wasn't just his handsome features and his tall body with its combination of power and grace. There was something about him that seemed to proclaim him skilful at everything he attempted. And so men regarded him with envy, women with interest.

Frances Callam watched with the others, but her eyes held a peculiar intentness. Ali Ben Saleem was the man she had come here to study.

She was a freelance journalist, much in demand for her skill at profiling people. Editors knew that she was unbeatable in stories where large sums of money were concerned. And Ali was one of the wealthiest men in the world.

'Will you look at that?' Joey Baines breathed in awe, watching Ali's imperial progress to the tables. Joey was a private detective whom she sometimes hired as an assistant. She'd brought him along tonight as cover while she visited the casino and watched Ali at play.

'I'm looking,' Fran murmured. 'He certainly lives up to the legend, doesn't he? In appearance anyway.'

'What's the rest of the legend?'

'He's a law unto himself, accountable to nobody for where his money comes from or where it goes to.'

'But we know where it comes from,' Joey objected. 'Those oil wells he's got gushing away in the desert.'

'And a lot of it vanishes in places like this,' Fran said, looking around her with disapproval.

'Hey, Fran, lighten up. Can't we enjoy life among the fleshpots for just one night? It's in a good cause.'

'It's in the cause of nailing a man who doesn't like answering questions about himself, and finding out what he has to hide,' Fran said firmly.

Joey ran a finger around the inside of his collar. His short, undistinguished person looked uncomfortable in the black tie and dinner jacket that was *de rigueur* for the men.

'I can't believe you came here looking like a goddess just to work,' he said, eyeing her slender figure, pale skin and red-gold hair with wistful lust.

'Down, Fido,' Fran said amiably. 'Tonight this is my work outfit. I need to look as if I belong in this place.'

She'd succeeded in her aim. Her dress seemed to be solid gold glitter with a neckline that plunged low, and a side slit that came up to her thigh. She was rather disconcerted by the dress's frank immodesty, and had hired it only with misgiving. But she was glad now that she'd done so. In the glittering, sophisticated ambience of The Golden Chance, London's premier casino, this was how to look.

As well as the dress, she'd hired the solid gold jewellery that went with it. Hanging earrings accentuated the length of her neck, heavy gold bracelets weighed down her wrists, and a long gold pendant plunged between her breasts, emphasising her *décolletage*.

I look like a kept woman, she thought, faintly shocked at herself.

But so did every other woman here, and in that respect the outfit was a success.

Certainly she could have held her own among the women who crowded around Sheikh Ali, competing for his attention, and being rewarded with a smile, or a kiss of the fingers in their direction. The sight made her seethe.

'Arrogant so-and-so,' she muttered. 'Men like that are supposed to be extinct.'

'Only the ones who can't get away with it,' Joey told her wisely. 'Those who can are as bad as ever.'

'You're jealous,' she said indignantly.

'We all are, Fran! Look around you. Every man in the place wants to be him, and every woman wants to sleep with him.'

'Not every one,' she said firmly. 'Not me.'

Ali had finished his royal progress and was settling at one of the tables. Fran edged nearer, trying to observe him without looking too interested.

He played for very high stakes, and when he lost he merely shrugged. Fran gulped at the sums he tossed away as though they were nothing. She noticed, too, that once play started he forgot about the women at his elbow. One minute he was flirting madly with them. The next they didn't exist. Her annoyance grew.

It grew even more when play stopped and he turned on the charm again, clearly expecting to take up with them where he'd left off. Worse still, they let him.

'You see that?' she muttered to Joey. 'Why doesn't one of them spit in his eye?'

'You try spitting in the eye of a hundred billion,' Joey said. 'See how easy it is. Why must you be such a puritan, Fran?'

'I can't help it. It's how I was raised. It's not decent

for one man to have so much—so much—just so
much.'

She'd been going to say 'so much money', but
Sheikh Ali had so much of everything. From the mo-
ment of his birth it had all fallen into his lap. His
father, the late Sheikh Saleem, had married an
Englishwoman and remained faithful to her all his life.
Ali was their only son.

He'd inherited his little principality at the age of
twenty-one. His first act had been to cancel all deals
with the world's mighty oil corporations, and to re-
negotiate them, giving Kamar a far larger slice of the
profits. The companies had raged but given in.
Kamar's oil was of priceless quality.

In the ten years since then he'd multiplied his country's wealth more than ten times. He lived a charmed
life between two worlds. He had apartments in both
London and New York, and he commuted between
them in his private jet, making huge, complex deals.

When not enjoying the high life in the west he returned to his domain to live in one of his palaces, or
to visit Wadi Sita, a top secret retreat in the desert,
where he was reputed to indulge in all manner of ex-
cesses. He never contradicted these rumours, nor even
deigned to acknowledge them, and because no journalist had ever been allowed to glimpse the truth the
stories flourished unchecked.

'Does Howard know you're here tonight?' Joey
asked, naming the man whom Fran usually dated.

'Of course not. He'd never approve. In fact he
doesn't approve of my doing this story. I asked him
what he could tell me about Ali, and he just gave me
the PR line about how important he was, and how
Kamar was a valuable ally. When I said there were

too many mysteries, Howard went pale and said, ''For pity's sake, don't offend him.'''

'What a wimp!' Joey said provocatively.

'Howard isn't a wimp, but he is a merchant banker, and he has a banker's priorities.'

'And you're going to marry this guy?'

'I never said that,' Fran answered quickly. 'Probably. One day. Maybe.'

'Boy, you're really head over heels about him, aren't you?'

'Can we concentrate on what we're here for?' she asked frostily.

'Place your bets, please!'

Ali pushed a large stake out over the board to red twenty-seven, then leaned back with an air of supreme indifference. He maintained it throughout the spinning of the wheel as the little ball bounced merrily from red to black, from one number to another. Fran found she was holding her breath, her eyes riveted on the wheel, until at last it stopped.

Red twenty-two.

The croupier raked the stakes in. Fran watched Sheikh Ali, frowning. He didn't even look at the fortune that was vanishing. All his attention was for his new stake.

Suddenly he looked up at her.

She gasped. Two points of light pierced her, held her imprisoned.

Then he smiled, and it was the most wickedly charming smile she had ever seen. It invited her into a conspiracy of delight and something in her leaped to accept. She discovered that she was smiling back; she didn't know how or why. Simply that the smile had taken over her mouth, then her eyes, then her whole body.

Common sense told her that only pure chance had made him look in her direction, but somehow she didn't believe it. He'd sensed her there. Among so many others, he'd known that she was watching him, and been impelled to meet her eyes.

Ali leaned forward to her, stretching out his hand across the narrow table. As if hypnotised she placed her own slender hand in his. He held it for a moment and she had the unnerving sense of steely strength in those long fingers. There was power enough there to break a man—or a woman.

Then he raised her hand to his lips. Fran drew in a sharp breath as his mouth brushed her skin. It was the lightest touch, but it was enough for her to sense the whole male animal, vibrant, sensual, dangerous.

'Place your bets, please.'

He released her, reached for his stake and pushed it out onto the table. It stopped at black twenty-two, but he didn't look to see. He'd forgotten the other women as soon as the wheel spun, but he kept his eyes on Fran, ignoring the wheel. She watched him back, meaning to tear her eyes away, but mysteriously unable to do so.

Black twenty-two.

Ali seemed to come out of a dream to realise that the croupier was pushing the chips towards him. It had been a large stake and with one win he'd recouped almost all his losses. He grinned, showing white teeth, and indicated the place beside him with the slightest inclination of his head.

She edged around the table towards him. The other

women pouted and sulked, reluctant to give way to her, but he dismissed them with a faint gesture.

Fran felt as if she was moving in a dream. Luck had fallen her way with stunning suddenness. She had meant to study Ali tonight, and now fate had presented her with the perfect opportunity.

'You have brought me luck,' he said as she reached him and sat down. 'Now you must stay close by me so that my luck remains.'

'Surely you're not superstitious?' she asked with a smile. 'Your luck will come and go. It has nothing to do with me.'

'I think otherwise,' he pronounced in a tone that silenced further argument. 'The spell you cast is for me alone. Not for any other man. Remember that.'

Arrogant beast, she thought. If this didn't happen to suit me I'd enjoy taking him down a peg.

'Place your bets.'

With a gesture of his hand Ali indicated for her to place the stake for him. She put the counters on red fifteen, and held her breath as the wheel spun.

Red fifteen.

A sigh went up from everyone around the table.

Almost everyone.

Ali alone was not watching. His eyes were fixed admiringly on Fran. As the counters were pushed towards him he gave a shrug which said, 'Of course.'

'I don't believe that happened,' she breathed.

'You made it happen,' he assured her, 'and you will make it happen again.'

'No, it was chance. You should stop now. Take it while you have it.'

His smile said that it was for petty men to worry about such things. Princes controlled their own fate.

Under his hypnotic glance Fran found herself believing it.

'Put it on for me again,' he said. 'All of it.'

Dazed, she piled up all his winnings and went to put them on—on—

'I can't decide,' she said frantically.

'What day of the month is your birthday?'

'The twenty-third.'

'Red or black? Choose.'

'Black,' she said recklessly.

'Then black twenty-three it is.'

She watched in agony as the wheel began to spin.

'Don't look,' he said, smiling. 'Look only at me, and let the little gods of the tables take care of the matter.'

'Can you make them do your pleasure as well?' she whispered.

'I can make anyone and anything do my pleasure,' he said simply.

The wheel stopped.

Black twenty-three.

A prickle went up Fran's spine. This was eerie. Ali saw her startled look and laughed.

'Witchcraft,' he said. 'And you are the most beautiful witch of all.'

'I—I don't believe it,' she stammered. 'It can't happen like that.'

'It happened because you are magic. And I can't resist magic.'

On the words he dropped his head and laid his lips against her palm. Instantly Fran felt as though she was being scorched, although the touch of his lips was teasingly soft. The sensation started in her skin and swiftly pervaded her. She had a sense of alarm and would have snatched her hand back, but she remembered in time that such gaucheness wouldn't fit the role she was playing. She smiled, hoping she looked as though such tributes happened every day.

The croupier pushed over the winnings. 'I'll take them,' Ali announced.

A man standing behind his chair counted up and wrote the total on a piece of paper. Fran gasped as she saw it.

While the man went to cash the chips Ali rose and drew Fran away from the table. 'Now we will dine together,' he announced.

Fran hesitated. Ancient female wisdom told her that it wasn't clever to accept such an abrupt invitation from a man she'd known barely half an hour. But she was in pursuit of a story, and she wouldn't succeed by refusing the first real break she'd been given. Besides, a restaurant was public enough.

Out of the corner of her eye she saw Joey, his jaw dropping. She gave him a wink and swept out on Ali's arm.

His Rolls-Royce was waiting outside, the chauffeur already standing with the door open. Ali handed her gallantly inside. The chauffeur got in and started the car without waiting for instructions.

When they were moving Ali turned to her, smiling mischievously, and reached into his pockets. From one he produced a necklace of priceless pearls, from the other, a diamond necklace.

'Which?' he asked.

'Whi—?'

'One of them is yours. Take your pick.'

She gaped. He carried such things around with him, in his pockets?

Feeling as though she'd been transported to another planet, she said, 'I'll take the diamonds.' The voice didn't sound like her own.

'Turn your neck so that I can remove that gold pendant,' he commanded. 'The man who gives you such trumpery baubles doesn't know how to value you.'

His fingers brushed her neck, and she took a shuddering, uncontrollable breath. This wasn't how the evening was supposed to go. She'd come prepared to analyse Sheikh Ali, to dislike and despise him. But she hadn't come prepared to be overwhelmed by him. It had simply happened.

She felt the chill on her flesh as he draped a king's ransom in diamonds about her neck. His fingertips brushed against her nape and she had to struggle not to tremble at that soft, devastating impact. Then there was another sensation, so light that she couldn't be sure of it. Had he kissed the back of her neck or not? How dared he? If he had…

'They were made for you,' he declared, turning her to face him. 'No woman has ever looked better in diamonds.'

'And you speak from a wide experience?' she said demurely.

He laughed, neither offended nor ashamed. 'Wider than you can imagine,' he assured her. 'But tonight none of the others exist. There is only you in the world. Now tell me your name.'

'My name—' She had a sudden inspiration. 'My name is Diamond.'

His eyes lit up. 'You have wit. Excellent. That will do for now. Before the night is over you will tell me your real name.'

He held her left hand in both of his and studied the fingers.

'No rings,' he observed. 'You are neither married nor promised, unless you are one of those modern women who scorn to tell the world that you belong to a man. Or maybe you scorn to let yourself belong?'

'I belong to no man,' she said. 'I belong to myself, and no man will ever own me.'

'Then you have never known love. When you do, you'll find that your aloof ideas mean nothing. When you love, you will give, and it must be all of yourself, or the gift means nothing.'

'And who do you belong to?' she demanded with spirit.

He laughed. 'That is quite another matter. But I could say that I belong to a million people.' Kamar had a population of one million. 'No part of my life is entirely my own. Even my heart is not mine to give. Tell me about the little man with you. I wondered if he might have been your lover.'

'Would that have made any difference to you?'

'None at all, since he made no effort to protect you from me. A man who cannot hold onto his woman is no man.'

'Do I need protecting from you?' Fran mused, teasing him with her eyes.

He laid his lips against her hand. 'I wonder if we'll discover that we each need protection from the other?' he said thoughtfully.

'Who knows?' she murmured, replying as she felt her role required. 'The pleasure will come in discovering.'

'And you are a woman made for pleasure.'

Fran drew a slow breath, shocked at how much the

words affected her. She was used to hearing her brains praised. Howard admired her looks but was just as likely to acclaim her common sense. And her common sense told her that, while passion mattered, it wasn't the whole of life. Suddenly she was no longer sure of that.

He listened to her silence and added, 'You're not going to pretend not to know what I mean.'

'There are many kinds of pleasure,' she fenced.

'Not for us. For you and I there is only one kind—the pleasure to be shared by a man and a woman in the heat of desire.'

'Isn't it a little soon to be thinking of desire?'

'We were thinking of desire the moment our eyes met. Don't try to deny it.'

She couldn't have begun to deny it. The truth was shocking but it was still the truth. She wondered wildly if she could jump out of the car and flee, but he was holding her hand in a grip that was only superficially gentle. Underneath, it was unbreakable.

He touched her face with his fingertips. The next thing she knew, his lips were on hers in the lightest kiss she'd ever known. It was so light that it might not have happened, except that it was followed by another on her chin, her jaw, her eyes, and again on her lips. She barely felt them, but she felt their effects in the tingling excitement they produced all over her body.

This was alarming. If he'd tried to overwhelm her with power she could have defended herself. But Sheikh Ali was an artist, putting out all his artistry to bring her under his spell. And there seemed to be no defence against that.

She moved helplessly against him, neither returning his kisses nor fending him off. He looked down into her face, but it was too dark in the car for him to find what he wanted to know. Nor could she see the little frown of uncertainty between his eyes.

The long, sleek car glided to a halt in a quiet street in London's most exclusive area. Slowly he released her. The chauffeur opened the door and Ali took her hand to assist her out. Then she was stepping out onto the pavement, and realising what she ought to have thought of before—that he had brought her not to a restaurant but to his home.

She knew this was the moment when she should act sensibly and run, but what kind of journalist ran away at the first hint of danger?

She gave herself a little shake. Of course there was no danger. What had put that thought into her head?

The tall windows of the mansion were filled with light. One on the ground floor had the curtains pulled back, revealing crystal chandeliers and lavish furnishings.

Slowly the front door opened. A tall man in Arab robes and headdress stood there massively.

'Welcome to my humble home,' said Prince Ali Ben Saleem.

CHAPTER TWO

As SHE entered the house Fran blinked at her gorgeous surroundings. She was in a large hallway, dominated by a huge, sweeping staircase, and with double doors on either side. There were exotic tiles beneath her feet, and more of them covering the walls. It was bewildering but gorgeous.

Every set of doors leading off the hall was closed, but at that moment one pair was thrown open and a man emerged. He approached Ali, not appearing to notice Fran, and addressed him in a language she didn't understand. While the two men talked she glanced through the doors and saw that the room was an office. The walls were covered with charts and maps, there were three fax machines, a row of telephones and a computer unlike any she had ever seen. Fran guessed that it was state of the art. So that was where he did the deals that earned him a million a day.

Ali noticed the direction of her glance and spoke sharply to the man, who retreated into the office and closed the door. Ali put his arm about Fran's shoulder, guiding her firmly away. He was smiling, but there was no mistaking the irresistible pressure he was exerting.

'That is only my office,' he said. 'In there I do very dull things that wouldn't interest you.'

'Who knows? Perhaps I would be interested?' Fran said provocatively.

18

Ali laughed. 'Such a beautiful woman need think only how to be more beautiful still, and to please the man who is enchanted by her.'

How about that? Fran thought, annoyed. Prehistoric, male chauvinist—

Ali threw open another set of doors and Fran gasped at the sight that met her eyes. It was a large, luxuriously decorated room with a bay window, in which stood a table laid for two. The plates were the finest porcelain with heavy gold bands around the edge. By each place stood three glasses of priceless crystal. The cutlery was solid gold.

'It's beautiful,' she murmured.

'For you, nothing is too good,' Ali declared.

For me—or for whoever you happened to pick up, Fran thought, determined to keep her wits about her. But aloud all she said was, 'You're too kind.'

He led her to the table and pulled a chair out for her like the humblest of attendants. Part of the act, Fran decided, amused. All her journalistic instincts were on full alert, and while she seemed to be merely languidly accepting whatever happened she was actually observing every detail.

At the same time, she couldn't deny that she was enjoying herself. Ali was simply the most handsome man she'd ever seen. In the casino she'd seen him mainly sitting at the table, or at a distance. Now he was on his feet and close to her she felt the full impact of his magnificence.

He was about six feet two in height, with long legs and broad shoulders. Yet he didn't give the impression of being heavily built. He walked softly, making no sound, but nobody could have overlooked him. His movements had the lightness of a panther ready to spring.

His face was more than merely good-looking. It was a study in contradictions. At first glance it was European, inherited from his mother. Yet his Arab father was also there. Fran had read about Prince Saleem, a fierce man who inspired terror and devotion among his people. He too was in Ali's face in the dark chocolate eyes, the curved, stubborn mouth, and the air of proud authority.

Yet Ali had more than looks. His charisma was so strong that it was practically a force field. He radiated strength and intensity. And, while some of it must have come from having been born to rule, her instincts told her that his vibrant, emotional power was all his own.

He showed her to a seat, drawing the chair out and deferring to her. 'I will serve you myself, if that is agreeable to you?' he said smoothly.

'I am honoured to be attended by a prince,' Fran murmured.

She saw him smile, and guessed what he was thinking: this woman had fallen for his line, just like all the others. Well, if he thought that, he was in for a shock.

A heated trolley stood nearby, and he ladled a pale yellow liquid into a dish. It was thick, like porridge, mixed with rice, and it tasted delicious.

'Pumpkin soup,' Ali explained. 'I have a weakness for it, so when I'm here my chef keeps some permanently ready.' He served himself and sat facing her. The table was small, so even on opposite sides they were still close. 'Have you ever tasted Arabic food before?' he asked.

'A little. There's a restaurant I sometimes go to. It

has the most delicious chicken with dates and honey, and I can't resist it. But the surroundings are vulgar. The walls are covered with murals of the desert, with oases that light up in neon.'

Ali winced. 'I know the kind of place you mean. They make a great play of the desert, but none of them knows what the desert is really like.'

'What is it like?' Fran asked eagerly. 'Tell me about the desert.'

'How shall I know what to say? There are so many deserts. There is the desert in the evening when the sun turns to blood and is swallowed up by the sand. In England you have long twilights, but in my country it can be broad daylight, and then pitch darkness a few minutes later.

'Then, in the early hours, dawn lays a cool light on the land for a few moments, then rises in pale glory, and we all give thanks for the renewed blessing. But at noon the desert can be a enemy, and the sun turns to a furnace, driving you back into the sand.

'But they all have one thing in common, and that is the silence: a deeper silence than you can imagine. Until you have stood in the desert and watched the stars wheel overhead, you have never heard the silence of the earth as it spins on its axis.'

'Yes,' she whispered. 'That's what I thought.'

Without her knowing, a dreamy, far-away look had come into her eyes. Ali saw it, and a small frown of interest creased his brows. 'You thought?' he asked.

'I used to dream about places like that,' she admitted. 'When I was a child that dream was very important to me.'

'Tell me,' Ali said intently. 'What happened in your childhood?'

'It's strange, but whenever I think about that time I remember rain. I suppose it couldn't have rained every day, but all I can see is grey, drizzly skies, and people to match.'

'People were unkind to you?'

'No, I'm not being fair. After my parents died I was raised by some distant cousins on their farm. They meant well, but they were old and very serious, and knew nothing about children. They did their best for me, encouraged me to do well at school. But there was no excitement, and I longed for it.' She gave a small embarrassed laugh. 'You'll probably think this is silly, but I started to read *The Arabian Nights*.'

'I don't think that's silly. Why should I? I read it myself as a boy. I loved those fantastical tales, with their magic and drama.'

'There was certainly plenty of that,' Fran remembered. 'A sultan who took a new wife every night and killed her in the morning.'

'Until he found Scheherazade, who teased his mind with fantastic tales, so that he had to let her live to find out what came next,' Ali supplied. 'I loved the stories, but I loved Scheherazade's wit even more.

'I used to read that book in the desert, looking out at the horizon as the sun blazed its last before dying. How sad for you to yearn for the sun in this cold country.'

She nodded. 'Yes, and living in a chilly house, watching the rain outside, always short of pocket money because—I quote—"we mustn't be extravagant".'

She hadn't meant to make herself sound quite so deprived as it came out. Her elderly cousins hadn't been mean, simply determined to teach her the value of money. While rebelling at their frugal standards she'd somehow imbibed them. She'd gone on to achieve a first-class degree in economics, but pure economics had been too dry for her. So she'd switched to journalism, specialising in stories where scandal mingled with money. She'd found the excitement she secretly yearned for through investigating the shady secrets of high-profile figures. But she couldn't tell Ali Ben Saleem that.

There was a great deal more she couldn't tell him—like Uncle Dan's teachings about 'money and morality'. The God-fearing old man had never bought himself or his family any little treat without donating a similar amount to charity.

His wife had shared his views about thrifty living until Fran was sixteen and had suddenly blossomed into a beauty. Aunt Jean had yearned to celebrate the girl's looks with a new wardrobe, but it had taken many earnest discussions before Dan could be brought into the right frame of mind. The local charities had done well that summer.

They were both dead now, but their austere, kindly influence lingered. Fran had a passion for lovely clothes, but she never treated herself without also giving to a good cause. It was bred in the bone, and she wouldn't have known how to stop. It was hardly surprising that Sheikh Ali's lifestyle roused her to indignation.

'I know what you mean about restaurants that play up to stereotypes,' Ali said. 'I've been in places over here called Ye Old English Waterwheel, with waiters dressed as yeomen, tugging their forelocks, and saying, ''What be thoy pleasure, maister?''' His stage yokel accent was so talented that Fran bubbled with laughter. He laughed with her and added, 'I nearly told them my pleasure would be to have them vanish from the face of the earth.'

'I suppose we both suffer from that kind of cliché about our countries,' Fran said.

'But England is also my country. I have an English mother, I attended Oxford University and learned soldiering at Sandhurst.'

She almost said, Yes, I know, but stopped herself in time. It wouldn't do to let him know she'd done her homework on him.

They had finished the pumpkin soup and Ali indicated a choice of dishes.

'If I had known your preference, I would have arranged for chicken with dates and honey,' he said. 'I promise it shall be served the next time we dine. Until then, perhaps you can find something in this humble selection.'

'This humble selection' stretched right down a long table. Fran was almost overwhelmed with choice. At last she picked a dish of long green beans.

'It's very hot,' he warned.

'The hotter the better,' she said recklessly.

But the first bite told her she'd made a mistake. The beans were spiced with onions, garlic, tomatoes and cayenne pepper.

'It's—it's delicious,' she said valiantly.

Ali grinned. 'You have steam coming out of your ears. Don't finish it if it's too much for you.'

'No, it's fine.' But she accepted some of the sliced tomatoes he pushed over to her, and to her relief they quenched the fire in her mouth.

'Try this instead,' Ali suggested, helping her to another dish. It was a cod liver salad and presented no problems. She began to relax even more. It was tempting to give herself up to the night's seductive spell.

And then, without warning, something disastrous happened. Glancing up, Fran met his eyes and found in them the last qualities she would have expected: real warmth, charm and—incredibly—a sense of fun. He was smiling at her, not seductively or cynically, but as though his mind danced in time with hers, and he was glad of it. And suddenly she suspected that this might be a truly delightful, great-hearted, funny, entrancing man. It was total disaster.

She struggled to clear her mind, but it persisted in lingering on the curve of his mouth, which was wide and flexible and made for kisses. It was smiling at her now in a special way that started a glow inside her.

And when she forced her attention away from his mouth his eyes were lying in wait to tease and entice her. There was a wicked promise in them and it was tempting to speculate what would happen to a woman who called that promise in. Of course, that could never be herself. She was here on serious business. But some lucky woman…

She pulled herself together.

'You have a lovely home,' she said, sounding slightly forced.

'Yes, it's beautiful,' he agreed. 'But I'm not sure it could be called a home. I have many dwellings, but I spend so little time in each one that—' He finished with a shrug.

'None of them is home?' Fran asked.

He gave a rueful smile. 'I feel like a small boy saying this, but wherever my mother is feels like my home. In her presence there is warmth and graciousness, and a sense of calm benevolence. You would like her very much.'

'I'm sure I should. She sounds like a great lady. Does she live in Kamar all the time?'

'Mostly. Sometimes she travels, but she doesn't care for flying. And—' he looked a little self-conscious '—she doesn't approve of some of my pleasures, so—'

'You mean like going to the casino?' Fran supplied, laughing.

'And other small indulgences,' he said outrageously. 'But mostly the casino. She says a man should have better things to do with his time.'

'She's right,' Fran said immediately.

'But how could I have spent this evening better than in meeting you?'

'You're not going to start telling me it was fate again, are you?'

'Have you suddenly become a cynic? What about all that Arabian folklore you used to enjoy? Didn't it teach you to believe in magic?'

'Well,' she said thoughtfully, 'it taught me to want to believe in magic, and that's almost the same thing. Sometimes, when life was very dull, I'd dream that a flying carpet was going to come through the window and carry me off to the land where genies came out of lamps and magicians cast their spells in clouds of coloured smoke.'

'And the magic prince?' he teased.

'He came out of the smoke, of course. But he always vanished in the smoke again, and the dream ended.'

'But you never stopped hoping for the flying carpet,' Ali said gently. 'You pretend to be very sensible and grown-up, but in your heart you're sure that one day it will come.'

She blushed a little. It was disconcerting to have him read her thoughts so well.

'I think that for you,' he said thoughtfully, 'the carpet will come.'

'I don't believe in magic,' she said, with a little shake of her head.

'But what do you call magic? When I saw you standing there tonight, that was magic far more potent than casting spells. And from that moment everything went well with me.' He gave her a wry smile. 'Do you know how much your witchcraft made me win? One hundred thousand. Look.'

Ali reached into his inside pocket, drew out a cheque book and calmly proceeded to write out a cheque for the full amount.

'What are you doing?' Fran gasped.

'I am giving you what is rightfully yours. You won this. Do with it as you will.'

He signed it with a flourish, then looked up at her, his eyes teasing. 'Who shall I make it out to? Come, admit defeat. Now you will have to tell me your name.'

'Oh, I don't think so,' she mused. She raised the glass, letting her eyes flirt with him over the rim. 'I'd be very foolish to give in right this minute, wouldn't I?'

'But I must have a name to put on the cheque.'

She shrugged.

'Without a name I can't give it to you.'

'Then keep it,' she said with an elegant gesture. 'I didn't ask you for anything.'

His eyes showed his admiration. 'You're not afraid to play for high stakes.'

'But I'm not playing for anything,' she said with a laugh. 'I've lived very happily without wealth and I can go on doing so.'

He cast a wry glance at her neck which wore a fortune in diamonds. Without hesitation Fran removed the necklace and set it beside him. 'Just so that there's no misunderstanding,' she said. 'I seek nothing from you. Nothing at all.'

It wasn't strictly true, but what she wanted from him would have to be told at another time, and another place. And then she would call the shots.

Their eyes held for a moment. His held bemusement that she should take their duel right up to the line. Finally there was a glimmer of respect.

With a shrug that mirrored the ones he'd given at the gaming tables, he pushed the cheque over to her, with the name still blank. Then he rose to his feet and made as if to fasten the necklace back in place. But Fran prevented him.

'You keep that. I'll keep this,' she said, indicating the cheque. 'After all, I don't want to be greedy, do I?'

Ali returned to his place opposite her and raised her hand to his lips, watching her all the time with eyes that were heavy, yet curiously alert. They were always alert, she realised, no matter what he was saying.

'Not many women can claim they've bested me,' he confessed. 'But I see you're used to playing games, and very good at it. I like that. It intrigues me. But what intrigues me even more is that smile you're giving me.'

'Smiles can convey so much more than words, don't you think?' she asked innocently.

'But what is conveyed without words can so easily be denied. Is that what you're doing, Diamond? Protecting yourself against the moment when you'll want to deny what is passing between us?'

It was like being naked, she thought, alarmed. He saw too much.

To divert his attention from the dangerous point she put the cheque in her purse. 'It would be very hard to deny that that has passed between us,' she observed.

'How true. I was sure a sharp wit lurked behind those innocent eyes.'

'You don't trust me, do you?' she asked impulsively.

'Not an inch. But we're equally matched, for I have the strangest feeling that you do not trust me.'

Fran's wide-eyed stare was a masterpiece of innocence. 'How could anyone doubt Your Highness's probity, rectitude, virtue, morality, righteousness—?'

He laughed until he almost choked, his eyes alight with real amusement, and he kissed her hand again, not seductively this time, but with a kind of vigorous triumph, as though he'd just seen his best hope romp past the winning post.

'What man could resist you?' he asked. 'Certainly I cannot. But stop calling me "Your highness". My name is Ali.'

'And mine is—Diamond.'

'I wonder. I begin to think I shall call you Scheherazade, for your wit, which is beyond the wit of all other women.'

'I'm cleverer than quite a few men too,' she riposted, and couldn't resist adding, 'You wait and see.'

He nodded. 'The waiting is half the pleasure. Will she say yes or no? And if she says no will her voice contain a secret invitation nonetheless?'

'I can't believe you ever have that problem. Don't tell me that any woman denies you.'

He shrugged. 'A man can have all the women in the world, yet not the one he wants. If that one denies him, what are all the others?'

Fran regarded him with wry amusement, not fooled by this. The words were humble but the tone was arrogant. Implicit was the fact that no woman refused him, but he felt it was polite to pretend otherwise.

'I'd have thought all the others were a good deal,' she said. 'They'd leave him no time for pining.'

'You speak like a woman who has never had her heart broken. I wonder if that can really be true?'

'It's true.'

'Then you have never loved, and that I find impossible to believe. You are made for love. I saw it in your eyes when they met mine in the casino.'

'You weren't thinking of love. You were thinking of money,' she said lightly.

'I was thinking of you and the spell you cast. It was that spell that turned my luck.'

'Oh, please! That's very pretty talk, but it was just chance.'

'For some there is no chance,' he said seriously. 'Whatever is written in the book of fate is what they put there themselves. I try to discern my fate through the smoke that surrounds it, and I see your handwriting.'

'And what—what else do you see?' she faltered.

'Nothing. The rest is hidden. There is only you.'

As he spoke he drew her to her feet and straight

into his arms. Fran had believed herself prepared for this moment, but when it came her well-laid plans seemed to fall away. His little teasing kisses in the car had carried the promise of what was to come, and now she knew that there was no way she could ever have left Ali tonight, without discovering if the promise would be kept.

It was kept magnificently. He enfolded her in his arms in a way that shut out the rest of the world, as though only she mattered. That alone was a seductive experience. Fran bestowed a brief thought on Howard—the man in her life as far as there was one. Howard was a banker, and he kissed like a banker, as though estimating profit and loss. Strange that she'd never thought of that before. Then Ali Ben Saleem's lips moved decisively over hers, and there were no thoughts left for any other man.

She told herself that she was merely laying the ground for the piece she would write, but her honesty wouldn't let her get away with that. This was the kind of experience a woman dreamed of, and it was irresistible.

His mouth was curved, strong, yet immensely subtle, and it knew what she wanted it to do before she knew it herself. He lightly caressed her mouth before brushing his lips over her eyes, her jaw, her neck. With unerring precision he found the little spot beneath her ear where she was unbearably sensitive and drew a soft, whispering line down the length of her neck. Nothing could have made her repress the sigh of pleasure she gave.

Her head was cradled on his arm while he searched her face, seeking there the answer to some question that was beyond words.

'Are you playing with me now?' he growled.

'Of course. A game that you don't understand.'

He liked that. 'When will I understand?'

'When it is ended.'

'When will it be ended?'

'When I have won.'

'Tell me your secret,' he demanded.

A smile touched her lips. 'You know the secret as well as I do.'

'With you, there would always be a new secret,' he said huskily, and covered her mouth again.

He half urged, half carried her the few steps to the couch by the window. She felt the cushions beneath her back and the moonlight on her face. He was caressing her with his lips while his hands began a gentle exploration of her body. She gasped at those soft touches. She hadn't known that she had such a body until his reverent fingertips told her, and told her also what it was for.

It was for giving and taking in an ecstasy of pleasure, and she hadn't suspected until this moment, when he made her understand what was possible beyond anything she could have imagined.

Her mouth moved feverishly against his, not receiving now but seeking and demanding with an urgency that astonished him—delighted him too, if his response was anything to go by. His insistence became fierce, and suddenly she could feel the hot breeze of the desert against her skin, see the dark red sun in its last moments before oblivion. He carried these things with him and no woman could lie in his arms without being aware of them as part of his soul.

All through the grey, chilly years this had been waiting for her, and now she had found it there was no turning back. He had said she was made for pleasure, and he was showing her that it was true.

She gave a long sigh, part acceptance, part apprehension. This was a very dangerous man. He could kiss, and kiss, until she no longer knew what was happening to her, or even who she was. And after that? Faintly, as if from a great distance, her pride was calling to her to save herself, because soon it would be too late…

But it was something else that saved her. A buzzer on the wall sounded faintly but persistently. Ali drew back with a small sound of annoyance, picked up a telephone nearby, and snapped something into it.

Almost at once his voice changed. Obviously the message was urgent, for he sighed and rose.

'Forgive me,' he said courteously. 'Important business calls me away.' He indicated the table. 'Please, pour yourself some wine. I shall be with you as soon as possible.'

He hurried from the room.

Still in a daze, Fran couldn't, at first, understand what had happened. At the height of a sensual experience such as she had never known before, he had simply brushed her aside. Business called and she had ceased to matter, or even to exist.

But when he returned he would expect her to be instantly available, she realised.

Well, now I know, she thought, seething. I came here to learn about Ali Ben Saleem, and I've already learned his priorities. Oil wells, one. Women, nil.

As her pulses slowed and she came out of the erotic dream he had induced with such infuriating ease, her anger grew.

'Who does he think I am?' she muttered.

No, not who? What? A doll to be put back on the shelf until he was ready to take her down again. And, as with a doll, he would expect to find her lying in the same position.

It would teach him a lesson not to find her at all.

She was on her feet in an instant, groping around for her sandals and trying to remember when and how she'd lost them. It brought home to her how far this man had lured her, how easily he'd made her lose control. She must escape.

She looked cautiously out into the hall.

A man, evidently a porter, sat by the front door. Fran wondered nervously if he had instructions to prevent her leaving. There was only one way to find out.

Taking a deep breath, she strolled across the marble floor, a picture of supreme confidence. The porter rose to his feet, uncertainty written all over his face. But, as Fran had hoped, none of his orders covered this unprecedented situation. Her heart thumping, she made an imperious gesture, and he bowed low as he opened the door for her to sail out into the night.

CHAPTER THREE

'YOU'RE crazy, going back into the lion's den,' Joey protested for the hundredth time.

'That's where it's most fun,' Fran said, putting the final touches to her immaculate appearance.

'You were lucky I was there to rescue you the other night.'

'Cut it out, Joey,' Fran chuckled. 'I walked out of his house under my own steam.'

'And found me waiting outside, in my car. I'd been on your tail ever since you left the casino.'

'But I won't need rescuing today. He's agreed to give me an interview.'

'Only he doesn't know it's you. And when he finds out he'll have a fit.'

Fran's eyes gleamed. 'That's what I'm looking forward to.'

She was almost unrecognisable as the siren of the other night. Instead of the seductive dress she wore a plain white silk blouse and grey business suit, with silver buttons.

Her glorious hair was smoothed back against her head. Her appearance radiated businesslike chic and quiet elegance. This was Ms Frances Callam, financial journalist. Diamond, the gorgeous creature who'd briefly scorched across the horizon, had been a mirage. Looking in the mirror, Fran could see no trace of her.

Which was almost a pity, she mused. Diamond had had a lot of fun. True, she'd also got herself into a perilous situation, from which she'd only just escaped. But she had escaped, and the whole event now looked like a thrilling adventure.

She gave a little sigh that was almost regretful. Suddenly her life seemed very lacking in adventure.

She disapproved of Sheikh Ali with every fibre of her being. She must keep reminding herself of that to dispel the sensual dream he'd woven around her, and which still lingered disturbingly.

At the time she'd fancied herself in control, but looking back she could see how disgracefully quickly she'd succumbed to a little cheap magic and a practised line.

But the scorching intensity of his lips on hers wouldn't be dismissed so easily. It haunted her night and day, filling her dreams so that she awoke wondering if she would ever know such sensations again. At work she tried to concentrate on figures, but they danced and turned into diamonds.

'I just hope the cheque clears before he sees you,' Joey said now.

With a start, Fran came out of her dream. 'I didn't take that money for myself,' she said. 'I made it out in favour of the International Children's Fund and handed it over to them yesterday. They'll be writing to thank him. I'd like to see his face when he gets that.'

Joey was pale. 'You gave away all that money?'

'Well, I couldn't have kept it,' she said, genuinely shocked.

'I sure would have done.'

Fran chuckled. 'I don't think he'd have given it to you.'

'I just can't believe he agreed to this interview.'

'I spoke to his secretary, and said that Frances Callam wanted to interview him for *The Financial Review*. I was given an appointment with no trouble.'

'Your taxi's here,' Joey said, looking out of the window. 'Sure you don't want me to drive you?'

'I think this time I should beard the lion completely alone.'

'I think I should be there waiting when he throws you out.'

'He isn't going to throw me out.'

'After the way you vanished and left him looking silly?'

'That merely told him that I can't be trifled with. Trust me, Joey. I'm right on top of it this time.'

Afterwards she was to remember the supreme self-confidence with which she got into the taxi and had herself taken back to the house of Ali Ben Saleem. It seemed so simple at the time.

At first nothing happened to change her mind. As soon as she rung the bell outside Ali's house the door was pulled open by the porter, who inclined his head in a silent question.

'Good morning,' Fran said. 'I have an appointment with Prince Ali Ben Saleem.'

She walked past him as she spoke, and into the centre of the tiled hallway. The porter hastened after her. He looked alarmed.

'Will you please inform His Highness that Frances Callam is here?'

At that moment the door to the office opened and Ali walked out. The porter made a sign of relief and backed towards the door. Fran took a deep breath and faced Ali, smiling.

He frowned when he saw her, then his face lightened and he advanced towards her, both hands out-stretched, smiling in welcome.

Whatever she'd expected, it wasn't this. He should have been annoyed at the memory of her desertion. Perhaps he didn't recognise her. But his first words dispelled that illusion.

'Diamond! My beautiful Diamond. What a pleasure to see you again. Come.'

He gestured towards the dining room, and she followed him in.

'I know why you're here,' he said when he'd closed the door behind them.

'You—you do?'

'You're angry with me about the other night. My poor Diamond, it was so unchivalrous of me to leave you and not return. My only excuse is that I was over-whelmed with business. I sent my secretary to make sure you got home safely, but I would have liked to see you myself.'

Fran took a deep breath, struggling for words while various images flitted through her mind: kicking his shins was the best, but boiling him in oil wasn't far behind.

He hadn't come back at all.

All this time she'd been picturing his face when he found her gone, and he didn't even know. He'd just forgotten about her.

His secretary had probably been too afraid of his wrath to admit that she wasn't there, and had invented some story about having seen her home. The doorman, too, had probably kept very quiet.

Then she saw Ali's eyes, glinting behind his smile, and a doubt crept into her mind. Did he really not know that she'd left? Or did he know, and had invented this story to turn the tables on her?

With this unpredictable man, anything was possible.

'I hope that some day soon we'll be able to enjoy the evening that was interrupted,' Ali continued, 'but just for the moment I'm afraid I'm very busy. In fact, you must leave at once, as I have an appointment with a journalist.'

'I thought you never saw journalists,' Fran said, getting ready to enjoy the next few minutes.

'Normally I don't, but Mr Callam is from a serious newspaper.'

'Did—did you say Mr Callam?'

'Mr Francis Callam. I've agreed to the interview because there are things it would suit me to make clear in his pages.'

Fran's thoughts were in a whirl. When they settled she gazed with delight on the resulting pattern. He was about to get the shock of his life.

'What kind of things?' she asked innocently.

Ali's smile was like a locked door. 'I wouldn't dream of boring you with such details.'

'Well, I know I'm just a stupid woman,' she said humbly, 'but I know how to spell financial. F-E—no, it's I, isn't it?'

He laughed. 'Your wit enchants me. Now, I've no more time for games. Mr Callam will be here at any moment.'

'Don't you want to know my name first?'

'I've already taken my own steps to discover it. I'll be in touch with you when I have time.'

'I wouldn't put you to so much trouble,' Fran said, breathing hard. 'My name is Frances Callam. Ms Frances Callam.'

She was fully revenged in the look that crossed his face. It was compounded of alarm, horror and anger.

'Are you telling me...?' he asked slowly.

'That I am the journalist you're waiting for. And I can not only spell financial, but I can add up. You know, one and one are two, two and two are four. I have a first-class economics degree, you see, and they insisted on it.'

His voice was very hard. 'You deceived me.'

'No, I didn't. I spoke to your secretary, and said Frances Callam wanted to talk to you for an article in *The Financial Review*. You both took it for granted it was a man because it never occurred to you that a financial journalist could be a woman. You fell into the trap of your own prejudice.'

'And the other night? Was it mere coincidence that you turned up at The Golden Chance?'

'No, I was observing you.'

'And afterwards? Do you dare say that wasn't deception?'

'We-ell, I may have left a few things out. But you made it easy.'

'And all the time you were laughing at me.' His eyes narrowed. 'Do you know what would happen, in my country, to a woman who dared to do that?'

'Tell me. No, wait!' She rummaged in her bag and produced a notebook. 'Now tell me. Hey!' Ali had firmly removed the notebook from her hand and tossed it aside.

'You will not make notes about me,' he said through gritted teeth. 'You will not write about anything that happened the other night—'

'Oh, I wasn't going to. I write for a serious paper.

It wouldn't be interested in that corny line you handed me.'

'I—'

'Well, you have to admit—burning sunsets and tents flapping in the breeze? But I don't blame you.'

'You don't?' He sounded dazed.

'I'm sure most girls would fall for it. Well, you wouldn't keep using it if they didn't, would you?'

'That's right,' he said, his eyes kindling. 'You see, one thing I've learned about women is this—the sillier the better.'

'You don't say!'

'The more foolish the line, the more unconvincing the stage props, the more chance that some fluffy-headed little girl is going to believe it. Experience has taught me all I need to know about your sex.'

'Are you daring to call me a fluffy-headed little girl?'

'I don't know why that should bother you, since you went out of your way to make me think just that. You should stick to the role, Miss Callam. It suits you better than pretending to be a man.'

'I'm doing no such thing,' she said furiously. 'I earn my living as a journalist. You promised me an interview, and I'm here. Why don't we get started?'

'If,' Ali said, regarding her coldly, 'you imagine for one moment that I intend to discuss my private affairs with you—'

'Not your private affairs, your business affairs,' Fran said. She couldn't resist adding provocatively, 'I think we've already covered the private ones.'

'Let it be clearly understood that I do not discuss business with women. That is not a woman's role.'

'Woman's role?' she echoed, scandalised. 'Why, you prehistoric—'

'Think what you like of me. Do you imagine I care? I haven't been used to considering the opinions of women and I see no reason to start now. In my country women know their place and keep to it. It's an arrangement that works very well.'

'I wonder what your mother thinks of that?' Fran said, with spirit. 'She's English, isn't she? Brought up to be equal with men—'

'No woman is equal with men. And don't speak about my mother. You're not going to interview me by the back door. I will not talk to you and that's final.'

'You talked all right when you thought I was just a plaything,' Frances snapped.

'But of course. That is what women are for.'

'It's not what I'm for.'

'You think so, but in my arms you came alive like a true woman. Don't say you've forgotten.'

She faced him defiantly. 'I was acting a part.'

He smiled, and something about it disturbed her obscurely. 'I don't think so. I can tell when a woman is pretending. I can also tell when she's yielding to her own deepest desires, in the arms of the man who can inflame those desires. Something happened between us the other night, something that was true and real.'

'As though anything true and real could happen between me and a man from the Stone Age.'

'Why must you deny it? What are you afraid of? That your theories might be swept away by a passion that will show you your real self? Is that why you try to reduce me to words on your page, because you think like that you will bring the truth under your control?'

He was standing dangerously close. She took a step away, and knew instantly that she'd made a tactical mistake. He knew now that she was nervous of him.

'The only truth I'm interested in where you're concerned,' she said, 'is what really goes on in those back-room deals you keep so secret.'

'And I tell you not to interfere in what doesn't concern you, and which would certainly be beyond your understanding. Please—' he held up a hand '—don't bore me with lectures about your brain. A woman's brain, for pity's sake!'

His scornful tone almost made her blow a gasket. 'We do have brains, you know! We are members of the same species. And you were ready enough to concede that Scheherazade had a brain the other night.'

'No. Scheherazade had wit. A woman's wit that sparkles and dazzles a man. Not a bludgeon to challenge him. I thought then that you were witty and subtle, but now you seem determined to prove me wrong.

'If you want me to listen to you, Diamond, forget your degree, and speak to me of your hair which is like a river of molten gold in the sunset. Then you will have all my attention. Since that night I've been troubled by your hair, thinking how I would run my hands through it and delight in adorning it with priceless jewels.

'I'm haunted, too, by your skin, which has the smoothness of satin. I've dreamed of how it would feel pressed against me when we lie together in bed—'

'Never,' she whispered in outrage.

He took a step closer to her and looked directly into her eyes. His own were burning.

'At this moment I too feel like saying never. I will never take to my bed a woman who rejects her own womanhood, and therefore my manhood. I will never trouble myself with a female who knows nothing about men and women and what fate created between them. I will throw her out and say good riddance.

'But then I look into the depths of your eyes, and I know that it isn't so easy. You and I met because we had to, and at our final parting we will neither of us be the same. What exquisite pleasure there will be in giving and taking with you, and knowing that what you give me you will have given no other man because you did not know it existed. That will be a treasure worth fighting for.'

He wasn't even touching her, but her heart was thumping wildly from the effect of his words and the images they conjured up in her fevered brain. She was fully clothed, but the caressing way he'd spoken of her skin had made it come alive. She felt as though his fingers were tracing soft paths across it, lingering, teasing her, and his tongue was driving her wild with flickering movements everywhere—her mouth, her breasts…making her want everything in the world, knowing that he was the one man who had it in his power to give.

She wanted to turn away, to refuse to meet his eyes and see in them the destiny he planned for her, whether she consented or not. But that would be cowardly. Danger must be faced, not avoided. And so she gazed on the picture he painted, and felt it swallow her up.

'Don't you feel that too?' he asked. 'That it must be so?'

'No,' she said, taking another step back from him.

'No, it can't be. You can't make something like that happen by giving an order.'

He reached for her. She backed but struck against the sofa, lost her balance, and had to sit on it. She tried to rise but he held her down with a hand on her shoulder, and sat beside her.

'But the order has already been given,' he said. 'And it was you who gave it. You came to The Golden Chance in search of me, and I recognised you at once as the woman who would play a special part in my life. It's too late to turn back. And why should you want to? Can it be that you are afraid?'

She would not let him kiss her, because he would take that as proof of his chauvinistic belief that only passion counted between men and women. And that was one victory he mustn't win. But while her resolve was strong her bones felt as if they had been turned to water.

Nor did he try to kiss her. He merely raised his hand and touched her lips softly with one fingertip, tracing the outline of her wide mouth. The sensations he could evoke by that simple gesture were shocking. She was on fire, and there was no hope for her.

She wanted to speak, to make an angry protest, but her mouth was quiveringly alive for the next gentle touch. Somehow—she didn't recall doing it—she'd taken hold of his arms, as if to steady herself, and the pressure of her fingers was drawing him close to her, until his lips were on hers.

As though this was a signal he'd waited for he took possession of the kiss, claiming her like a conqueror accepting surrender. Nor could she refuse because the treachery came from within herself, and it was her own desire that had invited him.

He had said that anticipation was half the pleasure, and he was a man who knew how to go slowly, prolonging his own pleasure and hers, teasing her with her own longings. She moaned softly, and he entered her mouth with quick, exploring movements that made her dizzy. She wanted to explore him in return, wanted it so much it alarmed her.

Before Ali, Fran had thought of herself as a moderate person. Howard's kisses had pleased her but never tormented her with the longing for more. Now she was discovering that her own propriety was nothing but a mask, behind which another woman—hot-blooded and demanding—was waiting to break forth into a new life. And it was happening with a man who drove her to a fury of antagonism, hand in hand with desire.

He gave her mouth a final caress, implicit with the promise of another time, and slid his lips down her neck, then further down, slipping open the buttons of her V-neck blouse to lay his lips between her breasts. The delight was unimaginable and her hands closed behind his head in a gesture of acceptance and plea. Her heart was thumping wildly beneath his lips, and she knew he must be able to feel it, but she was beyond caring. It felt as though everything about her was disintegrating and reforming into a new shape, a new person.

Then Ali raised his head and his eyes were hovering above her, reassured her that all was well as long as she was in his arms.

Slowly he lowered her back onto the cushions.

'You see?' he said, in a voice that shook a little.

'See?' she asked vaguely.

'When we are together—something happens—to you and to me—you can't deny it.'

'I don't,' she murmured. 'But it isn't—' She struggled to get the word out. 'Isn't important.'

'Passion is always important.'

Fran forced her head to clear. She didn't trust this man. And the more her body yearned for him, the more she distrusted him.

'But you feel passion for so many,' she managed to say.

He shook his head. 'Not—like that,' he said. And something in his voice told her that he was troubled. He'd done what he wanted, yet he too had been taken by surprise. He was shaking, and when he spoke again he sounded as though he was trying to force himself back to reality, because the realms of pleasure had alarmed him.

'Now you must go,' he said. 'For the moment. When the time is right for us to meet again, I will let you know.'

His arrogance had a usefully cooling effect on her. Angrily she freed herself and hastened to button up her blouse.

'You will let me know—when you have decided?'

'When the fates have decided,' he corrected her gently.

'Oh, no, you don't. I want the interview you promised me. If I leave without it, I won't come back, ever.'

'We'll see,' he said, smiling. 'But you will certainly leave without it.'

The world was resuming its normal shape. She changed tack. 'Now look, why don't you just be reasonable and we can—?'

'It's no use, Diamond. The answer is no.'

'And don't call me Diamond.'

'No, your name is Frances Callam. So, I needn't have gone to such lengths to find it out.'

'Didn't your secretary tell you? The one who saw me home?'

'It was no part of his duties to ask your name,' Ali said smoothly.

'But he must have told you where I lived,' she insisted. 'You could have discovered my name that way.'

His eyes flashed, and now she was certain that he had returned to find her gone, and this tale was an invention, so that she shouldn't know she'd successfully snubbed him.

'Why should I need such methods when I had a much better way?' he asked with a shrug. 'I have a small confession to make—about that cheque.'

'The one for a hundred thousand?'

'That's right.' He smiled straight into her eyes, and despite her annoyance Fran felt the return of disturbance deep within her, which had less to do with his sexual charisma than with his sheer charm. He shouldn't be allowed to smile like that.

'I'm afraid I stopped it,' Ali admitted. 'My bank will refuse to pay, but they will tell me who it's made out to. And so, if you hadn't come here today, I would have learned your name anyway.'

'Would you really?' she said slowly.

'Very unkind of me, wasn't it?'

'Very. But I did something rather unkind too. I didn't try to cash that cheque myself. I made it out to the International Children's Fund, and gave it to them yesterday, with your compliments.'

He laughed out loud, showing strong white teeth.

'That's very good, an excellent story. But, my dear Diamond, did you really think I'd believe that any woman could refuse such a sum of money?'

'I returned the necklace.'

'Worth about a tenth of the cheque. Giving away a hundred thousand would have been another matter.'

'Well, I did,' she said, getting cross. 'As you'll soon find out. When the cheque bounces, your name will be mud—probably in world headlines.'

'No, no, don't keep it up. It was a good try, but I'm not that easily fooled. Now I'm afraid you must go. You've caused me to waste too much time.'

'Yes, I mustn't disturb you from making money, must I?'

He saw her to the front door. 'Till our next meeting?'

'I wonder if there'll be one?'

'In my country we say—the answer is written in the sand.'

'And in my country we say—don't count your chickens before they're hatched.'

Ali watched her until she'd vanished from sight. As he turned back into the house his secretary was hurrying from the office, very pale.

'Excellency, someone from the ICF is on the phone to say they are most grateful for your generous cheque, but owing to a misunderstanding at the bank—'

Ali swore and vanished into the study. It took all his charm to smooth away the problem, and within five minutes a new cheque had been made out to the charity. As he sealed the envelope his eyes were unreadable.

'She fooled me,' he murmured. 'A hundred thousand, and nothing given in return.'

He took a sheet of paper and wrote on it 'Frances Callam'.

After regarding the name for a moment he crossed it out and wrote 'Diamond'.

Then he crossed that out, and wrote 'Scheherazade'.

CHAPTER FOUR

ALI BEN SALEEM'S house was quiet for a few days while he took a flying trip to New York. He returned in a hurry and spent the next week on the telephone, confirming deals and setting up new ones. Apart from his secretary, the staff saw very little of him, and he saw little of them. He certainly had no time to notice the new maid, which was what Fran had counted on.

It had been surprisingly easy to set up. Joey had mobilised his contacts to find an employment agency in the area. Using bribery and persuasion, he'd arranged for them to send out an advertisement to all the houses in the area, and Ali's chief steward had taken the bait. The house needed a live-in maid. Fran had applied, carefully disguised in a long, dark wig, drab clothes and flat shoes, and calling herself Jane. She'd been hired at once.

She'd thought long and hard before going under cover in Ali's house. It wasn't the way she liked to work, and she'd very nearly backed off.

But then the Sheikh had spoken in her mind: 'I do not discuss business with women... In my country women know their place and keep to it... No woman is equal with men.'

It was the memory of his imperious tone, as much as his words, that made her temper rise and her resolve harden. She knew she would have no peace until she'd made him unsay those words, and give her some respect.

51

She'd started on the day Ali departed. To begin with, her work had been downstairs, mostly in the kitchen. Once she was allowed upstairs, to clean Ali's bedroom, but only under the steward's supervision.

She'd found the room disappointingly austere. There was none of the silk-curtained luxury of downstairs, where Ali entertained ladies with names like Diamond. In his private domain Ali had plain white walls, polished floors and a large mahogany bed. Three pictures adorned the walls, all of them of horses. The steward had informed her that these were His Excellency's racehorses, shown at their moments of triumph in the Derby, the Grand National and at Ascot. Then he'd remembered his dignity, and told her sharply to get on with her work.

Fran wasn't sure exactly what she was looking for. Apart from getting a general picture of his life, she wanted something that would let him know she couldn't be simply dismissed, as he had done. It was proving hard to find.

She was working alone now. Joey had left London to take up another assignment in the north. She'd told Howard that she had to be out of town for a few weeks. Nobody knew where she was. She felt safer that way. But she was growing depressed by her lack of progress.

When Ali returned she kept well out of his sight, but it was hardly necessary. Sheikh Ali didn't notice servant girls.

But tonight it seemed he'd made a mistake. Watching from above, Fran had seen him go to his bedroom with files tucked under his arm. An hour later he'd been summoned downstairs by a late visitor, and gone down without locking his door.

This was her chance. Those files might contain some detail that would prove to be the key to the whole, involved oil empire. This man who spent a fortune on his pleasures and gave his people no say in the running of his little country must be made accountable. And she was the person to do it. If she also made him sorry he'd patronised her, that would merely be a bonus.

As soon as she saw him vanish she slipped down the stairs and into his room. The files were spread out on the bed. To her disappointment only one was in English, but she started on that.

She read rapidly, and as she did so her eyes widened with indignation. The documents concerned The Golden Choice, the casino where she and Ali had met, and they made it clear, beyond any misunderstanding, that Ali was the owner.

'The unscrupulous—' Words failed her, but she hurried to read as much as possible, her indignation growing.

Then, from behind her, came the ominous sound of a door being closed. Appalled, she looked up and found Ali standing there, regarding her with a cynically tolerant smile.

'I have to take my hat off to you,' he said. 'You don't give up, do you?'

Fran rose to her feet, trying to look dignified. It was difficult in the circumstances, but she did her best.

'You should have known I wouldn't give up,' she said defiantly.

'But I did know. The interest has been in seeing how far you were prepared to go. My dear Diamond—Frances—Jane—whatever you're calling yourself today—did you think I'd be so easily fooled?'

'You—knew it was me?'

'The advertisement that came through my door so conveniently, directing me to an employment agency? Of course I knew. I warned my steward to look out for you, and sure enough you turned up. To be fair, you did a good job. He barely recognised you. I knew you at once. There's something about you that no drab clothes can disguise.'

'You knew all along,' she repeated, in a daze.

'Poor Diamond. You thought you were doing so well.'

His smile never wavered as he spoke, but behind it lurked something that troubled her, something that would have frightened her if she'd been easily scared. Inside, he wasn't smiling. She was sure of it the next moment when he turned the key in the lock, and put it in his pocket.

'Hey, now, let me out of here,' she said, as firmly as she could.

'You want to rush away? Isn't that a little premature, seeing how much trouble you took to get in here?' He indicated the file she'd been reading. 'I do hope the result was worth it.'

That reminded her that she was aggrieved. 'You deceived me,' she said.

He began to laugh. 'I deceived you? You smuggled yourself into my house under false pretences, and I deceived you?'

'At the casino. It was a set-up. You own the place. No wonder you didn't mind losing. You were losing to yourself. And you fixed the winning too, making me think I was a lucky charm. Just another way of recycling the money to spend on enjoying yourself.'

'I didn't fix the winning,' he said. 'That would be

cheating, and beneath me. It just happened that way.'
He saw her sceptical look and snapped, 'I do not lie.'

'Of course not; I'm sorry.'

'You seem to have a very poor opinion of me. But
after everything that's happened I think we should declare a draw and be friends.'

As he spoke he opened a mahogany cupboard, revealing a refrigerator within it. From it he took a bottle
of champagne, which he opened and poured into two
glasses.

'You won't refuse to drink champagne with me, will
you?' he asked. 'Or would you prefer a nice cup of
tea?'

'Tea would be very dull,' she said, recovering her
poise and accepting the glass.

She'd been surprised to find Ali taking this in good
part, but, after all, she hardly knew his character.
Doubtless he was feeling pleased at having wrong-
footed her, and the matter would end here.

'You're a most extraordinary woman, Diamond,' he
said affably, beginning to tidy away the files.

'My name is Fran,' she pointed out.

'I know, but I can't help thinking of you as
Diamond. Fran is such an abrupt name, but my
Diamond is the jewel who glittered for me that first
night, and has teased and tormented me ever since.
You must admit that after that cheque you owed me
the chance to get my revenge.'

Fran couldn't resist a smile. 'Yes,' she said. 'I read
in the paper about your generous donation. I really did
get the better of you, didn't I?'

She heard him give a swift intake of breath. He was
looking at her strangely, and for one moment she
thought she saw something in his eyes that he would

rather have concealed. Briefly it flashed in his eyes—
a look of cold menace, warning her to beware.

Then it was gone as completely as a desert mirage.
He was smiling as he said, 'No woman ever managed
that before.'

'I'm beginning to realise that I didn't know you at
all,' Fran admitted. 'I never dreamed that you'd be as
reasonable as this about it.'

'What did you expect?' he asked, amused.

'I'm not sure, but something outrageous and outside
the normal rules.'

'In other words, you thought I'd act like a stage
foreigner out of a cheap novelette,' he said, sounding
nettled. 'I'm a civilised man.'

'I know. It was very unfair of me.'

'So now that's settled I think we should toast each
other, as equal combatants.'

They chinked glasses.

'I wonder what you'll tell your confederates?' Ali
mused, sitting beside her on the bed.

'Luckily I have no confederates. I prefer to work
alone.'

'What about the little man who was with you at the
casino? Don't tell me you haven't been sending him
reports?'

'I only employ him occasionally. He's far away on
another job right now.'

'But your family—oh, no, you have none. What a
sad life!'

'It isn't sad at all.'

'But there's nobody to praise your successes, and
nobody to sympathise with your failures. It does seem
hard that you should have so little to show for your
efforts.' He looked at her thoughtfully, and seemed to

reach a sudden decision. 'All right! Perhaps I've been unreasonable. You may have your interview. There.'

'Do you mean that?' she asked eagerly.

'You can come and talk to me as soon as I return. That's a promise.'

'Return?'

'The man who just came to see me warned me of a crisis in Kamar that needs my immediate attention. I have to leave at once. But we'll talk when I get back.'

'When will that be?'

He shrugged. 'How can I tell?'

'Oh, I see,' she said in a deflated voice. 'That kind of promise. One day, never.'

'How suspicious you are! You think I mean never to return?'

'Well, if you do it'll be a long time, and you'll have forgotten we ever had this talk.'

'You may be right. In that case, you'll have to come with me.'

She gasped with delight. 'You mean that?'

'I'm a man of my word. You will be my guest in Kamar.' His eyes held a curious light. 'You will be privileged as no woman has ever been before, and I promise you an experience you will never forget.'

'When do we leave?'

'In half an hour.'

'But I don't have my passport.'

His ironic smile reminded her that he was a head of state. 'Leave me to worry about that. Hurry now! If you're not ready on time I'll depart without you.'

Fran didn't need any further encouragement. Filled with joy and relief, she bounded up and headed for the door. Laughing, Ali turned the key and let her out.

In her own room she threw her few clothes together and had just zipped up her bag when there was a knock on her door. Outside, she found a beautiful Arab girl, who bowed gracefully to her.

'I bring you these,' she said, holding out her arms which were filled with dark green robes. You wear— and you will be me.'

Through her fractured English she explained a little more, and Fran gathered that she was a Kamari servant in Ali's household, allowed to enter the country only to work for him. Fran would assume her identity, and her passport for both the outward and return journeys.

The girl helped her on with the robes, and showed her how to cover her head and swathe her face so that only the eyes were visible.

'But you must look down so that nobody sees your blue eyes,' she advised. 'Also, that is how a woman must walk, with eyes downcast. Not raise to master.'

Really, thought Fran ironically. It was a black mark against Ali, but she was feeling too much in charity with him to brood on it.

A few minutes later she was ready to join Ali's car, waiting at the front. He was already seated in the back, and she stared at the sight of him. He had discarded western clothes, and now looked every inch an Arab prince in splendid flowing white robes and headdress. He was absorbed in papers, but he looked up and indicated for her to sit beside him.

When she was settled the door slammed behind her, and the car began to move.

'You'll have to forgive me if I work,' he said. 'This crisis is going to take much of my attention.'

'What kind of crisis?' she ventured to ask.

'Don't ask me questions now.' A brief smile flitted

across his face. 'When we reach Kamar, all will be made clear to you.'

In half an hour they were at the airport. The car swung away from the main terminals towards the area where cargo planes and private aircraft operated. Looking out of the window, Fran saw the chauffeur get out and approach an official, handing him some documents which, she supposed, were the passports. The official glanced at the Rolls with its Kamari flag, proclaiming that the head of state was on board, and indicated for them to go through. It was easy if you were royalty.

The Rolls swung in a great arc and finally stopped. The chauffeur opened the door on Ali's side and bowed as his master got out. Fran followed and found herself standing before a private jet, painted in the blue and silver colours of Kamar. Ali was already headed up the steps without waiting to see if she followed, and she hurried to catch up with him.

The interior of the aircraft took her breath away. It was hung with silk curtains and the seats were large armchairs. A thick, multicoloured carpet covered the floor.

Ali seated himself alone, while someone waved Fran to a separate section of the plane. She guessed he'd retreated into loftiness because his employees were there, and for the moment she was prepared to play along with it.

The engines were already running, and as soon as the doors were closed the plane began to taxi. In another few minutes they were airborne.

Soon after take-off the steward fixed a small table in front of her, and served wine and almond biscuits. It was some time since she'd eaten, and she devoured them. Ali joined her for a few minutes, smiling at her excitement.

'I shall have to spend most of my time on the phone,' he said, 'but I have ordered that your needs should be attended to. There is a bed if you wish to sleep. It's gone midnight and this is quite a long flight.'

She yawned. 'I guess you're right. Perhaps a lie-down would be nice.'

He gestured with his head and the steward showed her the way to a separate compartment. Her jaw dropped as she saw the satin-draped double bed. This was more like a luxury hotel than an aircraft. But then, Sheikh Ali was like no other man.

She was almost ready for sleep, but she found that as soon as she lay down her yawns vanished. She was too excited to miss a moment, and she lay by the window, gazing through it at the lights on the wings, until the first gleam of dawn appeared on the far horizon.

She watched, transfixed, as the light grew until she could see the world, and she took a long breath of sheer wonder. Below her was sand as far as the eye could see. The sun was rising, and the desert lay in a pale half light, dim, mysterious. For the first time she realised its immense size. It was huge, featureless, and potentially as dangerous as the man who was taking her to it.

But danger was only a small part of the story. The fierce beauty of the desert struck some people like a fever from which they could never really be cured, and in that instant she knew that she was one of the af-flicted. With joy she realised that she had come to the land of her dreams, the land that had haunted her ever since that lonely, rain-drenched childhood. And nothing in her life would ever be the same again.

She heard the door open, and the next minute Ali had dropped down beside her.

'There is my land,' he said. 'Waiting to welcome you.'

'It beautiful,' she said, awed. 'More beautiful than anything I could ever have imagined. It's so big and lonely—so—so self-sufficient.'

He looked at her with quick interest. 'You're right. That is what I have felt myself. The desert needs none of us. It is complete unto itself. How clever of you to understand that at once. Many people who are born here take a lifetime.'

She smiled, glad that he felt she was on his wavelength. It was a good start to her trip.

And then the sun finally appeared fully over the horizon, and the sand was flooded with smouldering light. Before her eyes it blossomed into deep yellow. The sky became a vivid, incredible blue, and the whole world seemed to glow.

'Thank you,' she murmured. 'Thank you for bringing me here.'

He shot her a troubled look that she didn't see.

'Come and sit down,' he said. 'We'll be landing any moment.'

She took her seat, still looking eagerly out of the window. Then the desert vanished, and they were coming in to land at Kamar's main airport, which looked exactly like every other airport. Another Rolls, with blacked-out windows, was waiting for them at the bottom of the steps.

Fran hastily adjusted her veil, lowered her eyes, and followed Ali demurely down the steps and into the back of the car. The door slammed, and they were moving.

The first part of the journey was uninteresting, along a long straight road that led from the airport to the city. Looking out of the darkened window, Fran saw the squat buildings of refineries.

But then they reached the city, full of early morning bustling, and at once her interest quickened. There was no time to see very much, for the car moved quickly, but she noticed that some of the people smiled and waved at the sight of the official flag. Whatever Ali was like as a ruler, his people were glad to have him among them again. Unless…

'Do they do that of their own free will?' she challenged Ali.

'Do what?'

'Wave and smile.'

She thought she heard him mutter, 'Give me patience!' Aloud he said sardonically, 'No, of course not. I issued a decree that anyone who doesn't look pleased to see me is beheaded in the market-place.'

'Sorry,' she said ruefully.

Ali glared, but relaxed into a sigh.

'I ought to have you beheaded for daring to insult me,' he said. 'But you'd only come back as a ghost and lecture me. Now be quiet and cover your face. We're nearly there.'

A few minutes later they swept beneath a huge archway and up to a broad flight of steps where several men in robes were waiting. One of them pulled open the car door.

'Remain here,' Ali commanded, and Fran stayed in her seat.

As he walked away someone else got into the car,

which moved off immediately. It was a tall woman, who removed her veil.

'I am Rasheeda,' she said. 'I am to take you to your apartments.'

She reached out and unhooked Fran's veil, fixing a long, hard look on her face. Her lips pursed critically, as though she disapproved of what she saw, and Fran began to feel that this was rather rude. But she concealed her indignation. With Ali's authority behind her, she had nothing to fear.

The car seemed to move for a long time, and she sensed that they were travelling right round to the back of the palace. Just before it came to a halt Rasheeda replaced her own veil, and nodded to Fran to do the same.

'Follow me,' she said as she left the car.

The way led up a flight of stairs, less ornate than at the front, and into a long, tiled corridor that was mercifully cool. In the few minutes between the car and the building Fran had felt the heat of the day that was rising fast. She breathed out, and Rasheeda gave her a quick glance.

'In your apartment you will find servants ready to make you comfortable,' she said.

'Thank you. You were expecting me, then?'

Rasheeda shrugged. 'We are always prepared for one more.'

It seemed a curious thing to say, but after puzzling it for a moment Fran shrugged. She would find her way around in time.

She had little time to look around, except to see that the building was exactly her idea of a traditional eastern palace. But the next moment they came to a lift.

Rasheeda pressed a button and soon they were flying upwards.

They walked along another corridor, until they stopped outside a door, bearing the number 37, which she pushed open. Inside Fran found a luxurious apartment, opening onto a balcony. An archway led to an ornate bathroom, covered in elaborate mosaics. Dazed, she realised that every fitting was solid gold. Rasheeda followed her gaze.

'You are much favoured,' she said briefly. 'I will summon your maidservants to prepare your bath now. You must be tired from your journey.'

'I don't seem to have my bag,' Fran said. 'Will it get here soon?'

'You will not be needing it.'

'But I will. All my things are in there.'

'Everything you could possibly need is here. His Highness prefers that his concubines accept only from his hands.'

'Excuse me? Did you say concubines? Look, there's been some mistake. I'm not a concubine. I'm a journalist.'

'I do not know what word you use in the west to describe such a woman as yourself.'

'But didn't Ali tell you—?'

'His Highness,' Rasheeda said, emphasising the words, 'telephoned me from the plane, giving me precise instructions for your reception. I am his mistress of concubines. I have followed my master's orders, and that is the end of the matter.'

'It certainly is not,' Fran said wrathfully. 'Are you saying that he dared to put me with his—his—?'

'It is a great honour for you,' Rasheeda said coldly. 'He will be most displeased at your ingratitude.'

'He's not the only one displeased,' Fran said. 'I'm going to see him now, and he's going to hear about my displeasure.'

She ran to the door and tried to pull it open, but it stayed firmly shut.

'Open this door at once,' she raged.

'His Highness's orders are that you remain here,' Rasheeda said firmly. 'Until he can find the time for you.'

'And just how long is that likely to be?'

'How can I tell? A week? A month? He has important things to attend to first.'

'Does he think he can get away with this?'

'His Highness is all-powerful and does as he pleases.'

Fran cast her a look of fury and ran past her, out onto the balcony.

'Help!' she cried. 'Help!'

She was four storeys up. Far below her stretched out a vast carpet of flowers and lawns. One or two men, presumably gardeners, glanced up at the sound of her voice, looked at each other, shrugged, and returned to their work.

Fran turned back into the room. The terrible truth was beginning to dawn on her. It was impossible, and yet, in her heart, she'd known that Ali was capable of anything, no matter how outrageous.

Rasheeda was standing beside the door.

'I shall leave you now,' she said, 'and send your attendants when you are more composed.'

She opened the door and quickly retreated. Fran made a desperate run, but she was too far away. By the time she reached the door it was already closed and locked. She hammered at it frantically.

'Let me out,' she cried. 'Let me out. You've got no right to do this!'

She listened, but there was only silence. She hammered again, harder this time.

'Let me out! *Let me out*!'

There was no response. She was left alone as the full horror of her situation dawned on her.

Ali had never meant to give her an interview. To him she was merely a woman who had dared to outwit him, and must be taught a lesson. He had tricked her into coming here, and now she was his prisoner, friendless, alone, with nobody to hear her cries.

In this country where he was all-powerful he might wreak what vengeance he pleased on her, and there was nothing she could do about it.

CHAPTER FIVE

WHEN she'd calmed down a little Fran began to explore her surroundings. Clearly there was no escape from the balcony, but she might find some other way.

She investigated her bathroom which, at any other time, would have delighted her with its luxury. The bath was sunk into the floor, and the smooth marble was delicious to the touch.

The main room was also opulent, with lavish hangings and a large bed, covered with rich crimson brocade and thick cushions. There were several doors, but they all led to closets. The only way out was by the main door, which was firmly locked. Fran groaned to think how stupidly she'd walked, wide-eyed, into what anyone could have seen was a trap.

And yet how could she possibly have anticipated such an outrageous action? In the modern world people just didn't do this kind of thing!

But Ali Ben Saleem wasn't a modern man. He was a sovereign ruler with absolute power, and he felt free to do exactly as he pleased.

She heard a key turn in the lock and looked up quickly, but it wasn't Ali. Two girls, dressed in the plain garb of maids, entered and inclined their heads respectfully towards her. One of them glided into the bathroom and began to run water into the sunken bath. Fran silenced her instinctive rebellion. She felt hot, sticky and tired, and the idea of a bath was suddenly very attractive.

The water was deliciously scented. Fran sank down into it and began to soap herself. Outwardly she was acquiescent. Inwardly she was planning just what she would say to Ali when she saw him. But when would that be? Rasheeda had hinted that she might be left here for a long time before that happened.

When she was ready to climb out of the bath the two maids held up a white towel to wrap around her. She finished drying and looked around for her clothes. There was no sign of the plain green tunic she had worn to enter the country.

Instead, one of the maids made a smiling gesture to some elaborate robes in peacock-blue that were hung up ready for her.

'I'd rather wear my own clothes,' Fran said firmly. 'They're in my bag. Where is it, please?'

One of the maids frowned. 'Bag is missing,' she said. 'These are your clothes.'

'Oh, no, they're not. If your master thinks he's going to dress me as one of his fancy women, he can think again!'

'Please,' the maid begged, 'do not speak disrespectfully of master.'

'I'll say a few disrespectful things to his face when I see him. I want my bag.'

They stared at her blankly.

Against all reason Fran dug her heels in. 'I'll wear my own clothes or nothing,' she said firmly.

Turning her back on them, she sat down on one of the heavily cushioned sofas, pulling the towel around her, and wishing it were larger.

Behind her she could hear whispering, as though the maids were conferring together about how best to cope with her rebellion.

'I am not giving in about this,' she said, as decisively as she could manage.

'That's my Diamond,' said an amused voice.

Fran leapt up and whirled around. Ali stood there, arms akimbo, regarding her sardonically. The maids had vanished.

'You!' she said angrily. 'How dare you?'

Ali grinned. 'How dare I what?'

How dared he stand there looking so handsome, and so assured? That was the thought that scorched across her brain before she could stop it, but she quickly substituted, How dared he behave so disgracefully?

'If this is your idea of a joke, then it's misfired badly,' she said with dignity.

'Tell me.' He folded his arms and regarded her.

'I'm here to write a story—the one you promised me. You thought it would be very funny to dump me in this place and lock the door. All right. It was funny. But now it's "joke over" time and I want to start getting serious.'

He looked her up and down, taking in the towel and the bits of her that it left uncovered. It reached only just to the top of her thighs. At the upper edge it was twisted into a makeshift knot just above her breasts, but with every breath she took Fran could feel it threatening to come loose. She put a protective hand over the knot, wishing Ali would stop looking at her in a way that showed he understood the danger as well as she did.

'But I am serious,' he said at last. 'Diamond, for a woman who prides herself on having a brain, you are easily deluded. I told you once there would be no interview and no story. I haven't budged from that position, and you were naive to imagine that I would.'

She heard the words but could hardly take in their meaning. It was simply too monstrous. 'You—never meant to talk to me?' she breathed.

'Not for a moment. Money, business, politics—these things are not the concern of women. I told you that, but you wouldn't believe me.'

'You lured me here on false pretences. You had no right—'

'But you should have guessed that I'd do something like this. You knew I was the kind of man who would never forgive an injury.' He took a step closer, looking down at her. For a moment there was a hint of menace in his soft voice. 'How foolish of you to forget that.'

'What injury? I've never harmed you.'

'You forced my hand over the cheque. That stung my pride.'

'Your pride!' she scoffed.

His voice changed, became harder. 'The ruler of a country must be a man of pride. If not, he is unfit to rule. I could not allow an insult to go unpunished. You invaded my home in disguise—two disguises if you include the night we met. You thought you were very clever, but you weren't as clever as you imagined. I decided it was time you had a lesson in reality.'

'Reality?' she echoed, hardly able to believe her ears. 'You call this reality? Putting me with your concubines?'

'You have only yourself to blame. You challenged me, and I took up your challenge. The next move is yours.'

'Yes, and it will be, when people start asking questions about my disappearance.'

'But when will that be? You told me yourself, nobody knows you came to work under cover in my house. Your friend Joey is away on another job. You have no family. Who will know that you are gone?'

'And bringing me here on someone else's passport...?' she whispered.

Ali nodded. 'Nobody will know that you have left the country, much less where you are.'

With mounting anger she realised the full horror of her situation.

'All those questions you asked me last night about how I was going to tell my confederates?—you were checking whether it was safe to kidnap me. You were planning this then.'

'I'm a man of foresight.'

She made one last attempt.

'Ali, this has gone far enough. I want my bag, my clothes, and I want to get out of here.'

He laughed softly. 'Oh, my Diamond, you are wonderful. You have no weapons, you are completely helpless in my power. Yet you speak with such authority, as though you had only to command and I must obey. I tremble in my shoes.'

'I don't believe this,' she said in a shaking voice. 'I'm dreaming, and I'll wake up soon.'

'I wish you the sweetest of dreams, and I hope they will all be of me. But when you awake you will still be here. And you will remain here, at my pleasure, until I decide otherwise.'

'You're utterly mad,' she breathed. 'You must be, to imagine that you can turn me into a concubine— number 37!'

He laughed. 'Well, I have to admit that I don't actually have thirty-seven. This is simply the only room with a lock on the door. The others don't have to be locked in. They enjoy serving their country.'

'Well, this isn't my country, and I have no intention of serving it in your bed,' Fran said emphatically. 'If the others are so keen, why not stick to them?'

'If you knew how often I've asked myself the same question. But you tease and provoke me as they do not.'

As he spoke he placed the back of one finger on her shoulder, and trailed it down the length of her arm. The touch was light, almost imperceptible, but it was enough to send tremors through her whole body. When he removed his hand she could still feel the tingling all down her arm.

She took a deep breath, trying to stop herself from shaking. It dismayed her to discover that her physical response to Ali was as intense as ever, even now when she was furiously angry with him. Of course he'd counted on that. He expected her to collapse before his male potency, and if it was the last thing she did she would prove him wrong. She lifted her head and met his eyes defiantly.

'I demand that you release me,' she said.

'Magnificent,' Ali murmured. 'At this moment I admire you more than ever.'

'Did you hear what I said?'

'Of course I heard, as I hear the splash of rain on the windows. I hear the sound, but it doesn't stop me in my course.' He lifted her chin. 'Be patient, Diamond. Did I not tell you that the pleasure lies in the anticipation? And we have much to look forward to. When the moment comes, we will be as no man and woman have ever been before.'

It was hard to deny it when his fingertips were stroking her mouth, but she forced herself.

'That will never happen,' she said. 'I refuse. If you

think that this—' she made a sweeping gesture around the room '—and all your power makes any difference, you're fooling yourself.'

He laughed softly. 'I think you'll find that it does make a difference. But fight me if you like. It will only make my eventual victory the sweeter.' He sighed ruefully. 'Let's hope that affairs of state don't detain me too long, and I can find time for you soon.'

She stared as his incredible meaning sank in. Then something in her snapped.

'No!' she screamed. *'No!'*

Evading his grasp, she darted to the door and began to hammer on it. 'Somebody—help!'

In a flash he was with her, putting both arms around her and lifting her off the floor to carry her into the middle of the room. She thrashed and kicked but his grasp was unbreakable, and all she achieved was to loosen the towel, which began to slip away from her.

'Let me go!' she screamed. *'Let me—'*

The sound was cut off by his mouth over hers, in the most ruthless kiss he had ever given her. It was not a caress but an assertion of dominance, silencing her completely. She put out all her strength to resist him. She would not let herself be kissed like this.

But he kissed her anyway, as never before. Their other kisses had been like fencing matches, with the power evenly balanced. This time he was determined to overcome her. The towel fell, unnoticed, to the floor, and he was holding her naked body in his arms, while his lips told her silently that she belonged to him, whatever she might say.

When he felt her still trying to struggle he murmured, 'Don't be foolish, my Diamond. You could overcome me more easily than you know, but not by force. You have weapons that could enslave a man.'

He turned her in his arms, putting a hand under her knees and raising her to carry her to the bed. Without removing his mouth from hers he lowered her onto the satin cushions. She clung to him, perhaps to steady herself, perhaps because she couldn't do anything else.

She became aware that his embrace had changed. The fierceness had gone out of it, leaving behind only tenderness, and coaxing. Something deep in her took fright at that coaxing. It contained a greater power than any threat. His lips were seductive, teasing her into compliance, persuading her that there was nothing she wanted to do but this.

He left her mouth and began to kiss her down the length of her neck, then down further to the place between her breasts. He lingered a moment, and Fran knew he must be able to feel the hammering of her heart.

'Does your heart beat with love or hate, Diamond?' he whispered.

'With hate,' she managed to say.

'And mine?' He took her hand and placed it over his own heart, which was beating as strongly as her own. 'What of mine? Is that love or hate you feel there?'

'Neither,' she gasped. 'All you want is possession.'

'Perhaps. There has never been a woman I wanted to possess as much as you, or for whom I would take such risks. Ask whatever you will of me.'

'Let me go,' she said fiercely.

The words stopped him in his tracks. He released her and drew back, his face a cold mask.

'You ask the impossible,' he grated. 'It's time you faced the truth. You'll stay here until I'm satisfied.'

'And when will that be?'

A strange, distant look came into his eyes, as though he was communicating with a vision only he could see.

'When you yield to me completely, in your heart as well as your body. When you say that you are mine for all time and desire only to remain with me. Then, and only then, will I be satisfied.'

Moving quickly, he rose and backed away.

'But I won't stay here,' she raged. 'I'll escape and expose you to the world.'

She was talking to a closed door.

Fran was too intelligent to keep fighting the same battle with the same discredited weapons. So she calmed her temper and assumed an attitude of compliance, to hide her inner rebellion and her determination to escape.

She realised she was exhausted. She hadn't slept the night before. Now she was determined to keep up her strength, so she slipped between the sheets of the lavish bed, and slept the sleep of the jet-lagged.

When she awoke her maids were present, bowing and smiling, and indicating a meal that was ready for her. It was a meal for an honoured guest—veal and apricots, followed by stuffed dates and wine. It was delicious and she realised that she was very hungry.

While she'd slept her bag had been returned to her. Diving into it, she discovered that something was missing. Her notebooks and Dictaphone machine were there, but not her mobile phone.

So, no chance to call for help.

The maid who understood some English, and whose name was Leena, explained that the rest of the afternoon would be taken up by a visit from a maker of materials, who would produce samples for her choice.

'Then make—to your liking,' she said.

Fran would have liked to say that she wasn't going to be here long enough to make a new wardrobe necessary, but she merely nodded and smiled. An appearance of agreement was simply part of the role she was playing for the moment.

But her pose was shaken when the merchant appeared and tossed bolt after bolt of fabric at her feet, until the floor was covered with a myriad colours.

'Where do I start?' she gasped.

'My master says—everything you wish,' Leena said, smiling.

Fran pulled herself together. She absolutely would not let herself weaken because of a few bolts of silk, even if one of them was guaranteed to highlight her eyes, and another would bring a peachy glow to her skin.

Since it was clearly expected of her she ran her hands over the material, feeling the luxurious sensation against her skin. It was her undoing. Suddenly she was a teenager again, pressing her nose against the shop window, yearning for the clothes within. Only this time someone had removed the window, and the clothes were hers.

A subtle intelligence had been at work here. Somebody understood what would make her weaken—if anything could. She would select only the bare minimum.

Two hours later the merchant departed jubilantly,

with the largest order he'd ever been given, even from the palace.

Fran was left aghast, wondering what had come over her. It wasn't just the material, but the fortune in jewels that Leena had calmly ordered to be sewn into the garments. When Fran had asked if these were real jewels Leena had been shocked. As though the Prince of Kamar would give anything less!

'But of course these are only little jewels,' she had explained. 'The master will present you with the big ones himself.'

'The—big ones?' Fran had said, dazed.

'You are to be greatly honoured. He has said so.'

Honoured with everything but my freedom, Fran thought.

But she held her tongue. When she next saw Ali she would have plenty to say.

It was early evening. Fran went out onto the balcony and watched the last few minutes of daylight before the light vanished and it was pitch-dark, almost as though somebody had thrown a switch.

Even in her present mood she had to admit that this was a magic place at night. Below her were the palace gardens, hung with a thousand coloured lamps, glowing against the velvety blackness. Beyond that was the city, with its own lights, hinting at a rich, busy life. From somewhere below the sound of music floated up to her.

Looking down, she could see the paths that criss-crossed in the garden, and the figures that strolled in the blessed cool of the evening. One of them might almost have been Ali.

She peered at the tall figure in the white robes and gold agal. She couldn't see his face, but his bearing

and the way he moved made her sure that it was Ali.
He was talking to someone by his side, someone
smaller, whose head was covered and who might have
been a woman…

Fran didn't even realise that she'd tensed, leaning
forward a little more, and a little more, until the figure
turned—and she saw his beard. Then she discovered
that she was gripping the rail with all her strength. She
released it, feeling the waves of relief wash through
her so fiercely that she felt faint.

To make it worse, Ali looked up at that moment.
She stepped away so that he shouldn't catch her look-
ing at him. But she was sure he would have seen her.
She turned quickly back into the room.

To pass the time she pulled out some of the books
she found on a shelf near her bed. They were in
English, and all about Kamar.

She had already learned a good deal about the country in her preparation for the feature, but this book
concentrated more on the men who had shaped the
principality.

Kamar was barely sixty years old. It had become a
self-governing state because one determined man,
Najeeb, had appeared out of the desert, sat himself and
his tribe down on the first oil well, and refused to
budge. He was the man the oil companies had had to
deal with, and when he'd declared himself sovereign
it had been easier not to argue.

He didn't sound a very pleasant man, Fran thought,
but he'd had vision, courage, determination and obsti-
nacy. He'd been Ali's grandfather.

His son, Najeeb the second, had made money easily
and spent it easily. He'd had two sons, who had quar-
relled for the throne, and the younger, Saleem, had

triumphed. Saleem had opened up Kamar to modern technology, and seemed to have been an enlightened ruler.

The photographs showed men with curiously similar faces, fierce, hard, seeming to look out on far desert horizons. They all had a noticeable unyielding quality about the mouth and chin, the same quality Fran had seen in Ali's face. He came from a line of men who were ruthless by nature, and also because ruthlessness was the only thing that paid. And he was one of them.

She was suddenly unwilling to read any more. She closed the book sharply. At once Leena was on her feet, urging that it was time to retire. Fran agreed.

It seemed that Leena would stay with her, sleeping on a small truckle bed, in case she should want anything during the night. Fran's attempts to shoo her away proved fruitless, so she resigned herself. And when she awoke in the early hours, with a parched throat, it was pleasant to have someone make her some herbal tea that sent her back to a dreamless sleep.

CHAPTER SIX

In the morning Leena had a surprise for her.

'We can go to the bazaar and do some shopping, if it is your wish,' she suggested.

So she wasn't to be kept locked in the palace all the time, Fran reflected. Perhaps while she was out she would find a chance to contact the British ambassador.

The maids dressed her in the peacock robes, and set the matching turban on her head. The veil was connected to one side of this, and could be drawn across her face to be hooked onto the other side.

Outside the door she found four large men waiting, their arms folded.

'They are your guard of honour,' Leena explained.

'Oh, I see,' Fran said wryly.

A stretch limousine waited below. One of the guards drove, the other three settled into the first compartment. Fran and Leena went into the second compartment. The car began to draw away.

But before they had travelled a couple of yards there was the sound of footsteps outside and one of the doors to the rear compartment was wrenched open. Next moment, a man had settled himself on the seat facing Fran, and pulled the door shut.

'Get out!' shrieked Leena. Then her hands flew to her mouth and she whispered, 'My lord!'

It wasn't Ali but a young man who resembled him, except that his expression was lighter and his eyes twinkled with merriment.

'I couldn't resist having a look at my cousin's latest acquisition,' he said cheerfully.

'Your veil,' Leena gasped to Fran.

'Too late, I've seen her face now,' the young man said. He smiled at Fran. 'I am Prince Yasir, Ali's cousin. Tell me, are the stories true? Did Ali really pay a hundred thousand for you?'

'Pay?' Fran gasped.

'That's what the rumours say. Most women don't come so expensive. I've never paid more than thirty thousand myself, but Ali acquires only the best, and I can see you're something out of the ordinary.'

'Get out of here at once!' Fran exploded. 'Go on! Get out before I kick you out.'

Leena shrieked, but the young man merely roared with laughter. 'And with the spirit of the devil. You were worth every penny. Goodbye—until we meet again.'

The next moment he opened the door and jumped out while the car was still moving.

'He is a prince,' Leena moaned, 'and you threatened him. The royal displeasure will fall on us.'

'Nonsense!' Fran said robustly. 'How dare he suggest that I was bought?'

'But everyone says you cost Prince Ali a hundred thousand,' Leena protested.

'He gave that much to charity because—that is—to please me,' Fran said, choosing her words carefully.

Leena gasped. 'Then he must value you greatly.'

So now she knew how she was regarded here, Fran thought: as a high-priced acquisition, on a level with a jewel or a racehorse. No doubt Ali saw her in the same light.

Then she forgot her indignation in her excitement

at being in the bazaar. As the limousine glided through the streets people backed away and bowed to the royal flag, although the darkened windows meant that they couldn't see inside. They drew to a halt. Leena settled Fran's veil back in place, and they stepped out of the car.

She gasped as she felt the noonday sun beating down on her. But when she'd had a few minutes to accustom herself she enjoyed the heat, the brilliant light and the dazzling colours. If this had been a holiday she would have revelled in it. As it was, the guard of honour constantly reminded her that she was a prisoner, although an honoured one.

Since she could order anything she wanted at the palace, there was little for her to buy in the street, but she chose a pair of white doves, whose cooing and friendly ways enchanted her. The vendor assured her, through Leena, that no cage was necessary.

'Win their love, and they will stay with you,' he promised.

'He means they will fly back to him and he can sell them again,' Leena said indignantly. 'We'll have a cage.'

'No,' Fran said. 'No cage.'

Leena started to argue, but Fran silenced her. She took a bag of food from the vendor, and used it to entice the doves into the car. As they got in, Fran could see the driver talking into the car phone. She discovered why when she reached her room to find a dovecote already set up on the balcony.

To her delight the doves seemed pleased with their new home, and showed no inclination to fly away.

'Not like me,' she murmured to them. 'I'll fly at the first opportunity.'

There was a light snack, then Leena seemed mysteriously anxious for Fran to take a nap. But she refused to say why this was so important, until Fran had awoken and was taking a cooling bath.

'What's that?' she demanded as Leena poured a sweet-smelling lotion into the water. Eyes closed, she breathed it in, and instantly strange thoughts began to float through her mind. It was a heady, erotic scent, hinting of passion incited and fulfilled. It was a perfume for lovers, and she breathed it in with relish.

Then abruptly she opened her eyes, assailed by suspicion. 'I'm getting out of here,' she said firmly, and climbed out of the tub. 'And when I've had supper I'm going to bed for a very early night.'

'But I have to prepare you for the master. He has chosen you to be his companion tonight. You are most honoured among women.'

'Fiddlesticks!' Fran said shortly. 'If you think I'm going to let you do me up like a turkey being prepared for the table, you're very much mistaken.'

'But it is the custom,' Leena wailed. 'To be chosen by the great lord is the finest thing that can happen to a concubine.'

'I'm not a concubine!'

'The chosen one is bowed down with honour.'

'Not this chosen one!' Fran snapped. 'I'm not going to be bowed down with anything. I shall go with my head up, look him in the eye and tell him what I think of him.'

'But properly attired,' Leena begged. 'Or I am in trouble.'

'Very well. Only for your sake.'

The seamstresses had worked through the night and the first of Fran's new clothes was ready. It was a marvel in pale fawn satin and brocade, with a wide, jewel-encrusted sash around the tiny waist. Over it was a tunic of diaphanous silk gauze, also glittering with jewels. When the matching turban was in place Fran drew a disbelieving breath at the sight of the Arab beauty who looked back at her from the mirror.

Ali seemed to be there with her, whispering 'I told you so', his eyes glowing with desire...

She drew a sharp breath and castigated herself. She was furious with Ali, set on leaving him at the first chance and never seeing him again. She must remember that.

The door opened and Rasheeda entered. It was the first time Fran had seen the mistress of concubines since the first day. Rasheeda regarded her loftily, then nodded her approval. Leena visibly relaxed.

From outside the door came the melancholy, mysterious sound of a horn being blown.

'Your litter is here,' Rasheeda said, adjusting Fran's veil. 'You will travel inside it to His Highness's apartments, and I will walk ahead proclaiming your coming. When you see the prince, remember to bow low and say, ''Your humble servant greets you, my lord.'' Do not meet his eyes unless he tells you to. To look at him without his permission is a grave offence. Do you understand?'

'I understand,' Fran said, breathing hard.

Rasheeda opened the door, four large men carried a curtained litter inside, and set it down. Leena parted the curtains for Fran to step in, closed the curtains firmly again, and they were on their way.

The litter was carried by men chosen for their size and strength. The inside was fitted with gold, inlaid with rubies and emeralds, and furnished with gold satin. The sides were shielded by curtains of white and gold brocade.

The journey seemed to take for ever. Shut away behind the curtains, Fran could only guess what was happening. In front of her she could hear the sound of the horn, followed by Rasheeda crying out words in Arabic.

She spent the time trying to sort out her thoughts and prepare what she was going to say to Ali. It would be like him, she thought crossly, not to be there when she arrived.

But he was there. She heard him speaking to the bearers, then the sound of feet retreating, the door closing.

'You can get out now,' came Ali's amused voice.

Fran leapt out of the litter and looked around for him, but Ali had retreated to a safe distance and was watching her with laughing eyes. Fran snatched away her veil and faced him.

'If you have the nerve to think that "your humble servant" is going to bow to you—'

'But I don't,' he said, laughing. 'That's why I took the precaution of making sure we were alone first. If my servants had seen you greet me disrespectfully I should have had to cast you into a snakepit, which would rather have spoiled our evening.'

Fran regarded him. 'How dare you send for me as though you had only to snap your fingers and I must jump to attention?' she seethed.

'But I'm afraid that's exactly true,' Ali said apologetically. 'I appreciate that you are unfamiliar with this arrangement, but don't worry. You'll get used to it.'

'Not in a million years!'

'Will you and I be provoking each other for a mil-

lion years, my Diamond? What a wonderful prospect.'
His eyes smiled at her, in a way that almost made her
forget her anger. 'How beautiful you are!'

'Don't try to change the subject.'

'To me, your beauty is always the subject. How
your eyes enthral me!' He deftly removed the turban,
letting her hair fall freely about her shoulders, and
running his hands through it. 'And your hair! How I
have dreamed of your hair!' He drew her into his arms.
'And of your lips,' he said, covering them.

A thousand answers jostled in her brain, but with
her mouth engaged with his possessive kisses she
could make none of them. She tried to hold onto rational thought, but she was just realising that she had
secretly longed for his embrace. Throughout all her
justified indignation, that yearning had been there, like
a subtle, endlessly repeated chord. Now she had what
her flesh wanted and her mind resisted.

'Tell me,' he whispered, 'haven't you dreamed of
me, just a little?'

'Yes,' she said, and watched the eager light come
into his eyes. 'I've dreamed of how I was going to
make you very, very sorry. I enjoyed those dreams.'

'How hard-hearted you are!' he chided her softly.

'I'm—?'

Whatever else she was going to say was cut off by
his mouth on hers. She should have been ready for
him, but nothing could have prepared her for the
scorching intensity with which he caressed her lips
again and again, until she gasped from the sensation.

'Such a battle we will have,' he whispered. 'And
how we will enjoy the victory!'

'Whose victory?'

'When we lie in each other's arms it will be a victory for both of us. Otherwise it will not be a true loving. We must look to the night ahead with joy.'

'We—'

'But for a while we must wait,' he added, releasing her. 'Passion, like many things, must be deferred so that it's full savour can be appreciated. Try to be a little patient.'

Fran was speechless. To give herself the relief of exercise she began to pace Ali's apartment, which was stupendous in its luxury. It was a kind of labyrinth, with horseshoe arches leading off in all directions. The mosaics on the walls were inlaid with intricately worked gold that gleamed richly in the soft light.

They were in a large room with several tables, laden with every possible variety of food. Instead of chairs, long couches were strewn around, as though for an orgy. But there were just the two of them.

'It's shocking, isn't it?' Ali said, reading her face.

'Yes, it is,' she responded indignantly. 'Nobody has the right to live like this when there are people starving.' She studied one of the walls and added, 'It looks new.'

'You sound as though that made it worse.'

'It does. If this was an old palace I might—'

'Forgive me?'

'Understand the need. I mean, if it's there anyway—but building from scratch—all that money—'

'Blame my great-grandfather, Najeeb. He built the first palace, but it wasn't big enough, so his son had to build this one.'

'The first palace?'

'I love you when your eyes pop with virtuous indignation. Come out onto the balcony and I'll show you the Sahar Palace. It's called that because Sahar means dawn, and with its high tower it catches the dawn sun before any other building.'

His balcony looked out over the city. Following his pointing finger, she just made out Sahar Palace. It was hard because the building was in darkness. Simply abandoned, she thought crossly. Her fingers itched to get at her Dictaphone and make notes of the waste and extravagance in this country. Luckily her memory was excellent.

'Can you put your puritan scruples aside long enough to eat something?' Ali asked, taking her hand and leading her to where a banquet was laid out on long tables decked with flowers.

'I hope the food is to your liking,' he said, pointing to one dish.

'Chicken with dates and honey,' Fran said in wonder.

'I promised that we would have your favourite dish the next time we dined together. Who would have thought it would be under such circumstances?'

'You would. You had this planned all the time.'

'Oh, no. Not until you threw down the gauntlet. I had no choice but to take it up. You insulted me, and you couldn't be allowed to get away with it.'

'Aren't you ashamed of yourself, seeking revenge?' she challenged. 'Only petty men do that.'

He laughed. 'In your country, maybe. But here a man who doesn't take revenge for an insult cannot hold up his head.'

'On a woman?'

He shrugged. 'The insult came from a woman. And, since a thousand women cannot be the equal of one man, a man who lets himself be bested by a woman is truly disgraced.'

She was about to explode when she saw his eyes twinkling at her, as though he knew exactly what she expected, and was playing up to it. And she remembered just what a very clever man Ali was. She was moving through a strange dream, where every reference was moved, the impossible became real and the solid ground dissolved beneath her feet. And he understood it all.

As he had done the first night, he handed her to her seat, and served her himself.

'It's a good thing your servants can't see you doing that,' she observed. 'I'm sure it's beneath your dignity to serve a woman.'

'*Touché*. But, as you are constantly reminding me, you are like no other woman.'

'No, I'm worth a good deal more, aren't I?' she riposted, remembering a grievance. 'I gather thirty thousand is the going rate.'

'Ah, yes, you've met my cousin. He's an engaging rascal, but he has no sense of responsibility. He acts first and thinks afterwards. He'd like me to give him a share in running the country, but he'll have to grow up first. It was improper of him to force himself on you this morning.'

'And see me without my veil; don't forget that.' She added primly, 'I nearly fainted with horror.'

He laughed at her irony. 'Yes, I guessed your delicate sensibilities would be offended.'

'My sensibilities were offended by discovering that you've let everyone think that a hundred thousand was my purchase price, as though I were one of your racehorses.'

'Certainly not!' Ali said, shocked. 'A first-class racehorse costs far more than that.'

Fran threw up her hands in despair. 'There's no talking to you.'

He grinned and filled her wine glass.

For the moment she gave up trying to bring him to a sense of his iniquity. The food was splendid, she knew she looked beautiful, and she was with the most attractive man she had ever met. It was useless to deny that, even if he was her enemy. And it was hard to think of him as an enemy when his eyes danced at her over his glass and told her that she entranced him.

'Come,' he said, when they had finished eating. 'I have something for you to see.'

He took her hand and led her to a chest that stood near the window. He flung it open and she gasped at the treasure that lay within. Rubies, emeralds, diamonds, pearls, gold and silver lay there, jumbled together.

Ali lifted a necklace of emeralds set in gold and held it up before her eyes.

'You have the kind of colouring that can wear all jewels,' he said. 'Diamonds and pearls, as well as rubies and emeralds. Today I think it will be emeralds; tomorrow—'

'Nothing,' Fran said. 'Neither today nor tomorrow. I won't take anything from you, Ali, because I have nothing to give back.'

She looked at him levelly. She wanted no misunderstanding.

He sighed. 'Why do you fight what is between us?'

'Because I'm here by force. As long as I'm a prisoner, there is nothing between us.'

'You're a hard, unforgiving woman—'

'I'm a *free* woman.' She tapped her breast. 'Free in

my heart, where it counts. In here I have something that you'll never conquer by force or trickery.'

Before she could say more the door was flung open and someone strode into the room. Fran started at the sight of Prince Yasir. His face was flushed, and he seemed on the verge of losing control.

Ali's face darkened, and he said something in Arabic that sounded like a command. Yasir replied in the same tongue, obviously furious. He pointed to Fran, and held up two, then three fingers. She stared at him, wondering if she'd understood properly, and which of them she was angrier with if she had.

Ali was clearly giving a refusal, and Yasir's temper increased. Ali made a gesture of finality. Yasir pointed at Fran and held up four fingers.

'You do and you're dead!' she muttered.

'Don't worry,' Ali replied coolly. 'When I sell you, I shall demand much more than four times the original price.'

'How much?' Yasir demanded at once. 'For her I pay whatever you ask.'

He reached for Fran, who drew back a fist in readiness. But Ali was there before her. The next moment Yasir was reeling back against the wall, rubbing his chin.

Ali gave him no chance to recover. Seizing Yasir's collar, he hauled him to the door and threw him out. He turned back into the room before the look in his eyes had changed, and Fran backed away, astounded at what she saw there. Ali was ready to commit murder.

In two steps he was beside her, pulling her into his arms.

'He dared to offer me money for you,' he grated. 'He thinks money can buy anything.'

'Not me,' she said breathlessly. 'Neither his nor yours.'

She wasn't sure that he heard her. His eyes were searching her with the brooding intensity of a man who'd seen a prize almost snatched from him, but had recovered it in time.

'From the moment I first saw you I knew you had to be mine,' he murmured. 'I can wait no longer.'

She stiffened in alarm. She had resolved not to yield, and if she didn't assert herself now it would be too late.

'Ali, let me go,' she breathed.

'Never in life. You're mine, and you'll be mine for ever.'

The prospect was seductively sweet. For a moment her senses swam. To give him all of herself on a tide of passion, if only…

Putting out all her strength, she broke from him and turned away quickly.

'This isn't going to happen,' she gasped.

Ali's eyes kindled as he reached for her, and Fran knew he was at danger point. There was only one thing to do. Throwing caution to the winds, she fended him off and boxed his ears hard enough to make his eyes water.

It was safe to assume that no woman had ever treated his royal person in such a way before. Ali was motionless through sheer astonishment.

'You forced me,' Fran said breathlessly.

'You—'

'Don't look at me like that.' She swiftly put a table

between them. 'It was your own fault for not acting like a gentleman.'

'I don't have to be a gentleman,' he snapped. 'I'm the prince.'

'That's where you're wrong. The prince should always be a gentleman.'

Ali breathed hard. 'You picked a wonderful time to start lecturing me. Your recklessness will lead you into trouble one day.'

'One day? What do you think this is? So now what happens? Do I get thrown into a dungeon for daring to strike the prince?'

'Don't tempt me,' Ali said through gritted teeth. He turned sharply away, less he see the confusion in his eyes as he brought his temper under control. When he felt he could speak calmly he turned back and regarded her with frosty eyes.

'*Now* will you release me?' Fran demanded.

'Release you?' he echoed in amazement. 'After this?' He took a long, hard breath. 'Much as I would like to let you feel the full weight of my displeasure, I have to approach the matter more subtly. Tomorrow you will be taken to a different apartment.'

'Aha!' she said triumphantly. 'The dungeon!'

Ali gritted his teeth. 'Your new apartment will be of the greatest comfort and luxury. You will have eight maidservants with instructions to attend to your every whim. Wherever you go, people will bow. I shall shower you with jewels, which you will wear at all times.'

'What is this?' Fran demanded suspiciously. 'If you're hoping to change my mind, let me tell you—'

'From this moment you are my official favourite,

entitled to the special treatment of one who has exerted herself to please me.'

'But I didn't exert myself to please you. Nor will I, ever!'

'Well, if you think I want the world knowing *that*—!' he said savagely.

Fran stared at him, her jaw dropping as the implications of this washed over her.

'Oh, my goodness!' she breathed. 'You're caught, aren't you? You can't let anyone suspect that Prince Ali Ben Saleem had his face slapped by a woman he'd deigned to honour.' She gave a peal of laughter.

'If you don't stop that,' he grated, 'I really will throw you into a dungeon.'

'No, you won't,' she choked. 'It would give too much away. And after you paid all that money for me you wouldn't want people to know that your judgement was slipping. Oh, heavens! This is wonderful!'

'That's enough!' There was real menace in his eyes this time. 'You're very sure of yourself, but suppose I decided to dispense with your consent? Who do you think would help you?'

She met his eyes, unafraid, defiant. 'You won't do that.'

'Let me remind you who I am, and what my powers are.'

'But that's why you won't,' she said breathlessly. 'It would be an admission of failure, an admission that you can't win me. Nobody else might know, but you and I would, and you couldn't live with that.'

His face was black with anger and she knew she'd touched a nerve.

'And there's another reason,' she added. 'You couldn't do it. You're a tyrant, a scheming manipulator and an arrogant, conceited dictator, but you're fundamentally a decent man, and it isn't in you.'

He regarded her. The fury had died out of his face but his eyes were still unforgiving.

'You have the tongue of a serpent,' he said bitterly. 'Let me warn you that a woman who can discern a man's weaknesses should have the good sense not to taunt him with them.'

'So you admit you have weaknesses? Well, that's a step in the right direction.'

'Does nothing make you afraid?' he snapped.

'Would I tell you?'

'Even you have weaknesses.'

'But perhaps I'm better at keeping them hidden.'

Ali breathed hard. 'To think that I—' He checked himself, on the verge of putting something into words that shocked him.

'That you what?'

'Nothing. But one day I shall have sons. And I shall tell them about women like you, and warn them to avoid such women like scorpions.'

'Pity someone didn't warn you,' Fran said affably. 'I think I'll be going now. Will you summon the bearers?'

'Are you mad?' he demanded. 'You can't leave before morning or the whole palace will know.'

'And your reputation will be shot to pieces,' she teased.

'Do you realise that you've condemned us to a night of making small talk?'

'You could give me that interview.'

'Be very careful!'

'All right, then I'm going to sit down and finish my

supper. And why shouldn't we make small talk? I'll bet you've never done that with a woman before.'

'Nonsense.'

'It isn't nonsense. You only have two attitudes to women—seductive and dismissive. But you can't seduce me and for a few hours you can't dismiss me, so you'll have to talk to me properly, about something that really matters.'

'I've told you I don't do that with women.'

'Exactly my point. So we seem to be faced with a long, boring night, chatting about the weather.'

He merely scowled and seated himself. When Fran poured him some wine he scowled again, but accepted it. She had a sudden conviction that he was longing to rub his cheek, but would die rather than let her see him do it.

Her lips twitched. On the face of it nothing had changed. She was still Ali's prisoner, subject to his power. But she had challenged that power, and discovered its limits, and her confidence was coming back.

CHAPTER SEVEN

'TELL me some more about Yasir,' Fran suggested.

'His father was my father's brother—his elder brother, unfortunately, so Yasir thinks that his father should have taken the throne, instead of mine.'

'Doesn't the eldest son take over automatically?'

'No. This part of the world is dangerous, and a ruler must be strong. My father was the stronger, so he took the throne as was his right. But Yasir feels that he, not I, should rule, and the result is a scene such as you saw tonight, for which I apologise. He had no right to burst in here, and I shall make sure he knows it.'

'I think he already does. Were you wise to strike him?'

'Most unwise. Luckily he's a good-natured fellow, and will forgive me easily.'

Fran decided to say no more. But she had seen a burning resentment in Yasir's expression that told her Ali had misread his cousin. She became thoughtful.

As she watched Ali's scowling countenance an imp of mischief was taking possession of her. It might be reckless and unwise, but that was in her nature. She'd never run from a risk.

'Something amuses you?' Ali growled.

'I was just thinking about the fix you're in.'

'Then I advise you to keep your amusement to yourself.'

'All right, I've got an idea. Let's go back to the

beginning, and talk as we might have done that first night, if I could have told you everything.'

'I thought you told me a good deal,' Ali said. He added with a touch of bitterness, 'But of course it was all invented—all those pretty stories about the Arabian nights were planted, because you thought they would entice me to indiscretions that you could make use of.'

'Oh, no,' she said quickly. 'That was all true. I told you things about myself I've never told anyone else, and I'd hate you to think—that, at least, was real. Please, Your Highness, you must believe me.'

He gave a twisted smile. 'I think we've got a little beyond "Your Highness".' This time he did rub his cheek, and actually managed to return her smile. There was a touch of ruefulness in his eyes that almost made her start to like him again. Almost. She must guard against his charm, she told herself.

'I told you those things because I knew you'd understand. Nobody else ever could. Uncle Dan and Aunt Jean thought only solid things mattered. They didn't have any time for "fancy ideas". At school I took supposedly useful, worthwhile subjects, like mathematics and computing, because they wanted me to. And when I turned out to be good at them I was kind of set on my path for ever. After that nobody ever thought of me as having a fanciful side—until you.

'It was a glorious release, being able to talk about those things after all these years. It was like somebody opened a door.'

'Yes,' Ali said quietly. He wished she wouldn't say these things that reminded him of his own feelings that night. The certainty that he'd found a sympathetic soul, able to understand him without words, had almost overwhelmed him. Suddenly his loneliness—the loneliness of a man who had everything except that which he truly wanted—had seemed to fade.

They had said very little, but that little had opened up long vistas of understanding. Her beauty and sexual charisma had heightened her magic, but been only a small part of it. He had ached to take her into his bed, but also into his heart.

When he'd been called away on business, he had cursed inwardly, and cut the call as short as he dared. But he'd never doubted that this woman whose soul spoke to his own would be waiting, still held in the enchantment that was woven around them both.

When he'd found her gone, it had been as though she'd punched him in the heart. He'd had no experience of rejection, and he'd felt like a young boy, floundering to get his bearings. He'd been compelled to hide his feelings and laugh it off, lest his servants suspect that a woman had mocked the Prince of Kamar. It had been a lesson in reality, and like all the lessons of his life it had taken place in a cruel spotlight.

Later, of course, he'd understood that she had never meant to go through with it. When she'd reappeared as a journalist he'd realised that it was a set-up from start to finish.

And now here she was, ostensibly in his power, yet still teasing and challenging him, still leaving him empty-handed. A man couldn't win with this woman, and that was something he had to alter.

Fran was still talking, apparently oblivious to his mood.

'After that it was just taken for granted that I'd go on taking useful subjects because I was good at them. So I went to college and did economics, which I must admit was fascinating.

'You wouldn't think stocks and shares and financial forecasts could be as thrilling as all that, but they were. And when I discovered that I had a ''nose'' for the markets that sealed my fate. I've got a friend who never buys new shares without calling to ask what I think.'

'Indeed!' Ali said coldly. 'A little more wine?'

'No, thank you. I want to tell you what they say about your companies on the Stock Exchange.'

'I'm not interested in what a woman has to say about my companies, or the London Stock Exchange.'

'I can tell you what they're saying in Wall Street too,' Fran went on, unperturbed, 'and the Bourse in France.'

'But I have no wish to hear.'

'I'm sure you haven't. But there's not a lot you can do about it, is there?' she asked lightly.

'You are making a big mistake,' he informed her.

Instead of answering in words Fran extended her index finger and beckoned to him. Her smile was enticing and her eyes full of mischief. Ali felt his head swim, and before he knew what he was doing he had leaned towards her. Fran came closer, and when she spoke her warm breath whispered against his face.

'It's very simple, my darling,' she murmured. 'If you don't let me say what I want, *and* pay attention, I shall scream for help at the top of my voice.'

'And do you think anyone will come?'

'Of course not. But they'll hear, and they'll know that you paid a hundred thousand for nothing.'

Ali drew a long breath, a prey to conflicting emotions. The skittering of her breath on his face was sending tremors through him, causing reactions that infuriated him. It was maddening to know that this woman could make him want her to madness as the very moment she was mocking him. She must be resisted and taught a lesson.

But she had called him 'my darling'.

'You,' he said with deliberation, 'are descended from a rattlesnake. Your father was a vulture. A man foolish enough to love you will end up with his heart shrivelled and his bones bleached white in the desert.'

'And you,' she returned, 'are making a big mistake in trusting Lemford Securities. The man who runs it lives on the edge. He's borrowing short and lending long, and I'm sure you know that's a recipe for disaster. Or don't you? Well, let me explain—'

'I can follow that kind of kindergarten economics,' he snapped.

'I'm so glad, because then maybe you can understand the rest.'

'I'm warning you—'

'And I'm warning you that the man in charge of your Wall Street operation isn't what he seems. He's changed his name several times to hide his involvement in some very dubious operation—'

'I have men whose job it is to discover this kind of information—'

'Then fire them, because they're letting you down. Take this.'

She took out the notebook that had been returned to her. Ali regarded her grimly.

'I never travel without it,' she told him, tearing off a sheet on which were written some internet addresses and giving it to him.

'Visit these sites,' she said. 'You'll learn enough about him to alarm you. But *you* do it. Don't delegate to someone else.' She was too absorbed in what she was saying to realise that she'd fallen into her efficient 'business' voice. But Ali realised it, and he bristled.

'Do you have any further orders for me?' he asked frostily.

'Don't you dare come the heavy sheikh with me,' she warned him. 'If you do what I say, I've just saved you a fortune.' She couldn't resist adding, 'Much more than my purchase price.'

'I wish you'd stop talking as though I'd bought you like a commodity.'

'It's the impression you strove to give. I'm merely taking up where you left off.'

Ali took the paper, meaning to toss it contemptuously away. But he didn't, and at heart he knew he wasn't going to.

Fran was too wise to press her point any further, and they finished the meal in light, meaningless conversation.

'It is late and you will be tired,' he observed, leading her into the room where his great bed stood. His eyes met hers. 'Nobody will disturb you.'

She almost had a moment of regret as she saw him walk away into a small side room. The door opened just enough to reveal that this was an office. Then it closed, shutting her out.

The bed was so large and so empty even when she lay down. It was a bed made for passion, where two people could forget the world in each other. And deep inside part of her wanted to do exactly that with this intriguing, fascinating and disturbing man. But it must not be. Not yet. Perhaps not ever.

She lay worrying at this dismaying thought, until she went to sleep.

He woke her as the sun was rising. He looked tired,

like a man who'd spent all night in front of a computer and on the telephone. He didn't volunteer anything, but she thought she detected a new look of respect in his eyes.

'Your bearers will be here in a moment,' he said, 'and they will return you to your quarters for the last time. Later today you will be escorted to your new apartments.'

He took her hand to lead her to the litter.

'Don't think this is the end of the matter,' he said. 'Our battle has moved onto new ground, but it is far from over. You're not as cold as you want me to think. Before I have finished, you will beg for my love.'

'In your dreams,' she said softly, and the bearers arrived before he could reply.

All that day the palace was in a bustle. Everyone knew that the prince had taken his new concubine to his bed, and enjoyed a night of passion with her such as no man had known before. Rumour said that this western woman was possessed of exotic arts that had won his heart and soul, and no reward was too great for her.

Nobody knew her true identity, but that was unimportant, as the prince's favourite had no life beyond his pleasure. He had decreed that henceforth she would be known as the Lady Almas Faiza.

Leena explained to Fran that Almas meant diamond, and Faiza meant victorious. Fran brooded over the intriguing word. Was Ali saying that she had scored a victory over him, or referring to the victory he was determined to have over her? But he had hinted also that they would find victory together, and, try as she might, Fran couldn't escape a thrill of anticipation at the thought of that joint victory.

With awe the servants prepared the lavish apartments that were kept for the favourite. The mosaics were washed, the floors polished, all the hangings were replaced, and the air was sweetly scented.

Finally came the ceremony without which her status would not be official. A litter was brought to her door. It was unlike the other one, in that it had no curtains or roof, for in this one she must be seen.

Gorgeously dressed and veiled, she seated herself and was raised high in the air on the shoulders of her bearers. Four maids positioned themselves in front and four behind. Two of them bore large bowls, piled with jewels. The favourite held out one graceful hand, and two snow-white doves fluttered out and settled on her arm. Rasheeda placed herself at the head of the procession and cried out something in Arabic, which Fran now knew meant, 'She who has been honoured approaches.' Then they were moving.

Right through the palace they travelled, through long corridors, broken by horseshoe arches, decorated with mosaics, inlaid with gold. Everywhere she looked there was gold, silver, mother-of-pearl. The ceilings were high and often lit by windows above, so that the atmosphere was pleasantly cool and light.

Then it was time to go into the first courtyard, which, although enclosed, was almost as large as a garden, filled with flowers and small trees. Here were the children of the many palace officials, with their mothers and nurses. They all laughed and greeted her, and the children tossed sweets which landed on her satin cushions.

At the far side of the courtyard they re-entered the palace. Men appeared bearing gifts, which the maids graciously accepted on her behalf. The gifts were of the finest and most costly, for everyone wanted to show their respect for Sheikh Ali by honouring his favourite.

Fran's eyes opened wide at the sight of a delicate sherbet set, made of gold and multicoloured glass, set on a gold tray. Behind this came a huge bowl of the finest porcelain, then a perfume bottle encrusted with rubies.

The second courtyard was smaller, dominated by a large fountain in the centre. There was nobody here, but, looking up, Fran saw that all the windows were crowded with spectators.

Then it was back into the palace, where more people came out to stare, and bow low as she passed.

I don't believe this is happening to me, she thought.

At last they reached her own apartments, opposite the prince's. Here Ali himself was waiting, and in the sight of them all he inclined his head to her. For such a woman even the ruler made a gesture of reverence. And only the woman on the litter and the man waiting to receive her knew the true irony of the situation.

He handed her down from the litter, and she lowered her head to him very slightly. Her mind was full of a multitude of images, too many to understand at once, but she saw that she was facing a magnificent trio of floor-length windows, all in the shape of horseshoe arches.

'Allow me to show you your personal garden,' Ali said, leading her through the centre window.

Outside was truly a place of wonder. Awed by its beauty, she accompanied Ali along the paths between the four fountains, exclaiming over the peacocks and gazelles that wandered freely. Courtiers remained at a respectful distance, speculating on what the prince was saying to his lady, and she to him, and why they both smiled.

They would have been astonished to overhear the conversation.

'You bowed to me,' Ali murmured. 'My round, I think.'

'Nonsense!' she replied. 'You bowed to me first. I was just returning the courtesy.'

'The prince does not bow to a woman.'

'Nevertheless, you did.'

Turning her head, she was just in time to catch him doing the same thing. Unmistakably his lips twitched. The next moment he was staring ahead again, the model of propriety.

Among the spectators there was some interest as to how the lady would react to the prince's gift of welcome. Instead of a rivière of diamonds, or something equally fabulous, he had chosen to give her a carpet. It was a very nice carpet, the best to be had. But it was a strange choice, and they wondered if the favourite would be disappointed.

Instead, they saw her give a trill of laughter, and throw her arms about the prince's neck. His own laughter mingled with hers as he said, 'I wondered if you would understand.' That remark baffled the onlookers.

Sitting alone in her apartments that evening—alone, that was, except for her personal attendants, her hairdresser, her chief confectioner and her private chef—Fran regarded that carpet. It didn't fly, but apart from that it was exactly like the one of her dreams.

Her surroundings vanished and she was back again

in Ali's London house, telling him of her childhood dreams.

'…a flying carpet was going to come through the window and carry me off…'

She would never forget his reply. 'I think that for you the carpet will come.'

Neither of them could have foreseen this day, yet when the moment had come he'd known exactly what to give her. It strengthened her suspicion that Ali had secretly lured her here to fulfil her Arabian nights fantasy.

She smiled at the thought, but then the smile faded. Her attraction to him was powerful, real, and no part of a fantasy. It was like a holiday, except that Ali had compelled her to take it, because that was how he did things. But afterwards?

She wasn't the kind of woman who could be sent on her way with a few glamorous memories and gifts. If she loved, it would be for real, and not as part of a holiday fantasy.

Whatever she felt about Ali, and he felt about her, they wouldn't discover it in this place.

There was a small flutter near the door, and she turned to find Leena standing there. 'Prince Yasir begs your permission to approach.'

He was as meek as a schoolboy, but his eyes danced.

'I come to offer you my tribute,' he said. 'If, in your justified anger, you reject it, I shall be so ashamed that I shall ride into the desert and never be seen again.'

'Don't talk foolishness,' she laughed.

'Say that you forgive me for my unforgivable behaviour yesterday,' he begged outrageously.

'I shouldn't.'

'I know. But do it anyway. See what I have brought you.'

His gift was a lavishly jewelled sash, which oddly jarred her. It was too much. But this was a country of too much, she reflected, and perhaps this was his way of atoning. She smiled and praised the sash, and when he displayed considerable relief she felt that she had been right.

He accepted her invitation to tea and they were soon chatting like old friends.

'I expect Ali told you our family history,' Yasir said ruefully. 'Of course I have the greatest respect for him as our country's ruler, but I can't resist the temptation to tweak his nose now and then. He knows it doesn't mean anything, and I hope that you do too.'

'I'd like to believe it meant nothing,' she said, 'but when I saw you fighting, and your look when he struck you—'

He laughed merrily. 'We've been scrapping since we were boys. Sometimes we fight, sometimes we race. Ali has some wonderful horses, but mine are better.'

'Arab steeds!' she exclaimed. 'I've heard of them. They're said to be the finest horses in the world.'

'You should get Ali to show you his beauties. Can you ride?'

'Sort of. I learned on a farm when I was a child. But the pony was a bit slow.'

'Tell Ali you want to ride his best mares. If he's too mean to agree I'll let you ride one of mine.'

He gave her a cheery wave and departed, leaving her thoughtful. Leena reminded her that she hadn't finished ordering the evening meal, and it was important to serve what pleased His Highness. Luckily the chef knew what would please His Highness far better than Fran did, and she was able to leave the matter to him.

Ali arrived in thoughtful mood that evening. He enjoyed the meal, and thanked her courteously for paying so much attention to his requirements, but she could tell that there was something on his mind, and she thought she knew what it was.

'Yasir came to see me today,' she said. 'He wanted to apologise and bring me a gift—that jewelled sash over there.'

Ali examined it and grunted. 'Do you like this?'

'Not really. I think it's overdone, but I didn't like to hurt his feelings by saying so.'

'It's like Yasir to go a little further than he needs, but I'm glad he is showing you the proper respect at last.'

'Have you made your peace with him?'

'You mean has he made his peace with me?'

'Yes, of course.'

'He's apologised, and I've told him to behave himself in future. He asked my permission to visit you and I gave it, feeling certain you were now safe from his advances.'

'He didn't come within three feet of me,' she assured him.

'It would have surprised me if he had. He's fond of harking back to the past, reminding me that his father was the elder brother. I reminded him that in those days he could have been beheaded for what he did. In view of his contrition, you have my permission to receive him.'

'Thank you,' she said ironically. 'You're very poor company tonight. Yasir was far more entertaining.'

'May I ask why?' Ali enquired coolly.

'He told me of his horses. He said I should ask you to let me ride one of your best mares, and if you're too mean I can ride his.'

'There will be no need for that. My animals are at your disposal. We can travel to Wadi Sita whenever you wish.'

'Wadi Sita?' she echoed, trying to sound indifferent.

She knew the name well. Wadi Sita was the legendary oasis that no journalist had ever penetrated. Here Ali indulged himself in exotic orgies of pleasure, safely hidden from the world's prying eyes. And now he had invited her there. But he would withdraw the invitation if he knew her eagerness, so she kept all trace of it out of her voice.

'Sita is the Arabic word for six,' he explained. 'Wadi means a valley, usually a pleasant valley with trees and water. We have six such places in the Kamar desert, but Wadi Sita is my favourite. I shall mount you on Safiya. She is my best mare, white as milk, light and strong, but gentle.'

'It sounds wonderful. When can we leave?'

'Tomorrow.' He rose. 'I'll give orders immediately. In fact, I won't be back tonight at all. I have urgent matters to attend to.'

His eyes met hers, and he nodded slightly.

'I heeded your warning. I checked, as you said.'

'And you discovered that your men were letting you down.'

Ali's lips twisted in bitterness. 'Worse. They were engaged in an active conspiracy to steal from me. They are being brought here now to be questioned about the money they've taken—how much, and where it's hidden. That will occupy me for the next few hours.'

'Suppose they won't talk?'

His eyes were as bleak as a steel wall. 'They will,' he said simply, and Fran knew a fleeting moment of pity for those who had dared to cross Ali Ben Saleem.

He paused, and she could tell that the next words cost him an effort. 'I am in your debt for revealing their dishonesty.'

Fran smiled, but was too tactful to say anything.

'Thank you,' Ali said jerkily, and went away.

CHAPTER EIGHT

THEY left for Wadi Sita late the following afternoon, when the sun was already sinking. A helicopter took them direct from the roof of the palace to a landing pad in the oasis itself.

Fran spent the journey glued to the window, watching for her first glimpse of the famous oasis. At last Wadi Sita came in sight. Far below she could make out the glitter of water, palm trees and beautiful gardens. Surrounding this was what seemed to be a small town, with a few buildings and many tents.

'When in the desert I like to live simply,' Ali explained. 'So we live in tents.'

Because the oasis was so small they were met not by a car, but by Ali's favourite stallion, and also a dainty white mare for Fran, so beautiful that she cried out with delight.

'She is called Safiya, which means patient,' Ali told her.

Safiya lived up to her name. She had large, beautiful eyes, was silken-mouthed and moved with a soft, gliding step. Fran immediately felt safe on her back.

It was still very warm, but the sun was no longer at furnace heat, and a pleasant breeze sprang up. Fran glanced at Ali, enjoying the sight of him on his black horse. He rode proudly, with his head up, his white burnouse fluttering in the breeze, and the sunset gleaming off the gold cords that held it in place.

He glanced in her direction, and she quickly looked

away, dismayed to have been caught looking at him. She had an uneasy notion that she'd been smiling at the magnificent picture he presented, which might mislead him into thinking that she was weakening.

Looking around, she noticed a high building, larger than the others, where every window was covered with bars. They were elegant and ornate, and the last of the sun turned the brass to gold, making them beautiful. But still, this was obviously some kind of prison.

'You've noticed my harem,' Ali said casually. 'I keep a special one out here for the sake of convenience. My raiders travel far and wide kidnapping women who are kept locked up there, awaiting my pleasure.'

'What?' Then Fran noticed that he was grinning. 'You—!'

'I couldn't resist it. You're so ready to believe every tall tale about me.'

'There wouldn't be any tall tales if you came clean.'

'Why should I? I'm not accountable to the world for what I do in my own country.'

'Of all the arrogant—!'

He laughed aloud. 'You goose, that's the Water Extraction Company. The water here is rich in minerals and sulphur, and has unique properties for curing many ailments.

'The company works on finding new cures. But we have to look out for industrial spies. Several major drug companies have tried to steal our discoveries, so that they can patent them before we can do so ourselves. Then they could charge extortionate prices, whereas I only want a reasonable profit for my country. So the bars are part of the security arrangements.'

He glanced at her, his lips twitching. 'You're not

taking notes,' he complained. 'Of course, this isn't as interesting as the tales of the wicked sheikh who makes love to fifty women a night.'

'Only fifty? I'd heard a hundred.'

'No, no, I'm only human.'

She burst out laughing and he joined her.

At last they reached the edge of the oasis, where there was a village of tents, bounded by palm trees, and, beyond them, the desert. Darkness had fallen, but the village was lit by flaming torches held high by a hundred arms, illuminating a path as the Sheikh and his favourite rode side by side in majesty.

When they reached her tent he lifted her down himself, holding her high for a moment before lowering her slowly against his chest. Then he kissed her before all the world, and all the world cheered.

Her tent was a mini palace, thickly carpeted, hung with silken drapes and lavishly provided with huge cushions. Partitions divided it into rooms, one for eating, one for sleeping, one for washing away the hot dust. Her maids were already there, having been sent on ahead to prepare.

When she had bathed and Leena had anointed her with sweet-smelling oils, there was the serious process of deciding what to wear for the evening. Leena displayed several garments, but gently nudged her towards one of white and saffron, against which her skin glowed warmly.

Ali's eyes, too, glowed, when he saw her. He had come to fetch her for the feast that was to be given in her honour.

'Tonight we eat under the stars,' he said. 'And because this is an informal place there is no need for your veil. Many tribesmen are here. They are my friends, and they have come for miles across the desert for a glimpse of you.'

'But we only planned this trip last night. How did they know to make the journey?'

'For a woman who prides herself on being modern, you ask some remarkably silly questions. Even tribesmen have mobile phones these days.'

He took her hand and led her out of the tent. Fran's first thought was that the place had caught fire. Men stood as far as the eye could see, each carrying a torch. She put her head up and smiled.

Ali led her to two huge cushions, and they sat together, cross-legged, and presided over the feast. All the finest foods were spread before them, in such profusion that Fran felt giddy.

This was followed by the entertainment. A large space was cleared and suddenly the air was filled with whoops and yells. A troop of horsemen burst onto the scene, galloping around and around in a circle, performing amazing acrobatics. Ali explained that they were tribesmen who still lived in the desert and treasured the skills handed down from their ancestors.

There had never been such riders, doing handstands on the backs of fast galloping horses, leaping from horse to horse, landing perfectly every time. With each landing there were yells and yodels of triumph, until the air was filled with their cries.

Finally there came one horseman on his own. He was better dressed than the others and his face was covered, except for his eyes. He was the least skilled, but the crowd roared and cheered as if he was a star, and Fran understood why when he landed at her feet and revealed himself to be Yasir.

'What are you doing here, playing the fool?' Ali demanded cheerfully.

'I came to pay my respects,' Yasir said, sweeping an extravagant bow to Fran. She smiled and applauded, and he vanished into the crowd.

A young man appeared with a lyre, and began to sing. Fran didn't understand the words, but the music, with its poignant sound of happiness that was half sadness, seemed to take possession of her. Ali leaned close and whispered, 'It is an Arabic poem, hundreds of years old. It means, "My heart rides with the wild wind, my steed is fast, my love rides by my side…"'

'That's beautiful,' Fran said.

'"The wind is eternal,"' Ali continued. '"The sand is eternal. Our love is eternal."'

The singer's voice grew melancholy.

'"She is gone from me. But, in my heart, we shall ride in the moonlight, for ever,"' Ali translated. 'Come, my love, let us walk together.'

He took her hand, and the crowds melted away. He led her to the gardens where they could walk under the palm trees, watched through the leaves by parrots, and listen to the soft plashing of the fountains.

'This is such a perfect place,' she murmured.

'I hoped you would think so. I believe the Enchanted Gardens must be like this.'

'The Enchanted Gardens?' she echoed. 'Where are they?'

'Anywhere you like. They are where lovers meet when the storms and stress of life are over. Or they exist in your heart. My father built this garden as a gift for my mother. We all have our own Enchanted Gardens. Mine are with you.'

He kissed her tenderly, and led her away down

winding paths to where the desert began, and the brilliant moon threw black shadows among the dunes.

'Here it is,' he said, 'the desert you dreamed of. And tomorrow I shall show it to you. We shall leave very early in the morning, while it is cool and pleasant, and return when the sun climbs. At midday you will sleep, and in the evening we shall venture out again. Perhaps we shall ride on for ever, and never be seen again by human eyes. And the desert, which is so full of mysterious legends, will have another one.'

'When you talk such beautiful nonsense I could almost wish it to happen,' she whispered.

'It's a crime to accuse the prince of talking nonsense,' he told her with a smile.

'Beautiful nonsense,' she reminded him.

'Then I forgive you. There is much beauty for me to show you, but the greatest beauty of all is in you.'

She had never known him speak so simply and gently before, and her heart responded with joy. He drew her close and she went gladly into his arms. His kiss was like his speech, loving, almost reverent, not demanding but coaxing, and it was irresistible.

'Ali,' she whispered, melting against him.

'Say my name again,' he begged. 'I love to hear it on your lips.'

She said it again, and then again. It had a wonderful sound, until he silenced it by covering her mouth with his own. His lips were warm, firm yet tender. They spoke to her not only of passion, but of love, and something inside her flowered. If only he could always be like this.

She felt him lift her high in his arms and begin to walk back the way they had come. She clung to him, her eyes closed, for she wanted no images to intrude on the fever of longing that possessed her.

He laid her down. They were in darkness except for one small lamp. Fran reached up for him, caressing his face, eager for his love. If he wanted her now, she knew she had no will to refuse him.

But this was a clever man, as subtle as the serpent in the Garden of Eden. Instead of lying down beside her, he kissed her gently and rose again, leaving her longing.

'I shall be here for you before dawn,' he said. 'Be ready for me, for I shall bring a flying carpet to transport you to a magic land.'

Then he was gone, and she was alone, wondering what kind of man this was who always surprised her.

He was as good as his word, arriving in the cool early light, dressed for riding. She too was in riding breeches, which Leena had brought with her.

They mounted the waiting horses and headed out in the cool morning air to a world that belonged to them alone. The desert lay almost in darkness, but there was just enough light to see by, and soon the oasis was far behind them.

The sun climbed fast and the light grew every moment, flooding the land with colour. Ali spurred his horse and it streaked away over the sand. A light touch, and Safiya did the same, carrying her along like the wind until she almost caught up with him. But he went faster and faster, always keeping her at a little distance, until at last he pulled rein and wheeled to face her.

'Do you know where we are?' he asked, smiling.

She looked around and saw that in every direction the sand stretched as far as her eyes could see.

'We're lost,' she cried, bewildered.

'Of course we're not. We rode away from the sun, and we can return by riding towards it. But just for a little while we are alone in the world. And it can be ours, with only the two of us, and nobody else to tell us yea or nay. If we were on the moon together, I think it would be like this.'

'Oh, yes,' she said, looking about her in wonder.

Beneath their feet the sand rippled away in dunes of varying shades of yellow. Above them the blue, cloudless sky plunged down to meet it. She felt drunk with the vivid intensity of the colours.

He slipped an arm about her shoulders, drawing her sideways on Safiya's back so that she leaned against him, and looked searchingly into her face.

'Let us go on for ever,' he said, 'and seek our Enchanted Garden, where there will be no problems or fighting, and we can love each other as fate meant us to.'

'You make it sound so tempting,' she sighed. 'But we can't run away from the world.'

'Lady Almas Faiza, why must you be so serious?'

'Because things can never be as easy for me as for you.'

'Easy? Do you think it's easy for me to be with you day after day, and feel the distance you put between us?'

She shook her head. 'Not I. The distance is there. I only wish—' She checked herself.

'What do you wish?' he asked eagerly.

She touched his face with tender fingers, but shook her head.

He kissed her once more. 'The sun is high, and we must return. Tonight we will make this journey again as the moon rises. I want you to see my desert in all its moods, for you will understand them better than any other.'

She had thought nothing could be more beautiful than the desert at sunrise, but that night she discovered that she was wrong.

As they strolled to where the horses were waiting, Ali said, 'I used to come here as a child, with my parents. I was too young to understand about love, but I knew even then that the bond between them was very rare.

'I remember one night seeing them ride out together, to be alone, leaving me behind. I was jealous because they shared something that excluded me. And I promised myself that one day I too would ride out with my lady under the moon.'

She looked at him quickly, but he laid gentle fingers over her mouth, as if words would spoil this moment.

The full moon was shining brilliant and silver, draining the world of colour, and making the dunes mysterious and unearthly. They rode for a while and when they stopped Fran looked around, listening, wondering if there had ever been a silence like this one.

'Was it like this in your dreams?' Ali asked.

'Yes. The wizard always conjured his spells under the moon, and the desert was always blue-black. But I never dreamed the reality could be so wonderful.'

He said nothing and she turned her head. In the unearthly light she couldn't see his face, only feel his presence, and his hand holding hers. She was conscious of a wonderful contentment. Whatever else happened to her in the future, she would always have this glorious moment with Ali, when he had brought her only beauty and peace.

'Thank you,' she said at last.

He understood her. He turned without a word, and they retraced their steps to the oasis.

Leena was waiting for her with a cool bath. Afterwards Fran walked dreamily towards the bed, lost in some inner dream.

'Tonight I have new oils to make you beautiful for my lord,' Leena said.

She lay down and let the maid draw the soft towel away from her, revealing her nakedness. A delicious aroma began to pervade the air, like nothing she had ever known before. It was full of secrets and spells and it whispered to her of love and desire, of the most delicate eroticism, and unfulfilled yearning.

She thought of Ali, and how she ached for him. It had always been hard to refuse what she wanted as much as he, and now, after their magic moment of communion in the desert, she felt close to him as never before. She lay on her front, her chin on her arms, longing for him.

She felt hands on her shoulders, rubbing the oil softly into her skin with smooth, practised movements. Gradually Fran relaxed and gave herself up to the enjoyment, refusing to spoil it by looking too far ahead. She gave a long, contented sigh.

'I'm glad to know that I'm pleasing you,' said a soft voice.

'Ali!' She half rose and tried to turn, but his hands on her shoulders pressed her gently down again. 'How did you come to be here?'

'I slipped in a moment ago and sent your maid away.'

He was naked to the waist, wearing only riding breeches. But she herself was completely naked, she realised. This was another of his tricks to take shameless advantage of her, and she knew she should be indignant. But it was hard to summon up the proper emotions when his skilled hands were driving away every feeling but pleasure.

'You had no right to do that,' she murmured.

'I know. I'm a terrible fellow. Can you forgive me?'

'Only if you go away at once,' she said, smiling to herself.

'If that is your wish.'

'You mean—you will?' she asked, unable to keep a hint of dismay out of her voice.

'Of course. Just as soon as I have finished. Now lie still while I finish my work.'

She had no inclination to argue further. It was bliss to lie there while his fingers kneaded the back of her neck, her shoulder blades, then her spine. She drew a long, shuddering breath as he softly traced a line down the length of her back and over the curve of her behind.

'You are beautiful, Diamond,' he murmured into her ear. 'As beautiful as I dreamed of you, with a skin of satin, and a shape that is perfection.'

'You shouldn't be looking at my shape,' she chided him half-heartedly.

'How can I not look, when you display it as shamelessly as a nymph?'

He brushed aside her hair and kissed the back of her neck. She hadn't known she was so sensitive in that one particular spot, but her sudden gasp told him everything. He began to trail kisses down the length of her spine to the small of her back, then up again. The pleasure was light and delicate, and she felt herself melting into it, ready for anything that might happen next, but also ready to wait, as long as this delightful feeling continued.

His hands were gentle, turning her onto her back so that he could continue his work. There was witchcraft in his lips and tongue as they trailed lazily across her breasts, with a flickering movement now and then, heightening the sensation just enough to tantalise her.

'I've longed to see you naked,' he whispered against her fevered skin. 'I've dreamed that you would throw away your weapons, wanting me as I want you.'

She didn't dare to tell him just how much she wanted him. Whatever he thought, the battle wasn't over, and soon she must take up her weapons again. But tonight she would yield to her desire. She could fight him, but not her own mounting passion.

She might regret it tomorrow, but at this moment tomorrow was a day that would never come. The gambler, the risk-taker, rose in her, and said that if she never made love with him she would regret it a thousand times more.

He threw off the last of his clothes, and she saw the magnificence of his body, bronze in the lamplight. He was broad of shoulder and long of back, with a straight spine, lean hips and a firm, muscular behind. There was power in his loins. She could sense it in his strong, graceful movements, and it heightened the desire growing in her.

Then his nakedness was pressed against hers. She revelled in his magnificence, the muscular breadth of his shoulders, the long, straight spine, lean, hard hips and powerful thighs.

She could see now how much he wanted her, but he reached for her gently, loving her to desire by slow degrees until he was certain that her passion matched his.

For this he had many skills at his command. He was a subtle lover who knew how the lightest touch could cause a volcano of sensation, and the softest breath send excitement scurrying across her sensitised skin. He knew how to kiss her slowly, lingeringly, giving her time. There was genius in the kisses he bestowed all over her body, so that she was soon in a fever of sensation.

This was love carried to a point of high art. She felt invaded and possessed by him, although he had not yet claimed her, and was still revelling in the enjoyment of her beauty, as though everything he discovered enchanted him.

She could hold off no longer. 'Tell me that you want me,' she implored.

He told her with lips that brushed against her skin. And then he told her with actions that almost made her heart stop with joy. He told her with his hands, caressing her soft, rounded breasts. He told her with his arms which enfolded her against his chest. Finally he told her with his loins, and then she knew it was true.

Like him she'd dreamed of this, but no dream could be as beautiful as the reality. As soon as their bodies were united she knew that it was right. She clasped him in her arms and held him close, sharing his rhythm as the pleasure mounted.

His face was close to hers, smiling, holding her eyes

with his. She could hear him murmuring soft words. They were in Arabic, but she didn't have to understand them to know their meaning. They were the words of a man absorbed in a woman, for whom nothing existed but her. They held passion, adoration, perhaps even true and lasting love.

She tried to answer, but no words would come, only a sigh. Why had she waited so long to be in his arms, when it was where she belonged? She felt her defences falling away. She didn't want to fight him any more, only to be one with him.

Now it was happening, and her brain was telling her to beware the beauty of that oneness, while her heart was telling her that it was what she had been born for.

When she parted from him she wanted to weep, but the moment passed in the gentle pleasure of sleeping in his arms.

In the cool dawn Fran awoke to an unearthly silence. Ali lay naked beside her, on his front, one arm resting lightly across her, his face buried against her shoulder. He was breathing gently in a peaceful, contented sleep, like a man for whom everything in the world was good.

Fran lay staring into the distance, happy, but troubled. At last she knew the truth about herself that she had suspected, and feared. Cool, efficient Frances Callam, who'd always prided herself on her good sense, her rational approach to every situation, was actually a woman who became a slave to her sensations in her lover's arms. His touch, his kiss, could make the real world vanish. In his embrace she had no will but to stay there for ever. And that scared her.

Now she was herself again, passionately loving the

man who lay beside her, but still herself, separate from him, and knowing that this was right. For if she were not separate, what did she have to give him?

He stirred and woke, gazing directly at her, and at something she saw in his eyes she felt her resolve weaken. What did anything matter but being with him?

He touched her cheek. 'Is all well with you, my Lady Almas Faiza?'

'Almost too well,' she whispered.

'How can that be?'

'Because it's dangerous to be so happy.'

'Words. Happiness is every lover's right. You give me such joy. In return, everything I have is yours.'

Now she should demand her freedom, but she put it off. She couldn't bear to spoil this moment.

'I've wondered why you called me Faiza?' she said. 'Whose victory were you celebrating?'

He looked at her with lazy, contented eyes. 'And now you know the answer. Come here, lady, and conquer me again.'

Unable to resist, she did so, and in the sweetness of that loving all fears were forgotten. Their second loving was like their first in ardour, but with a new sense of discovery. They knew each other's bodies and explored them eagerly and with tenderness. Afterwards they fell asleep again. But when Fran awoke the problems were greater than ever, and she knew that they had to be faced.

'What shall we do today?' he murmured. 'The desert again?'

'No, not the desert.'

'What, then, my life?'

She took a deep breath and crossed her fingers.

'Ali, let me go home.'

He stared. 'Let you go? Now? When we have just truly found each other?'

'But what have we found? I can't love you as your prisoner.'

'As long as you love me, does it matter how?'

'It does to me.'

He yawned and stretched. 'I think I will keep you with me for ever. Never speak of leaving me.'

'But—'

'Silence, woman,' he said, drawing her into his arms and covering her mouth.

It was sweet to be there, sweeter still to kiss him and feel his desire. But there was a core of independence in her that wouldn't let her yield. Summoning all her strength, she freed herself from him.

'Come back to me,' he said, laughing and trying to take hold of her again.

'No! Ali, I'm serious. This is beautiful, but it's unreal.'

'Then enjoy it as unreality. But if you must be so serious I will do something to please you. You may visit the Water Company and ask them any questions you like. They will have my orders to tell you everything.'

'Oh, you're so clever,' she breathed. 'Buying me off with titbits.'

'It's what you wanted, isn't it?'

'Yes, but you think you can talk me round so easily.'

He tightened his arms, pulling her hard against his chest.

'What I think is that, while I'm stronger than you, I don't need to talk you round,' he growled.

He spoke humorously, but beneath the teasing it was still an assertion of power, one step short of outright tyranny.

And again he'd managed to confuse her. As a journalist she would give her eye-teeth to get into the Water Company, and he knew that. It also implied that he would soon release her to return home and write her story. So she had nothing to worry about. And yet...

She knew the next words were unwise, but nothing could stop her saying them.

'Aren't you afraid that while I'm in there I'll find a way of escape?'

He released her abruptly and sat up. When he turned, the change in his face shocked her. It was as though winter had come.

'If you ever tried to leave me,' he said in a hard voice, 'I would never forgive you.'

Rising, he pulled on his clothes, and left without looking at her.

CHAPTER NINE

AT ANY other time the visit to the Water Company would have thrilled Fran. As Ali had promised, everyone had orders to help her, and what she learned about the work was fascinating. Many women worked there, one of whom was deputed to accompany her, and who seemed extremely knowledgeable. Wryly, Fran thought she could hear Ali laughing at her.

But while she listened and smiled, and asked intelligent questions, she couldn't banish the picture of his face as she had seen it that morning, threatening never to forgive her.

She left in the early afternoon and settled in the gardens, writing up her notes. When she'd finished she put her notebook away and wandered about the gardens, watching the play of the fountains, wondering what would happen next. She and Ali should have talked about the problem this morning, but instead, after the most wonderful night of her life, he'd simply silenced discussion like a dictator, and walked out. A shiver went through her at the memory.

She sat on the edge of the largest fountain and leaned over to gaze down into the water. Suddenly another reflection joined hers, and she looked up, smiling, to find Yasir beside her.

'I believe in England you say "a penny for them",' he said merrily.

'That's right.'

'What strange thoughts you must be having to bring

such a melancholy smile to your face. Are you happy
or sad?'

'Both,' she said with a sigh.

'I'm a very good listener.'

He led her away from the fountain and they began
to stroll down winding paths.

'Isn't Ali treating you right?' Yasir asked sympa-
thetically. 'I'd heard that you please him so well that
he piles every luxury onto you.'

'But the thing I want most isn't a luxury,' she protested. 'It's a right. I want my freedom.'

'You seem free enough to me,' he said, looking
around. 'I see no guards.'

'Who needs guards in the middle of the desert?
Where could I run to?'

'True. But do you really want to run from Ali?'

'Not really,' she admitted. 'If I had my freedom, I'd
probably use it to come back to him.'

'But that would be your own choice, so it would be
different.'

'Yes, that's it!' she cried. 'You understand. Why
can't he?'

'My cousin Ali is a splendid fellow, but when he's
got what he wants he thinks that's the end of the matter.'

'I know,' Fran said with feeling. 'And it's never
going to be right with us unless I can come to him
freely.'

Yasir nodded. 'You two are perfect together. I hate
to think of him spoiling it through pigheadedness. I
have a little house near here. You can use my telephone to call the British ambassador.'

'Yasir, really? As simple as that?'

'As simple as that. We could go now.'

He took her hand and drew her away down a narrow path. She hurried with him, anxious not to lose this unexpected chance.

Yasir's 'little house' turned out to be a modest palace, overly ornate and generally too much like the rest of him. Fran hurried in after him and looked around for a telephone.

'Up there,' he said, grasping her hand and mounting the stairs.

She could hardly believe that she was going to find a way out at last. She had a brief moment of hesitation. It was tempting to stay here, living a dream of love with Ali, but she knew it was a temptation she must refuse.

'In here,' Yasir said, throwing open a door and drawing her through.

She found herself in an ornate bedroom, heavily hung in crimson brocade. One wall was bare of drapes, covered with knives of all kinds. Swords, daggers, scimitars, curved knives, long narrow knives, short thick knives. The air was heavy with some exotic perfume that Fran found vaguely displeasing, especially when joined to the disagreeable impression made by the weapons. But she had no time to worry about it.

There was a telephone by the bed and she snatched up the receiver.

'How do I call the ambassador?' she asked urgently.

She thought perhaps Yasir hadn't heard her, for he only smiled. Fran put the receiver to her ear, but heard nothing. The phone was dead.

Then she noticed that Yasir was holding the wire in his hand. He had pulled it out of the wall. As she watched, he turned the key in the door.

And now she realised that there was something horrible about his smile.

'I want to call the ambassador,' she said, more firmly than she felt.

'I'm afraid that wouldn't suit me. I prefer that you stay here—with me. Ali can have you back when I've finished. If he still wants you by then. Which is doubtful.'

Why had she ever thought this was a charming young man? Behind the handsome face his eyes were cold and dead.

'You're mad,' she breathed, backing away from him. 'What do you think Ali will do to you?'

'Oh, he'll be very angry at first, but I'll just make myself scarce for a while and he'll forget. Women matter very little in this country, and the idea of two men carrying on a feud because of one is ridiculous.'

'But it's not about that, is it?' she said to keep him talking. 'Not on your side.'

'How clever of you. No, you're just the instrument. Ali will get over this in time, but he'll suffer, and that's what matters. All my life he's taken everything from me, including the throne that ought to be mine. Now I've taken something from him. And I'm going to enjoy it.'

He made a determined move towards her. She backed off. Alarm was rising as she saw the dimensions of the trap she'd walked into. Yasir's apparent good nature was a mask that deceived even Ali. Beneath it was cold hatred, and it was all turned on her.

Yasir was smiling again, a cruel smile, as though he was relishing the fight to come. Fran forced herself to stay calm and stop backing away. Yasir looked at her breast rising and falling, clearly enjoying himself. He didn't see that she had changed the shape of her hand, so that it was balled into a fist except for two fingers. He came close, reached out to grab her.

The next moment he let out a yell of agony as Fran rammed her extended fingers into his solar plexus, with all her force. He doubled up, clutching his middle, his face contorted with pain and outrage.

But he was between her and the door. She was still trapped with a vicious man who no longer cared what he did, as long as he could show his hate.

'You are going to be very sorry for that,' he grated.

'Not as sorry as you'll be when Ali hears,' she said breathlessly.

'He won't care about you once he knows you came with me. You'll be so much waste to be disposed of.'

'You're lying to convince yourself. Ali loves me.'

He was still gasping, but he bared his teeth in a travesty of a grin. 'You westerners with your foolish notions about men and women. Women are playthings, and he knows that as well as any man, whatever he may have told you. He'll tell you himself, always assuming that he bothers to see you again. Now come here.'

Behind her was the wall with the knives. Unable to see what she was doing, she scrabbled and felt a hilt against her fingers. She wrenched, and to her relief it came off easily. Holding Yasir's eyes with her own, she brought it around to the front. It had a long, wicked-looking blade.

'I will use this if I have to,' she said deliberately.

'Don't be a fool,' he sneered. 'I'm a prince and Ali's cousin. Shed my blood and see what your lover does with you. It won't be pleasant.'

She had a terrible fear that he might be right, but she kept her face impassive while she raised the knife to the level of his eyes and thrust it towards him in a series of little jabbing movements. As she'd hoped, he jerked his head back. She kept coming forward, trying to get between him and the door, but she couldn't manage it. It was stalemate. She could keep him off, but not defeat him.

And then she heard a commotion below, the sound of footsteps running upstairs, a man's voice that sounded like Ali's— *Oh, please God!*

Yasir heard it too. His eyes glittered with spite. Moving too fast for her to follow, he grabbed the knife by the thin blade and pulled his hand down it. The next moment there was blood everywhere as the razor edge sliced his arm. He fell back to the floor at the exact moment that the door crashed in, and Ali stood there with a face as black as thunder. Behind him stood two huge men in the uniform of his personal guard.

'Arrest her!' Yasir shrieked. 'She tried to kill me. I'm bleeding to death.'

The guards made as if to move but Ali raised a hand and they fell back. He stood in silence, looking from Fran, stood holding the blood-stained knife, to his cousin.

'Give that to me,' he said to her.

'Ali—listen to me—'

'Give it to me,' he repeated in a voice of deadly quiet.

In despair she handed him the knife. He turned away from her, dropped to his knees beside Yasir, and examined his wound. At last he rose.

'Guards,' he said in a voice that was cold and bleak, 'arrest this man.'

'She's a murderess!' Yasir cried.

'If she had killed you, it would have been no more than you deserve,' Ali said. 'Think yourself lucky that I don't kill you myself. Take him away. Have his wound tended and see that he is watched at all times.'

Yasir set up a howl of rage, but the guards ignored it, raising him and hauling him off.

Fran leaned back against the wall, faint with relief.

'I thought you were going to—'

'You should have known me better,' Ali said. 'But we can talk later. Come.'

He was wearing long, flowing robes. He put an arm about her shoulders, enfolding her in a gesture of protection, and led her out of the house. He held her like that until they reached her tent.

'He only wanted to get me away from you to make you suffer,' she gasped, weeping. 'I took the knife from his wall to fend him off, but I never used it. He cut himself deliberately when he heard your voice. Ali, you must believe me—'

'Hush, I do believe you. He will be punished, never fear.'

'How did you know where I was?'

'Leena saw you speaking to him in the garden. She understood the danger better than you, and fetched me. You are shaking.'

She was trembling violently, from her own actions as much as Yasir's. Ali took her face between his hands.

'You were very foolish to go with him, but you were also wonderful. I am proud of you. My lady is a tigress.'

'I thought you were going to arrest me—'

'Then you did me an injustice. As though I could ever doubt you.'

His trust in her was unbearable. Fran forced herself to say, 'Ali, I have to be honest with you. I went to Yasir's house because I was trying to escape you.'

He stared at her blankly. 'You went from me to him?'

'No, of course not. I went because he told me I could telephone the British ambassador. *Don't look at me like that!* You knew I wanted to get away.'

'You—meant to leave me? Using the help of that creature?'

'I didn't know what he was like or I wouldn't have gone with him,' she cried. 'What was I to do? Ali, this has to end; I must leave here.'

'After last night—the closeness we discovered?'

'It's because of last night.'

'Are you saying I was wrong?' he asked in disbelief. 'That I only imagined what happened to us in each other's arms?'

'No, you didn't imagine it, but—this place is unreal. I'm not myself here, but somebody else that I don't know. And if I don't know who I am, how do I know what I have to give you?'

Looking into his face, she saw that he didn't understand a word. For all his western ways, Ali was still part of a culture where it didn't matter who—or what—the woman was, as long as she pleased the man. Fran's ideas about giving herself in freedom had no meaning for him.

'Ali, please try to understand,' she begged. 'This has to stop. It's been wonderful but—it's time for me to leave.'

To her dismay, his face hardened. 'That is for me to say.'

'But it's madness to think we can go on like this. Can't you see that—?'

'I see only that it's for me to make the decisions. I will not be dictated to by you or any other woman.'

'You said if I tried to leave you you'd never forgive me,' Fran cried in desperation. 'Well, I tried. So where does that leave us?'

'It leaves you exactly where you were before,' he said in an iron voice. 'Subject to my wishes. Did you imagine my anger would make me send you away? Don't think it for a moment. If we're enemies, that would make another reason for keeping you here. Do you understand me?'

The cold implacability in his face made his meaning all too clear. Fran shivered.

'I offered you a life as my favourite, honoured by everyone, including myself. And you threw it back in my face,' he said coldly. 'Beware lest you find that the life of a discarded favourite is even less to your liking.'

'That's all you understand, isn't it?' she asked. 'The language of force.'

'Diamond, I have no wish to quarrel with you. I prefer to think of this as an aberration, best forgotten on both sides. I said that I would not forgive you, but I do, because I can't help myself. Let us put this behind us, and return to that world where we are one.'

'I don't think we can ever return to that world,' she said sadly. 'It didn't really exist.'

She wasn't sure when he'd moved towards her, but suddenly he seemed very close, dominating her by his sheer intense vitality. Fran tried to step back from him but she couldn't move. When he touched her she trembled.

'Don't,' she whispered. 'Don't…'

'Don't ask me not to touch you, when touching you is all my joy. Don't ask me to believe there is no joy for you in my touch.'

'I have never denied it,' she said huskily. 'But there has to be more…or there is nothing…'

He silenced her by laying his fingers lightly on her lips. The touch burned her. She turned her head away but he laid his lips against her neck.

'There is this,' he murmured, his breath scorching her.

She tried to protest but the sensation aroused beautiful memories, and she had to fight not to succumb to them.

'Ali—no,' she pleaded. 'There's so much still to say—'

'But we are saying it,' he murmured, lifting her and carrying her to the bed.

He undressed her and himself quickly. Fran tried to fight her own sensations, but her body had changed since yesterday. Now it was a body that had known him in the bittersweet intimacy of passion. It had responded to him as to no other man, and as it never would again. It flowered for him. It loved him.

Her mind might be full of anger and despair, but his caresses made her want to weep tears of happiness. And he seemed to know it, and used his knowledge shamelessly to make her acknowledge him as her king, as she never would do in words.

When he began to kiss her breasts she arched helplessly against him, seeking the skilful movements of his tongue. As she felt him give what she craved the heat seemed to rise up and engulf her, melting resistance.

His hands caressed her everywhere, finding her intimately before he moved over her to claim her deeply. At the moment of union she sighed, and even she could not have said whether it was a sound of joy or anguish. She loved him so much, and she'd discovered her love in such heart-rending circumstances.

When he had left her, he did not turn away, but held her close, prolonging the intimacy of loving.

'You see,' he whispered, 'how it can be with us— how it must always be; you must never leave me— you belong to me.'

At the word 'belong' her mouth tried to shape the word 'no', but only silently. And what use was a word against the burning, joyful affirmation of her flesh.

He continued to hold her warmly, until the heat and the physical contentment overcame her and she slept in his arms. But even in sleep she was troubled. Ali's loving had been beautiful, ecstatic, but she knew in her heart that it had also been another assertion of his power. He had demonstrated that he could subdue her, not through his desire, but through her own. She was as much a prisoner as ever.

When she awoke he was still there, regarding her tenderly.

'I told you once that I would only be satisfied when you yielded to me completely, in your heart as well as your body,' he reminded her. 'When you said that you were mine for all time and desired only to remain with me. Say it, Diamond. Let me hear you say the words, and swear that they are true.'

She looked up at him from the pillow in despair.

'I will never say those words, Ali.'

She wept as she spoke, because her heart told her that it was true. She loved him beyond reason, loved him so much that she was engulfed by him. But she must resist her love and never, ever admit it to him.

He scowled as he heard her. He could see the glisten of her tears, and they caused an unfamiliar pain in his breast. But that was something he must conceal.

He rose, and turned away from the bed, hiding from her. Her power over him must be resisted and never acknowledged, lest she unman him. He had threatened her with his wrath, but then forgiven her. She would despise him, because no woman respected a man who allowed her to rule him.

There was a noise in the outer tent. Swiftly Ali pulled a robe about him and went out. Fran heard muttered voices. Then Ali's voice rose in command. A moment later he was back with her.

'We are returning to the city,' he said. 'There is a message to say that my mother is on her way home. I would like to be there before her, to show my respect.'

'Where has she been?'

'In New York. Hurry now.'

The flight back over the desert at night was magical. Far below them lights gleamed out of the velvety blackness. Gradually they went lower and lower, until the landing on the palace roof. Fran was escorted back to her apartment by a guard of honour that had mysteriously doubled in size since last time.

Ali's secretary greeted him with the news that Princess Elise had already arrived. He went straight to her apartments.

The princess was an elegant woman with snowy white hair and a beautiful, fine-boned face. She had been born in London, sixty years ago, but now she looked every inch eastern royalty. She rose and greeted Ali with open arms, and a brilliant smile that made her face young again.

'My son!' she said warmly.

He hugged her with enthusiasm. 'You look younger every time I see you. Did you enjoy your trip?'

'Yes, it was very satisfactory. You will find the fruit of my work in there.' She made a gesture towards a desk on which several files lay. 'I hope you'll approve of what I have done.'

'When have I ever questioned any decision of yours? Put business aside for the moment and let me look at you.'

He stood back, holding her at arm's length until he was satisfied. Then he grinned and hugged her again.

'You look remarkably well for a woman who's just flown all the way from New York,' he observed.

'Actually, I took a little detour to London. I seem to have arrived just after you left. And while I was there I heard some strange stories about you.'

He laughed and settled himself on the sofa, accepting the drink she offered him. 'People talk. When have I ever worried about that?'

'Perhaps you should have worried a little more. The servants in your house didn't know how to answer my questions. They shuffled their feet and tried to get away, until I had to be very firm. Now tell me about this English girl that you have ''invited'' to be your guest.'

Ali shrugged in a light-hearted way, but actually he was as uneasy as his own steward under his mother's piercing gaze. Here was one woman who saw through him and would tolerate nothing less than honesty, which made her uncomfortably like another woman, at this minute in his palace.

'Miss Frances Callam is enjoying my hospitality for a while,' he said. 'Tell me more about your trip.'

'All in good time, my son. I've had to play private detective to find my way through a garbled story about an employment agency, and a servant girl who vanished when you did. Through the agency I found myself talking to an enquiry agent called Joey, who is concerned because he cannot contact Miss Callam. I reassured him, hoping that I was right to do so.'

'Quite right, Mother. Miss Callam is in no danger.'

'Ali, why can't you meet my eye?'

'Believe me, Mother, you are making a fuss about nothing.' Elise was looking at him wryly, and he reddened under that all-seeing gaze.

'Ali, there are some laws that even you cannot ignore. I won't ask what you've done, because it might be better for me not to know. But I expect you to bring this young woman to meet me tomorrow.'

'Yes, Mother,' he said meekly.

CHAPTER TEN

ELISE'S apartment was a clever combination of royal luxury and English comfort. She was immediately above Fran's own rooms, looking out onto the Peacock Garden, and her sitting room was filled with light. Long net curtains filled the floor-length windows and wafted gently in the faint breeze.

She rose, a tall, graceful figure in white robes, and embraced Fran warmly.

'I have longed for this meeting,' she said, adding mysteriously, 'I've heard so much about you that it has made me most curious.'

Tea was served. It was good, solid English tea, because, as Elise explained, 'After thirty-five years in this country I still can't do without my cuppa.'

'Oh, yes,' Fran said, sipping gratefully.

They made polite small talk, with occasional interjections from Ali, until Elise said with a touch of exasperation, 'My son, I'm sure you have affairs of state to attend to.'

'No today,' he said, smiling at them both. 'If I leave you may talk about me.'

'Certainly we are going to talk about you. Please go away at once. Can't you see when you are not wanted?'

He gave a wry glance first to his mother, then Fran, before reluctantly leaving.

When they were alone Elise kissed Fran on both cheeks and smiled.

143

'I knew you would be beautiful,' she said, 'from the effect you have had on my son. But you are more than beautiful. Speak to me quite frankly, I beg you. Are you here of your own free will?'

'No,' Fran said, and Elise's face darkened.

'We will talk of that later,' she said heavily. 'For now, tell me how you met.'

Fran described the first evening, and what had happened subsequently. When she came to the part about the cheque, Elise said, 'Ah! Now I understand something that has been puzzling me. Come with me.'

She took Fran's hand and led her into the next room. Fran stopped dead on the threshold. This room didn't belong to a female forced to live in retirement. This was a business office, complete with desks, filing cabinets and all the latest equipment.

Two young women were busy at computers. They rose and bowed when the princess entered, and she waved them lightly away. Under Fran's astonished eye she went to a third computer and began to tap in some figures. A file opened on the screen and Elise beckoned her to look.

'Normally Ali gives the ICF one million a year,' Elise observed calmly. 'When he suddenly added another hundred thousand I couldn't understand it. He never does such things without first consulting me.'

'A million?' Fran echoed in dismay. 'And—consulting you?'

'I handle all his donations to foreign charities.'

'All his—?'

'About twenty million a year.' Elise gave her lovely smile again. 'My dear, have you fallen for the legend of the playboy who spends every penny on himself? How unwise of you!

'Ali maintains this grandiose palace because it's expected of him, but the oil revenues are spent first on his subjects, and only afterwards on himself. I must show you some of our hospitals. They are simply the best equipped in the world.'

'But why didn't he tell me this instead of just saying loftily that he wouldn't discuss it?' Fran said in frustration.

'Because he is a prince,' Elise said, amused. 'He doesn't feel he has to explain himself to anybody. You take him on his terms or not at all.'

'And all those things he told me about not discussing serious things with women—' Fran said with mounting indignation.

'He was probably trying to annoy you. And it's true that he wouldn't talk with a strange woman, nor does he appoint women to his cabinet. He makes an exception for me because I am his mother. In this country, a man who does not respect his mother is considered a disgrace.

'I remember years ago, in England, my own brother once quarrelling with our mother and telling her to shut up. No Kamari man would speak like that to the woman who gave him life.'

She gestured towards the computer.

'He takes his charities very seriously indeed, and they are all in my hands. If people wish to solicit donations they come to me, not to him. I visit them, and advise Ali according to what I discover. That is why I have been out of the country recently.'

'And I thought it was a shopping trip.'

'Well, I indulged myself with a little shopping as well.'

'I can't take all this in,' Fran said, dazed.

'Then I will give you some more.' Elise pressed a buzzer on her desk and spoke into an intercom. 'Be good enough to have my car brought around to the front.'

Ten minutes later the two women were seated in the back of the princess's personal limousine, gliding into the heart of town. They stopped outside a huge white-walled building, which Elise explained was the city hospital.

'We shall have to go through the private part first, but quickly.'

The private section was much like a private hospital anywhere, but it was the public wards that alerted Fran.

'These are for people who cannot afford to pay,' Elise explained. 'The money comes from state funds, or, in other words, Ali.'

Everywhere she looked Fran saw spotless cleanliness, the finest equipment and a high ratio of staff to patients. She had to admit that the place shamed a good many western hospitals.

'The people with money are charged heavily,' Elise said, 'and they partly pay for the poor patients. But only partly. The rest of the money comes from the royal coffers.'

'From the oil,' Fran mused.

'Not just from the oil. The casinos make a handsome profit.'

'Casinos? Plural?'

'In almost every capital city in the world, and several in Las Vegas. We need all the profit we can make because Ali has some very expensive ideas for irrigating the desert. So far most of the money has been soaked up by the sand, but he keeps trying one ex-

periment after another.' Elise smiled fondly. 'Sometimes there's a touch of the mad professor about my
son.'

She saw Fran craning her neck out of the window.
'Something interests you?'

'The Sahar Palace. Ali told me how it was built and
then abandoned as not being big enough.'

'Did he tell you what it's used for now?'

'No, I thought it was just standing empty.'

'And he let you think that,' Elise said with motherly
exasperation. She said something in Arabic to the
driver, and the car turned into the palace entrance.

As they went through the main gates the big front
door opened and two women came hurrying out, smiling as they saw their visitor. They were followed by
a stream of children who engulfed Elise, with scant
regard to her royalty.

'They all love it when Her Highness visits us,' one
of the women confided to Fran. 'They have no mothers
of their own, so in their hearts she is their mother.'

'This is an orphanage?' Fran asked.

'Of course,' Elise said. 'Ali insisted that this place
must be put to good use, and what better use can there
be than the future of our country? Come inside. I think
you will see things that will surprise you.'

But Fran was no longer surprised by any revelation.
The home clearly had a generous budget and was well
staffed and equipped, but it was the place's warm
atmosphere that delighted her. She had begun to realise that she knew nothing about Ali and the way he
ran his country.

At the rear of the orphanage were the classrooms.
Girls were taught apart from boys, but Fran's alert

eyes noted that their science equipment was equally good.

'My husband was an enlightened man,' Elise explained. 'Which is to say that he listened to me,' she added with a twinkle. 'I made him see the need for women to be properly educated. My son is the same. His ideas are old-fashioned, but the right woman could make him listen.'

She smiled, apparently not needing a reply to this, which was lucky because Fran was far from knowing what to say.

'Do the casinos pay for all this?' she asked, changing the subject.

'No, this is the London property portfolio.'

It wasn't until they returned to the palace that Elise demanded full details of Fran's presence in Kamar. She listened composedly, only a small furrow on her forehead betraying any sign of disturbance. When the story was finished she simply said, 'How charming.'

They had tea together, then Elise declared that she was tired and needed to lie down. But as soon as Fran had departed Elise picked up the phone and demanded, in a voice that promised trouble, to be connected to her son.

He arrived to find her pacing the floor, and her first words contained no welcome, and certainly no respect.

'My son, are you quite mad? This young woman is a writer for several internationally respected publications. She has friends in high places, and you have simply kidnapped her. Are you asking for an international incident?'

'There will be no incident that I can't smooth over,' Ali said arrogantly. 'They need our oil.'

'I like you least when you talk like that,' Elise snapped, and he had the grace to blush.

'You don't understand, Mother,' he said at last. 'Fran and I—understand each other. We have done so from the first moment when I met her in the casino.' His eyes kindled. 'At least, so I thought. Later I discovered that she went there on purpose to find out about me.'

'And so you fell in love with her and took her home,' Elise said wryly.

'Certainly not. I took her home but there was no question of falling in love. She was a pleasant companion for a night.'

'Really,' Elise said with a touch of scorn. 'Continue. I am agog!'

'When we talked—something changed. Her mind enchanted me. She took me back to my childhood, and the magic stories I loved to read. She knew them too. I could talk to her. We felt so close, but she wouldn't tell me her name.

'Then I was summoned away, on business, and when I returned she had gone.'

Elise's lips twitched. 'She just walked out on you?'

'Yes!' Ali's voice had an edge. 'But she returned two days later, as herself. I'd agreed to see a journalist; I was expecting a man. Naturally I refused to talk to her.'

'Naturally,' Elise murmured.

'While I was away, she gained entry to my house, pretending to be a maid.'

'And so you decided to teach her a lesson. For what, I wonder? For her methods, or for daring to reject you?'

Ali flung her a dark look, but made no comment.

'So,' Elise continued thoughtfully, 'if you're not afraid of an international incident, it seems that all you have to worry about is Mr Howard Marks.'

'Who is he? I've never heard of him.'

'I gather he is Miss Callam's fiancé.'

'Impossible,' Ali said at once. 'If that were true she would never have—' He stopped. His mother was looking at him with eyes raised. 'Never mind.'

'Perhaps I should have spoken of this last night, but first I wanted to meet this young woman, and see what kind of person she is. Now I think I know. Mr Marks is a banker. He has been going out with Miss Callam for some time, and has it in mind to marry her. He is evidently an extremely good match. Of course, I've been out of England for some time, but in my day a good match was the kind of thing a girl had to think of very seriously.'

'Then why did she never speak to me of this man?'

'From what I can see, you haven't given her much chance to tell you anything.'

'Then she can tell me now,' Ali said grimly, rising to his feet.

Fran was lying down with her hands clasped behind her head, brooding on what she had learned that day. Her picture of Ali as a self-indulgent playboy had been wrong all the time. That was merely what he allowed the world to think. Behind the scenes he was a true father to his people. She felt happiness stealing over her at being able to think the best of him.

She wondered when she would see him. He would probably want to devote some time to his mother, but later perhaps he might come to her. She was eager to see him in this new light, and to let him know how her heart had warmed to him.

At last she heard his footsteps outside, and sat up eagerly as he came into the room.

'Why didn't you tell me about—?' they both said together, and stopped.

'I've been talking with my mother,' Ali said. 'Why did you never speak to me of Howard Marks?'

For a moment Fran had to think who he meant. Howard and the life he represented was so far away.

'Ali—I don't understand—'

'Howard Marks—the man you were planning to marry. My mother knows all about him, so don't pretend that you don't. How could you have concealed such a thing from me?'

A moment ago she'd been full of tenderness towards him, but at this flash of the old, imperious Ali her temper rose quickly.

'How could I—? Well, you've got a nerve!' She bounded off the bed and confronted him. 'Don't tell me that my disappearance has been noticed after all?'

'Evidently. According to my mother, Mr Marks has been asking questions, claiming to be your future husband. This was something you should have told me.'

Fran stared at him, outraged beyond speech. She hadn't mentioned Howard because Ali had driven him right out of her mind. In Ali's arms no other man had existed. But there was no way she could say such a thing to this arrogant, overbearing man who barked out his unreasonable orders like a tyrant.

'You're very fond of telling people what they should do,' she seethed. 'Perhaps it's you that should listen. I never asked to come here; I was tricked into it. I don't recall you enquiring if there was a man in my life.'

'Are you saying that there is?'

'Are you saying it would have made a difference?'

They glared at each other, both furious.

'Was he the man with you at the casino?' he snapped.

'Of course not. That was Joey. I wouldn't take Howard on a job.'

'Ah, yes, you were on a job. A job entitled "the seduction of a prince". You naturally wouldn't want to tell Mr Marks about that.'

'There was nothing to tell. You may recall that there was no seduction—'

'Yes, you slipped out when my back was turned,' he said grimly.

'So you did know I'd gone,' she said triumphantly. 'That story of yours about not coming back was just to fool me.'

He regarded her coldly, and she guessed he was furious with himself for the slip.

'It seems we've both been playing a game of delusion,' he said at last, in a voice harsher than she'd ever heard him use before. 'You set out to trick me into thinking you were a true woman with a heart to offer, and you were very convincing, for a while.'

'Was it my heart you wanted, Ali? I wonder. Maybe we both played games at first, but we weren't playing for hearts.'

'Yes, I know the prize you were after,' he said grimly. 'Not a heart but a scoop for your paper. And I taught you that I'm not a man to be played with. Now tell me about this man who plans to marry you.

What kind of man is he who permits you to take such risks?'

'Howard doesn't permit or not permit. He understands that I'm my own woman, not subject to his orders.' Furious indignation made her say the next words. 'It will be a great relief to get back to him.'

Ali drew a sharp breath. 'Do you think I'm going to let you return to the west with the secrets you've discovered?'

'What secrets? I've learned about your charities, not your national security.'

He didn't answer in words, but he gave her a burning stare that told her his true meaning. Facts and figures weren't the only secrets. There were also the secrets of a man's heart that could be learned only in his arms, in his bed, when two eager bodies became one in the life of true passion. These were the secrets that lived in the night, in the incoherent words of love too deep to be spoken. They were secrets a man might turn away from by day because they confronted him with a self that he feared. But they couldn't be denied, and his eyes told her that he would kill them both before letting her expose them to a derisive world.

But how could he know her so little, she wondered wildly, as not to understand that he could trust her with these things, because for her too they were sacred?

'Even you must know by now that you can't keep me here for ever,' she said.

'But I can, and I will. My mother says that I have compromised you, and so deprived you of a good marriage. Very well. Then I have a duty towards you. I will replace a good marriage with a better one. As my wife you will have nothing to complain of.'

'Your wife?' she echoed, aghast.

'Our marriage will take place immediately.'

'Our marriage will never take place,' she flung at him. 'I won't stay with a man who informs me of our wedding as though he's doing me a favour.'

'You will stay,' Ali said, 'and you will become my wife. The truth that is between us will prevail and make our marriage a happy one. I shall give instructions immediately, and the ceremony will take place in three days' time.'

'It will not,' Fran cried wildly. 'Ali, understand once and for all that I won't marry you. Not in three days' time. Not ever.'

'My mind is made up. There is nothing further to discuss,' he said calmly, and walked out.

Marriage, for a ruler of Kamar, was a complex business. Officially it was a secular state. Three of the world's great religions lived peacefully side by side, with no one religion predominating.

So there would be, in effect, four weddings. The first was a civil ceremony, conducted in a small room in the palace. Then the ruler and his bride would present themselves at each of the three main religious headquarters in the city for the pronouncement of a blessing. These were riotous occasions, with the public thronging the entrances, clapping and cheering.

If this had been a normal wedding Fran would have enjoyed the buzz of preparation. From dawn to dusk she was engulfed in the making of a new wardrobe, and the selection of adornments for her state rooms. Instead, she floated through it all in an unhappy dream, wondering how she could be so miserable when her life was about to be joined to that of the man she loved. No, she amended that. The man she could have loved. For he seemed bent on destroying her feelings for him.

Elise had said the right woman could make Ali listen, but he showed no sign of listening. And in this tyranny Fran saw an ominous portent for their future.

Two days before the wedding Ali departed on a flying visit to the north of his little country, stating that he would return the following day. Elise came to spend the evening with her future daughter-in-law.

'You'll be glad to know that Yasir will not trouble you again,' she said. 'His wound is superficial and healing well, and he will have left the country before your wedding. Ali has banned him from returning in less than five years.'

'That's good,' Fran said.

Elise observed her critically. 'You don't look like a happy bride preparing for her big day.'

'Don't I?' Fran asked listlessly.

'Anyone would think you were going to your execution instead of your wedding.'

'Well, it feels like the end of my life.'

'How ungrateful you are! Ali will make you the princess of a wealthy country. You'll never have to lift a finger again.'

'Is that why you married?' Fran asked, regarding Elise levelly.

It fascinated her to observe that even now the mention of her late husband could bring a faint blush to Elise's cheek.

'I married the man I loved more than anything in life,' Elise said. 'And I knew that he loved me the same way.'

'You're lucky it was that easy for you,' Fran said wistfully.

Elise gave her rich laugh. 'It wasn't easy at all. We had terrible fights, especially in the first year. But we survived them all, because we knew that we couldn't bear to be apart. Whatever happened, we *knew* how much we loved and needed each other.'

She fell silent, leaving the implication hanging in the air. Fran met her eyes.

'Is that how you love my son?' Elise asked at last.

'I don't know,' Fran said desperately. 'How can I know when he's forcing me into this wedding? Because he knows his own feelings he thinks that's all that matters.'

'But what makes you think he knows his own feelings?' Elise asked.

'Well, he's certainly acting like a man who knows.'

'Nonsense. He's acting like a man in the depths of confusion. Does he really love you? Or does he only want you? Even he doesn't know. But he thinks if he acts firmly the confusion will sort itself out by magic. He's wrong, of course. He's merely ensuring that he'll never know the truth. And neither will you if this ridiculous marriage is allowed to go ahead.'

'I thought you approved of me,' Fran said.

'But I do. I think you're extremely good for him. You've got him not knowing whether he's coming or going, and he needs some uncertainty. He's had things all his own way for far too long. I want to see you married to Ali, but, oh, Fran, my dear—not like this.'

'Have you said all this to him?'

'Of course I have, and I might as well have been talking to a brick wall. The men of this family have always been distinguished for their stubbornness, and their inability to see beyond the ends of their noses. I'm sorry to say that my son is a chip off several unfortunate old blocks. Your sons will probably be the same.'

'You mean—my sons with Ali? Will they ever exist, I wonder?'

'They will if we act sensibly. You say you don't know how much you love Ali. But do you love him enough to leave him?'

A bleakness settled over Fran's heart. To leave him, perhaps for ever, never to ride beside him, never again to lie in his arms?

But the alternative was to live by his side as his chief concubine—for she would be little more than that—enjoying his desire but not his respect, never knowing the truth of his heart or her own, and seeing their love wither in that uncertainty.

'Yes,' she whispered. 'I love him enough for that.'

'In that case,' Elise said decisively, 'we have work to do.'

It was unlike the princess to act impulsively, but when she announced her immediate departure nobody dared to argue. Ali's chief adviser ventured to suggest that His Highness might prefer her to wait until his return, but she gave him her chilliest and most imperious stare until he faltered into silence. When he gathered his wits sufficiently to remind her that the wedding was set for two days hence, she informed him loftily, and with perfect truth, that she would have returned by then.

Instantly a smooth-running machine was set in motion. The princess's personal limousine was brought to the front to wait for her with its engine running. A message was sent to her state apartments and a moment later Her Highness emerged, accompanied by a heavily veiled maidservant. In a few minutes they were in the car, on their way to the airport, and the flight to London.

Another limousine was waiting at the other end, to take them to Ali's house. After a brief pause there, it set off again for the short journey to Fran's address, where it disgorged the 'maidservant', now without her Arab garb and veils. The whole business had taken under twelve hours.

CHAPTER ELEVEN

ELISE was back in Kamar by noon next day. Ali reached the palace an hour later. Within minutes he was on his way to his mother's room.

The thunder of his boots on the tiled floor caused a quaking everywhere, except in the princess's apartment. She sat calmly writing at her desk, waiting for her son to arrive. The slam of the door shook the building. She glanced up, then returned to what she was doing.

Ali cast a glowering look at her bent head, and set about pacing the floor. When he'd covered the ground several times he snapped, 'My grandfather would have fed you to the alligators for what you've done.'

'Your grandfather was an exceedingly foolish man,' Elise observed calmly. 'I regret to say that you seem to have inherited the worst of his foolishness. Of course I got her away. Whatever were you thinking of to let things get so far?'

'She is the bride I have chosen,' Ali growled.

'But has she chosen you? Marry her at the sword's point and you would never know.'

'Do you think I know nothing about her heart? There have been such things between us—I cannot tell even you—' He found himself reddening, and turned away from his mother's understanding eyes. 'I promise you, I know her heart.'

'No, my son, you know only her passion. Her heart is a secret to you. And when passion dies?'

'That will never happen.'

'For you, perhaps. But a woman's heart is different. For her, passion is nothing without love. How can she know that you love her when you have behaved with arrogance and unkindness, and treated her wishes as though they were nothing?'

'Everything I have is hers. What can she ask that it will not be my pleasure to give?'

'Her freedom. Freedom to choose you—or reject you.'

He paled. 'Reject me?'

'You must win her, so that she can choose you freely.'

'And if she does not?' he asked, almost inaudibly.

'Then you must let her go. Unless her happiness is more to you than your own, you do not truly love her, and she is right to refuse you.'

'You're asking me to beg from a woman.'

'If she's the woman I think her, she won't make you beg.'

'But to humble myself—to go to her as a suppliant, uncertain of her answer— I am the prince.'

'And have never had to ask for what you wanted. It's time you learned.'

'And if I can't?'

'Then she will never be yours,' Elise said simply.

He wheeled away from her sharply. His mother watched him with sympathy and pity. It was hard for her to do this to him. Only the knowledge that his eventual happiness depended on it had given her the courage.

When at last he spoke again his voice was shaking. 'I can't believe that she left without a message to me—not a single word.'

'Have you looked everywhere?'

He stared at her, and after a moment he hurried out of the room.

The maids were still in Fran's apartment. They took one look at his face and scattered. Ali raged through the rooms, looking for he knew not what. Somewhere, surely, there must be a sign that she hadn't simply turned her back on him. Because if she had done that then everything he'd thought was between them was no more than a mockery.

At last he found what he was looking for on a little inlaid table, held down by a gold box. He opened out the single sheet of paper and read:

My Darling,

I know you'll think it's a terrible betrayal, my leaving you, but try to understand that I have no choice. Nobody should get married like this. There would never be peace between us, and eventually there would be nothing at all.

Do you remember my dream of a flying carpet? Well, it happened, as you meant it to. The magician cast his spells and the prince came out of the coloured smoke. He was handsome and charming, and he showed me wonders that will live in my heart for ever.

It was a lovely dream and I shall always remember that I once had a little magic, all my own. But, sadly, magic doesn't last, and the carpet flies away again.

Goodbye, my darling. I wonder where we'll meet again? Will it be in the Enchanted Gardens? Were we ever destined to find them? Or maybe they don't really exist.

I've wondered how to sign this letter. You gave me so many names, and it was lovely pretending to be them for a while. But they were only illusions, and I can't live on illusions. If you can't love the woman I really am, let us forget each other.

No, not forget. Never. But put the dream aside as too beautiful to be true. I've signed this letter with the one name you never called me, but the only one that was true. Try to forgive me.

The letter was signed, 'Frances.'

When he'd finished reading Ali realised how quiet and empty the apartment was. Where once there had been her laughter, now there was nothing. Her defiance had enraged him, but he would have given all he had to have her there again, telling him that she would do as she pleased, no matter what he thought. With what courage she had opposed him, and how wonderful that courage seemed now.

Only the soft plashing of the fountains broke the silence, and suddenly he realised that another noise was missing. He'd grown used to the cooing of her white doves, the faithful birds that would never leave her. He strode out to the courtyard.

But the dovecote was empty. The doves had flown away.

He knew then that she had really gone.

It was strange, Fran thought, how you could love a man so much that it hurt. You could dream of him at night and yearn for him by day. The memory of his passion and your own could make your flesh ache with longing. He could fill your heart and thoughts until nothing else existed in the whole world.

And yet you could force yourself to leave him, and know that you'd done the right thing. You could struggle not to be crushed by your own heartbreak and resist the fierce temptation to run back to him.

For the first few days she flinched whenever the telephone rang, certain that it must be Ali. But it never was. She'd half expected an explosion of wrath at her defection. But perhaps he would simply ask her to talk, say that he understood, and wanted to start again, without coercion. If he truly loved her...

But there were no telegrams or letters, and nobody came to the door. It was as though he had wiped her out of his existence, and a shiver went through her. He'd planned to marry her out of duty, because he'd 'compromised' her. Her departure had actually been a relief to him, and now it was all over.

Barney, a kindly elderly man who ran *The Financial Review*, threw up his hands at the sight of her.

'So the prodigal returns! There was a crazy rumour that you were going to marry Prince Ali.'

'Crazy,' Fran agreed with her brightest smile. 'You shouldn't believe all you hear. But I have been in Kamar.'

'Great! So what really happens to all that money?'

'He spends it on his people.'

'Oh, c'mon; the story must be better than that.'

'It's the truth. He doesn't make a big fuss about it because he thinks it's nobody else's business. But he isn't the way we thought. In fact, I don't think there's a story there at all.'

The editor's jaw dropped. 'No story?'

'Well, if there is, I can't write it. I'm sorry.'

'Then I'll have to assign someone else.'

'I wish them luck,' Fran said with a wan little smile.

Once she would have thought herself crazy to give up an assignment, but what had happened to her was something that could never be mined as raw material for a feature. It was too precious, too sacred.

Howard called. After the volcanic emotions of the last few weeks his kindly, slightly pompous voice sounded very welcome, and she agreed to have dinner with him.

Luckily he was a man of little imagination, and he readily accepted the story that she had been in Kamar to work.

'You really have been the mystery woman,' he said, when he'd ordered an excellent supper at an expensive restaurant. Howard always ate at expensive restaurants. He felt it was expected of a man in his position. 'You might have given me a call, my dear.'

'I'm sorry, Howard, there was a lot going on.'

'Of course, of course. And I've been very busy myself. There's a bit of manoeuvring going on at the bank. The chief executive is retiring, and—er—' he coughed modestly '—it's between me and one other fellow.'

'I'm sure the other fellow doesn't have a chance,' Fran said dutifully.

'Well, if I could bring some spectacular new business it would certainly help.' He smiled at her. 'I've missed you, my dear. I enjoy taking you to dinner. You're a fine-looking woman, and you make me very proud.'

'Your hair…is like a river of molten gold… How your eyes enthral me!'

Fran closed her eyes against the sound of Ali's voice whispering passionate hymns to her beauty. When would those memories cease to torment her?

'Well,' Howard said, filling her wine glass, 'I hope it was all worth it.'

'Worth it?'

'I mean did you gather plenty of material?'

'Well—'

'You must brief me about Kamar. It's a big nut and I'd like to crack it. That would really be a feather in my cap.'

Fran repeated what she'd told the editor about how Ali handled the Kamari budget, and his lavish giving to charity. Howard listened with a gleam in his eye that told her he was mentally taking notes.

It was a dull evening because Howard was a dull man, but dullness was what she wanted right now. It relaxed her tortured nerves, even though nothing was going to ease the pain in her heart. He drove her home and gave her a brief kiss goodnight, but she escaped before it could develop into anything more intense.

She had been home a week when she received an excited call from Barney.

'I've just had a call from Prince Ali's office. We can do the feature with his co-operation, the lot.'

'That's wonderful, Barney. I'm very pleased for you.'

'Not me, love, you.'

'I've told you, I can't do it.'

'You have to. Prince Ali made it a condition. You or nobody.'

At the words 'You have to,' something inside Fran flinched. This was the old Ali, laying down the law, insisting on his own way, giving her no choice. He wanted to see her again, but it was beneath his dignity to ask, so he tried to coerce her. He'd learned nothing.

'It can't be me,' she said in a tense voice.

'Fran, if you turn down a scoop like this I'll have to say you're unreliable, and then I couldn't use you again.'

'All right,' Fran said in a smouldering voice, 'I'll do it.'

Even now the signs of Ali's power were all around her. She arrived home to discover that some files, containing a wealth of material about Kamar, had been delivered in her absence.

There was also a typewritten note, saying that she would be given twenty-four hours to master the material, and then Ali's secretary would see her.

Perhaps that meant he wouldn't be there himself. This was a farewell gift. Afterwards she would hear of him no more, and somehow she would try to persuade herself that it was for the best.

Reading the file, she felt as though somebody had let her into Aladdin's cave. All the doors she had knocked on fruitlessly were now open to her. With what she had learned while in Kamar, she had the basis for a splendid feature. Once that would have been enough.

She made a long list of questions, and on the appointed day she approached Ali's house. The huge front door opened while she was still halfway up the path.

Ali's secretary advanced to meet her with a bow. If he knew that this was the woman who'd jilted his master he gave no sign of it.

'His Highness regrets profoundly that he is unable to be present. He has instructed me to give you all the help you require.'

So she wouldn't see Ali. When her heart had recovered from its pang of disappointment she would feel relieved.

Everything was ready for her. Ali's secretary was prepared with answers to all her questions. At her request he opened computer files and explained everything with perfect courtesy. Finally, he said, 'I'll arrange for some tea to be served to you.'

He slipped quietly out, leaving Fran frowning at the screen, concentrating too hard to hear a movement in the room.

'I hope everything is to your liking.'

She looked up quickly to see Ali watching her, and now she realised that she'd always secretly known that he would be there.

'Your secretary told me you were away,' she said.

'I instructed him to say that. I was afraid that otherwise you would leave.'

'Still manipulating people,' she observed.

He gave a wry, mirthless smile. 'Well, I'm afraid the habit is ingrained by now.'

'That's what I was afraid of. I tried to tell you in my letter—'

'Yes, your letter. Let's not discuss that.'

'No, let's discuss why you pulled so many strings to get me here. Or is that simply what I should have expected of you?'

'I don't understand your attitude,' he said in a hard voice. 'You made a fool of me before my people. In return I'm giving you what you wanted.'

'Giving? Or commanding? You told my editor it had to be me and nobody else.'

'It didn't occur to me that you would refuse. I wanted to see you, to give you a chance to explain your behaviour.'

'Explain? You kidnapped me and I escaped. What is there to explain?'

'I offered you honourable marriage—'

'You didn't offer me, you ordered me, just as you're ordering now. I refused but you wouldn't listen.'

'Because I couldn't understand how you could prefer your cold-blooded Englishman—'

'He looks cold-blooded to you because he knows how to behave with some restraint. He doesn't just grab anything he wants. He respects me.'

'Respects!' Ali said scornfully. 'I despise his kind of respect which is nothing but another name for cowardice. He respects you so much that it was days before he knew you were missing.'

'Because Howard doesn't demand an account of every moment of my life. He doesn't treat me like a possession.'

'Oh, you westerners! You know nothing. "People aren't possessions", "People don't own each other", "You can't belong to someone else". You see, I know all the standard phrases. But I come from a hot country, with hot-blooded people, and I tell you that if a man really loves a woman he wants her to belong to him in every possible way.

'It's not liberal, it's not fashionable, it's not correct, but if the love is there he wants everything about her— her heart, her mind, her body, her soul. He wants her thoughts to be of him, her heart to beat for him, and her passion to throb only for him. When she bears children, they must be his children.

'If she betrays his love his heart breaks. If he turns to find her, and she is not there, he doesn't wait days and then ask a few mild questions. He goes insane.'

She could almost believe that he had gone insane

that moment. His eyes burned with a fierce light and seemed to see right through her.

'Do you understand?' he grated. 'Do you know what you have done?'

'Yes, I left you,' she said breathlessly. 'It was what I had to do. I hoped that I could make you understand, but you can't understand, can you?'

'I understand that you belong with me, and this nonsense has to stop—'

'Stop saying "belong",' she insisted desperately. 'I don't belong to you. I never will. I can't love that way.'

'What is your way of loving?' he asked savagely. 'To drive a man to distraction and then abandon him, laugh at him?'

'I didn't—'

'Do you enjoy showing your power? Is that why you did this?'

'If you think that, we'll never understand each other,' she said desperately.

'Talk!' he said contemptuously. 'All this is talk.' He seized her and tried to pull her into his arms. 'Come back with me, and I will make you the most envied woman in Kamar. We can forget this and all shall be well between us again. Come back with me, Diamond—'

'Don't call me that,' she cried. 'Diamond never really existed. She cared for nothing but jewels and having people bow to her. She enjoyed being known as your favourite, and she didn't mind that it wasn't going to last, as long as she had her moment of triumph.

'But that's not me. My name is Frances and I don't like being piled high with jewels. They could be made of plastic for all I care. You wanted Diamond, but you weren't interested in Frances. Ali, have you any idea how wretched we would have made each other?'

It was as though she had struck him. He let his hands fall and stepped back from her.

'You mean how wretched I would have made you,' he said in a shocked voice.

'Yes,' she said sadly. 'I think you would. And I'd have had to live with that wretchedness all my life. But you could have consoled yourself with a succession of favourites.'

His eyes were murderous.

'You should not have said that to me.' He wheeled away from her and began to stride the room. 'You shouldn't have said it, but perhaps it's as well you did. It shows how far apart we are. There would have been no other woman but you, no other wife, no favourites. That was how my father treated my mother, and how I would have treated you.

'Have you forgotten the day I found my cousin bleeding and you standing over him with a knife in your hand? I arrested him because I knew that, however it looked, you must be innocent. That was how much I trusted you. That was how close I thought we were. If you never understood that, then truly our minds never met.'

'No,' Fran said, nodding. 'That's exactly it. Our minds never met.'

'And this banker—your mind meets his? Of course you are half a banker yourself.'

'Luckily for you. How much did a mere woman save you, Ali?'

'A great deal. I admitted that at the time and thanked you. But I missed the real point—that you

have more in common with him than with me. You
always did have, and you always will.'

He regarded her strangely. 'My mother was right,
as she is about all things. He is a good marriage for
you.'

'He's a good banker, if that's what you mean,' Fran
said stiffly. 'Henderson & Carver is one of the most
highly regarded merchant banks in London, and any
day now he'll be appointed chief executive.'

It felt strange to hear herself talking in that stiff,
'proper' way when her heart was breaking at the distance that increased every moment between herself
and the man she loved. But she couldn't bridge that
distance, and only pride was left to sustain her.

There were lines of suffering etched on Ali's face,
yet the words that came out belied that suffering. She
had hurt him, and that hurt her, yet he would deny his
own pain to her, and so keep her at a distance. And
that was a denial of love.

'Chief executive,' Ali mused. 'What can I say to
the woman who will be the wife of such a powerful
man?'

'Don't jeer at me. I know he isn't as powerful as
you—'

'He is nothing like me at all. And that's why you've
chosen him, isn't it?'

'What's the point of talking about it?' she said wearily. 'Maybe I will marry Howard, maybe I won't—'

'Don't tell me he's hesitating?' Ali's face darkened
and he turned away quickly. 'He's a fool,' he said over
his shoulder.

'No, just a very cautious man.'

'If he was a clever man he would seize you while
he had the chance.'

'Exactly,' she said in despair. 'Seize. That will always be the way you think.'

Suddenly she realised what a dangerous thing she'd done in coming here. This was Ali's territory, where she could simply be taken prisoner again.

At that moment he turned and their eyes met. With a gasp Fran seized up her bag, ran for the door, pulled it open and hurried out into the hall.

The doorman on duty was the same one as last time. He'd learned his lesson by now, and stood in front of the front door, arms folded.

Ali came out behind her. Fran turned to look at him with a face full of accusation.

'Let her go,' he said.

The porter stared, not sure he'd heard properly.

'Let her go!'

The door opened, and the next moment Fran was gone.

CHAPTER TWELVE

THE buzzer went on Howard Marks's desk. 'Someone to see you, Mr Marks,' came his secretary's voice.

'You must forgive my arriving without an appointment,' said the man in the doorway. 'But my business is rather urgent.'

'Your Highness,' Howard said, rising hastily to his feet. 'This is an unexpected honour.'

Ali regarded him askance. A voice was running through his head, making an ironic commentary on what was happening. It was unnerving because it was unfamiliar. In fact, it had never happened before he met Fran.

But the voice was there now, observing coolly, *After the rumours this man has heard he should be wanting to sock me on the jaw, not declaring my company to be an honour.*

But his smile gave no sign of this as he approached Howard's desk and began to unload his briefcase.

'Recent disturbing events have compelled me to make alterations in my financial arrangements,' he said smoothly. 'Men that I thought I could trust have turned out to be thieves. For this revelation I am greatly indebted to Miss Frances Callam, whose visit to my country has been most beneficial.'

'I had heard that she'd been to Kamar,' Howard said cautiously.

Ask me about it, damn you! said the voice. *Threaten*

*to break my neck if I laid a finger on her, as I would
do with you.*

When Howard said nothing Ali continued, 'She persuaded me to break my normal rule and give her unprecedented access for her feature. I am now very glad
that I did so. I have learned to trust her judgement.'

'I have always admired Miss Callam's business
sense,' Howard said gravely.

'It was her recommendation that persuaded me to
seek you out and suggest that you take on some of
Kamar's business.'

'Indeed!' Howard said.

*Oh, Diamond, if you could see this man's face now!
At the mention of business his eyes light up as they
never did at the sound of your name.*

For an hour they went through papers together.
When they had finished Ali said casually, 'Miss
Callam informs me that you are in line to become
chief executive.'

'It should be a certainty now,' Howard observed
with a grin, looking at the papers.

'I hope so,' Ali said formally. 'It would please me
to help to promote your marriage with Miss Callam,
which I understand is imminent.'

'Did she say so?' Howard asked eagerly.

'She spoke of you in the highest possible terms.'

'I say! By Jove! Really? Always a bit hard to know
what's going on in Fran's mind. She keeps her secrets,
you know.'

'Not from you, I feel sure,' Ali said. 'But I am em-
boldened to touch on a delicate matter, so that there
may be no misunderstandings. I hope your mind is
entirely without suspicion regarding Miss Callam. Her
visit to my country was made solely in pursuit of her

feature. She never forgot what was due to you, and she was treated at all times with respect.'

In saying this Ali was not conscious of uttering a falsehood. Respect had always been a part of his feelings for Fran, and it was when she had lain in his arms in the throes of passion that his respect for her had been deepest.

'Well, naturally,' Howard said, with an awkward laugh. 'I never imagined anything else.'

Then you should have done. If such a beautiful woman were mine—as I once dreamed she was—I would suffer torments at the thought of her under the eyes of men.

Aloud Ali said, 'Then all is well. I look forward to hearing of your marriage. I return to Kamar tonight, and you will be hearing from me soon.'

He inclined his head and left the room. Howard stared at the door for a moment, puzzled. At last he muttered, 'Funny fellow!'

Fran's flat was tiny by the side of her palatial apartment in Kamar, but now it felt like a refuge, and she loved it. It was on the ground floor, with French windows that opened onto a garden. On summer evenings she could sit with them open, looking out at the garden and listening to soft music.

That was what she was doing when Howard phoned her. But as she listened to what he had to say her relaxed mood was shattered.

'He actually came to see you?' she asked, dazed.

'You should see the business he's putting my way. Every bank in the world is after Kamari money and this should just about clinch it for me getting the job.'

He droned on about the job for a few minutes. Fran

listened on automatic, trying to take in this astonishing new development.

'You seem to have made a big impression on him,' Howard said. 'I didn't follow everything but I gather this has something to do with you.'

'I helped to show that he was being defrauded,' Fran said, through stiff lips.

'That's it. When he talked about us handling some of his affairs, he almost made it sound like he was giving you a dowry.'

'A—dowry?'

'Yes, he said he hoped we'd be happy and all that. He seemed to think your reputation had been compromised, and he wanted to make sure I hadn't misunderstood. Good of him, wasn't it?'

'Very good,' Fran whispered.

'So, all that remains now is to set the date. Why don't we have lunch tomorrow?'

She answered mechanically and hung up as soon as she could.

It was over, and now she knew the truth. Ali had acted out of possessiveness, not love, and he was probably glad to be rid of her. He was certainly acting like a man who wanted to draw a line under the whole business. She had been right to leave him.

But the ache of regret in her heart, for what might have been, couldn't be stilled.

It was getting late, and the light in the garden was beginning to fade. Fran switched on a small lamp and went to close the curtains. Then she started back with a gasp.

'I came to say goodbye,' Ali said.

'You—'

'Forgive me for not coming to the front door. I preferred to be discreet, having already caused you so much trouble. I also wanted to return these.'

He held out the files she'd left behind when she'd fled his house.

'Thank you,' she said blankly.

An awkward silence fell. This was the last time she would ever see him, and she didn't know what to say.

'Howard called me,' she said at last.

'Good. So now all is well.'

'Is it?'

'I finally understood what you'd been trying to tell me all this time. I thought I could give you everything, but all you wanted was to be free of me, and I wouldn't see it. I can love you best by letting you go. So let this be the end.'

'The end?' she whispered.

'I shall never trouble you again; you have my word on that. That's why I had to seek this last meeting, and tell you what was in my heart. From you I have learned many things: that love is more than passion, and the freedom of the heart is beyond price. It is over, Scheherazade. And you have won.'

'Don't call me that,' she cried, her eyes stinging with tears. She turned away so that he shouldn't see.

'It is how I shall always think of you, what I shall always call you in my heart. My Scheherazade, who set all my power at nothing, and outwitted me in the end. You have defeated me. Go in peace. Remember me kindly if you can. Forget me if you will. You, I shall never forget.'

She drew a deep shuddering breath at a strange note she heard in his voice, something that had never been there before. She forced herself to turn and face him.

But there was nobody there, only the curtains waving gently in the breeze.

On the flight home to Kamar, the prince sat in heavy silence, and nobody dared to approach him. When they landed he got into the back of the car without speaking, and was conveyed quickly to the palace.

'You did right, my son,' Elise said when she heard the whole story. 'Doubtless this is the best thing for her.'

'Will she be happy, Mother?'

'How can I tell? Was she happy with you?'

'I thought so—sometimes. But I was deluding myself. I saw what I wanted to see. I thought because I wanted her she must want me. I am wiser now.'

He spoke with a calm simplicity that might have fooled a casual onlooker. But Elise was not fooled. She saw the wretchedness in his eyes, heard the despair in his voice, and knew that this was a man whose life had ended.

'I am feeling a little tired,' she said with a sigh.

Instantly he was beside her. 'Have you seen the doctor?'

'Goodness, no. I'm not ill, merely tired.'

'You must take care of yourself, Mother.' He gave a wan smile. 'You are all I have now.'

'And it's time that was changed. You have gone too long without an heir, and we should be thinking of your marriage.'

He started back. 'How can you—when you know—?'

'I spoke of marriage, not of love. Your heart concerns only yourself. Your marriage concerns your country.'

'You are right. Select a bride for me, and present her to me on our wedding day. Since I can't marry the one my heart chooses, what does it matter who it is?'

He dropped on one knee beside her chair. 'Pity the woman who marries me, Mother. She will get a wretched bargain—a hollow man with no heart to give.'

'Time may change your feelings,' she said, stroking his face.

But Ali shook his head. 'Time will not change me. But I shall try to do my duty.'

'Well, do another duty for your mother. Take me to Wadi Sita. It's a while since I was there, and I should like to remember the old days, when you were a little boy, and we went there with your father.'

'I remember those days too. They were very happy. Life was simpler then. When do you wish to go?'

'Tomorrow, I think.'

Next day they boarded the helicopter and set out for Wadi Sita, landing in the darkness of early evening. Elise went to her tent and Ali joined her for supper an hour later. She had personally overseen the arrangements, and everything was laid out to please him. All his favourite foods were offered, and he smiled and thanked her. Yet the servants who moved silently in and out noticed that His Highness was abstracted, and ate without knowing.

A young man appeared, bearing a lyre. He bowed low, sat cross-legged on the carpet and began to sing.

'My heart rides with the wild wind…'

Ali tensed as he heard the bittersweet notes of the song that he'd once listened to with his beloved. But then he realised that Elise could not have known that, and it would be an insult to her to silence the singer. He sat with his head bent, trying not to hear the words that brought back so many tormenting memories.

> *'My steed is fast,*
> *My love rides by my side.'*

She had ridden by his side in reality, as she still rode through his dreams, her hair tossed by the breeze, her eyes alight with something he had once dreamed was love.

But then she had ridden away from him, into the arms of a dullard. She had failed in courage at the last, but for that Ali blamed himself. It was he, with his selfishness, who had frightened her away. Everything might have been different, if only he had been different. That was the greatest pain of all.

The singer had reached the climax of the song. He had a powerful yet poignant voice, and he made it full of emotion.

> *'The wind is eternal,*
> *The sand is eternal.*
> *Our love is eternal.*
> *She is gone from me,*
> *But in my heart,*
> *We shall ride*
> *In the moonlight,*
> *For ever.'*

Ali bent his head so that nobody might see his suffering. He had forced himself to make the sacrifice, but he had not yet taught himself to endure the thought of life without the one woman who gave life meaning.

As the song ended he muttered, 'Forgive me,' to his mother, and strode out of the tent as if pursued by furies.

His feet seemed to find their own way to the place where they had stood together beneath the palm tress, looking out over the desert. As ill luck would have it there was a full moon tonight, as brilliant and beautiful as before. But now *she* was gone, and he saw only the moon's coldness.

After a moment Elise came to stand beside him.

'I'm sorry, Mother,' he said. 'It was a mistake for me to come here, where she was.'

'Perhaps you were wrong to give her up so easily,' Elise suggested. 'You could still return to England, overwhelm her.'

He shook his head. 'No, that isn't the way.'

'Do you doubt your ability to make her say yes?'

'I doubt my will to do so. I could never again want to make her do anything. She must come to me willingly, or not at all. And now that can never be.'

He didn't see his mother's smile of satisfaction. She said, 'Then what will you do now?'

'Live as befits the man who loves her, and who has learned from her. It will not have been in vain. She taught me things that will always be part of me, and others will benefit.'

'Good, my son. That is how it should be. Let us now retire to bed. In your tent you will find a gift from me.'

'A gift?' He smiled. 'Your gifts were always the best. You thought of things that nobody else would think of. What is it?'

'Go and see. But remember, it is a very special gift.'

Frowning and puzzled, Ali turned and strode off to his tent. He went straight in, too preoccupied to notice that two white doves had come to rest immediately over the entrance.

The light was dim, only one small lamp burned, and at first he was unsure where to look. But then he discerned the tall, elegant figure of a woman, and his heart sank. How could his mother have done this? Did she think him so fickle that he could forget the love of his life in the arms of a stranger?

The young woman turned at his entrance and inclined her head gracefully towards him. She was heavily veiled. Ali stopped a few feet away from her.

'My lord,' she murmured.

He was too troubled in his mind to wonder that she spoke in English, but he automatically replied in the same language.

'Did my mother send you here?'

'Yes, my lord,' the figure murmured.

'That was kind of her,' he said with difficulty, 'but she did not understand. It is not my wish—' He stopped. 'That is—' He pulled himself together. 'You are kind and gracious, and I am sure you are very beautiful. Some man will be fortunate, but it cannot be me.'

The figure bent her head and raised her hands to cover her face.

'I beg you not to distress yourself,' Ali said gently. 'I must refuse this, because it would be a betrayal of the woman I love. That is something I can never do. Even on my wedding day, I shall not betray her in my heart. She'll never know that, nor will she care. But it will remain true, all my life.'

The figure lowered her hands from her face and held them clasped. Her head remained lowered, but her breast rose and fell as if from some violent emotion.

'Why do I tell you this?' Ali mused. 'Perhaps it's because you are a stranger and I cannot see your face that I can open my heart to you. I loved her, and I failed her—yes, truly, I did…' For the woman had shaken her head. 'When she was with me, there were many things I did not understand. Now it is too late.

'And so she left me, and I shall—' a shudder went through him '—shall never see her again. But she will live in my heart until my last breath. She is with me still, in every breeze that whispers. In the night her voice sings to me, in the morning her kiss awakens me. Her shadow will always be beside me.'

His voice had the quietness of heartbreak. The listening figure was very still, but in the flickering light from the lamp Ali saw a tear glistening on her cheek.

'Why do you weep?' he asked, taking a step towards her. 'Not for her. She is free of a man she couldn't love. Not for me, for I shall always have the joy of loving her.'

'Always?' the figure asked softly.

'Always, until I lie in my grave and she lies in hers, and the wind blows the sand to infinity, and there is no trace of our lives. Perhaps somewhere there is a garden where we shall meet again, without pain or misunderstanding. So you see, you must leave me, for I have nothing to offer.'

At last she raised her head.

'But I have not come to take,' she whispered. 'Only to give.'

Her veil fell. Ali stared in thunderstruck silence, then a glad cry broke from him.

'You!' he said. *'You!'*

The next moment Fran was in his arms, crushed by a kiss that felt like the first he had ever given her.

'You!' he said again. 'You all the time. You came back to me. But how—?'

This time Fran silenced him with lips that never spoke a word, yet told him all he wanted to know.

'How could I leave you?' she said at last. 'I thought I wanted to, but then you released me to marry Howard and I knew you loved me.'

'I have always loved you,' he said humbly. 'But I never learned how to ask, only to take. If not for you, I might have gone through life without knowing that the greatest prizes can only be won, not seized. But for your wisdom, my sweet life, we might have married and yet lost each other on our wedding day.

'Now we shall never lose each other, and our wedding day will be a time of joy and triumph. At least—' he checked himself '—I beg you to marry me...'

She smiled. 'Your mother is already arranging our wedding.'

'My mother—?'

'I telephoned her when you left me that day in England. She told me to fly out here, and arranged everything.'

'Then—you love me?' He said the words softly, as though he hardly dared to believe them. 'After everything I've done—how can you love me?'

'It's only now that I know how much I love you. Now that I can *be* myself, I can *give* myself. A prisoner has nothing to give. And I want to give only to you. But you must tell me something. You spoke of a woman you loved, but you didn't say her name. Tell me who you love.'

'Frances,' he said. 'It is Frances that I love. The others—' he gave a rueful smile '—perhaps they'll return sometimes, for you are a woman of variety, and will always have a new self to bemuse me. But it is Frances that I love, and always will.

'Be your true self. Come to me in freedom, and leave also in freedom, for I know—' his face darkened, as though it was hard for him to say this '—you will wish to return sometimes to your own country. As long as you always come back to me.'

'Always,' she said. 'Always. My darling, let us too build an Enchanted Garden.'

Looking into her eyes, he divined her true meaning.

'One that we shall carry with us all our lives,' he said, 'until the time comes for us to wander in the Enchanted Garden for ever.'

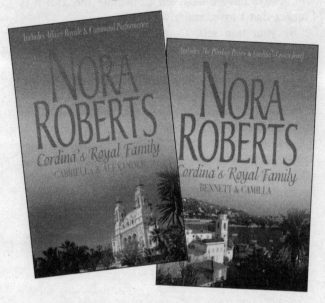

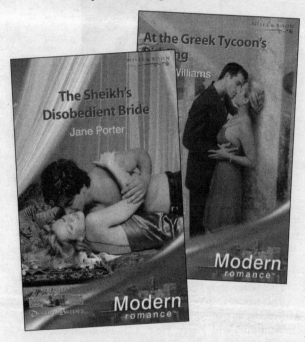

0207/01a V2

MILLS & BOON®

Live the emotion

Modern
romance™

ROYALLY BEDDED, REGALLY WEDDED
by Julia James

Lizzy Mitchell is an ordinary girl, but she has something Prince Rico Ceraldi wants: she's the adoptive mother of the heir to the throne of his principality! Lizzy will do anything to keep her son – then Rico demands a marriage of convenience…

THE SHEIKH'S ENGLISH BRIDE *by Sharon Kendrick*

When billionaire Xavier de Maistre discovers he could inherit the kingdom of Kharastan, it's a surprise. But more surprising is Laura Cottingham, the lawyer who delivered the news. Xavier wants her – but is she ready to be tamed and tempted by this desert prince…?

SICILIAN HUSBAND, BLACKMAILED BRIDE
by Kate Walker

Sinfully gorgeous Guido Corsentino is determined to reclaim his wife! Outwardly Amber is untouchable – only Guido knows the passionate woman inside. But Amber ran away from him once, and Guido resolves to protect her from the consequences of her actions…in his bed!

AT THE GREEK BOSS'S BIDDING *by Jane Porter*

Arrogant Greek billionaire Kristian Koumantaros won't be at the mercy of anyone…especially his nurse Elizabeth! Elizabeth realises she'll have to leave, as the sexual chemistry between them is too strong… But Kristian resolves to fight for her with every weapon he still has…

On sale 2nd March 2007

Available at WHSmith, Tesco, ASDA, and all good bookshops
www.millsandboon.co.uk